Marta couldn't help herself...
she was going back to the gym
to see him!

The dancing had already started when she walked
in. The music was good. Vince had rehearsed the
band until they sounded clean, sharp, and professional.
He stood with his back to the dancers as usual. Then
he turned and casually took the mike. "Hope you like
this," he said. That was all. He sat down at the piano
and began the opening chords of "New Love." As
she stood against the far wall of the gym watching
him play, listening, she suddenly felt his eyes on her.
All the way across the room. Without knowing exactly
why or how, she began to walk toward the bandstand.
She climbed the little flight of steps, and Russ the
trumpet player lowered the mike for her. With her
hand cupping the cold metal, she sang the song Fanetti
had written for her.

Hello, new love,
Won't you say my name?
We hardly know each other,
    but we're really just the same.
Our eyes will tell us what we cannot say.
You'll call me your love, I know, one day.

Look, new love, at the moonlight shining
    through the tree
We need no words to tell us
    it's for you and me.
Let me touch your hand, your lips, your cheek.
Let me hold you close
And you'll hear it speak, this new love.

All She Wants

Suzanne Diamond

WARNER BOOKS

A Warner Communications Company

For Frank

All She Wants

All she wants is what she wants.
A great big slice of everything. My heart and soul
Will not suffice.
She wants it all. She wants it whole.

All she wants is what she wants.
She says I'll never know.
My deepest dreams become the taunts
Of hopes too frail, too weak to grow.

Where are the answers I seek all alone
Searching old hangouts for leads?
The music is playing, the saxophone
Saying what it was, what it is, that she needs.

All she wants is what she wants,
A melody to twist and bend.
She will not take what I offer her,
A song without an end.

Vincent Fanetti

CHAPTER 1

March 1946

HIS LETTER TO HER CAME IN THE MORNING MAIL AND everybody in the Resnick household saw it before Marta. Whatever feelings they might have had against his staying in touch with her, they kept to themselves, and left his letter sealed in the pile of mail on the dining-room table, the usual place.

He had made no effort to hide his name: First Lieutenant Vincent Fanetti, M.D. 6073311, Twenty-fourth Infantry Division, Army Station 704, Camp Hood, Texas. It was in the upper-left-hand corner of the thin airmail envelope, in his big, bold, sloping handwriting.

Marta had been staying late at the university, trying to get caught up. She was in the last months of her senior year, her accelerated program speeding to its June finish. The work had begun to pile up in merciless mountains, partly because she was in love with Dan Reiter and tried to be with him every second he was free. After he was discharged from the army, she spent that winter trailing around with him, talking, comparing ideas, embracing, and petting.

Instead of studying! Instead of writing thoughtful dissertations on the music of the baroque; instead of reading the scholar-critics and music historians; instead of listening with the musician's inner ear to the sounds and rhythms of the nineteenth and twentieth centuries. On all of which she would be tested in order to graduate.

Vincent Fanetti's letter had been carefully placed by Mrs. Resnick on top of the others in the middle of the table where the day's mail was always left. Both Steven, Marta's younger brother, who was in his freshman year at City University, and her father, Dr. Resnick, coming home exhausted as usual from his grinding, daily general practice, had picked up the letter, looked at it, and put it back down. Nobody mentioned it.

Welcome or not, a letter from somebody still in the service brought it all back. You could visualize again the ugly headlines, the fear in the eyes of people with kids and lovers fighting in Belgium or in the South Pacific, the rationing, the lean, careful, work-directed years that had come on them unsought.

When Marta pushed open the front door at 6:00 P.M., she was greeted by the familiar Friday aroma of brisket and fruit schnecken, and wearily tossing her books on the living-room couch, she went to hang her coat in the dining-room closet. She saw the handwriting halfway across the room. Almost as if Vince were saying her name out loud, the envelope beckoned to her. She picked it up, read the celebratory title before his name and the achieved distinctions after it, and grinned spontaneously. He had made it!

"Come . . ." Her mother was standing in the doorway to the kitchen, her face flushed from bending over the stove,

2

her apron tied high around her thickening waist. "We're ready to eat. We were waiting for you. Steven is starved...."

"Steven is always starved." Marta took the letter, gathered her books, and started up the stairs to her bedroom. "I'll wash my hands and be right back down." Her mother stood staring after her, a small frown between her brows.

Nothing changed. To her family even his letters were still an intrusion. She smoothed the envelope. "Okay, Fanetti," she said softly; and without trying to conjure him, there he was in her line of vision, the big tough kid with the strange gray eyes, the maker of songs, the spinner of melodies and dreams. He had dreamed himself right where he wanted to be!

She didn't open the letter right away. Her instinct told her that some dreams get ground under, leaving a fine, dusty residue to settle in the bottom of the heart. Sudden storms, old tunes, the taste of a tiny tea cake or the fragrance of an early spring afternoon, any one might raise the forgotten, powdery past.

But you hesitate to do the stirring-up deliberately. So Marta put the letter on her dressing table, propped up; and as she hung up her clothes and stacked her books on her desk, it was as if she could see his eyes watching her, following her, narrowed and intense.

World War II was over. But she knew that Vince Fanetti would be staying in the army, serving out his time, the time they gave him to become a doctor. Captain Daniel Reiter had been honorably discharged after spending two and a half years chasing the Germans eastward across Europe. The war was behind him, and everyday life was about to begin again. The Germans had capitulated in April 1945, when Hitler disappeared, with V-E Day, the official surrender date, coming on May 9. V-J Day was four months later, when a Japanese delegation boarded the

U.S. battleship *Missouri* on September 2 in Tokyo Bay, accepting all the Allied terms laid down in the Potsdam ultimatum.

It had been one hell of a war. It had left over fifteen million men killed or missing in action. Fifty-seven nations, scattered around the globe, were directly involved. If anybody cared, the cost to the United States had been more than $350 billion, spent generously, prodigiously, and steadily between 1939 and 1946. Roosevelt had died exhausted before the end. Truman had taken over and dropped the first atom bomb in history.

But it was all over. The pent-up energy of the American people, emotional, intellectual, and economic, was exploding into immediate plans for new houses, nylon stockings, gorgeous cars, and brand-new electronics. The time biding, the limited expectations of the war years had come to an end, and in Woodlyn, like other middle-class suburban communities, the road led up.

Marta helped her mother serve dinner at the kitchen table. The conversation as usual revolved around the day's news, the family discussing President Truman's increasing difficulties in dealing with the Russians and the terrible revelations about the concentration camps uncovered by the liberating armies.

Marta picked at the pot roast, carrots, and potatoes, refusing the sour tomatoes and garlic pickles that sat in their usual place on the dinner table, and tried not to think about Vincent Fanetti. It was almost as if he were waiting for her in her bedroom, quietly, not too patiently, just the way he had waited for her after school on the sidewalk outside her entrance to Hillcrest High, shifting about lightly on the balls of his feet, the musician in him supplying silent rhythm for the athlete's restless movements.

"Is Daniel coming over tonight?" asked Mrs. Resnick.

When Marta looked sharply at her mother, who was serving Steven another portion of thick-sliced meat, she could see that Mrs. Resnick too had been thinking about Vincent's letter.

"I don't know," Marta answered stubbornly.

Dr. Resnick, as much a party to the subtleties as her mother, said quickly, "Look, he hasn't been out of the army that long! Give the boy a chance to spend some time with his own family."

"Well, he'll probably call," said Mrs. Resnick, and tried to ladle more meat and potatoes onto Marta's plate.

"No more, Ma," she said. Seeing the sagging of her mother's shoulders and the long lines that dragged at her father's mouth, she relented. "Dan did say he'd call. We may go visit some of his friends tonight. A guy he knows who just got out of the navy . . ." She began to get up from the table.

"What's your hurry? I made delicious schnecken. Steven tasted them. Aren't they good, Steven?"

"Yeah, Ma . . ." Steven remained neutral. He had missed none of the byplay. To be a Resnick meant that you operated simultaneously on three separate levels: the mechanical, which was polite and all surface; the technical, which was strategic, making use of the family's high verbal IQ; and the subterranean, which was where the emotional was giving out the straight stuff. Steven was engaged in using all techniques in his own struggle with his parents. His head remained down over his plate, his glasses steamy from the heat rising off the meat and vegetables.

Marta sighed and settled back in her chair. Her father, his food half-uneaten, pushed back his own chair and said to her, "There's a   Philharmonic rebroadcast of the

Shostakovitch Seventh tonight. If you want to hear it at eight-thirty . . ."

"If we're still here," she said.

As Marta helped stack the dishes, her mother began a new line of attack to create collusion among them, to encourage team enterprise. "We'll have Dan's parents to dinner one night," said Mrs. Resnick, piling the dishes on the drainboard. While Steven stood washing them at the sink, getting his shirt front soaked, Dr. Resnick made a halfhearted swipe at the pots with a wet towel.

"Whenever you like," the doctor said softly. Mrs. Resnick relieved him of the towel. He sighed and reached into his pocket for his cigarettes. "We could take them out, of course," he said in the doorway to the kitchen.

"Oh, a dinner at home is much nicer," Mrs. Resnick contended.

Marta said, "Sure," and, quickly storing the clean dishes in the cupboard, pushed past her father and went upstairs.

It was premature to ask Dan's parents for dinner, and they all knew it. She shut her bedroom door with a snap. She and Dan weren't engaged. They hadn't even discussed their future, and the whole damned family acted as if the two of them already had an understanding. Well, they did have some kind of an understanding, but Marta had no idea what it was.

Fanetti's letter was still there, waiting. She knew why he had written it. She knew all the reasons: to keep her up-to-date on his achievements; to let her know where he was, so that somehow, even out-of-touch, each could locate the other in his mind's eye; and finally to give her a chance to write back and tell him what he wanted to hear.

She clicked on her little radio, getting her favorite

popular-music station. Holding his letter, she sat down at her desk. Dick Haymes was singing, "I'll Get By..." while Harry James's trumpet blew sweet and soft in the background. "As Long As I Have You..." With care she opened the thin airmail envelope. Before she began to read, her eyes roamed the two sheets filled with the familiar, optimistic, uphill scrawl. He could be sitting right there....

> 4th A.M.C.
> 24th Infantry Division
> Camp Hood, Texas
> March 15, 1946

Dear Marta:

I guess you can see by the return address that I'm finished with my medical training. I graduated a week ago and received my commission as a first lieutenant. Technically I'm in the army, but I will be doing my internship in a civilian hospital for the next year. Right now I'm waiting to hear which hospital it will be. Actually I may have two choices, which is pretty damned decent of the army, I think. It's possible that I'll be back in Philadelphia to serve my residency year at Municipal Hospital. Or I may decide to go out to California. I spent a brief period out there on R and R last year, and I really liked it. There's a rawness about life that is so different from home, where everything has been worked over and over...like soil that needs a rest from too much planting.

Anyway, the war is finished! You and I often talked about what it would be like...afterward. I always believed everything would be completely different. Now I'm not so sure. Some things seem to be constant.

I think about you often. At crazy times! It's usually some piece of music. Last week I heard Jimmy Dorsey doing "Green Eyes," and I remember you singing it for the first time in the gym. Your own green eyes were blazing with excitement on the double time! I don't think I ever knew anyone who reacted to the music quite like you. Your feelings were infectious, and I think I did more original music during those years than I ever did before or since. (Who am I kidding with that "during those years"? Actually it was less than a year, wasn't it!) I guess you'll never give up the music, and you shouldn't. You have a gift for song, for wonderful lyrics that flow with the melody. Maybe one of these days I'll be sitting in the canteen and I'll hear you on the juke. I'd like that, Marta.

But I'd like it better if it were really you I was listening to. In person. Sometimes when I'm thinking about you, I pick up the telephone to call . . . but then I decide that if you had wanted it to be different, you would have made it happen differently!

I'm not blaming you or judging you. I care for you too much to do that. And believe it or not, I do understand. I know that magic circle, invisible to us ordinary mortals, that was drawn around your life very young. It wasn't anybody's fault, I guess (at least I try not to think so!). I've seen a lot of basic human nature during these years of medical study, and all my initial impressions (from the collective wisdom of my big-hearted Italian family) have been altered somewhat. I used to think it was a wide-open world and you picked your own direction. If you wanted the prize at the end of the trip, all you had to do was get on the road, keep trying, and sooner or later you'd have it.

But I've seen too many losers . . . too many disappointed people, too many hopeless hopers. (And my medical career has only begun!) I'm not so certain anymore that the wide-open world is anything but an illusion, a product of some pretty powerful propaganda.

8

I was taught, I guess like you, that I could *be* anything, *have* anything, anyone, if I wanted it enough. Well, we know, don't we, Marta, that we have to subtract that "anyone" from the list right away. Because if wanting you could have made it happen, nothing, nothing would've stopped us!

I'm still not sure I'm going to mail this letter. As I read it over I realize that Big Doc Freud-Fraud here is not telling the whole truth. Some part of me seems to nourish faint hopes never forgotten, that you and I—

Although I haven't decided yet, I have already been accepted at the hospital in LA. I'm just sort of taking it easy here in this camp, with really no duties, for a couple of weeks. If you want to, you can write to me here. I figure you must be at the university knocking them dead with that brain of yours. I always liked the fact that you didn't try to hide your "smarts" with me, the way I saw you cover it up with other people. That was a big compliment. It meant that you had the same confidence in me, in my intelligence, in my integrity, as I had in yours.

We're alike, you and I. We pour our basic essences into the things we love, with no reservations, no holding back.

Even if I send this, I know I can't hope you'll answer. And if you do answer, out of gentility, niceness, whatever crap you want to call it, it will be a big mistake! There never was any halfway for you and me.

I'm listening to Les Brown at this moment on the radio playing "Sentimental Journey." I've taken plenty of them, as you know. And I'd do one more—

                                                              Vince

Dick Haymes softly crooned the refrain, "I'll Get By...." "It's great for you, Vincent," Marta said aloud, and was startled by the unexpected sound of her voice over Harry

James's silky trumpet. Old songs, new songs, any music could be used to conjure dreams. She could see Vincent almost as if he were sitting across from her, with his glittering gray eyes fringed by black lashes, the thick brows drawn together as he concentrated, the strong structure of his face and neck, the stubborn mouth. . . .

She had to tell him right away that it was great what he had accomplished. Reaching into her desk drawer, she took out a box of stationery, which wasn't getting much use anymore. She had bought it and had it imprinted with her name and address for writing letters to Daniel overseas. She hesitated only a second and then began her letter:

March 18, 1946

Dear Vincent,

I'm so happy for you, and of course not surprised that you are now a doctor. I would never be surprised at anything you achieved. I hope your work is everything you want it to be.

I am, as you thought, at the university, getting ready to graduate in June. I can't believe it all went so quickly. I probably made a mistake in speeding through in three years, but it seemed the "ambitious, clever" thing to do. And then the war hurried up everything, didn't it? We all felt the need to move faster here at home, to do more. I can only say now that I know I missed a lot in college. I majored in music and, of course, had to concentrate on that. But there were wonderful courses in poetry and literature, and even in political science, that I just couldn't work into my heavy schedule.

I haven't given up on the popular-music field as a vocation. I'm not quite sure how to go about it because I don't want to wade into the deep water in New York. But I'm told that the business doesn't allow for long-distance floating! As far as performing, I'm not interested in that at all anymore. I'd rather be the one that writes the lyrics . . . and perhaps some of the music. Anyway, I still haven't satisfied myself yet that there is no way to do it—from Philadelphia!

These next two paragraphs I've rewritten three times. I'm not sure why . . . because I was always able to level with you. I guess the big question is, exactly what is the truth? of yesterday, as well as today.

I loved growing up, Vincent, and you were part of it. I do not understand the process, but I believe that for me the choices were simple. You would say that's because I chose the easy way, and, of course, that may be the truth. Or the truth may be that I never could have attempted the tough way. It's possible that the tough road, in that sense, was never a real option for me.

Or maybe everything is true at one and the same time. And it's only the blindness of the moment that prevents us from picking Road A instead of Road B. But (I guess you can see what I've learned in Philosophy 29!) there seems to be a logical paradox here, isn't that so? How could I choose if I didn't see? How could I see if the circumstances were blinding?

You would say, cut out the bull, Marty! But I've got this unwieldy load of rational argument cluttering up my head and it won't let me off that easy! I tour around all the sides and can always see some other facet of the truth. You would say, if you want to be a perennial tourist, Marta, that's okay. But if you want to be a player, stop talking and get in the game!

Well, Vincent, I have. I'm going with a guy . . . and it's right for me.

I shared so much with you, but I can't share this. It doesn't belong to the high-school Marta who was testing, testing all the time, discovering the limits and chipping away at them.

I will never forget you. You're part of the music I love and part of my life. Even though I may never see you again . . .

Would it help if I tell you I can't stop crying, Vince, that the ink is splotching all over this paper, that all the philosophy courses can't help. I don't know why or how, but I learned awfully young the lesson that some things have to be lived with. There's a great future out there waiting for you. And if that road you talked about is not quite as wide or as open as we once thought, yours is a boulevard compared to everybody else's back alley!

I don't know how to end this. And yet I must. Don't think of me, Vince. And I will try not to think of you.

Marta

Her throat hurt with trying not to weep anymore. When she turned her desk chair around and caught sight of herself across the room in her dressing-table mirror, she was shocked by her contorted features and the mottled flush that had spread up her neck and cheeks. She turned back to the desk and addressed the envelope, carefully copying the numbers and information. There was no instantaneous way to mitigate pain. The trick was to resettle the dust of memories somewhere out of harm's way, to deactivate the mechanism that did the stirring. Nothing disappeared, only new layers hid the past . . . would someday hide the present.

When the letter was sealed, she went through her desk drawers searching for an airmail stamp and couldn't find one. The steady letter writing, the efficiency of the war years, no longer existed. She would have to ask her father . . . and immediately decided that he would somehow know the letter was for Vincent. She would have to stamp and mail it herself. Tucking the sealed letter underneath the desk blotter along with his, she sat staring out through the venetian blinds into the cold, clear, winter night, into the backs of the houses across the way where lights were still burning in kitchens and dining rooms. Cooking, eating, cleaning up, nothing had changed from the years before or during the war. Oh, the blackout shades were gone now, those that had finally been hung! There was plenty of sugar and coffee and meat in those kitchens across the way. But the people hadn't changed. Sighing again and again, Marta felt the fatigue of the week, of the winter, of the term, of old emotions, settling across her shoulders.

She suddenly heard the ring of the telephone out in the hallway. It rang twice more and stopped. Somebody had answered it downstairs. Mrs. Resnick's voice came from the foot of the stairs, faint but audible through the closed bedroom door. "Mart-a! It's Daniel! Can you hear me?"

She was at once on her feet and rushing to the door, out into the hall. She grabbed for the telephone, which stood on a small chest, and the extra-long cord spilled like spaghetti onto the floor. She wound it around her arm and removed the receiver. "Hi, Dan!"

"Busy, Mart?" The familiar deep voice filled with masculine secrets.

"Not busy!" She would find out what those secrets were someday. Dragging the cord, she went back into her room, shut the door again, and stretched out on her bed with the phone balanced on her belly. "A little tired is all."

13

"Too tired to go out tonight?" There was a tinge of disappointment.

She didn't hesitate a second. "Oh no! Of course not!"

His laughter resounded back over the wire, coming from a place down in his chest, a happy rumble. "Well, great!"

"What do you want to do?" she asked, wanting to prolong the conversation, not ready to let him go.

"We'll see." Daniel-type arrangements. "I'll pick you up at eight-thirty. Of course," he added, "if there's something special you want to do . . ."

"It doesn't matter to me at all what we do, Dan." She was already halfway out her bedroom door, ready to jump into the shower as soon as she hung up.

With the water rushing hot and needle sharp on her shoulders and breasts, she tried to rinse away the fatigue and pressures of the day. She let the spray hit her hard on the forehead, chin, and closed eyes. The heat was lovely, and she felt herself relaxing as she lathered her tall slender body, soaping the delicately molded rib cage above the slim waist, the rounded hips, the full bosom. Daniel! He had held her and touched her and kissed her. But they had never . . . She had not stopped him. She had felt his breath coming hot and fast against her mouth, his tongue probing hers, and then suddenly he had moved back, sighing, not letting her go, but taking it down three decibels. Cutting off the volume. She had used the same technique with others many times. With him she wanted more. But Daniel would go at his own pace. She breathed deeply in the steamy cubicle, gently touching herself all over, making believe they were at last his hands. . . .

"Hey, Mart!" Steven was right outside the bathroom door, pounding with his fist and shouting. "Don't use up all the hot water! I'm goin' out too, you know."

14

She rubbed herself pink and dry with a big old towel. "Take it easy, Steven. I'm coming right out."

Polished and powdered, perfumed, brushed and all made-up, in her best navy woolen slacks and argyle sweater, she went downstairs to wait for Dan. Her mother and father were sitting in the living room, reading, giving the new TV a rest. They both looked up as she came down the last step, and she saw her own glow reflected in their tired eyes. Both smiled with satisfaction, never taking their focus from her as she sat down as usual at the piano and began to run her long fingers over the keys.

"So, how about a little of the new Schubert," said Dr. Resnick. "Can you get through it yet?"

She opened the music of the "Impromptu in F Minor" and played the first bars. She glanced over her shoulder. "No comments now, Daddy!"

"Who me?" Pleasure, absolute parental pleasure!

"She's doing it beautifully," murmured Mrs. Resnick behind her as Marta sailed on through the music, aware that it was mechanically okay and passionless. She knew her father knew it too. She stopped on the third page. "And so on." She laughed.

"You're doing fine," said Dr. Resnick. "Keep going!"

But instead her fingers doodled over the keys, echoing aloud something she was hearing within. The melody was Steven's latest song. She couldn't have said at that moment why she was hearing and playing it. Some instinct to explore the old sadness was still operating in spite of the fact that her blond hair was curled and gleaming, that the fair skin was rouged and radiant, and that the hazel eyes, mascaraed and shadowed in pale blue, were bright with visions of the evening ahead. Maybe it was because this sad ballad that her brother had just completed had no lyrics yet, and hung suspended, waiting for her. Or maybe it was

15

because the dust of memory just wasn't ready to settle. She sang softly to herself as she fitted an accompaniment to the tender melody: "Don't think of me. And I'll try not to think of you. . . ."

Dan arrived, bringing into the living room the cold breath of the March night that clung to his new tweed sport jacket and scarf. Ready to leave at once, Marta started to put on her coat. But her parents had to examine and admire Dan's civvies, to talk to him about his course at the university and his new job at a local bank. Ever polite, at ease with them and fond, he obliged by lingering in the living room, making himself comfortable on the easy chair opposite Dr. Resnick. Marta's mother got up to serve tea and cake.

Marta lunged after her. "Absolutely not!" she said firmly, fixing Daniel with a glower that said, Now you'll see how long it will take! "Dan already ate, Mom, and I'm still full from dinner. We have to go."

"All right, all right." Mrs. Resnick reluctantly came back and sat down across from Dan, then pushed on with more questions. "It feels good to be home?"

"Oh yes," he said, and glancing at Marta with a half-grin. "I can't begin to tell you. . . ."

Dr. Resnick nodded. "Some things you can't describe." The clock in the dining room chimed the half-hour. Her father motioned at once to Marta. "Get WCAU on!" he said. "We'll miss the beginning of the Shostakovitch. Quick!"

She adjusted the dials of the big old Majestic that was destined for the Salvation Army the following week, now that they had the new TV and a small, efficient table radio. The opening bars of the symphony filled the room. Sighing, Marta sat down again and listened. After a few minutes she reached over and tugged at Dan's sleeve, whispering,

ALL SHE WANTS

"This goes on for quite a while, friend! If you've got some plans for tonight . . ." He stood up.

Driving into town, he said, "What was that music?"

"The Shostakovitch Seventh Symphony, the Leningrad. Program music. It describes the seige, the defense . . . very big sound . . . very brave and monumental!"

"What does that mean exactly?" He glanced sideways at her, his face serious.

"Oh, Daniel! I have no idea what that means." She laughed merrily. "That was just a little artistic mumbo jumbo!" She watched the chiseled features move into a frown.

"Come on," she coaxed. "You know."

His profile was sharp and clean against the black glitter of the car window, the straight nose and cleft chin, the curly hair that had been slicked down earlier in the evening but now brushed his brow. "You don't indulge in fakery," he said somberly.

She shrugged and looked out at the brightly lighted buildings of the city in front of them beyond the river. "Sometimes," she said, "it's a mistake to try to describe music anyway. Just listen to it. That's enough."

"Aren't those odd sentiments, coming from a scholar?" He glanced at her and she saw that a teasing half-grin was back on his lips.

"Well . . . I'm in a dopey mood tonight," she said lightly.

"But you don't really believe you can't describe the music, do you?"

She sighed. "You can do whatever you want to do. If you do it authoritatively enough, everybody will agree that you're an expert. And experts have special dispensation to say all sorts of nonsense. But God help you if you fumble it! You get pounced on! There's nothing more pathetic than an expert who fumbles. All those words, just running on and on . . ."

They had reached the center of the city and he drove slowly circling Rittenhouse Square. "Would you mind, Mart, if we stopped in to say hello to my parents for a few minutes?"

She stared at him, disappointed, wondering why he wanted to kill more of their evening together. "No, I don't mind," she said quietly.

He reached for her arm as he turned into the garage of the highrise apartment house, steering with his left hand. "My mother thinks I don't bring you around enough, Marta. My parents want to get to know you," he said, the familiar playful smile pulling at the corner of his mouth.

"Well . . ." she said, returning the grin. "I'd certainly like to get to know them too, Dan."

"They think you're very special." He was still holding her hand while the attendant waited for them to get out of the car. On the way up in the elevator, he stood behind her, both arms wrapped around her as they looked into each other's eyes reflected in the mirror.

The Reiters' apartment was elegant. They had closed up their big house in the suburbs during the war because it took too many servants and too much heat.

"Will you move back into your old house?" Marta asked Mrs. Reiter when they were seated in the big, lavish living room with its view of the city lights and the treetops of the square.

"Probably not," said Mrs. Reiter. "We like living in town. I think we may sell it."

"Or . . ." Mr. Reiter cleared his throat. "We may hold on to it."

Daniel laughed. "Don't hold on to it for me!" he said.

"Why not?" His mother was offering them both a plate of candy and nuts.

"Okay, Mom." He took a handful of the nuts. "Save it for me!"

"Who said for you?" Mr. Reiter smiled. "We may have other plans. To rent it, for example."

Marta was surprised when Mrs. Reiter went into the bedroom after several minutes and came out wearing her mink coat and hat. She began pulling on her gloves. "I really wish we weren't going out," she said.

"I'd rather stay and talk to Marta." Mr. Reiter got reluctantly to his feet. "You're the first real musicologist I've met!"

Marta giggled. "No big deal!"

Dan said, "Very big deal! She knows more about music . . ." Marta glared at him and felt her face flushing.

When his parents had left, she stood up, preparing to get her own coat. "Well," she said. "That was a nice visit, short and sweet."

He had come up behind her, his arms around her waist, his head close down near hers. He kissed her neck and turned her around in his arms. "Ummm." She sighed as he brought his lips down on hers, gently, then harder. And harder. He moved her back toward the big soft couch, reached behind him, and turned off the lamp. Only a dim glow from the foyer wall candelabra remained in the big room.

"Marta," he said softly. "I'm crazy about you."

"Oh, Daniel." She sighed. His hands were caressing her breasts, her waist, her legs. He unhooked her slacks and slid them down, gently stroking the smooth skin of her bare thigh. Without a word, they stretched out together on the couch. Time began to spin its web, lightly, softly, obliterating the world around them. She

19

expected that he would pull himself back as he always did at some point, breathing hot and fast. But he didn't even try to stop. She helped him as he drew down her silk panties. He rubbed her soft stomach, touched the curling hair below, and gently pushed apart her legs. He unzipped his trousers.

"Do you have . . . ?" she whispered.

"Yes." His voice was hoarse with desire. And then he was inside her, moving carefully, slowly, deeper and deeper. His hands reached under her buttocks, holding her high off the cushions, and his teeth bit into her lips. "Oh God!" she cried. She felt the rush, the dam exploding and filling her pelvis with heat. "Daniel . . . Daniel!" Wet with their mingling juices.

He held her tightly as they relaxed together, but she was suddenly aware of his full weight atop her. Trying to breathe naturally, she moved his shoulder and he reluctantly lifted himself from her chest. He peered down into her eyes.

"I love you," he said.

"I love you," she said.

They came down later in the elevator, still clinging to each other. Leaving the car parked in the garage, they wandered out into the cold March night, arms and hands linked. They found a tiny coffee shop open on a side street; and when they were side by side in a narrow booth, his heavy thigh pressing against hers, she tucked her arm through his. "You knew they were going out!" she said in his ear.

He turned his head and kissed her nose lightly.

"Didn't you?" she insisted.

"What do you want to eat?" He laughed.

She tried to move away from him a little. "You think you're going to get your own way all the time with me,

20

don't you! You think, Mr. Big Banker, that you're going to move me around like a chess piece and strong-arm me and . . .'' He kissed her hard on the lips as the waitress stood beside their cramped booth, order book in hand, grinning down at them.

She never got a denial or affirmation from him. It was all pure Daniel.

When he drove her home, the streets of Woodlyn were deserted and dark. The war was over, but it was still an early-to-bed community. A perfect half-moon sailed through the clear night sky over the roof of her house, throwing the whole row of attached dwellings into stark silhouette. The air was pungent. ''It's almost spring,'' she said, taking a deep breath as they walked up to the front door.

''Perennial spring,'' he said softly, shoving open the door, folding her again in his arms. He began to move her toward the porch couch. But she heard stirrings upstairs.

''They're still up,'' she whispered.

''Tomorrow?''

''What time?''

''I'll pick you up in the afternoon. We can be together, and have dinner later.''

She grinned at him. ''Be together where, Don Giovanni?''

He was holding her tightly, locked against his chest. ''My family will be out all afternoon.''

They moved together to the front door, reluctant to part. Suddenly serious and sober, she looked up into his eyes. ''Daniel, I won't let you always have your way.'' She needed to warn him of her own willfulness, her own needs, the strong tides that tugged her.

He kissed her again, bending over her, his hands holding her shoulders, pressing her hard against him.

''Good night, beautiful,'' he said softly.

While she undressed, she played her radio very quietly

21

so as not to wake her brother, who was asleep in the next room. The old Ray Eberle version of "Moon Love" drifted around the room. What would Tchaikovsky have to say about the liberty they had taken with his Fifth Symphony? Dropping all her clothes in a heap at her feet, she stared at the tall slim form in the glass. "That's the way it is, Peter Ilyitch," she said softly nodding to her golden, happy reflection. "All's fair in music and love!"

She was about to slip into the cold sheets when she stopped suddenly beside the bed, then slowly walked around the footboard to the desk. Beneath the blotter were the two letters, Vincent's and hers. She looked at them for a second, then, with a sigh, ripped them into tiny pieces, dropped them into the wastebasket, and climbed into bed.

CHAPTER 2

October 1981

WHEN THEY ENTERED THE HOTEL SHE HEARD THE MUSIC playing, big string sound. She appreciated the committee's taste in bands. It was exactly what she would have chosen for this kind of charity affair, given the average age of the partygoers. Music from the forties, her own emotional springboard. Marta handed her fur coat to her husband, Daniel; but when she saw that he had to wait in line to check it, she walked with him to the booth and stood beside him.

She always had mixed emotions at these big dances. It was a little silly—dressing up in fancy, expensive ball gowns to strut around with teased, sprayed, perfect coiffure; jewels (out of the vault for the night) strung around neck and wrist, dotting fingers (toes too if it was possible). All to make a public statement concerning the status of one's checkbook.

Yet, it had its purposes. You were reconfirming your spot in the social hierarchy; you were trying to forget your age, that the kids were somewhere in California (Utah,

Vermont, New Mexico, killing time, as if time didn't do that for itself). You were trying to remember that the beautiful girl you once were hadn't disappeared. She was still there, layered over with concerns and responsibilities, the accumulation of thirty-three years of married life.

Marta looked around the entrance to the ballroom foyer, all marble and crystal and perfumed ladies. In spite of herself, the excitement took hold. The music was perfect, lots of saxophone and trumpet. And those strings . . . Before the evening was over, she would be tired, bored, and faintly revolted by the extra drinks and extra food, the endless need to chatter, the strain of looking glamorous (God, Marty, how do you do it? Once a beauty always a . . .), and longing for the quiet bedroom, the few minutes of reading before sleep, the little bit of classical music on the radio, and Dan, turning out the light and holding her. "Good night, Marty, my love. You were the most beautiful tonight." And her whispered, "Will you always tell me that, even when it isn't true?" "It will always be true," and fast asleep he would be, instantly. With his clear conscience.

As if that's what facilitated quick sleep and pleasant dreams! She would toss and turn as always after one of those big energy-depleting jousts. Strung up and conscience clear too, but sleepless all the same.

They had come alone, in their own car, to the dance. Although the moment of festivity was delayed a little, and they had to join the crowd at the hotel instead of packing into somebody's Cadillac as they used to, this was what Dan wanted. When he was ready to leave at the evening's end, he hated to stand around waiting for friends. It was better for her too. She and Dan were alike in that need for privacy, for the ability to move under one's own steam.

They were alike in other ways too; background, interests, tastes.

Dan was handing the hat-check girl their coats. He was in pretty fine shape himself, his waist still lean, his back and arms still muscled like a young man's. His hair had turned gray, but it made him look distinguished, every bit the important banker that he was.

She knew she was lucky. Her marriage was solid, full of love and understanding. She had known, almost from their very first date, that he was the one. He told her often that he had known instantly too, when he first saw her singing at the canteen for GI's where she performed every weekend during the war.

World War II, many wars ago. A lot of ammunition over the horizon, a lot of pain in the psyche. They had been able, thank God, to sit out the Korean mess; but Vietnam had caught them with a son who didn't want to stay in college, who was wild for adventure, who had the face and body of a man and the judgment of a ten-year-old.

They had survived it all. They had fought to keep him out of the army; they had fought to keep him in school. He had made it through and he was all right.

She sighed and Dan caught her in mid-breath. He raised his brow questioningly. She slipped her arm through his, smiled up at him, appreciating the way he looked in his elegant black tuxedo, approving how he had resisted floppy ties and cummerbunds and ruffled shirts.

"Okay," she said, and they headed into the ballroom.

They had gotten only as far as the first table when they spotted their friends. They knew almost everyone at the dance by name or on sight, but their own special close friends had two tables pushed together, all carefully planned in advance.

Suzanne Diamond

"The Reiters!" A short, dark woman in blue chiffon rushed toward them, kissed Marta, and then turned and threw her arms around Dan, while he allowed himself to be pressed into her embrace. With a noticeable hesitation, he bent and kissed her cheek. "Hi, Doris," he said. The kissing ritual was distasteful to him, and Marta wondered why her friends persisted in it when Dan showed the same resistance. All the men kissed her. And Dan didn't like that either, but only she was able to read his quick glance and the slight stiffening of his back. Greeting everyone, he shook hands all around with the men.

Doris Brenner, Marta's closest friend, pulled her by the hand to the end of the table. "I have your seats here, near Herb and me."

The small talk, the laughter, and the clinking ice cubes from the first highballs of the evening mingled with the music and the general buzz in the large ballroom.

Doris inspected Marta from head to toe, then followed Marta's eyes as she looked around. "These damned lights," Doris said irritably. "The way they flood this place with glare is murder! For me, anyway. You, with your skin...you have some secret."

Marta smiled. "No secrets," she said. "They'll bring the lighting down soon. After it gets going. They always do."

Doris sighed. "As our eyes turn bleary and our hair droops, they'll kindly lower the voltage."

Marta stayed seated while Dan went to the bar to get their drinks. She ignored the plaintive tone of Doris's lament. What was the point of commenting? They had been friends from girlhood, and she had been listening to Doris complain for years. It wasn't easy to maintain relationships with people past a certain time. Jealousies, worries, and differing interests intervened, separating them.

To keep old friendships alive took a certain dedication to continuity, a belief that the flow of life depended on an ever-increasing toleration. It was easier for Dan. He had done business with most of these men. He was respected and sought out socially, undoubtedly because he was wealthy and influential. And, through no addition or subtraction of her own, she basked in his acceptability. Well, not quite. She had learned to be attentive to people's needs and to overlook their shortcomings. She knew she was all right as a friend, and gave a small internal nod to herself in her own behalf.

People were still trickling into the room, filling it to capacity.

"Some crowd," Doris commented. "You wouldn't believe it, considering the price of the tickets."

Her husband leaned across her toward Marta. "Who decided on three-fifty a couple?" he asked.

Marta shook her head. "The hospital dance committee, I guess. That's what this kind of shindig costs these days."

Doris said, "No matter. They're not going to make enough on this party. The hospital's in trouble." She looked directly at Marta. "But you know that. Dan's on the board. He must have told you all the details."

When Marta stared back at her blankly, Doris said, "It's Dan's bank that's involved; I mean, the problems are with the hospital's expansion-and-building program. I hear they can't repay their loan to the bank." She looked at Marta questioningly.

Marta said, "He never discussed it with me, Doris."

"The trustees fired the president of the hospital and half the board," said Herb. "The cost overruns were incredible!"

Doris added, "A lot of prominent doctors are leaving. Fortunately, mine's still here."

"I really don't know about any of this," said Marta. "I

27

did read something in the paper about the president of the hospital . . . but I didn't know he was fired.''

"Well," Herb said. "This may be our last year of dancing for charity! At three hundred and fifty bucks a throw, yet! It's 1981, the year of the breaking point!" he murmured, and his wife turned to argue with him.

Marta looked away. She was uncomfortable that she was so ignorant of Dan's affairs. Knowing that he preferred to handle his business completely on his own didn't help when her ignorance became a social embarrassment. It was wrong of him to keep so much from her. She regretted again that they were here at the dance. It would probably be better to send the money directly to the hospital anyway. Who needed all this hoopla!

The band had begun to play a soft, slow number and couples were drifting onto the dance floor. Marta, in spite of herself, listened with a smile and slow-mounting pleasure to the vocalist as she crooned, "I'll Be Seeing You. . . ." The old familiar lyrics filling the room . . . with all the old familiar feelings. Standing up, restlessly peering around for Dan, Marta wondered why it was taking him so long to return. She wanted to dance, knowing that would help start the evening off for her. Then across the dance floor, as the dancers shifted, a space opened and she could see to the opposite side. A tall, broad-shouldered man was leaning against a table, his back to his own group, eyes narrowed, arms crossed on his chest. There was something about him that was immediately familiar. She stared at him and knew that he was staring back at her.

CHAPTER 3

October 1940

SHE KNEW THAT HE WAS STARING AT HER. BUT YOU
weren't supposed to notice. It didn't matter that you both
went to the same school, that you might be attracted to
each other, that you were down here in the gymnasium at
lunchtime, for God's sake, to dance with your fellow
students, to get to know everybody, as the *Student Associa-
tion Bulletin* said. You still didn't do it. You were supposed to ignore Fanetti's intense eyes following you as you
made your way around the big echoing room, looking for
your girl friends. It was the usual draggy blue Monday and
the only thing that made school worthwhile that dumb day
of the week was the lunchtime dance.

The Jewish kids from across the bridge in Woodlyn, her
neighborhood, all clustered together in a large group on
one side, and the Italian kids from the Hillcrest neighborhood right around the high school fanned out over the rest
of the gym. This was their project. They played in the
band, crowded the dance floor, were the best jitter-
bugs, laughed, screamed, and sneaked secret cigarettes in

the corners with their backs turned to the teachers who were the chaperons. Oh, it was their show all right, the dark-haired guys with their peg pants and shiny pompadour haircuts, the black-eyed girls who wore red-purple lipstick and bright blue eye shadow, the laughing girls with the dark, high-combed upswept hairdos who hung around Vince Fanetti whenever he was free, who stared adoringly up at him from the dance floor and trailed after him in the halls and on the athletic field. Marta knew her friends would die laughing if she ever showed up with their kind of makeup at school. To begin with, she'd be reluctant to let her parents see her. Not that they were really strict. But her father didn't like any artifice, and Marta always wanted to please him. So she applied her cosmetics lightly, with a skill born of hours of practice, standing before her brilliantly lit bedroom mirror every morning before school, the glass reflecting back to her the pretty face that was surely on its way to beauty, once it had emerged from the lingering childhood roundness. She knew all the tricks. She patted and toned the pancake, never making the sponge too wet or the applications too thick, gently worked the dry red rouge high on the cheeks where those prominent bones would one day make fascinating angles, spread the blue eye shadow over eyes that were a clear emerald green, and with a moist, pinky lipstick, rounded the lines of the delicate mouth (à la Lana Turner) arching the upper bow and filling in the full, sensual lower lip. She made pouty little kisses to the glamour girl in the mirror, practicing for the male mouth that would claim that soft eager flower. One day soon, she hoped. A light dusting of powder here and there, never completely covering the shine of the camelia skin; a quick feathering of the golden winged brows with a soft brown pencil, and the job was done. Bending way over, she would brush the long, heavy

30

honey-blond hair. And as her head hung down below her waist every weekday morning at seven forty-five and the blood was rushing to her face, she often giggled out loud. She couldn't help visualizing the countless bedrooms of Woodlyn where other striving young beauties, all hung upside down, were brushing away like maniacs, while downstairs their mothers prepared oatmeal and French toast that they would refuse to eat. If they could get away with it.

Her father would never have stopped her in the morning even if her makeup had been wild instead of so subtle, and Mom, taking her usual cue from him, would have peered at her and not said anything either. But Marta always wanted to please them, especially her father, that soft-spoken, graying general practitioner who sat day after day in his little office, reading books while the patients stayed away in droves. He would not approve of all that high color for his Marta, his exceptional, beautiful, talented . . .

She tried never to disappoint him. Her mother said, "Don't worry about it. He knows all about disappointment." He had once been the busiest doctor in the neighborhood. But the Depression had sapped his drive. What's more, her mother insisted, he was too honest. He didn't give his patients enough medication. He didn't elaborate enough on their minor ills. When he finally got around to sending them bills, they stopped coming. "Believe me, disappointment is his middle name," said her mother.

Marta's middle name was Portia; and until she was ten she loved it, because her father had told her over and over the story of the lady lawyer's eloquent stand against injustice. Quality of mercy . . . How he loved to tell her about the old man who operated within *their* laws and was accepted by *them* as *they* needed him. And not a whit more! Her father's voice would lower three tones and

31

increase in decibels when he did the "If you prick us" bit. God, how that man loved theater! Drama!

Her girl friends said, "Oh, Marta dramatizes everything. The same things happen to us, but when they happen to her, oh brother, oh baby, oh baloney, Marty!"

It didn't offend her even though the comments shut her up and turned her inward. She dropped the Portia and used the P. alone. But they all sat up and listened when Marta Resnick got the floor at a party and began to sing, eyes closed, swaying to the music, as dramatic as she liked. They all watched her too when she danced with Solly Grayeboyes, her present jitterbug partner. Because she was so good at that fast footwork, because she was so "sharp," and a focal point for all of them, so sure of herself!

The gang ignored (if they knew) that she was an A student, a lover of painting and literature and languages and . . . well, you grew up with that. The combination of heredity and advantages, Mom said, you can't beat it!

She never discussed art or poetry with any of her friends, boys or girls. None of them would have cared. She was a private learner and had a secret kinship with the little scholarly boys who wore thick glasses and the fat boys who didn't play at sports and the weirdo girls with stringy hair and flat chests who adored Latin and could recite Virgil by heart.

So could she. Daddy and she had traced Caesar's conquests as she continued to study the classical language, following the power thrusts up and down the length of Europe and across the map toward the Middle East. "There," he said to her one evening, stabbing the map with his finger. "That is where Caesar first saw Cleopatra, and there is where Antony lost his heart to her. And there is where the empire began to crumble."

She looked at his jabbing finger as if it were the verdict itself of a relentless history, and in her mind's eye she saw the legions twice come, twice conquer, and finally fail.

Her brother, Steven Resnick, had no interest whatsoever in academics. At fourteen, two years her junior, he was already bigger and heavier than she (although Marta thought of her own five feet six in flats as above average, almost "model height"). Her handsome, quick-smiling brother was in love with ball games. All kinds. Football, baseball, basketball (his best sport), even soccer, which was as high class as tennis and almost as uncommon.

But his real first love was popular music. The sounds and rhythms, lyrics and vocalizing became their commons as well as their field of battle. They listened together; the singers were analyzed; they argued the merits of the bands, taking them apart (the use of brass versus strings, the wonders of the piano players . . . Count Basie, The Duke, whew!). They both took piano lessons. She learned more, but Steven was a natural. Of course, he wouldn't practice. He could pick up the melody of any pop song from the radio and beat it out in the key of C with a thumpy bass that was all right, but he could never play even the basic Mozart.

Mozart seized at Marta's brain. It was so difficult. It seemed so easy. It held, she would discover, a kind of key she could apply to life situations later on, taking all the richness and complications and making them look simple. That was the hallmark of the master. She understood it almost at once when she first started to play some of the early sonatas at about the age of nine, and she never stopped marveling at the complexities of the designs, the layering of the sonorities, the purity of the melodies.

Her brother, Steven, just shrugged and ran out of the house when his mother tried to make him practice. Marta

33

would hear him out in the back, in the alleyway, shooting baskets, hitting the wall over the garage door where he had put up the rim. Snap! Bang! He had the most amazing deadeye for a little kid.

Her father didn't like their intensity about popular music. Her mother said to him, "What's the difference?" But to make him happy she insisted that Marta and Steven start again on their violin lessons, which had ended several years before. They had good ears; the teacher said their intonations were amazing for beginners. But Marta, just turned twelve, didn't have time, what with homework and piano and learning to be beautiful (makeup at least an hour a day after school with the girls). And Steven, who could play tunes after his first three lessons and was only ten years old at the time, never picked up the instrument between his sessions with the teacher. Good money after bad. They had stopped after a year or so. But both of them sailed into the string sections of their school orchestras. The violin wasn't their instrument, they both knew, but music itself was an irresistible lure. In his school, Steven made the last of the second fiddles, and of course when Marta tried out for her orchestra she was made a second too. Steven was happy sawing away back near the corner of the stage, but Marta, who was more competitive, would challenge the chair in front of her (a fat senior girl with long, oily black hair who got on Marta's nerves), and occasionally she was the better of the two and got herself moved up. But it was always a struggle for both Steven and Marta to maintain their facility. The music teachers in their respective schools put up with them because most kids wanted the brass, and the string sections were woefully small.

Classical music and the orchestra never interfered

with their devotion to the hit parade. Pop music was a steady, exhilarating presence in their lives.

What their father really didn't like was when Marta stood up in the living room making believe she had her hand on the mike, eyes closed, rocking around on the balls of her feet, singing her lungs out like the professional vocalists she heard on records. She and Steven shared a record player, but their record collections were private. Their tastes were close but not identical, and Marta was generous in lending Steven her records, although he sometimes gave them back with little scratches on them. She'd yell; he'd murmur an apology, eyes cast down, and wag his blond head; and Marta would feel like a louse and wind up buying him a new release.

He was her perpetually admiring audience. When Marta did her Kitty Kallen bit, Steven would sprawl on the floor, never taking his eyes off her face, his fingers beating time on the carpet. She would sing over Kitty's recorded voice, tossing the imaginary wire from the mike around the imaginary stage. In heaven!

But the real thing happened so fast and so unexpectedly that afterward she wasn't sure exactly how well she had done. There was an opening senior hop the very first week of high school. Marta and her girl friend Doris Molner got themselves invited through the devious process of promoting Doris's dead-head older brother, Sid. Very few tenth graders were asked; they were too new to the school to have met the senior boys yet. Not only was Marta invited; but by a series of impossible events (she told Steven afterward), one of the guys in Fanetti's band asked her to sing a number. Her heart pounding like Gene Krupa's drum, and hanging on to the microphone, she let it fly, hitting the high notes of "Frenesi" right on the mark.

As luck would have it, her mother and father, coming

home from a movie, stopped in to see what these dances were all about; and there was Marta up on the stage, swaying and singing, too surprised and excited to be scared.

Her mother said afterward that she had done fine. Her father agreed. But very quietly. Marta understood. The next morning, over late breakfast and the Sunday paper, she asked, "Didn't you like the way I sang, Dad?"

He put down the paper, took a sip of his coffee, cleared his throat, and said softly, "That sort of thing isn't good enough for you, Mart. You're a real musician. You don't need that kind of—noise."

She wasn't offended. But Steven, who was dunking his bagel in his milk and coffee and slopping it all over the table, made a loud, unpleasant sound. "Whatta you mean 'noise'? That band she sang with was okay. That's Fanetti's group. They've got some rep."

She tried to explain to her father that really there was no conflict. It was all music. As long as it did something to you, touched your feelings, it was good. The doctor didn't agree. But she went on loving it all; classical sounds were sharp little needles piercing the skin, locating special nerve endings. But, oh God, that Glenn Miller surge, that Harry James trumpet wail! Popular music beat her heart to a pulp like a great sledgehammer.

Fanetti's group was a replica of those hot or syrupy big brass combos whose records everybody collected. Fanetti was good. He was all business, ignoring the black-eyed girls begging him to "come on down and dance, Vince." He stood up there leading the band, or sat quietly at the piano, no theatrics in his style, big and solid like a football player.

She found out the following week that, in fact, he was a football player, their team's first-string quarterback. She had never seen a game before the fall of 1940. And when she finally did go (with curiosity about him in action and lots of confused emotions), the game seemed demonically brutal to her. There was that first golden Sunday afternoon in October when she sat with her girl friends in the stands, in the hollow across from the school, and saw him run with the ball for the first time. It was snapped back to him. He went back for the throw, was rushed, and then ran twenty yards for the touchdown, leaving the opposition in confusion behind. Without any conscious effort, she suddenly saw the scoring as an act of total courage.

Marta never stopped loving music, but she never learned to like football. The game frightened her and she couldn't enjoy it, although it always held a fascination for her, compounded mainly of apprehension and disbelief that human bodies would want to expose themselves to that kind of punishment.

Her brother was a complete fan of Fanetti in both his roles. Steven saw every Hillcrest game all through the 1940 season, and Fanetti's combo played all during the year at Steven's junior high. "He's practically a professional," Steven told Marta at the opening performance in September. Shaking his fair head, trying to convince his sister, Steven wanted her to know how superior his idol was. "He plays in a club too," he said. "And he gets paid!"

"What kind of club? What do you mean? How do you know all this?" she asked.

"His sister's in my geometry class. And she's a real good trumpet player."

"Are you kidding?" Marta stared at him.

"Honest, Mart. She's terrific." Steven had no reason to discriminate against female brass players. It was the sound coming out of the polished horn he was concerned with.

But Marta, who accepted girl flutists in her own orchestra, was enough her father's daughter to be faintly bothered by the notion of a girl playing the trumpet.

"What do you mean a club? Where is it?"

Steven looked pleased that he had information his big sister wanted. He liked getting and holding her attention. He took his time about answering.

"Steven!"

"It's some dance place or bar or something in West Philly. How do I know? Ask him! You see him more than I do."

She saw him every Monday and Friday at lunchtime. She could have gone up to the bandstand and started to talk to him. But she didn't. The time she had performed at the prom, he had simply asked her what key she sang in, told her to listen for the first ten bars and to come in when the brasses got soft. It was a nice arrangement of "I'll Be Seeing You." She heard later that he did all the arranging himself, although she never told him how impressed she was that night. He said to her casually after her two numbers, "Pretty good," and left the bandstand for a smoke break out in the yard with the other musicians. Marie DiVito, supposed to be the prettiest girl in the senior class, walked with him, laughing and tugging at his arm.

You just weren't supposed to have much to do with one another. In school or out, everybody understood it. They weren't exactly different species, of course, and there *was* an acceptance of coexistence (cooperation in school matters, for example, although the Italian kids had absolutely nothing to do with school government and never went near the literary magazine or newspaper). There was just never any hanging around together. How could there be? Their paths didn't cross either in or out of school. The Jewish kids took the academic course (education being both the springboard and the trophy of success, the means to all ends). The Italian kids mostly took commercial, or one of the other vocational subjects offered in their high school: auto mechanics, woodworking, mechanical drawing, courses designed to lead directly into jobs after graduation. And many of them didn't even make it through these courses. A couple of years of training in the school, and they made a fast shift out into the real world where the money was.

They came from poor families, the Hillcrest kids. Not that most of Woodlyn didn't too. But things hadn't always been tough for them. The 1920s had been golden for most of their families, and one way or another they had made this dazzling one-generation leap from downtown Jewish immigrant parents, (some of them had themselves been immigrants) to suburban householders. The pride in telling it! And even if they all faced the same battle of the lean thirties and the struggle to hang on to their homes, there remained for the Woodlynites the conviction of their specialness as people and the wonder at their second-generation assimilation into this best-of-all-possible-worlds.

The Depression hit everybody. But not equally. Some Woodlyn families had no cars, for example. (Dr. Resnick couldn't do without his because he had to call on his sick patients every day, although his ancient and temperamental Buick was always in need of repair). Some families even continued to have a maid. The Resnicks had an occasional someone to move furniture and clean corners, to do the ironing that Mom couldn't finish, although she was always home cleaning too, waxing and polishing, cooking up a storm for the doctor, who, unlike his children and wife, was a picky, uncaring eater.

There were many mixed signals flying around those Woodlyn households, Marta realized years later, after she was grown up and away from it all. You thought your brand of poverty was special to you, some small peculiar failure, not quite understood. And not quite inevitable either. "He could open a second office," Mom had once told Marta, "like Dr. Melman. I see cars parked outside his office here. Sure they're willing to wait for him to come in, in the afternoon. They're impressed with that second office."

There was no way of knowing just what the Depression, or anything else for that matter, meant to the Italian families. There was no contact. Even if you had some rare and odd reason for going through their neighborhood, you got in and out, with no monkeying around; you were in alien territory, not particularly dangerous but not comfortable either. Not that the Hillcrest neighborhood was bad in any way. It had trees and nice row houses too, and corner drug and grocery stores, but it was still part of West Philly and the streets were narrower and the houses seemed closer to the sidewalk, older, darker, and teeming with little kids. Oh, it just wasn't Woodlyn.

They learned the word *suburban* young, as the ultimate accolade for describing the upward flight toward success. Their own suburb was unique, they were sure, despite its proximity to the city. It still had unbuilt stretches of open fields and stands of buttonball trees, and here and there on special streets, the houses of the really rich, big single stone homes, set back, with gardens all around and full-time maids and even an occasional chauffeur.

Woodlyn's separation, its containment as a community, was reinforced by the deep natural valley, some forty feet below the surface of the street, that divided it from the rest of West Philadelphia. This wide and deep moat was the roadbed for the tracks of the Main Line branch of the Pennsylvania Railroad. The school sat on the Hillcrest side, and the Woodlyn kids had to walk across a long bridge to get there every day. They entered Hillcrest High through the special big wooden double doors nearest the bridge. Only they used this entrance, naturally. And only they came out of it at the end of the school day, trooping back, or wandering back, or laughing and running back, about four hundred of them, crossing their bridge (back to Paradise) every afternoon at two-fifteen, the official end of the school day. The sidewalk in front of their entrance and the bridge itself were their social arenas where infatuations started, dates were made, love affairs ended, friendships deepened, and where everybody learned how to smoke cigarettes. A soft pretzel coated in mustard in one hand (unless she was dieting) her books poised on her hip, as a Chesterfield passed from girl to girl, is how Marta Resnick pictured herself going home every day.

The seniors that year, in the fall of 1940, were a dance-crazy bunch. They won permission to have four dances over the year, aside naturally from the lunch-hour hops, and excitedly scheduled the first affair for the first week of school. To Marta's joy and astonishment, she was invited (sort of) to that dance by Sid Molner, her girl friend Doris's older brother. He was a shy and studious senior who never would have dared to ask one of the girls in his own twelfth-grade class. And in fact he wouldn't have had the nerve to ask Marta either, but Doris had arranged it. Dragging him across the bridge with her and Marta on the way home one afternoon, his sister said uncompromisingly, "You want to take Marta to the opener, don't you, Sid?" He was ambling beside Doris, looking uncomfortable, but he nodded silently and the date was set. Marta was thrilled to be going, even with a stiff like Sidney. She responded brightly, "Oh, Sid, I'd love it. It'll be neat!"

When poor Sid, flushed and almost collapsing from

nerves, picked her up Saturday night, Marta swore to herself that she'd make sure they both had a terrific time. But fate intervened in the way of Louis Morrow, a big-shot senior who somehow spotted her, asked her to dance, and pow!—that was it for Sid. He stood around looking forlorn while Marta, all dressed up in a pink taffeta gown, whirled around the dance floor. To add insult to injury, one of the guys in the band, out of the blue, asked her to perform! He had heard her singing in music class, a solo part, one of those peppy hallelujahs that she loved. So there she had been at that first dance, a little nobody tenth grader, dancing four numbers with Lou Morrow (the best-looking guy in the school!) and topping it off by singing from the bandstand, mike in hand, while Mom and Dad, who had stopped in to check out the evening, stood in the rear of the gym, listening.

She and Sid never went out again. In fact, he was so embarrassed by her popularity and by the mistake he had made in taking out a winner rather than another shrinking violet that she couldn't even get him to exchange a few civil words when they met in the Molner living room.

Lou Morrow became a part of her life. Not an absolutely constant part, because he was busy and popular and dating (often if not steadily) a particular girl in his class. Marta looked for him out of the corner of her eye at lunch dances and after school. Finally he began to call her on the telephone, and she went out occasionally on a Friday night with him and his gang to the Hot Shoppe for milkshakes and hamburgers, after hanging around somebody's house, dancing, smoking, and laughing a lot.

They all lived in Woodlyn, close to one another, and though their circumstances obviously varied, row house, or semidetached, or big single with grounds, they all "belonged." Falling in and out of love with one another was what you were supposed to do.

You weren't supposed to get involved with the kids from Hillcrest. The contact between the two main groups was minimal by design and intent. Just like the contact between either of those groups and the small band of Negro children from down the hill in the city. The groups hardly even saw one another, except in homeroom, which was arranged alphabetically and which lasted only ten minutes for roll calling every morning at eight-fifteen. All the academic classes were ability grouped, and the Woodlyn kids seemed destined to be stuck together. Of six or seven sections in each of the tenth, eleventh, and twelfth grades, they always filled the top three.

Marta knew that the Italian kids detested the Negro kids. During her three years in the high school, there were several minor skirmishes between them and one open terrible clash that took place down in the hollow between the railroad tracks and the football stadium after an athletic meet. A lot of the kids got banged up, and Louis Morrow, Bob Goldin, and another of the senior boys, who had intervened to try to stop the fight, themselves got bloodied.

Mostly they just avoided one another. Of course, Fanetti did have two black boys in his band: Mackie, a sax, and Jones, a trumpet. They were really good. Once a group of the black girls came to a lunchtime dance, heating up the floor with the most amazing jitterbugging Marta and her friends had ever seen, sliding under one another's legs and writhing all over the place until one of the teachers had to come onto the floor to stop them. They left and never came back. But Marta never forgot the abandonment, the mad inflation of spirit that she saw in that performance. She herself was a good dancer and she thought she could

43

learn to do it their way. But it scared her, for some reason. It was too wild; it was too free. It was too sexy, and sex was off limits in any and all forms for the girls. Even the necking-kissing and petting-touching that went on in the backs of automobiles were discussed only with best friends, and all secret, dark, deep desires were glossed over or kept private. Marta was just a tenth grader when she saw that dancing, taking it all in, but she got the message quick!

There were various messages being sent out all the time by the grouping off, by the behavior patterns, by the advice and small talk that buzzed among her friends, and by all the arcane, cryptic little codes that prohibited, prevented, even condemned certain practices. You learned what to do and what not to do.

Marta was always one of the fastest learners around. In school and out.

That first time she noticed Fanetti's eyes on her in the gym, she thought he was just remembering the accident of a new little tenth grader taking off on his big-deal bandstand at an opening senior dance. But each time she came down for the after-lunch dances, while she herself was subtly peering around for Lou Morrow, she became aware of the musician staring at her. Once or twice she and Fanetti passed in the hall at the change of classes, and she nodded to him and smiled. He looked startled and turned away quickly. So he understood the rules too. She was to tell herself that many times over the next years. He watched her, but he never approached. And he frequently had Marie DiVito or some other pretty girl trailing beside him, a senior from his own crowd.

It was on a Monday that they finally met and talked. Marta always hated Mondays. Never coming to school unprepared, she nevertheless found it a drag to get to work on Sunday. She'd push herself, but still she never felt quite ready for the new week. She liked to be right on top of her schoolwork, and she didn't mind studying. But Sunday was such a glorious fun day, what with sleeping late, and big wonderful breakfasts (the only morning of the week that she really ate, stuffing herself with smoked fish and Danish pastries) and the Sunday newspapers, and the beginning of the New York Philharmonic on the radio. She listened to just the first number because she had to meet the kids at the Woodlyn movie for the afternoon show to look at guys rather than the screen, to giggle and sneak a smoke. And afterward, the quick Sunday-night supper, and the greatest thing of all, her Beta Gamma sorority meeting. There the girls were like her, "sharp," all Beta-type, all privy to the subtleties of dress, decorum, and orientation that gave them their special cachet.

That Monday had been particularly difficult for Marta. After the Beta Gamma meeting the Sunday night before, she had stayed up late, trying to finish an English-composition paper that somehow just wouldn't come right. The language remained awkward and stilted, her point getting lost in a lot of fancy verbiage. At midnight she was still crossing out and rewriting, so that it was after one before she finally got to bed. In the morning, she was dopey, trailing over the bridge after Doris Molner, her best friend, who gave her a tin ear with her running commentary on everybody and everything that had happened to her over the weekend.

She did a lousy job on a surprise Latin quiz, and when she went to the girls' room before lunch and looked at herself in the mirror as she repaired her makeup, her face was pale and tired.

She never thought, though, about skipping the lunch-hour dance. That twice-a-week whirling around the gym to the drum-heated beats of the band set her up in some mysterious way, making her feel light and charged.

She walked into the big high-roofed gymnasium, looking first for Lou, then for her girl friends, and finally for Solly Grayeboys, who was by far the best dancer in the school, although God knows he was no beauty! He was too small and thin. Actually Marta was almost two inches taller than he. Solly had further ruined whatever looks he had by aping the current fashion and practically shaving his scalp. Lou Morrow was one of the guys who looked good in the faddish Ivy League crew cut, because you had to have the physique, the bone structure, and of course the right kind of thick straight hair—the blonder the better. Solly's black hair was curly and his crew came out of his scalp in little steel-wool spikes that didn't go at all with his large-featured face. He certainly wasn't the sort of guy Marta could ever be attracted to. But how that boy could move! "Snake-hips" the others called him. He had double-quick reflexes and a miraculous sense of timing. Strong arms and legs. Marta felt totally controlled by him on the dance floor as he went through his fast-paced gyrations, giving her sharp signals in advance, twirling her out and pulling her back with his sinewy strength. Right on beat. He never lost a step and she learned to keep up with him! There were very few girls who could. Sooner or later during the Monday or Friday lunch-hour dance, there would be a really fast number and one by one the couples would drop back; and wherever he was, Solly would come find her, and they would more or less have the floor to themselves with everybody looking at them.

She didn't see any of her friends when she walked into the gym that Monday. The room wasn't very full, because there was a pep rally taking place in the auditorium for the biggest game of the football season. Although the players didn't attend (Fanetti was up on his usual spot on the bandstand, she saw), a lot of the kids had gone to the auditorium to learn the new cheers. There was no sign of Lou or Solly. She walked slowly about the perimeter of the big gym, seeing who was around, saying hi to some of the kids, and not quite being able to make up her mind whether to stay or go. It was disappointing. While she was wandering back and forth, she looked up, and sure enough Fanetti was watching her, seated at the piano, playing softly, his intense eyes peering around the room, she just knew, following her.

She thought she saw Doris coming in at the entrance and began to amble over there. The number had ended and just as she walked past, Fanetti jumped off the bandstand and came toward her. "Hi," he said.

She hadn't realized how tall he was. Of course, she was in flats, polished brown moccasins that she really didn't like as much as her high heels. You had to wear the flats to school with argyle socks or other heavy-knit anklets, though, because that was the collegiate dictum you obeyed, the price for being "smart."

"Hi," she answered.

"How 'bout doing a number for us at the dance Friday night?"

"I didn't know there was a dance," she said.

"It's a special. . . ."

"Oh . . . okay. What did you have in mind?"

"Do you know 'Green Eyes'?"

"I can do that."

"What kind of tempo do you like?"

"Well, you know the way Helen O'Connell does it?"

"A slow verse and then a fast one, ending fast?"

"That's it."

"Well . . ." he said.

They stood facing, looking past each other.

"Okay," she said after another awkward minute and began to walk away.

"Hey," he called. "Can you rehearse after school?"

"Today?" She took a couple of steps back toward him.

"Well . . . I got football practice. . . ."

"Well, you tell me."

"Actually, it's gonna be every day this week after school, because of the West Philly game on Sunday."

"Sure," she said, and out of the corner of her eye she saw that her two friends, Doris Molner and Phyllis Cooper, were standing in the doorway, their eyes pinned on her and Fanetti.

"Look," he said, "can you be down here this afternoon at two-fifteen?"

"Soon as I get out of my last class."

"Two-twenty. Okay?"

She looked up at him and noticed the wide spacing of his even features, the heavy, clear line of the cheek bones and jaw bones, the dark brows and straight nose.

She said, "I thought you had to go to practice."

For the first time their glances met and held. His eyes were gray. She had never seen anything like them; the irises were tinged with amber and ringed in black. He had the kind of thick dark lashes the girls tried to create with oils and lotions and mascara. He could be considered a very handsome guy, by some standards.

"I can be ten minutes late," he said, his eyes now searching her face. She looked away in embarrassment. There was an intensity to his stare that unnerved her.

"I don't want to get you in any trouble," she said.

"It's okay," he said. "Just get here as soon as you can."

"We're not gonna have much time," she said.

"It's all right."

Just as Marta started to move away, a small, dark-haired girl rushed over to him. "Hey, Vince," she said, grabbing his arm, "going to dance?"

"No. I'm not, Marie."

Marie DiVito, with her dark eyes, was the seniors' glamour girl. She didn't let go of Vincent's arm and he grinned down at her.

"Come on, boss man, break the rules for just this once! For me!" Marie insisted.

He shook his head. Pulling away gently from her, he turned and jumped back up on the stand.

The band went into "Chattanooga Choo Choo," which they did with a lot of clarinet and really fast. Marta wanted to dance, but the girls were waving so she threaded her way between the dancers, headed in their direction. She didn't make it all the way across the floor, because Solly tapped her on the shoulder.

"How you doin', Mart?" He reached for her hand; she smiled, nodded, eyes bright, her chin up. All ready. Pulling her into the sharp rhythm, her feet flying, her hips loose. The music seemed to keep picking up tempo; and as she was twisted out and sprung back by her partner, she saw Fanetti glance her way, stare for a second, and then turn his back to the dance floor. His hands were beating time for the band to follow, held low in front of him: he didn't go in for a lot of gyrations up there, but the band paid attention to him. She swore it was the fastest "Choo Choo" she had ever danced to, and when it finally ended with a big flourish, she and Solly were both panting and sweating.

"Gee, that was something," she said.

Solly was looking back and forth between her and the band. "Wonder what the hay he was tryin' to prove."

She was going to walk away when Solly unexpectedly

49

pulled her back for a slow number, "I'll Never Smile Again," which was really a freaker because she never danced slow ones with him. Doris danced by and Marta said hello over Solly's shoulder. Way over! She stood at least two and a half inches taller than he did, and she knew she must look goofy. But she didn't slump like the girls usually did when they were stuck with a short guy. Instead she put on her dancer's back, arrow straight, with the shoulders dropped nice and square, as she had been taught in ballet. Her left hand dropped gracefully against the back of Solly's thin neck. What the heck, it wasn't her fault that he was such a shrimp!

The whole day was peculiar because when she went to leave him at the end of the number, Solly held on to her hand and said, "What's your hurry?"

"Later, Solly," she said. Doris and Phyllis were standing close by, round faces eager.

"What'd Fanetti want?" Phyllis asked as soon as Marta was with them.

"I thought for a sec he was gonna ask you to dance, Mart." Doris looked back and forth from the bandstand to Marta.

"He wants me to sing on Friday night."

"What's Friday night?"

"You've got me!" Marta shrugged.

"Two days before the West Philly game," Phyllis said.

"So what's that got to do with Marty singing?" asked Doris.

"Special dance, maybe, or something," said Phyllis.

"He likes you, Mart." Doris smirked, her full face wise and amused.

"Don't be silly," Marta answered, but somehow without looking back at the bandstand she could feel Fanetti's eyes on her again.

"Kid, he's still staring," said Phyllis.

When they left the gym for their algebra class, Doris said to her suddenly, "Would you dance with him if he asked you?"

Marta shrugged. "He never leaves the bandstand."

"But suppose he did. What would you do?"

"What do you mean what would I do? I've been properly introduced, Mommy. I can dance with the guy. So what?"

"I don't know . . . I mean, you know."

Marta turned to face her at the classroom door. "No, I don't know," she said, surprising herself with a sudden flash of anger. "I don't understand. Is it some kind of crime to dance with him?"

"He's . . . Italian!"

"No kidding." Marta pushed through the door, leaving Doris standing puzzled out in the hall.

She couldn't have said herself just what had gotten into her. It was something about Doris's certainty of her sure-negative response that set her teeth on edge and got to her in some strange way.

Seated at her desk, she stopped thinking about the whole episode because the new algebra was difficult and she hadn't done sufficient study the night before. Her attention was riveted on the teacher and the board; she was confused, but not worried that she didn't quite understand her work. Her father would explain it to her. There was some design, some little principle that she wasn't getting. She had a pretty good instinct for math, and she had done the homework correctly. But she didn't have it down cold. She'd get it by tomorrow.

When the bell rang at two-fifteen, she skipped going to the locker room and took off instead for the gym. He was there, all alone at the piano, when she walked in.

"Hi." She was suddenly very shy with him.

51

He nodded, glanced up, then went on with some noodling around at the keyboard. It was a soft and pretty melody she didn't know. She stood beside the piano for a minute, and then he looked up suddenly and said, "Well, okay. Let's hear it!" and went into a swinging tempo, the first chorus of "Green Eyes." She picked up after the intro, keeping the rhythm sexy like O'Connell did it, and then when he broke into double time, she was right there on top of it.

"Try the key of C," he said, making no comment on how she sounded.

"Why?"

"You're pushing your voice on the top notes." He looked up at her briefly. "That's bad for the throat."

"I'm not pushing."

He played the verse again in the key of C and she picked it up and it felt pretty good. Actually more comfortable.

"Now try to phrase it a little better on the slow time. Take a breath. Don't try to push it out all at once."

She followed what he said and it felt a little peculiar to be lagging a hair's-breadth of a beat behind the piano; but he kept nodding that it was all right, and she thought the effect was interesting, with a kind of tension in it.

They went over the music two or three more times, and then he looked up at the clock. She followed his eyes. It was past two-thirty. "Gee, you better go," she said.

He stood up but didn't hurry. "You walkin' the bridge?" he asked.

"I have to go to my locker," she answered.

Out in the hall he said, "So long," but suddenly turned back to her. "Let's try it again tomorrow."

She avoided his eyes. "If you think it's necessary."

"It can't hurt," he said, and then he was gone, on the double.

She stood in the hall, bewildered, looking after him as he ran lightly through the doorway and down the sidewalk. She stood staring until he had disappeared from view.

Shaking her head, all kinds of confused feelings playing havoc in her throat and chest, she got her things out of the locker and headed for home with the few other late stragglers across the bridge. Halfway over, she stopped. Down in the hollow the players were divided into four-man practice groups, running, shoving, pouncing, falling on one another. Even from the distance, up on the bridge, it appeared violent to her. As she watched, fascinated, leaning on the concrete railing, looking past the railroad tracks toward the Hillcrest stands and playing field, she saw a single figure off by himself, away from the groups that were exercising. He had his hands on his hips and he seemed to be looking directly up at her. She turned her head quickly and jogged the rest of the way home.

CHAPTER 4

October 1981

IT WAS HE. SHE STOOD ROOTED NEXT TO THE TABLE FULL of her laughing, joking friends as the dancers on the hotel floor closed off her view of the man on the other side of the room. It was Vincent Fanetti. She was sure. This time it was not her crazy imagination playing now-you-see-him-now-you-don't. That game had gone on, uninvited, unwanted, for a long time. Sometimes wandering around in the market, reluctantly pushing a metal wagon full of groceries, or across a jammed theater, or during the intermission at a concert, she would think she saw his tall form, the angular face, the narrowed, intense stare. But it was never he. Many years earlier he had gone to California to practice medicine. That much she had learned after their final meeting, their final parting.

But tonight was different. The setting was possible, a charity dance for the Philadelphia Municipal Hospital. For some reason he had come east and was here this evening. Marta looked around for her husband. If she had spotted Dan at that moment, she might have turned away from

Vincent Fanetti and the meeting that was not inevitable. But Dan was nowhere in sight.

Almost without volition, she moved toward the dance floor and began to push through the crowd swaying in time to the music. They met right in the middle, shoved and bumped by the dancers.

"Well," she said softly.

"Hello, Marta." His voice was the same. His eyes were the same. His face was . . . older, of course, she thought, lined, tanned from the California sun, his hair gray, even the dark brows a little gray. Still handsome, movie-star looks, a gypsy in a perfectly tailored tux. You would never mistake Vince Fanetti for a banker. Though she wasn't sure why.

He reached for her and she was in his arms, dancing. And as she was waiting for it to happen, the years began to slip away. Yet, they were two strangers on a hotel dance floor with a wall of time and events separating them.

"I was hoping I would see you here," he said.

"Dan . . . my husband is on the board of the hospital," she said, hating the unctuous tone that crept into her voice.

"I know."

"Oh! When did you get back to Philly?" She had to know, for some reason.

"A couple of weeks ago."

"Are you going back to California? Or staying?"

He looked over her head and then down into her eyes again. "That depends," he said softly.

She didn't ask the question, and he didn't volunteer the answer. The music was ending. Her mind raced, trying to figure what she wanted: to be with him? to play catch-up? to let it go? To walk away right now was impossible. Even as she considered saying lightly and brightly, "Welcome

56

back to Philly, Vince, permanently or not. I wish you luck.''

And he was saying, "I'll meet you in the bar up in the mezzanine in about half an hour."

"Well . . . I . . .'' He was holding on to her arm. She felt the long fingers gripping the soft flesh of her upper arm. "All right," she mumbled.

But as she left the dance floor he was still beside her. "I'd like to meet your husband."

She stopped as the music began again and the dancers bumped into them. "What for?"

But they couldn't stay where they were and Vince was propelling her by the elbow back to her table. "Do you think there's any point . . . ?'' she asked, hardly turning her head.

Whatever his reasons, he was intent on the meeting. She took a deep breath and her eyes located Dan, with his back to the dance floor, sitting next to Doris. There was no time to warn her friend Doris, and Marta quickly positioned herself next to her husband so that when Dan rose, his back would be to the others.

"It took you forever," she said by way of explanation, smiling up at him.

"Huge mob at the bar." He was looking over her shoulder at Fanetti.

"Dan, I'd like you to meet an old high-school friend, Vincent Fanetti. Dr. Fanetti." And half-turning, "My husband, Daniel Reiter."

The two men shook hands, measuring each other. They were the same height, but Dan was heavier and broader.

They appeared to be the same age, although Marta knew that Dan was three years older. She thought she heard Doris gasp, and she deliberately turned away from the group at the table to avoid further introductions. The two men were discussing the hospital.

"Are you coming onto the staff?" Dan asked.

"I'm considering it."

"What's your specialty?"

"Thoracic surgery." Fanetti was silent for a second. "I understand you're on the board of directors."

"That's right," Dan said. "Where are you practicing now?"

"Doctors' Hospital in LA."

"I see." Dan looked out over the ballroom. "Well, this is a fine hospital."

Fanetti's mouth curled at one corner into a wry smile. "I'm sure," he said, "in spite of the present problems."

Dan's gaze focused narrowly back on him. "They'll work out," he said shortly.

Fanetti shrugged. And then he said more loudly and distinctly, "My wife is from California. She would prefer to remain out there. So . . . I'm not certain yet."

"Well, good luck. Nice meeting you." Dan had ended it. He was holding the chair for Marta to sit down. Her drink stood at her empty place, the ice melting.

Fanetti was gone, behind her, swallowed up in the crowd somewhere on the other side of the huge room. For a few minutes, with the noise blasting all around her, Marta had an overwhelming sense of dislocation, and she thought, Yes, I concocted this one too. But Doris was trying to catch her eye, reaching around Dan to touch her shoulder. Doris's face was awash with amazement. And Marta knew it was all real. She sighed and shrugged, raising her eyebrows at Doris, behind Dan's broad back. Then she touched his shoulder and said, "The hospital has some serious problems?" He nodded, interrupting the conversation he had begun with the Moyers, the couple seated across from them.

"And your bank? What's the connection, Dan?"

"Be okay," he said, and leaned across the table to resume with Mike Moyers.

Twenty-five minutes later, playing around with another watery Scotch and soda, she said to Dan, "I'm going to the ladies' room. I think it'll be a little while before they start serving dinner."

He stood up formally as she left the table, pushing back his cuff to glance at his watch. "Won't be long now." He winked at her. He meant, she knew, We can leave pretty soon.

She hurried toward the ladies' room and was about to slip past it when Doris caught her, grabbing her shoulder from behind and almost knocking her off balance.

"My God, Mart! That was Fanetti, wasn't it!"

Marta stopped, her mind racing, wondering how she could escape.

"Yes. What do you know!" She laughed. "After all these many, many years!"

"What'd he say?"

"He's married. He's thinking about moving back to Philadelphia."

"Who'd he marry?"

She gave Doris a playful shove and said as breezily as she could, "Go see!"

Trying to think of a way to leave Doris quickly, she found herself entering the ladies' room with her friend. There was a line waiting for the booths. Doris went in first, and the second she closed the door behind her, Marta called to her, "Meet you back at the table, Dor," and went spinning out before Doris could answer.

She turned toward the mezzanine steps, making sure

that there was no one she knew in the lobby. Her heart was pounding as she entered the small, darkened bar off the quiet, carpeted hall. Music was piping in softly and Vincent stood at the bar, holding a drink, watching for her. He motioned to the back of the lounge. "There's a table back there."

"I can't linger. . . ."

"Five minutes . . ."

They sat down together in the dim corner. "I'm still not sure it's you," she said.

He looked at her for a second before answering. "And me. . . . I'm always sure. It's you, Marta. I was hoping you'd be here tonight."

She drew back in her seat. "Please, Vince . . ."

He leaned across the table. "Are you happy?"

"Yes. Oh yes!"

"He's a . . . nice guy . . . solid. . . ."

"Exactly . . . He's a wonderful person."

"I was most expressly not . . . a wonderful person. Was I, Marta?"

She moved forward in her chair and leaned across the table toward him. The table was tiny and their heads were close. "You were special. Always special."

"Too special for comfort?"

"Let's not . . . tilt at old windmills, Vince. . . ."

"Same old battleground . . ."

"No. No. We're not the same people. You know that. How can we be?"

"Some things don't change."

"Everything changes," she said. "I have two children, a son and a daughter."

"Do they look like you?"

"No. Not really. More like Dan's family. They're terrific kids. My daughter's in graduate school. My son . . . is a lawyer.''

"That's nice."

"And yours?"

"I have a son. And sad for him, he does look like me."

"Still modest!" She laughed and touched his arm. But it was a mistake. He grabbed her hand.

"False modesty was never my game," he said. "I had something to offer you. And you knew it."

She pulled her hand away from his and sat back in her chair.

"I guess you're right," she said softly. "Some things just don't seem to change. The part of me that couldn't make it then probably still couldn't!"

"You never gave it a fair shot. Don't you often think—''

"No," she interrupted. "The past is . . . just that, the past."

"You don't believe in second chances?"

She said gently, "I don't think so. . . ."

"I wrote you letters and tore them up."

"Just as well . . .''

"Once I actually started to make a long-distance call . . . I had your home number. . . .''

"What's the point, Vince?"

"I wanted to see you, Marta. I wanted to talk to you . . . really talk."

"You said you had an offer from Municipal Hospital."

He shrugged. "It's not the first offer I've had."

"Why now? Why come back now?"

He leaned closer to her and reached again for her hand. This time he crushed it in his strong fingers. "Because time is flowing fast and I can't hold on to it. It's rushing past us, Marta."

"Yes," she said. "But seeing each other won't stop it, Vince."

"I don't want to stop it," he said solemnly. "I have no reason to. I want to get in those things that I lost . . . that I missed. That's all."

"Oh, that I do understand." She sighed. "I do understand that."

"I know you understand. You always did."

She stood up, next to him. He was still holding her hand. "I'm not sure I'm going to see you again. I have to think about it."

He was looking up at her gently pressing her fingertips. "Do you have everything you want?"

She smiled. "Steven once asked me about that song . . . 'All She Wants.' I made believe I didn't remember."

"I wrote it for you."

"Yes, but you never saw the story as I did."

"You tried to change the lyrics. . . ."

"I wanted to tell it my way. . . ."

"Still kidding yourself, Mart?"

"Whatever that means! Tell me, what's the prize for total truth?"

He shook his head. "I often wonder. Maybe total happiness."

She drew her hand away from him. "Dr. Fanetti, I'm terribly proud of you. I know you earned it all . . . everything you are, everything you have! But one thing is for sure, you were always the romantic. Not I!"

He began to rise, and she touched his shoulder. "Please stay here till I leave."

He handed her a card. "You can get me at this number. Leave a message. It's okay. It's an answering service in the hospital."

She shook her head, but she took the card and put it in

her evening bag. "I don't know. Good night." Without glancing back, she went down to the crowded, noisy ballroom.

Her husband got up and held her chair as she sat down. She was jumping inside. "Well," she said, "no dinner in sight yet." She laughed nervously.

"Are you hungry? You usually dislike these hotel meals."

"I'm not hungry. I really hate this kind of plastic food. It seems to come rolling out of a canned-goods factory back there somewhere." She leaned toward her husband. "What I'd really like is another drink. This one is all diluted."

He got up and she said, "Make it a double. They're all ice anyway."

He looked at her curiously for a second and said, "I'll be right back."

When he had gone, she finished the last of the watery Scotch and soda, trying to calm her shaking limbs. Her bare arms and shoulders were cold and the room seemed suddenly drafty to her in spite of the mob filling it. She turned in her chair, staring off blindly at the dancers on the floor, avoiding Doris's attempts to signal her.

When Dan returned with her drink, she kept sipping at it until it was gone and she had begun to feel the warmth flowing back into her legs and the trembling in her thighs stopped. At last the waiters started to serve the meal, wheeling in trays of waxy crudités, baskets of small cardboard rolls, and cups of pale, unidentifiable fruit. The glasses on the table were filled with red wine and she picked hers up and sniffed it, but she was unable to tell after the whiskey if it was any good or not. She listened to the conversation at their end of the table, trying to pick up the threads. It was difficult to pay attention, to reenter the party.

Across from her and Dan sat close friends, the Moyerses, who were discussing Carole Moyers's new job. "My wife, the family counselor," gibed Mike Moyers with a sheepish grin. His voice held a mixture of pride and embarrassment.

"How did you get to be a family counselor?" Dan asked curiously.

"I went back to graduate school," Carole said, her chin lifted. "I got a master's degree in social-service work. And now I'm employed by a local agency." She added emphatically to Marta, "I love it!"

"Sounds great!" Marta pushed away the warm fruit cocktail and sipped her wine.

"Everybody's doing something now," Carole said. "It's miserable to feel useless."

"Why useless?" asked Dan softly. He glanced sideways at Marta. Then, turning, he said to the group, "My wife has been involved in the local music scene for years. She's contributed an enormous amount!" And directly to her, "Think of all the great things you helped get started...."

She reviewed to herself: the chamber group she had formed, with which she had played the piano; years of steady practicing, performing in the libraries and schools. It had been pleasant. It had ended when she got bored. And the musical theater she had joined at the community center...the big productions that she did the music for every year, much of it her own original stuff. Everyone said their shows were better than the usual fare at the commercial theaters in town. Because of her...that outpouring of time and energy. Oh, she had been a busy musical bee all right. And not once had she gone into the kind of really tough, challenging, rewarding, professional field she had always dreamed of....

Dan said, "And don't forget how active you girls were in the PTA. That was important for all of our kids. And the work for this hospital. It's been very much appreciated. I know that for a fact."

"Yeah, yeah." Carole had won her battle. She refused to be drawn in.

"It wasn't easy, you know," said her husband, Mike; and then, laughing, "Particularly running back and forth to MacDonald's for dinner for two years."

"You survived," said Carole.

Marta's old friend Phyllis Bogin and her husband, Arnold, were seated next to the Moyerses. Leaning in toward the group, Phyllis said, "I just got a job."

"Some job!" mocked her husband.

"Well . . . it's not much yet."

"Not much money. Just much time!" Arnie Bogin laughed.

"That's right. That's how it is when you first start out." Phyllis, who had never worked in her life and had spent most of her married years in quest of clothes and fancy home furnishings, lunches in town, and tennis lessons, was enthused about her new role. She leaned across Mike Moyers and said to Carole, "I love it too! I feel like I'm alive!" She turned to her husband. "You just wait," she said confidently. "One of these days I'm going to really start selling my novelties." She turned back to the others. "They pay me a small salary to start with; it's a new business, but these gals who run it are really on the ball. And I'm about to start making commissions. I won't be working for peanuts much longer!" She said directly to Marta, "I never got one-tenth the gratification out of the volunteer work I did all those years that I get from one day of making my rounds."

Marta returned her earnest look. "Are you sorry you didn't go to work before?"

Phyllis shrugged. "Why think about the past? My kids

got what they needed from me." She half-turned to her husband. "I did my bit for home, school, and charity. Now it's my turn!"

"How about you, Mart?" asked Carole. "Got any plans to join the business world?"

The waiter was refilling Marta's wineglass, and she didn't stop him although she was already light-headed. "As a matter of fact," she said, "I'm having serious thoughts on the subject. My brother, Steven, wants me to do some work with him on music and lyrics for the big TV spring special he's preparing for NBC."

Carole said, "God, that's exciting! On a major network! Would you have to go to New York?" She glanced obliquely at Dan. His expression never changed.

Marta giggled. "Oh sure! I'm planning to take an apartment in the Dakota and spend hours with Woody and Mia and Yoko."

"You may be kidding around," said Mike Moyers, "but I read about your brother, Steve, all the time. They call him Mr. Music in all those TV gossip columns."

Dan said softly, "He really doesn't make the gossip columns that often. Steve is one of those people who found a sane and stable spot in that crazy world up there."

"He's with Darby and Colt," Marta added. "It's a big ad agency. They do most of their work for TV."

"Gee," said Phyllis, "what a great spot he must have!"

Marta nodded. "He records, he composes. He's the music director and conductor for all the specials done by his agency. He made it all happen himself!" Dizzy as she felt from all the alcohol, Marta had the familiar surge of pride as always when she spoke about her brother. "He had to swim upstream to get where he is. And Dan's right about one thing," nodding vehemently, "Steven's life is as normal as ours. Just a heck of a lot more interesting!"

Doris, sitting next to Daniel, was leaning on her elbows, her face in her hands, listening intently to the conversation. Bending across Dan, she said, "Boy, I remember like yesterday how Marta's mother had fits because Steven wouldn't apply to medical school. But I guess he showed them all, didn't he, Mart?"

Marta sighed. Her gentle brother had waged his own tireless battle against the programs prescribed for him. Against family. They were a tough combo to fight, Aaron and Lillian. You were beating on love. You were betraying the people who believed in you the most. You were disappointing the people who never disappointed you. Marta had caved in. Steven, with his shy smile and weak eyes, his tender manner and funny-little-kid laugh, had gone his own way, leaving her parents, sad and bewildered, behind.

"Music was always his life . . ." she said, and her voice was beginning to sound soppy in her own ears. Still she sipped at the second glass of wine.

"Who'd he marry?" asked Mike Moyers. "A Philadelphia girl?"

"No," said Dan. "She's from New York. A very nice person."

"She was a gorgeous showgirl." Marta giggled. "My poor mother almost died!" She was laughing loudly and Dan touched her arm under the table. She looked at him and saw the irritation and concern in his eyes. "Maureen is gorgeous," she enunciated slowly. "A real Irish knockout! And you know what? She's a doll. An angel. She's been the perfect wife. They have three great kids, and two of them will be doctors! How do you like that!" She said it defiantly and directly to her husband.

There was a moment of uncomfortable silence at the table. The music had begun again, softly now because the waiters were circulating, finally, with steaming platters of food. Dan made no answer to her gibe. He was looking down at his plate, sliding the silverware back and forth.

Marta leaned forward and across him, calling to Doris, "Get the music, kid? 'Moonlight Cocktail'! Big year, Dor, 1942!"

"It never happened," said Doris sourly. "There was no 1942."

"It happened!" cried Marta, and Dan watched her as she put down her wineglass. He carefully moved it away from her.

She immediately reached for the glass, tilted and drained it. With a small shrug, Dan began to eat his dinner.

Carole Moyers asked, "So . . . you still writing music?"

"Up till now I haven't done much of anything . . . outside of a few things for the community-center theater," Marta answered. "Not anything to speak of . . . certainly nothing that made real demands on my ability . . . whatever it may be! I never considered dabbling around here in local music circles as anything but . . . dabbling! After all, my time and energy were given for thanks alone! None of it was very important. Actually, all I've been is a little housewife." She laughed and looked up at Dan, who was buttering a roll. "There you are! There's a neat little lyric right there, to the tiny tune of 'Little Teapot.' Remember that one, girls! I'm a little housewife . . . bump, bump, bump." That tickled her and she started to laugh again. "I like to do lyrics," she said to Carole. "Steven was always better than I was at the music. But I do get ideas for both music and lyrics . . . now and then. Steven knows. He's been asking me to work with him for a long time. He's just never been happy with any of the assistants provided by the agency."

Her dinner was beginning to grow cold in front of her.

She sighed, picked up her fork, and stabbed a piece of gray roast beef. Whatever appetite she had had earlier was completely gone. She pushed the food around on her plate, picking at the wild rice and dried-up little mushrooms. A headache was beginning at the back of her head, and her eyes felt weepy. When the waiter tried to refill her wineglass she covered it with her palm. "No, thanks," she said somberly.

After dessert and coffee, the others at the long table got up to dance. She and Dan sat in silence for a minute. "Let's go home, Marta." She got to her feet, her head heavy on her shoulders. He took her firmly by the elbow and propelled her to the door. As they left the room, he half-turned and waved to their friends on the dance floor. He and Marta were, as usual, the first to leave. Out in the lobby he helped her into her mink coat. As he was tipping the hat-check girl and putting on his own coat, Marta thought she saw Vince standing in the entrance to the ballroom. He was with a slender blond woman and a group of men whom Marta knew were doctors on the staff of Municipal Hospital. She turned away quickly, and Dan took her arm again. They went down the steps out under the hotel canopy, the cold autumn wind suddenly striking her flushed face. Heads down against the unexpected northerly, they walked quickly to their car, and then Dan headed for the parkway, home. The interior of the car was chilly and Marta huddled down into her coat as Dan adjusted the heat.

On impulse she reached over and touched his arm. "Go through West Philly. Please. Turn around and go up Market over Lancaster Avenue. I want to go through Hillcrest . . . and Woodlyn. . . ."

He didn't respond but continued to make his way around

the planted circles in the almost-empty park, until he reached the Schuylkill River Drive.

"Dan . . ." she said crankily. "Didn't you hear me?"

"I heard you," he said. "But it's not a good idea."

"Why not?"

He shrugged, going toward the river.

She said, "We're locked in the car. For God's sake, why the hell are you so determinedly careful . . . all the time! So . . . so proper! So . . . correct!"

He answered evenly, "It's a bad idea at night, Marta. I don't see any sense in driving through that part of the city. I can be home this way in fifteen minutes or so."

"Oh Jesus! One lousy little favor I ask of you. . . ."

But they were already spinning along under the arching trees on the drive. The autumn sky over the river was high and filled with fast-moving clouds. The stars, small icy dots, disappeared and then suddenly glittered again as the clouds sailed on.

"You think you can't get rammed, bammed, and hijacked here?" she said petulantly. "All I wanted was to look at my poor old part of the city."

"Look at it during the day. And keep your car doors locked."

"You hate to do what I want." She knew her grumbling would be ignored. He made no answer; instead, he switched on the radio. When loud disco music blasted out, he grabbed for the knob and turned it off. She reached forward and switched it back on. Blaring, despite the diminished volume, was the number-three song of the moment, pumping the blood, the base guitar going like the systolic and the drum thumping the diastolic. If you had any blood left to pump! If you hadn't sat by and let it all evaporate. If you hadn't . . . "Oh crap!" she said, and

70

heard him mutter his disapproval. She put back her head and dozed.

He stopped the car in the driveway, and she got out wearily and stood sniffing the breeze, getting the faint scent of the last summer flowers and the first cold from the north. The wind was whipping the leaves off the trees, blowing them all over the grounds behind and alongside the big stone house. The fall had come on fast. Everything came on fast now. Just as Vince had said, you couldn't stop it. He had said he didn't want to. What he wanted . . .

They undressed in silence, and she went without comment into the bathroom for a steaming hot shower. She brushed her hair. She rubbed herself, face and neck and arms and breasts and belly, with perfumed lotion. Bleary-eyed, she examined her still-slender body in the mirrors on the walls and door of the bathroom. In the excessively bright light her eyes were reddened and heavy, but her skin glowed and her hair shone. All was not lost, she thought, nodding to the exhausted lady nodding to her. Petted and patted, she thought. Nevertheless, Mom had been correct too, all along. It was mainly a question of heredity.

She took two aspirin and when she came out of the bathroom, floating toward bed in her blue chiffon gown, she was somehow amused at herself, though she was so tired. Dan had found some soft Haydn on the radio that stood on the nighttable on his side of the bed. There was a tall glass of club soda with ice in it on the table on her side. He was sitting up in bed, reading a market letter, and he smiled to her as she climbed in. "Feel better?"

"I'm okay." She sipped her cold drink. "Thanks for the soda. It helps the head!"

He clicked off his light and lay on his side, looking up at her. The music had stopped and news had come on.

"President Reagan appears to have won his battle to sell AWACS to the Saudis," said the commentator.

He reached back and turned off the radio. "I love you, Marta. You're beautiful." She switched off her light and moved close to him. She fell asleep in his arms.

CHAPTER 5

October 1940

A LOT OF THE NEWS WAS UPSETTING. DR. AND MRS. RESNICK listened to H.V. Kaltenborn, who assured them that "Peace in our time" was still possible. They clucked to each other, Dad's normal pessimism making him shake his head with concern and Mother's usual optimism rescuing them both. "It'll be all right," she insisted.

"If the English can hold out," said Dr. Resnick.

"We're sending 'em destroyers," Steven reminded them.

"Let's hope it helps." Dr. Resnick got up to put his cup of coffee, half-finished as usual, back on the table. "The Germans will have to come to terms eventually. . . ."

"God, I hope so!" murmured Mrs. Resnick.

"But with the French out of it, and the Belgians! The Dutch and the Scandinavian countries . . ." The doctor sighed, seeing, as he always did, first one side of the problem and then the other.

"And the lousy Russians as their partners yet!"

"I don't know, Lilly. I think that was a move to buy time. But who knows?"

"The Russians are brutes," said Mother.

"And the Germans are rational, sensitive, caring. . . ."

Steven looked up from his math paper. "I saw in the newsreel at the movies on Saturday that they locked up a lot of the Jews." He searched his father's face. "Do you think that's true, Dad?"

Dr. Resnick shrugged. "It wouldn't be the first time," he murmured.

Mrs. Resnick said, "The Germans always treated the Jews better than the Russians did. Or the Poles, for that matter. The Rosenzweigs owned a lot of property in and around Berlin. You remember?" she asked her husband.

"Something's going on there. Something terrible. The Rosenzweigs better kiss their property goodbye."

"Eva Rosenzweig's brother and his family are still there. He's a very successful manufacturer. I can't imagine that they would bother him."

Dr. Resnick shook his shaggy gray head. His face was lined and there were bluish pouches under his hazel eyes. Marta tried to remember her father in a younger, bouncier version, but she wasn't successful. For a long time now he had looked older than his years. Why did time weigh on him like that? She often wondered why Mom appeared younger than he did when they were the same age. It hurt her that Daddy seemed old and burdened. But when he smiled his funny, quizzical half-smile and made some clever, right-on-target remark, he looked so distinguished and sharp. Mother always said, "Don't paint such unrealistic pictures, Marta. You'll have a husband someday. And believe me, perfect he won't be!"

But Marta knew that daughters weren't wives. And fathers weren't husbands. There were rivers of love and tenderness that flowed between her and her father. Who cared if there was less than perfect understanding! She didn't expect that. She thought she shared a reasonable amount with her parents, both of her own life and of theirs.

"There's no place in Europe that it's good to be today," said the doctor, sadly. He stood beside Marta's chair and looked down at her work. Steven glanced up from his paper. "How 'bout Uncle Max?"

Dr. Resnick shrugged but didn't answer. Communication with his old uncle in Liverpool, the last of his family that he knew about, had ceased months before. Letters were unanswered.

Marta looked up into her father's face. He never answered any questions directly about his uncle, or in fact about anything concerning his family. When Marta asked him, he said he didn't know, didn't remember, it was too long ago. His mother and father had died young, and Marta knew them only by the few photographs taken in their backyard. Sturdy, smiling people, Grandpop Resnick with a big white walrus mustache and Grandmom Resnick with a funny 1910-style bonnet on her head. But the smiles and solid appearances were deceiving. They had not lived long enough to enjoy the fruits of their children's accomplishments. The only remaining family now, besides old Uncle Max in England, were Dr. Resnick's two spinster sisters, who lived together in West Philly in the house they had bought for their parents many years ago. They didn't seem to know much about their family history either, although they all loved to talk and joke about their terribly poor, but hilariously happy, childhood in South Philly. Back so far and no further. And Aunt Moll, the intellectual sister, swore to Marta that she just didn't know anything about their own two sets of grandparents and what had gone on in their mother's and father's lives in Europe. All history began with the immigration to America, the land of dreams, the home of the free and talented, the land of opportunity and public education. And poverty. God, had they been poor in 1900! The year after the big arrival. Marta could recite by heart the dozens of stories of peeing in the privy on freezing nights, living on potatoes for weeks in the wintertime, relatives just off the boat, sleeping all over the floor in the tiny parlor at Second and Christian streets, just two blocks from the river where all the greenhorns came in. What a life it must have been!

But Daddy learned to swim in the Delaware on hot summer nights, and to defend himself against the Irish bullies from Fifth Street, and made it to Central High for specially gifted boys. And of course went on to medical school. And everybody had piano and violin lessons. Aunts Min and Molly went to Normal School, paying out of their salaries as elementary teachers for the new house in West Philly and for courses at Temple University at night. So it all meant something. It meant that Grandpop Resnick, who was working for nickles and dimes as an interpreter, and Grandma Resnick, who was running a butter-and-egg store for the Himmelfarbs, were inspiring their kids with a desire for learning.

They all loved music and the arts. Marta knew why she herself adored the theater and poetry. Deeply buried in the family was a lyric pulse, a zest for drama and life.

Despite the closeness of her family and the love they shared, there was a deep reluctance to discuss personalities, sexual relationships, and emotional intimacies. They were verbal enough for ten families when it came to discussing politics and literature and achievements. But certain barriers were there, erected in early childhood, among and between them all. Private lives were private. One's own, and everybody else's.

Dr. Resnick was pointing at the equations she was working on. "Trouble?"

"I get the answers, but I'm not really sure what I'm doing."

"Always try to figure that out, Marta. If you can." He pulled another dining-room chair over beside her. "Let me see the book." He looked down through his bifocals, scanning the explanations at the beginning of the chapter. Then he picked up a pencil and began to do some figuring on a piece of scratch paper.

"Dad?" Steven needed help too.

"Just a minute," he said. "I'll be right there. In a minute." He turned to his daughter. "Look here, Marta. Let me explain something to you." He did some equations on the paper as he read aloud the word problems from her book. "Think about what the problem asks. Think about what the problem tells you. Think about the methods you've been taught to pursue the answer."

Marta was nodding as he figured.

The doctor looked directly at her. "Abstract the principle. There's always some new factor added to what you already know. That's how you're brought along to solve more and more complicated problems. You see, sweetheart?" He was smiling at her and she caught the sharp, sweet smell of tobacco on his breath. Don't smoke, he cautioned his patients, his son, and his daughter, everybody who would listen; and he himself smoked like a chimney. Before she could answer, he had turned to the preceding chapter in her book. "Read here." He pointed at a paragraph.

"You're too far back," she said. "That's old work."

"I know. I know. Read it."

Obediently she read what she thought she had read and understood the week before; and as he explained what the problems in the preceding chapter were aiming at, the whole new set of equations became clearer.

"Yeah," she said and picked up her pencil. She figured some more of the new problems, saw the patterns more clearly, and with delight threw her arms around her father's neck. "Doll baby!" she cried. "Got it! Thank you, Papa!"

His nicotine-stained finger raised and wagging under her nose, he smiled as he reminded her, "Stop every once in a while and ask yourself some key questions. For example: This facility I seem to have . . . at anything, any kind of problem solving, is it based on knowledge, understanding? Or am I sliding along on the varnished surface of my intelligence. You can get by on that. But if you don't dig for the basics, you'll always be gliding over the real meaning. Algebra's like anything else."

Steven's nose was practically pressed to the paper as he struggled with his biology. "If you're going to be a doctor, Steven, you'll have to go at this stuff more slowly and more thoroughly."

Steven peered up at his father. "Who says I'm going to be a doctor?"

"I said," Mother answered from the living room. Not often, but emphatically when the occasion arose, she reiterated her determination that Steven would be a doctor like his father. And as usual, Steven made no reply.

"Why are you bending so close to that paper?" asked the doctor.

Steven looked up, surprised. "I don't know."

"What's the matter? Can't you see it so well?"

"I can see it."

"It's just a habit he's gotten into," said Mother.

"You come into the office tomorrow, Steven; I want you to read the eye charts. You may need glasses."

"Oh, Pop . . ."

"Now what's the trouble with this biology?"

"I don't understand about this cell. What do they mean by the nucleus filled with chromosomes?"

"A single cell, Steven, is the basic bit of life. Everything organic is made up of cells. And there's matter inside those cells. A nucleus, a center." He went on, pointing at the diagrams in Steven's book, and explaining it to the boy who was already looking over his shoulder at the grandfather clock that stood in the corner of the dining room.

"Steven?"

"Yes, Dad."

"Doesn't this interest you? It's fascinating stuff."

"Yeah . . . I'm interested. . . ."

"You come into the office right after school tomorrow. I'll set up the microscope for you. I'll put various things— a little piece of your nail, a little piece of cuticle—on a slide and you can see for yourself what they mean by a living cell. You'll find it interesting, son. Give it a chance to make some meaning to you. You're too bright to be so impatient with schoolwork."

Steven shrugged, and Marta knew he would show up at Dad's office as expected. And she knew that someday he'd outshine them all with his intelligence ablaze. What her parents couldn't see was that despite his size and physical maturity, Steven was still a little boy. Marta understood it well. She was the one he sometimes came to late at night when there was a thunder storm, uneasy, still a child in need of reassurance. She always sat and talked to him, even if he had awakened her out of a deep sleep to yak about dumb things like baseball and Stan Kowalsky, his best friend and rival, who always seemed to be outsmarting, outperforming, and outshining poor Steven.

Girls grew up faster than boys. She had found out when she was very young how to please everybody; how to be good at everything; how to be a star. It wasn't a trick exactly; it was figuring out in advance what was expected of you; it was feeling competent to deliver. The more you succeeded, the better you got, and the better you liked it. And the better they all thought you were. Someplace along the line, you had to get on the train.

Steven didn't even know yet that there was a train. It wasn't something you could tell him. Or anybody. It had to come to you. Out of nowhere. You had to wake up one day and say to yourself, I can do it all. Big me! And then you hopped aboard and went sailing out of the station. On your way! Steven had to find it himself.

The telephone rang at eight-thirty, just as "Lux Theater" was about to start and Mom was in the kitchen fixing them a bowl of fruit, which calorie-counting Marta and Dr. Resnick, who didn't eat between meals, ignored every evening, and which Mrs. Resnick and Steven polished off in no time between them. "Kitchen call," her mother signaled to her. That meant a male was on the line.

"I'll take it upstairs," she answered, already on her way. There were three bedrooms, and one bathroom on the second floor of their house, and the upstairs phone was out in the hall on a small table. But luck had been with her when the phone company installed it; they had added a cord that was at least fifteen feet long. Long enough anyway for her to pull the line after her, shut her door, and hop on her bed to talk.

"'Lo," she said, and heard Mom hang up downstairs.

"Hi ya, Marta."

"Well . . . How you doin', Lou?"

80

"Not bad. You goin' to Sandy Lopersteen's party Saturday night?"

Sandy was one of the cute, popular girls whom Marta and her friends held in such high esteem. Sandy practically ran Bêta Gamma, and all the girls copied her hairstyle and her sweater-and-skirt combinations. Lou had taken her out on dates.

"I don't think so, Lou."

"Why not?"

"I wasn't invited. Not yet, anyway!"

"Well, how 'bout goin' with us?"

Marta stared into the mirror over her dressing table and saw herself frowning. She unwrinkled her brow. What the hay! "Who's 'us,' Lou?"

"Well, you know. Bobby, and Al . . . the whole gang."

"Oh, well. Sandy may not be so thrilled about my coming along, you know."

"You're comin' with me, kid!"

And then Marta said something that was to astound her for the next week: "What happened to the 'us'?"

There was a full minute of silence. Lou was clearly weighing his options. "You heard me, Marty. You're comin' with me. That's what happened to the 'us.'"

She laughed happily, right into the mouthpiece. "Okay, big shot."

"Listen, little shot, you're gonna get some of that brass taken out of you. . . ."

"Oh yeah! By whom?"

"By me."

"Okay, wise guy!"

"Just wait till Saturday night."

"Hey, I'm really scared!"

"You better be!"

They ribbed back and forth, Marta on top of it, beside

herself with the joy of being asked, of being wanted, of being envied by all the girls in her class and resented by the big girls in her sorority who would all be at Sandy Lopersteen's party. Even though she was crazy about those grown-up, wise-cracking, cigarette-smoking sorors, she knew there were limits. Oh, she was part of their group; they had looked her over and accepted her . . . but with reservations. She was supposed to copy their style, not usurp it. She was to envy their territory, not tramp on it. She was to hang around them, buttering them up, giving back, in poor imitation, their superstyle and the chic they had evolved out of knowing that their parents had nice houses and cars and that they were getting sheared-beaver coats. "Geeze, Marta, Sandy's has got thirteen stripes," Doris was to tell her after a meeting one winter night. Those girls drove convertibles with the tops down and smoked Chesterfield cigarettes right out in the open! She was, in short, to stand at rapt and admiring attention, but at a slight distance. Marta understood. Just as her girl friends Marilyn and Doris and Phyllis did. But there was this geyser inside Marta and it upset all her plans for decorum. Its source was a secret thing; it sprang up spontaneously every now and then and almost shot her crazy heart out of her newly developed chest! It made her want to get up there and sing as loud and saucy as she could. (The sorority sisters made her sing her way all through her initiation, but once she was admitted to Beta Gam, they never asked her again.) She had given it all some thought. One afternoon, running across the bridge all alone, coming from a *Hillcrest Lit.* meeting, jogging rhythmically like she saw the lean track athletes do, the knowledge of her own power and how it would work against her often as not suddenly popped right into the clearest chamber of consciousness. She was so knocked out by the certainty of the revelation that she just stopped right there and stood in the middle of the bridge, hearing the trains chug and toot their way underneath her out of the city toward the Main Line. It wasn't easy to make a decision, and she wasn't sure just how far she would go in testing the limits of her own strength. But some message kept on coming through, pretty darned plain: "Do it your way, Marta P. Resnick! It'll have to be okay."

She was ready to hang up the phone. "I'll be seein' you, Lou."

"In Apple Blossom Time, kid."

"Not quite." She laughed.

"Huh?"

"Wrong season, hon!" She was loving every second of her own cleverness. Lou didn't get it. He was big and good-looking, but she wondered a little how smart he was. He didn't seem to be on top of it nor as quick as she was. She shoved the thought right out of her head because it made him seem less attractive.

"What time, Lou?"

"Pick you up at eight-thirty."

When she came out of her room, coiling the long telephone cord back against the wall in the hall, she heard male voices and her mother's bright laughter from downstairs. She ran eagerly down the steps. Everybody was in the kitchen, laughing and gathered around her mother's younger brother, Uncle Hank, who had come in with a big box of ice cream from the corner drugstore. He turned and kissed Marta.

"Hi ya, beautiful."

"Ho, Uncle Hank. Chocolate?"

"For you, chocolate. For Steve, vanilla. For Lilly," patting his sister's plump shoulder, "coffee. And for Aaron, butter pecan."

"For me you don't have to bother," said the doctor.

"How come you don't like ice cream, Aaron?" Uncle Hank Caplan was young and handsome. The Caplan grandparents complained to Mother that he was footloose and careless about his life, but to Marta and Steven he was a hero.

The doctor shrugged. "I guess I didn't grow up with it," he said. "In my time hot sweet potatoes and Mama's mandel bread were what made my mouth water."

"Your mouth hasn't watered in thirty years," said Mrs. Resnick. Then quickly, to take the sting out of her words, she leaned over and kissed her husband's cheek. "Aaron is interested in food for thought, not for the stomach," she said proudly.

"I'll take ice cream," murmured Steven.

Uncle Hank handed him a plate of melting vanilla that Mrs. Resnick had ladled into a soup bowl. "You listen to your father, young fella." He punched Steve's shoulder with a light tap.

Uncle Hank never stayed very long; he always seemed to be on his way somewhere exciting, with his dark hair glued down, the white part glistening with perfumed oil, his olive skin smooth from a fresh shave. His suits were sharp and carefully pressed, but never extreme as the current "zoot" fashion that Marta and her friends disdained. Everything about him was different from Marta's parents. He wasn't a kid, but he wasn't in the grown-up camp either. His square fingers beat drum tattoos on the table when they sat drinking tea or on the arms of the chair when he visited with them in the living room. On his pinkie he wore a big star sapphire that Marta loved to look into, as if it were Uncle Hank's private crystal ball. He always whistled the current hit-parade number, and he walked with a bounce that showed how he had rhythm inside him all the time. When she was little, Marta would be whisked up into Uncle Hank's strong arms, and he would dance with her around the porch and through the living room; she could remember giggling hysterically, her head bobbing and whirling, as Mom trailed them yelling, "Stop, for God's sake, Hank!"

In the last year Marta often showed him the new steps she and her friends had picked up, and every once in a while he astounded her by doing some wonderful, intricate things that must have taken practice to perfect. He showed her willingly, but laughed in the back of his throat in his modest way, as if it was just nothing.

She thought he had a secret life. She and Steven had discussed it, but at this point she suspected certain things about life that Steven did not. She wasn't about to discuss these embarrassing speculations about Uncle Hank's activities—not with Steven, certainly never with her parents; and some peculiar, loyal, persistent notion of family privacy kept her from talking to her best girl friends about Uncle Hank. The girls were all "in love" with him. He wasn't quite as inaccessible as the movie stars they idolized (oh God, Tyrone Power!) but still it was worship from a safe, adoring distance.

While they all sat around the kitchen table, everybody chattering and vying for Uncle Hank's attention, Mother said, "How are things?"

Uncle Hank shrugged, reached over and squeezed her arm, and said, "Business will pick up, Lil. You can see it all over, little indications."

Dr. Resnick said, "I don't see it, quite frankly."

"They're not paying Aaron's bills any quicker," said Mom, and added under her breath, "if at all."

"There are collection agencies, Aaron," said Uncle Hank. "Perfectly respectable," he added quickly when the

85

doctor drew his mouth down and made a gesture of dismissal.

"I'm a doctor," he said softly, "not a car salesman."

"Even doctors have to eat," said Uncle Hank, laughing. He couldn't be serious for long. "Of course, between my mother and my sister," patting Mrs. Resnick again, "they can make a banquet out of nothing. Right, Lil?"

Mom smiled with pleasure. "We're not starving, Hank. Don't worry about it. Worry about yourself. And maybe worry a little about Mom and Pop."

The Caplan grandparents had sailed into the Depression with the energy if not the capital amassed during the golden twenties. Grandpop had been an operator in real estate and had made a bundle, Mom said, but the kids really couldn't remember all the affluence. The bundle went when Grandpop traveled to Florida to look into the land boom there in the late twenties. All the Florida property and money disappeared, and then in order to make good on debts (while his flimflam partners beat it, declaring bankruptcy), he dug into his holdings in the Philadelphia area. Where he had made it in the first place. Poor Grandpop. He was left with some little properties that had big mortgages. Overextended in every direction, he paid off what he owed and became a poor man for the second time in his life. The first time was when he was carried off the boat as a babe in arms, at the Philadelphia wharf in 1873. He was supporting himself and Grandmom, but barely. He had grown tired and old while both he and Uncle Hank worked for Morris Abramavitz, a small realtor in West Philadelphia. Nobody was selling much. They collected rents and occasionally tried to put together a deal. Uncle Hank eked out a living, according to Dr. Resnick. Fond of his brother-in-law, worried about his future, the doctor had for many years urged the young man to go back to school to study something that would give him some future chance. Uncle Hank said he had never been much of a student and he couldn't go back to the books now. And then there was more of a peculiar, elliptical kind of talk that had been going on between Mom and Hank for a couple of months now. The kids were aware that something special was in the wind, but the remarks were abbreviated in front of them. It was clear that they were being excluded and should ask no more questions.

"Maybe we'll be over Sunday afternoon?" Uncle Hank never asked permission to stop in. Steven looked up from his bowl of ice cream; his chin had a dripping white beard and his mouth was surrounded by a milky mustache. He and Marta glanced at each other. Uncle Hank had said "we."

Mother had caught the verbal shorthand. She sighed, pursed her lips, and looked over Uncle Hank's head. "We may be going out for dinner."

Dr. Resnick sank back into his easy chair. He had played around with his ice cream and finally gone back to his book, leaving the mushy mess on the table next to him. He never raised his eyes. Whatever the matter was, it didn't concern him.

Uncle Hank sighed. His handsome face was serious and grave, Marta thought. Then he shrugged, and no more was said about why in God's name this most adored and favorite person would have to get his sister's permission, suddenly, to come to visit on a Sunday afternoon when it was the most natural and usual thing in the world.

They got one more clue as he was leaving, horsing around first with Steven, then brushing Marta lightly on the forehead with his lips and stroking her hair for a second. He kissed his sister Lilly on her plump cheek and said softly, "Sunday's the only day Kathy's got free. She's on this special case now. Nurses have tough schedules, you know."

Without looking back at him, Mom nodded and said, "We'll make it some other time soon, Hank. I wouldn't want to have you come by Sunday and we shouldn't be here."

Uncle Hank's face was unfamiliarly serious as he said good night. Nevertheless, he gave them a big wave and strode down the front steps with his usual energy, slamming the door so loudly behind him that the glass trembled.

Marta said softly to her mother, "Who's Kathy?"

Her mother shook her head, not looking up from her sewing. "His current girl friend. Who knows? They come and go. . . ."

Marta wondered why her father buried his head deep into his book and her mother frowned as her needle flew.

The music was echoing in the big empty gym when Marta pushed open the door and hesitated a moment in the entrance. The band was playing "Imagination," a good swing arrangement. The lyric was saying it all: imagination could turn the world upside down. It made you see everything inside out. She stood listening, concentrating. One of the guys in the band, she thought it was Dom Perrina, the clarinet player, was at the mike singing. It was 8:00 A.M. and she had come in early to see if Fanetti wanted her to rehearse again after school, although he hadn't asked her to. She kept surprising herself. He and his band had been on her mind, as the song said, working on her imagination.

For the first time she felt hesitant in approaching him. Something had altered, and she wasn't sure she knew exactly what it was. He was somebody from another dimension, or on another plane, or, more reasonably, a foreigner with whom one had to deal carefully for fear of being misunderstood.

There was no problem in the language itself. It was how it was used that made her stop and think before she entered the empty, vaulted gym. What they had to say to each other had to remain free of ambiguities. But two problems existed right at the outset. She was aware of the little nuances subverting the meanings of everyday speech, aware that they were talking on more than one level; and of course there was the language of the music. It was a special form of communication that could zing you in the solar plexis even while your smart-sharp mind was denying it all.

So what was she doing here, coming in ahead of time, when he didn't even expect her? She wasn't sure she knew how to keep it one-dimensional. She had already accepted the fact that nobody ever said exactly what he was feeling. Or rarely, anyway. And now she wasn't sure what she was feeling. Obviously, she was rising to the challenge! But why the devil did she need such challenges?

There were plenty of situations in her life that called for brains and a little daring; there was the mayor's scholarship, for example. She could win it, she was sure. With a little push here and a little shove there: the honors paper in Latin, the contest on the nineteenth-century novel, the extra work on the Lincoln project in her special history class. She had plenty of chances to shine. Plenty of opportunities to compete. So why did she need to complicate her life and interfere with the priorities she and her parents had already set up for her? Yet, how far different from her own were her parents' dreams for her? Wasn't she just like them? Wasn't she that proverbial apple that Aunt Molly said never fell far from the tree?

But the apple, at the moment, was rolling out of the

orchard. She slowly approached the bandstand and saw Fanetti turn toward her as one of the boys told him she was there. Her hips felt awkward, malconnected to her thighs, and her knees were bending out of rhythm. Even the beat of her swinging arms was wrong, and the dancer-artist in her told her that she looked terrible, thumping up to him instead of gliding gorgeously like Rita Hayworth.

He jumped nimbly down from the stand. "Okay, Dom," he said to the singer at the mike.

"You want me to try it once more, Vince?" The clarinetist lingered with the small group still sitting over their instruments, watching Marta and Fanetti.

"No need," he said. He gestured to the others. "That'll do it. We're ready for Friday."

The big old grand that Fanetti usually played up on the stage was still surrounded by a group of musicians laughing and talking among themselves. Fanetti gestured to her with his thumb, pointing toward the side of the gym. Without a word, just a quick exchange of glances and a nod, they walked over to the battered upright in the far corner against the wall.

"I just took a chance coming in this early," she said hesitantly.

"We practice every morning." He looked back at the bandstand and then suddenly appeared to make up his mind about something. He reached into his shirt pocket and took out two folded sheets of paper. He handed one of them to her. "I'd like you to try this."

She read over the lyrics on the sheet of notebook paper. "You wrote this?" she asked. It was good. She liked it.

"I monkey around a little."

He gave her the second folded sheet, the melody carefully notated on the upper staff. "You don't really need it." He had sketched in the lyrics over the bars in an almost illegible scrawl. "You just need the words," he said. "You'll pick up the tune."

She read aloud softly, " 'Hello, new love. / Won't you smile and say hi to me? / What are you waitin' around to see? / Let your eyes lead you on to me. / To the heart of a new love.' "

She glanced his way. "You do both? Words and music?"

He nodded and sat down at the upright. It had a tinny, metallic ring as his long fingers hit the keys. He was playing very softly, every now and then glancing back over his shoulder to see if the musicians had left the gym yet.

She began to hum along with it. "It's nice." She listened to the break; and when he repeated it for her, nodding that she should come in on the verse, she sang the lyric.

The guys were still hanging around near the gym door, laughing and kidding. Fanetti suddenly stopped playing. "Let's use the big piano," he said, and walked off, leaving her standing there. She stared at his back and wondered what suddenly had made it so rigid. Why was he angry? She followed him to the bandstand. But it wasn't anger she saw in his eyes as he sat down at the big grand and looked at her while his fingers picked up the "New Love" melody again. The gym was finally empty, the big doors slamming shut behind the musicians. Fanetti's eyes never left her face as he started at the top and she came in after one chorus, glancing down at the paper he had given her. He wasn't angry at all. He was intent. He was focusing on the music, on her, on the sound. Abruptly he stopped. "I'm gonna have to make a few changes in that last verse. It's not right."

"Gee, I think it's swell."

"I want it longer. I want the melody to rise a little bit

more. It's too clipped. I don't know. I have to work on it. By this afternoon I'll have it."

She waited for him to suggest that she come in again after school. But he was playing the song over and over, stopping and starting, fiddling around with combinations of phrases. She wasn't going to be the one to suggest it, she decided. Still, she hung around a minute or two. He seemed almost to have forgotten that she was there.

"So long," she said, and went down the steps of the little stage.

He looked at her. "Wait a minute." He gathered up his books from a chair and jumped down beside her. "I'll walk up with you."

"It's a good song," she said as they pushed through the crowd of kids on their way to homeroom. "But don't play around with it! I wouldn't change it too much."

He laughed and all at once was very handsome. Fascinated, she watched the white teeth and the smile. Was he laughing at her? Suddenly embarrassed, she started to move away.

"Hey," he said, and caught her arm. The kids were pushing and shoving all around them. Fanetti, still holding her arm, pulled her toward the window. "You really think you're a big expert on music, huh?" His voice was teasing.

She shrugged. "I know something."

"You know what's in my head?" A little half-smile played around his mouth.

"What brilliant thing is that supposed to mean?" He was making her sore, making her feel ill at ease and silly.

"How can you tell me what to write down?"

"Who told you what to write?"

"You said, don't change anything!"

"Okay, Paderewski, you're the expert. Sorry I said a

word." This time she turned, pulled away from him, and followed the mob up the steps to her classroom. She never looked back. Big deal! She was only trying to compliment him. Big shot! She tossed her head, her long honey-blond hair swishing on her slender shoulders. Vince Fanetti . . . Big nothin'!

The October weather was golden and balmy, and at lunchtime she went out their special school entrance with her girl friends to hang around the steps. Maybe Lou Morrow would be out here. Their date for Saturday night had almost dropped out of her mind when she was concentrating on that nutty Italian. Chewing on an apple and sipping an orangeade (her newest diet) she spotted Lou tossing a football with his gang out near the street.

With a wink to Doris and Marilyn, she put down the food and ambled over to him. Suddenly the ball was coming right at her! She ducked and tilted just in time as Lou's buddy, Bobby Goldin, made a lunge for it, just grazing her shoulder as he thundered by.

She took a breath. These guys went at it like pros!

"Hey, Marty!" Lou jogged over to her. "You wanta play?"

"C'mon, Marty!" Bobby tossed the football to her before she could protest, and laughingly she caught it. Hugging it to her chest, she turned and ran back toward the entrance with it. As she got close to the crowd of girls on the steps she turned and with all her strength threw it over Lou Morrow's head. He was right behind her, yelling and coming on fast. Al Rosenberg caught it, leaping up and grabbing it right over the hood of an old Chevy that was illegally parked at the curb.

"Nice catch, Al!" she sang out, and Lou Morrow deliberately slammed into her, making believe he couldn't stop after her pivot and toss. "Lou!" she screamed. The girls were howling and holding up their arms to brace her as she fell backward with Lou hanging on. There was a scramble and lots of giggling with Lou's friends running over and everybody knocking into everybody else.

Marta was the only one in her crowd who had gotten friendly with these seniors and the girls had been urging her for days to introduce them. She smiled with satisfaction, untangling herself from the rhubarb on the steps. They were introduced all right! Arms grazed, hands grabbed, legs rubbed, and whatever else the guys could get away with. The girls bubbled and screamed, and each tried to spot the boy that interested her the most. Marta jousted a little with Lou, backing off as he grabbed for her in the free-for-all.

At that moment, Mr. "Prig-Preston," five-foot-nothing math teacher, big spy, showed up, waving his arms angrily. "What's going on here?" he shouted, and the guys and girls scattered as if there had been an explosion. Marta was so fascinated by the vanishing act that she stood rooted to the spot.

"I am surprised at you, Marta," she heard Preston say by her side. He only came up to her shoulder. His small white hands were waving nervously in front of his small red face, and she tried to keep herself from bursting into laughter. He was blotchy with anger.

"Gee, Mr. Preston. You just missed the most spectacular catch you ever saw." She was talking fast. "One of the boys made this sensational recovery, by the steps here, and the others came after him and sort of fell over the gang sitting here minding their own business on the steps. Like they always do. But gee, Mr. Preston," she bobbed excitedly around in front of him, talking to the usual dumb look that was erasing the anger from his silly face, "we're gonna win that big game on Sunday. I just know it. Our passing—wow! It's great!''

Preston looked up at her, pursing his thin lips. He waggled his finger at her. "Those boys shouldn't be out here with a football. They know that. And I know who was here, too!"

"They were just practicing, Mr. Preston."

"That belongs on the football field."

"But we're all so excited about the game on Sunday. We want to win!"

Mr. Preston seemed to have calmed down but he was still chewing on his lips with barely contained irritation. He stared at the empty spot where the gang had had their melee. "It's too bad some of that crowd doesn't have a little more enthusiasm for their mathematics. Football won't get them graduated." Before Marta could cajole him any more, he turned and hurried back into the school.

She ran into Bobby Goldin on her way to her next class. "Did he see us?" he stopped to ask Marta in the hall.

"He says he knows who was there."

"Oh jeez."

"He won't do anything."

"The little skunk!"

She shrugged. "Don't worry about it!"

"Listen, we have a game to play on Sunday. It's damn important."

Inching her way past a group in the doorway to her classroom, she twisted her head and stared back at him incredulously. "He knows that!"

"He could . . ."

"He won't. Stop worrying!"

When she sat down at her desk and took out her English paper, she thought momentarily about how dumb, or was it naïve, the kids could be. Didn't these hot-shot football players know what she knew, little tenth-grade beginner! Namely, that Cartwright, the principal, was a sports nut. And Billings, the assistant principal, was even more gung ho. Nobody was about to ruin Hillcrest's chances for the West Philly game on Sunday. There was nothing Prig-Preston could do. She shook her head and pushed the whole incident out of her mind.

She decided against going down to the gym after school. Let Fanetti cool his heels. Big-shot Fanetti! Big musicologist!

The girls were giggling and chattering all around her on the way home but she was caught up in her own thoughts. The melody of "New Love" kept slipping back into her consciousness, and she found herself impatient to get home to try to pick it out on the piano. She checked in her pocketbook, which was slung over her shoulder, to see if she still had the two sheets of paper he had given her with the music and lyrics on them.

"Hey, wait up, Mart!" The girls had stopped to watch the football scrimmage down in the hollow. The second and third teams were tossing the ball, and guys were still trailing down the hill on the path from school. "I have to get home," she called and broke into a trot. She wanted to be alone. That music was the darnedest thing! The melody was a bright moth flapping around in her mind. It wanted to be heard, to be expressed.

When she got home she went right to the piano and began to pick out the notes with one hand. Steven came wandering out of the kitchen, his mouth full of chocolate cake, the crumbs clinging to his chin. "Whatzat?" he asked, chomping.

"Wipe your mouth, Steven." Their mother was drying dishes in the doorway to the kitchen.

He sat down on the piano bench next to Marta, first

taking her pile of books and dropping them carelessly on the floor. "What is it?" he repeated.

"It's a new song."

"Yeah? Whose record?"

She looked at her brother. "It's good, isn't it? Sort of grabs you!"

"So, whose record is it?"

She stood and gathered up her books from the floor. "Fanetti just wrote it. He wants me to sing it." She took the music out of her pocketbook and handed it to her brother.

Steven's fair eyebrows had risen and his blue eyes were wide. "Lemme see."

He began to play the right hand and almost at once the chords to the accompaniment were right there holding up the melody. "Boy, it's good!"

She ran upstairs before her mother could catch her and start pushing the freshly baked chocolate cake. The house smelled good, as it always did when her mother had prepared something special. Home was a warm and comforting nest. And at this moment it was the last place she wanted to be. She left her bedroom door open just enough to hear the music from downstairs. She could tell that Steven really went for it. He was playing around with little grace notes and glides that meant he was connecting with the melody. Then her mother called her and Steven began to yell for her. With an angry thrust, she tossed her books onto her desk and went back downstairs. You couldn't get away from them! Not in this house you couldn't.

"Be back soon, Mom," she called, and was out the front door and halfway down the steps when her mother's voice stopped her.

"What's the matter with you?"

She stopped and turned back to face the door. "Nothing. I have to get something at the drugstore."

"So have some milk first. I just cut the cake. You got a whole afternoon."

"I'm not hungry, Ma."

"You don't have to be hungry for cake and milk."

She kept on walking down the steps to the sidewalk. "I'll be back soon. I need loose-leaf paper and stuff. Be right back, Mom."

And she escaped into the Indian-summer afternoon. She walked toward the drugstore, went past it, then rounded the corner. She had to be by herself for a while. Something was nagging at her, pulling at her, and it worried her because she couldn't tell whether it was something good or bad.

An old man was raking and burning leaves at the curb. The air up and down the street was pungent as the aromatic smoke rose thick and creamy. The autumn sunlight slanted through the big shade trees, making golden patches on the sloping lawns. It was the best time of the year. The holidays had just passed this week; to her it was the true New Year, not January when the world was frozen and living things felt isolated from one another.

A group of kids was gathered in front of the candy store. She knew who they were, and she quickly crossed to the opposite side of the street and jogged past, her head down. She didn't want to see anybody or talk to anybody right now. What was it? Why did she feel so peculiar?

There was a guy walking toward her and she slowed up, her heart suddenly knocking like a little tommy gun. He was tall and broad-shouldered and had dark hair, and she was all at once sure it was Vince Fanetti. He had forded the moat, he had battled the bridge, he had invaded their territory. Her breathing became ragged, and she had decid-

98

ed to run across the street again to avoid him when she realized it was not he.

The man walked past and a curious flatness took the place of the alarming excitement she had felt. What did Vincent Fanetti mean to her? Nothing! He had to mean nothing! She didn't know him and didn't want to know him. What was this perversity that had suddenly attacked her in her sixteenth year, when she was very close to being a woman, was a woman in most important ways?

She had to knock it off. She'd tell Fanetti that she couldn't sing on Friday and then skip the dance altogether. Better still, she just wouldn't say anything, just wouldn't show up. That would end it all right there. Whatever it was!

Saturday night was Sandy Lopersteen's big party; she had just the right skirt and cashmere sweater. Lou Morrow, the biggest-shot senior, was picking her up, and she'd walk right into that party with him and love every second of it. She began to calm down again, the old Marta.

She turned and started for home. Yes, that was the way it would be!

Marta did homework all Friday night. After she had finished, she sat curled up in the armchair in her bedroom, trying to concentrate on *The Return of the Native* for English. But her eyes kept straying back to the electric clock on her desk. Fanetti would know by now that she wasn't going to show for the performance. He would wonder. Too bad! But Eustacia Vye's problems couldn't keep her mind riveted on Wessex and the heavy, Hardy hand of fate. She gave up at about ten o'clock and went over the clothes she was planning to wear for the party the next night.

*   *   *

A big crowd filled Sandy Lopersteen's paneled basement playroom when Marta walked in with Lou Morrow and his buddy Al Rosenberg. Although there was a lot of movement and music and everybody was laughing and cracking jokes, about halfway through the evening, Marta knew it was just a mixed success. Lou Morrow was hooked all right, coming over and hanging around her every time some other guy talked to her, cutting in every time she danced with somebody else, but the girls were resentful. They let her know it, in the main, by ignoring her. She smiled and danced and kidded around with all the boys; but as far as her older sorority sisters were concerned, she wasn't there at all. Toward the middle of the evening, she decided she had had enough; she couldn't afford to antagonize these important senior girls—not because they had any power in the school; most of them were playgirls, butterflies, disinterested students. But the social year had just begun and they could make that aspect of life terrible for her. Besides, she understood how they felt. She had moved in too fast with one of their favorite guys. She wasn't sure exactly whose special interest Lou had been, but the girls banded together in their resentment.

She ducked the boys for the rest of the evening as well as she could, and buttered up the sorors who were sitting or standing by themselves in little groups. They were cool. They shut up as soon as she came over to them. She toned down her personality and began the kind of toadying she had seen her girl friends affect when they wanted to get into the sorority. She had never tried it before. It was interesting. It was revolting! But she managed to mend a few fences, particularly with Sandy Lopersteen, who at first kept moving away as Marta approached. Then she found the one correct little ploy. She asked Sandy's advice about her (mythical) tenth-grade boy friend who was going to be really sore that she, Marta, had come to a senior party on a Saturday night. What did Sandy think she ought to do? Tell, or not tell? Sandy didn't quite say, "Go home, kid, and don't come back to any of our gatherings," but with a saccharine smile on her pretty face, she made it clear to Marta (who kept nodding sadly and seriously) that really she was better off plowing the sophomore field. Remember, they would all be gone by the spring, all these glamorous seniors, and next year and the year after that, you had to have some social life in the school. You needed those classmate boyfriends.

Marta wanted to respond, "Look, Sandy baby, you only bother with these senior-classmate guys of yours when you haven't been invited down to the university to a frat house on the weekend." That was what all the high-school seniors who were cute were always aiming for. But nevertheless she agreed out loud with every dumb word Sandy Lopersteen uttered and followed her around for a good half-hour, helping her pick up glasses and put the sandwiches on the dining-room table, and tried to sweet-mouth the other girls into believing that she was really just a little tenth-grade pet and not to be taken seriously as competition.

By the time the evening ended, she had made them all a little more accepting; and the boys were still hanging over her shoulder as they all piled into Lou's car to go for a fast spin around the neighborhood.

She knew she had problems when Lou pulled into the churchyard, near an old cemetery, turned off the motor and the lights, and began to grab for her. The couple in the back were bumping around, and she didn't hear anybody back there protesting.

His mouth was open and his tongue was a mile long as he tried to flatten himself against her. His hands never stopped moving and she kept trying to figure out where next to put her elbow to defend herself. There really wasn't any way. He was an expert with his huge paws and probing tongue, and before she could prevent him he had covered her breast with his palm and was squeezing her. His other hand, fingers crawling, began to reach under her skirt.

"Cut it out!" she said between clenched teeth.

He ignored her. There were squeals of laughter from the backseat. "Lou!" she whispered. "I want to go home."

"Come on, Mart. Loosen up." His head was down on her shoulder and he began to bite her neck.

Desperate, she said, "Lou, I'm sick!"

It took a minute, but she heard him sigh and he pulled off her. "What is it?" he asked with disgust.

"I don't know. I feel nauseated. I think it was the tuna. God!" She sighed deeply, simulating, as well as she could remember, aches and pains in the belly.

He moved over, started the motor, and took her home. When she got out of the car and said good night to the entwined duo in the backseat, she did some deep breathing.

"Feel better?" he said and began to move in on her again as they stood in her doorway.

Just then Dr. Resnick, God bless him, saved the night, calling from the upstairs, "Marta, is that you?"

"It's me, Dad."

"Please lock the door, dear, when you come up."

"Good night Lou."

"Put the light out, Mart." Lou was reaching for her.

"Can't, Lou, my dad . . ."

"He won't know."

"Are you crazy! He knows your car's out front. It was terrific, Lou. See ya." She shoved him out the front door, flicked off the porch lamp, and beat it up the stairs into her bedroom. What a stupid night! What a waste of time and energy! She looked at her tall, slender reflection in the door mirror. Her mouth was pale and swollen, her lipstick gone, smeared all over Lou Morrow's big puss. Her hair had lost the curl she had so tediously set in all afternoon. Her good sweater was stained, and there were pulled threads in her new wool skirt!

When she was ready for bed, she suddenly noticed a note on her pillow in Steven's oversized handwriting. "Vince F. called. He wanted to know where you were Friday night. I told him I played his song. He sounded mad at first. But when I told him I thought it was really good, he liked that!"

On her night table Steven had left the two sheets of music, by now rumpled and stained with his chocolate fingerprints and God knows what else. Brushing her hair, she climbed into bed and sat propped up looking over the lyrics. She could hear the melody as she slid down, turned off the light, and fell asleep at once.

CHAPTER 6

October 1981

SHE HEARD DAN MOVING AROUND THE BEDROOM BEFORE she opened her eyes. The bathroom door creaked and closed, opened again, and then the bedroom was silent. He hadn't pulled the draperies and the room was still dim, strips of sunlight creeping in along the edges. It would be a lovely fall Sunday. She stretched under the thick comforter, testing her head gently to see what damage remained from the night before. That was the last time she'd pull that damn-fool stunt: Scotch and wine didn't mix for her. She hadn't enjoyed any of it anyway. And she had made an idiot of herself in front of her friends. And what she had done to Dan . . . A wave of embarrassment and remorse hit her and she sank down deeper into the bed.

She lay there reviewing the jumbled events at the hotel the night before. The card that Vincent Fanetti had given her was in her evening bag on the bureau, where she had carelessly tossed it. It had been a terrible evening! She had to set things right. About to throw the covers off and get up, she sank back against the headboard as Dan came into the bedroom holding two steaming mugs of coffee. He handed her one, sat down in the easy chair opposite, and began to sip his coffee.

"You shouldn't have," she said. "But, boy, does that smell good! Thanks a million." She took an eager swallow.

"Want to take a ride up to see Diane today?" Dan asked. "The countryside will be turning color now."

Their daughter, Diane, was in graduate school just far enough away to make frequent visits difficult. She gave them days stingily, and they accepted the gift of her presence with pleasure and poorly camouflaged eagerness. They understood how attached she was to them and how hard she was trying to separate herself. Maybe they were all too attached: their son, Allen, who was delaying his entrance into a local law practice by dallying in the sun of New Mexico; Diane, who had turned down the large university right in the city for a smaller one at a safe distance from her parents; Dan and Marta themselves. They loved one another, she was sure; but the kids needed to be set free, had a right to be.

Marta sat in bed inhaling the fragrance of her morning coffee and sighing. "I'd love to go see Di," she said. "But she's bound to be busy. It's the beginning of the new term. Tell you what I think, Daniel." She began to hum, "It's just you and me babe. . . ."

He smiled. "That's okay with me. Why don't we take a ride to the seashore then. I'd rather do that anyway. We can take a walk on the beach, have lunch, and come home early. Does that appeal to you, Mart?"

She didn't answer. Her mind was hobbling about among the ruins of last night's memories. "Listen, Dan," she said softly, "I'm sorry I was such a . . . big mouth last night."

He laughed. "You weren't."

She viewed him solemnly. His hair was disheveled, shaggy on his brow, and his plaid pajamas and bare feet made him look very young, very carefree. A very attractive man. He was her young and attractive man. A sudden surge of love for him spilled into her chest and caught at her throat.

He must have felt it across the room, because he put down his coffee and came back to their bed. Gently he took her cup out of her hand and lay down beside her, pulling her into his arms, murmuring her name, stroking her breasts until the nipples began to firm. One hand held her head while his other caressed her back; and then he eased up her nightgown and ran his palm over the length of her inner thigh.

"Oh, Dan." She sighed. "What's the matter with me?"

He moved his head so that he could look directly into her eyes, and the smile that creased his cheek continued to play around his lips. "Not the tiniest thing," he said.

"You don't see me as I am," she said, and knew that she sounded like a petulant child.

He put his mouth down on hers and silenced her.

She wanted to respond completely to him because some instinct informed her that she had to empty herself of troubling emotions and petty irritations. But her mind refused to allow her body to perform. She knew she wasn't ready, couldn't be now, when he gently mounted her, pushing her long legs apart, his mouth on hers. Her arms went around his neck, her fingers in the thick hair, the male scent of him filling her nostrils with pleasure. Everything was right. Why was everything wrong?

She never pretended with him. It was a matter of pride to her that her senses were reliable and that her tie to her husband was based on honesty and real need. When her blood ran warm, and her thoughts were preoccupied with love, he would be there. Sooner or later, they would be together in bed, arms entwined, his firm muscled body pumping against her in the fashion they had evolved together over the years for bringing each other pleasure. And if their needs did not run perfectly concurrent, well, so what! They ignored the imperfect timing, the textbook rules for togetherness. There were misses but rare disappointments. In the beginning Dan was an eager lover, and coming first, he would then turn to her, massaging, pressing, rubbing her to a climax. And she would do the same for him, if he wanted it. . . . "Oddball stuff tonight, Dan?" she would whisper then and go down on him willingly when he asked, mouth, tongue, hands all moving on him.

But the years had created rhythms and they were together almost all the time, as if nature had adjusted his streaming hormones to the ebb and flow of hers. Glances, sounds, fingertip brushes, were all that was necessary to induce the rushing sensations they had both come to expect.

There had never been any need to pretend. Her young body had responded to his right from the start. He had found her an active and hungry partner. "Let go!" she had whispered in the beginning to him. "If you don't, I can't!"

And he had understood. They each had to take directly from the other in order to give. "Don't bother about me," she said, when he hesitated on the brink himself, and she was too far to plunge with him. "Later for me," she would murmur, and her silent, loving young husband would rush to a climax. "I'm a selfish little beastie," she would whisper. "And I'll get you yet, boy!" And laughing like a crazy wanton, she would grab his head and push his face into her crotch, sighing, and heaving, shamelessly enraptured.

They had always been lovers. Even when he had to be the general and she was the private. Even when they were adversaries. Even when there was disappointment and anguish. Lovers, she saw to that. "Switch my gears, baby!" she had laughed in his ear when the children were tiresome infants and she was exhausted from boredom and overwork. "Oh love me!" she had crooned to her young husband, who had held her adoringly and emptied himself in her with an ecstasy he had never expected.

"I corrupted such a nice fella," she used to giggle in his ear as she pushed and squeezed him, stroking and probing until he moaned with pleasure.

He had always been her nice fella. He filled her with love and tenderness and answered her deepest needs. And if their style of lovemaking became over the years less brothel and more missionary, who cared! There was nobody to whom they had to account. Not even to each other. They were alike, she and Dan. Each had a small air space around his psyche, not to be breached.

Fanetti had written, "All she wants is what she wants," and wouldn't heed his own insight. Daniel Reiter marched into her life in his soldier's uniform and got the picture right away. He was happy with her mind and body. Fanetti would have wanted her soul. . . .

She felt Dan's temperature rising and his breathing become hoarser, and still she couldn't react. When he rolled off her, lying peacefully on his back, eyes closed, hands holding hers, she began to get out of bed. "Your turn," he said, pulling her back.

"No," she said softly, kissing his ear.

"Why not?"

She sat up looking at herself in the mirror over her bureau on the far wall.

"I don't know. . . ." And then, because he seemed

uncertain and disturbed, she added, "Maybe I'm hung over."

"That'll do it." He laughed and got up with her. He helped her pull the gown over her head and held her lightly, gently, naked in his arms. "See you later?"

"Dan . . ." she murmured, and wondered what it was she had to tell him. When she saw the troubled spot in his eye, she laughed. "You bet! Later!"

Speeding down the empty highway through the brilliant sunshine, she heard herself sighing. Once Dan turned around to glance at her; she stared out the side window; he turned on the radio.

Side by side they walked in bare feet on the windy beach, the sand cold and crisp. The sea was glassy and shimmering, solid enough to slide across.

"Wanta race?" she said and took off into the stiff breeze. He came up alongside her, pulled her hair, shoved her shoulder, and loped past her.

"Show-off!" she screamed.

He stopped and waited for her. "Gad!" She puffed. "I'm out of breath! And old!".

Standing by the water's edge, with the breakers curling onto the clam shells and slapping at the wet beach, he held her in his arms. "You're nineteen years old, and draped around a microphone, making all kinds of obvious sexy gestures and singing your little heart out."

"Did you think I was sexy?"

"I thought you were delicious. . . ."

"Dan . . ." she held his hand and they walked back with the wind at their shoulders now, "I want something."

He looked at her. "Okay."

"You won't like it. . . ."

He was silent.

"I want to go to work for Steven."

He released her hand and bent to pick up his shoes where they had left them at the foot of the wooden stairs leading from the beach up to the street. She stood beside him while he sat on the step tying his shoes; hers were cradled in her arms.

"Put your shoes on," he said.

"Dan, please. Talk to me about this...."

"It's not a good idea, Marta."

"Why not?"

"You'll have to spend a lot of time in New York."

"Not a lot of time, Dan. Two days a week in the beginning. After this spring special, maybe I can just go up and back once a week."

"You're kidding yourself. Nobody can work like that. It's just a game."

"You think I want to play games?"

"I think you're a little bored. The kids are out from under. Your friends are taking themselves seriously as working women."

"Well, why the hell not?" She felt anger rising and her temples had started to throb again.

She recognized the shuttered blankness in his eyes and the stubborn thrust of his jaw. Brushing her feet, she bent to put on her shoes. He tried to hold her elbow to support her, but she moved away from him. Silently they walked to the car and drove to the seafood place they both liked, a little dive on the bay that smelled like seaweed and pepper. She picked at her shrimp while he devoured his crab and gulped his beer.

"No good?" He watched her pushing her food around.

She took a big bite. "It's fine." She sipped her coffee. "The problem is my problem won't go away. Which is a stupid thing on this wonderful day...." She gestured to the bay beyond the window, glittering in the afternoon sunlight. Gulls wheeled and shrieked over the purple surface, dipping their bills in and out as they spotted their prey; the sky was high and wide, paint-box blue, with a few lacy clouds stretched across the horizon. It was a day for celebration and joy. It was a day for counting blessings.

"Oh damn!" she said, put down her fork, and stared out at the serenity beyond the window.

He reached across the table and took her hand. "Maybe you ought to make an appointment to see the doctor."

She jerked her hand away and stared at him. "What in heaven's name are you saying!"

"There's something the matter, Marta. And I think you might get your health checked. What's wrong with that suggestion?"

She finished her coffee without answering. She was determined to ignore him for the rest of the day. Until she was alone, she could think of no other way to handle her seething anger.

Without touching or speaking, they walked along the bay for an hour until the sun began to lose its warmth and the winds from the north came skittering across the water, stirring it up into waves and ripples that made little flapping sounds against the sea wall.

On the way home, as the shadows of the trees lengthened on the empty roadway, he fished around for something on the radio, twisting the dial this way and that until in exasperation she muttered, "For God's sake, get what you want and leave it alone already!" She sank back in sulky gloom against the car seat.

He ignored her complaint, found the classical-music station he had been looking for, and turned down the Brahms piano concerto until it was gentled into being semiaudible. He drove with his usual concentration and ease, whistling the familiar melody each time it repeated.

He heard the tunes accurately in his head although he couldn't play a note on any instrument, something he regretted aloud from time to time. Often when she was angry with him and reaching for meannesses she would say, "Too bad your busy mother didn't find time to get you music lessons. But she would have had to skip her precious bridge afternoons."

He rarely retorted. Only once had he reacted as violently and openly as she would have done after a frontal verbal assault. She was doing all the accusing, typically, during a long, drawn-out argument. "Who appointed you king? Why do we always have to do everything your way?" His answer had been mild, reasonable. "We often do what you want, Marta. You just forget easily." Vexed beyond control, she had lashed out, "Oh Mr. Goddamn Perfect! Your shitty mother was too self-preoccupied to put any brakes on you. . . . You have to . . ." But she never got the rest out because he smacked her hard across the mouth, turned, and, ashen-faced, stalked out of the room. He did not apologize. She didn't either, but she knew that she had gone too far and tried to stop herself in future arguments. Most of the time she could, and when she pushed too hard, he simply ducked out on her. His wild reaction had frightened them both. They silently acknowledged the temper he kept under tight rein, and, with varying success, she tried to respect it.

Now on the way home he was attempting to make up for the frustration of the afternoon. They had crossed the Delaware River from Jersey and were back in the city. A kid selling flowers in the middle of the busy downtown street approached their car as they stopped for a red light. Dan rolled down the window, reached into his pocket for money, and soberly handed her four red roses wrapped in green tissue.

"Thank you," she said.

"Are we friends?" he asked as they drove along the parkway in the fading afternoon light.

"We're best friends, Dan." She sighed. "But if we are," she added earnestly, "why don't you give me a total hearing? Why won't you listen the way you would at the bank if somebody had a problem? No really," she insisted when he shook his head, as if the cases were too unlike to be compared. "You think you have more at stake down there, is that it?"

"You know that isn't true, Marta," he said softly.

"You think I'm just a dumb dame, somebody to shove around, somebody to take from and forget about. . . ." All her resolutions to keep quiet had disappeared.

"I don't think that at all."

"Then talk to me, Damnit!"

He was pulling into their driveway. "All right," he said. "Let's go in the house and talk about it."

With the Sunday papers spread around him, his hand straying now and then to the business section, lifting the corner to catch the headline, he sat opposite her in the den. She stared at him, trying to get her thoughts in order.

She said finally, "I'm not sick. I'm not depressed." She repeated hastily when she saw him start to respond, "No, I'm not, Dan. I am not lamenting the departure of our children. I am not bored. I'll tell you what I am, and if it sounds like a cliché, it is! I am unfulfilled." She sighed. "God how I hate that word. Give me some time, Dan, and I could come up with a nifty synonym. But it'll have to do for now."

He returned her look, deeply and steadily. "I don't doubt you," he said.

"Do you understand?"

"Yes," he said. "I understand. Unfortunately, the talent you believe is unfulfilled can't get fulfilled here on the

114

Philadelphia Main Line. Your talent seems to need the big city and the big spot to actualize itself." He stood up, hands in pockets, and began to pace around the room. "We've got a real conflict of interests here, Mart, because I don't want a part-time wife. I want my wife here, near me, with me."

"Taking care of you . . ."

"Exactly."

"Have I ever shirked that job, Dan?"

"Never." He put his hand under her chin and tilted her face up to his.

"I'll never neglect you," she said softly.

"It's inevitable if you get involved in Steven's business."

"Dan . . ."

"I want you here. Where you've always been. I don't want any dramatic changes in our life." He sat down again and she gazed at him thoughtfully. "What will you do when I do what I want?" she asked softly.

He opened the newspaper on his lap, put on his glasses, and began to read. "I don't know," he said.

She left Vincent Fanetti's card in her evening bag when she removed her cosmetics, comb, and tissues. Shoving the card down into the small satin side pocket, she replaced the bag in its plastic box at the top of her closet. But she didn't forget about it, and when Dan left for work on Monday morning, kissing her as usual, no sign of any tension on his part, she retrieved the card. Sipping her second cup of coffee at the kitchen table, she sat staring at it as memories flooded back. "Why can't you sing anymore?" he had asked when she didn't come back to the club, far away in the past of 1941. "Are you out of your mind?" she had snapped. "I got in trouble with my folks!" He had responded that a career was trouble, that

115

anything difficult, worth doing in fact, was bound to be trouble. She had answered rapidly and sharply that he didn't have a clue as to what it was all about, that the variety of trouble she had gotten into couldn't be repeated. He had called her gutless. He had told her bluntly that she overestimated her own toughness, that, in fact, she couldn't make it on her own. Ever.

And she had never for one minute agreed with him. The music was the same for them both, but the libretto was as different as *Das Rhinegold* was from *Mame*. There was no way he could know, she had told herself, the kind of person she really was, from what kind of family she had come, with what kind of goals she had been taught, et cetera, et cetera.

Et cetera, she thought, staring down at Dr. Fanetti's private number on the little white card. Dan would never know if she called him. No one would ever know.

What was it after all, between her and Vince, but a little unfinished business. A little unfinished affair that cropped up, if only at the back of her mind, over the years, making her wonder where he was and whom he loved and what kind of view he now had of the world.

She put her empty cup in the sink and again she tucked the card away, this time in her desk, in a calendar. She placed it carefully at the beginning of November, as if by then she might have decided.

She had started putting in time at the piano every morning, first letting her fingers settle on the keys, allowing feelings to surface with wisps of melodies that sprang into existence entwined with lyrics. Then she would swing her long legs off the end of the padded velvet piano bench and, staring out the expanse of picture window into the sweep of garden beyond, would hold her tablet and pencil on her knees and copy down the words that came from someplace inside.

She thought about thinking, and tried to stop. It didn't do to question the wellspring, but only to catch the flow. Steven had told her that they needed five or six big production numbers for the two-hour special. He wanted to do at least two originals, or three if they were any good.

"How do you see them?" she had asked in their usual shorthand language.

"Two upbeat, and at least one biggie, sentimental, lotta ooze."

And she understood what he was after. "Should I send you ideas?"

"You come up to New York with the ideas." He needed help in putting it together. "I'm running dry," he said, puzzling her because he never complained and had never before run out.

"Not you!" she had said, laughing.

His answer was simply, "Talk to Dan. See what you can do."

She was humming the words, not satisfied yet with the rhythm, when Doris called her on the phone.

"You got away awfully quick Saturday night," Doris said.

"I think I had too much to drink."

"Maybe we're all drinking too much these days."

"I don't know . . . I don't, as a rule."

"You weren't puttin' it behind your ear, Mart!"

"Don't you ever feel like tying one on . . . a little?"

"Yes. Every morning at eleven and every afternoon at four."

"Oh come on . . ."

"I got troubles."

"Who hasn't?"

"Mine are scary."

"What are you saying, Dor?"

"I have to have a little operation. Or maybe not so little!"

Marta stared out the window, frowning. "What is it?"

"It's a lady-type thing. The payoff for all these piker years of being such a good little piker of a girl."

"You'll be okay."

"Sure."

There were a few seconds of silence between them and then Marta heard Doris sigh.

"It'll be okay," Marta repeated and sounded lame to herself.

"Can you have lunch?" Doris asked. "I really can't stand being alone today."

"When do you have to . . . ?"

"I go into the hospital over the weekend. I was going to tell you about it at the dance Saturday night, but you were so preoccupied with Mr. Italian Hero of 1941 that I couldn't get your attention."

They both began to laugh. "I was so surprised!" Marta said.

"Surprised!" Doris was herself again, chuckling, wry. "You were flattened, kid!"

Marta tried to remember. "Who noticed?" she asked finally.

"Who cares?"

"No, really . . . was it that obvious?"

"No! Absolutely not. Only kidding! Well, maybe Dan . . . Had they ever met before?"

"Oh no. This is the first time I've seen him in all these years."

"So you trysted in the lobby. . . ."

"A couple of minutes . . ."

"And you decided . . . ?"

"Nothing. Nothing's changed."

"He's changed. For God's sake. Marta, he looks like a movie star."

"I'm not in the market, Dor."

Doris sighed. "No," she said. "Nor am I, at this moment. Unfortunately!"

"We'll talk over lunch."

Marta hated the thought of talking over lunch. She had stopped sharing secrets with friends way back in 1941. Around the age of sixteen the need to share had evaporated. She always seemed to require space and time to work around ideas and events. Words spoken, however lightly, became commitments to ideas. And ideas ought to be negotiable. Getting into her car and driving to the restaurant to meet her best friend, she wondered if maybe she was just concerned about appearing vulnerable. But she shook her head, pulling into the parking lot. "You're a private flyer, kid!" She believed in her own direction toward the solitary recharging of energy, toward the single solving of problems.

The restaurant with its gingham cloths and bright geraniums was filled with ladies lunching, and Marta smiled and waved to friends as she made her way to the table where Doris was sitting somberly, pointing at her highball as she said, "Anxious to get started."

"All right . . . it's okay, Dor!"

"You'll join me, won't you?"

Marta didn't want to but she ordered white wine when the waiter came, and Doris sighed with relief. "God, how I hate to drink alone!"

"That's a good sign."

119

"I don't know. I'm doing a lot of lunching out. I'm real nervous, Mart."

"You'll be fine. You'll see."

"Jeez, I hope so! They have to take out some damned thing. I think I may be in trouble."

"Oh, Doris!"

"They tell me it's an easy operation and they can get it all. . . ."

They sat staring at each other, their drinks forgotten in front of them on the table. "You're catching it early," Marta murmured.

"They say . . ."

When their lunch came, it was apparent that neither woman wanted to eat, or even could, and the food sat before them growing cold. Doris was making little pellets of bread from the roll on her plate, rolling them around and dropping them on the table.

Breaking her own rules, Marta said, "Fanetti's got a super offer from Municipal Hospital. Chief of surgery . . ."

"Not bad for an Italian piano banger from Hillcrest."

"He was always more than that, Dor."

"In what way was he more?"

"He . . . was a sensitive, talented guy . . . even then."

"Were you in love with him, Marty?"

Her eyebrows raised, her brow wrinkling, Marta said, "I've often asked myself that. How can I say what I felt when I was sixteen? Anyway, we came from different worlds."

"Not anymore . . ."

"No. Not anymore."

When they parted, each walking to her own car, Marta wasn't sure she had done anything at all for Doris, and she was very sure she had aggravated her own uneasy state of mind. At home she went right to the piano, trying to figure out the melody to the lyrics she had begun that morning and got so involved that she lost track of the time. She was going over the music when she heard Dan at the front door and realized that the evening had come while she was working, lost in her own thoughts.

"For heaven's sake." She laughed. "I forgot about dinner."

"We can go out."

"No. I had enough of that today. With Doris."

"It's up to you," he said and seemed very quiet. He hung up his coat and disappeared upstairs.

He never came down again until she called to tell him that dinner was on the table. Pouring himself a glass of wine, he sat down while she fixed his plate. "Drink?" he asked.

"No, thanks," she said. "I had wine with lunch. I think Doris is very upset."

He smiled at her. "Why not? It's the thing to be, apparently."

She ate her dinner without another word, anger knotting under her esophagus. He didn't try to josh her out of it as he usually did. He was preoccupied and at the end of the silent meal he said stiffly, "If you don't mind, I'll take my coffee into the den. I have some work to do."

She shoved the dishes, clattering and banging them, into the dishwasher. "Selfish bastard," she muttered; and without wiping the sink or doing any of the neat little housewifely chores she usually enjoyed, she went back into the living room to work on her song again.

She thought he was asleep when she climbed into bed, but he reached for her and kissed her face and smoothed her hair. "I love you," he said.

"You're nuts about me," she answered.

"That's right. I am."

121

"You have a very strange way of showing it."

"I just have the same old way, Mart."

"Some things have to change, Dan. Everything can't stay the same."

"My love for you stays the same." He pressed her into his arms and she sighed and listened to his even breathing as he fell asleep first. He always did, quietly, efficiently. She thought her machinery must be a damn sight less efficient than his. Things were always charging her up or letting her down. Dan operated in a steady state.

She poked him hard and he jumped awake. "What is it?"

"I want to talk to you."

"Now?... For God's sake, Mart..."

"Dan, exactly what does your bank have to do with the problems at Municipal Hospital?"

"It'll all work out...."

"Honey, can you stop being a brave bully boy for just a couple of minutes?"

"Your timing is peculiar, Mart."

"That's true," she said. "But we're stuck with it, you and I." She turned to face him, their faces close together on his pillow. "We're stuck with each other...."

He smoothed her hair and touched her cheek. "I wouldn't put it that way," he said softly.

"What I mean is, we're the way we are. By now, we both know it, don't we!"

"We know it."

"What happened down at Municipal? I want you to tell me."

He stretched, reached over to put on his light, and got out of bed. He went into the bathroom and she heard water running. "Do you want a cold drink?" he called.

"No." She was sitting up and her patience was wearing thin again. "Dan?"

"Okay . . . I don't know why it matters to you. But I'll discuss it with you if it makes you happy."

"I hate being treated like an orphan child who boards here."

"I never quite visualized you like that," he said, laughing.

"Why did the president get canned?"

"He quit. He had spent too much money. His cost for the new building and the improvements on the old structures went way out of line."

"Did they borrow a lot from Philadelphia Federal?"

"I approved a loan of fifteen million."

"And they can't pay it back?"

He nodded. "Not right now. Not the amount they're supposed to pay back."

"So what will happen?"

He shrugged and raised his brows. "We'll wait," he said. "We'll reschedule the loan and assume that eventually they're going to pay it all back."

"Do you think they're good for it?"

Without hesitating he said, "Yes, I think they're good for it."

"Why did some of the doctors leave?"

"Because they were on the board and were instrumental in making the original decisions with the president."

"Was it their fault?"

Dan shrugged. "The people who make decisions have to take the responsibility."

"And you . . ."

"I didn't take any position."

"But you must have. You lent them the money."

"I thought it was a decent loan."

"And they couldn't throw you off the hospital board?"

He laughed. "Not very well."

"Are you terribly upset?"

"No. I took a big shot here . . . and I don't think we're sunk. We just have to finish the building program now and get on with some new staff members and some new board members. I am concerned, of course. And I'm doing a lot of figuring and a lot of work on it. Every day. But I think we're going to come out okay, the bank and the hospital."

He had sat down in the easy chair across from the bed and put his feet up on the ottoman where he had left his newspaper. He pulled the paper out and, holding it up, slipped on his glasses and began to read.

"Dan . . . ?"

"Do you ever read the financial news, Mart?"

"You know I don't."

He pointed at the paper. "Everything costs more than it should. Including the price of money . . . money borrowed for building. I tried to keep the interest rates within reason, but there's a market, and they had to pay the current price."

"But what did the president and his cohorts think when they allowed the budget to be exceeded?"

He shrugged. "Who knows? They claim they had to okay the cost overruns or the new buildings couldn't be finished."

"Is that true, do you think?"

"I don't know. But now it's all over. They got caught in a bad market. Construction has just about ground to a halt all over the country. We got caught too—the bank, that is—right at the tail end."

"You thought the boom would last?"

He sighed. "No, I didn't. I thought they understood that they had to trim their budget, if need be, to bring the finished project in within the terms of the loan. And there's no point in asking why they didn't. If they'd had a satisfactory answer, they'd all still be employed at the hospital."

"So what will happen now?"

He sat thinking for a minute and then raised his brows. "We have to wait longer for our money. They went twenty percent over their budget. That's an additional three million they owe us. They'll have to raise their rates. And the hospital board has to try to get more grant funds from the federal and state governments."

"Will they get it?"

"If we can justify the need. I think so. Philadelphia Municipal is a major city medical center. And Philadelphia Federal is a major bank. Nobody wants either of us in trouble." He sighed again. "Okay? Are you satisfied now?"

"Not quite," she said. "Why do you hate to discuss this with me?"

"Because I discuss finances all day long. When I come home I want relief from it."

"Yes," she said softly. "That's fair enough."

If the moment had eased, if his explanations to her had been impulsive and self-generating, she would have told him that she was unsettled too, like the late fall weather. She was upset about Doris's illness and worried about how to work with Steven, to do what she had to do, without causing a storm.

But he sat across from her quietly reading *The Wall Street Journal* and asking her nothing. When he finally got up, slipping his glasses into his bathrobe pocket, he neatly folded the newspaper so that only the headline was visible: POLISH AUTHORITIES TRY TO STOP SOLIDARITY. Tapping it with his index finger, he said, "You think we got problems. You see this head. The Polish government is about to collapse. There's no food over there and an energy shortage. Some top American banks have big loans outstanding to that weak Polish government.'' He stood looking down at her. ''And the Soviet Union perches nearby like a bird of prey.'' He got into bed and turned out the light.

''My problems seem terrible to me too,. Dan. Even though they're not on the scale of yours,'' she murmured softly, moving into his enfolding clasp.

''Of course,'' he said, and again within minutes he was breathing evenly, on his way to a deep, comforting sleep.

She lay quietly for a while and knew that sleep would not come that easily to her tonight. Slipping out of bed, she found his robe and the newspaper he had been reading. She took them into the adjoining bedroom, climbed on the cold twin bed with his robe wrapped around her, and read about the Polish resistance to the pressures of their Communist government.

CHAPTER 7

October 1940

THE HEADLINES IN THE SUNDAY PAPER WERE TERRIFYING: HEAVY BOMBING CAUSES LOSSES IN LONDON. And the subhead: INVASION POSSIBLE AT ANY TIME. British intelligence was reporting that the Germans had assembled a whole fleet of landing barges on the French and Belgian coasts. Would England fall to Hitler's might as easily as the low countries had?

Marta turned to the comics. The war seemed far away this lovely fall morning, although her mother had bought blackout shades and there was talk of air-raid wardens being selected in each neighborhood, and of course everybody was discussing the draft. Daddy still said it wouldn't happen. Out loud he said it, but his eyes were cloudy. Aunt Moll said it was inevitable and that the Atlantic Ocean wouldn't stop those insane Germans and that sooner or later they'd turn on the Russians too.

"You get my message?" Steven asked, eating his breakfast at the kitchen table. "I left it on your pillow last night.

Fanetti wanted to know why you didn't show up at the dance.''

She nodded.

"I like Fanetti."

She glanced at her brother. "You don't even know him."

"I played in his band on Thursday."

She stared at Steven. "What are you talking about?"

"He came over with his band for a morning assembly, and I went up to him beforehand and told him I was your brother. So he let me fill in on trumpet."

"You can't play the trumpet," Marta said, laughing.

Steven shrugged. "I managed." Then he added, "He's really a terrific musician, Mart. You oughta hear some of those arrangements. They do 'Chattanooga Choo Choo' as good as Miller. Honest to God!"

"Don't exaggerate, Steven!"

"No, really, Mart."

She took her coffee and sat down at the table.

Her mother was standing at the stove, holding an egg. "Scrambled or sunnyside?"

"Not hungry."

"What do you mean?"

"I must have eaten something at the party last night that didn't agree with me," she lied.

Her mother glanced at her. "Who's this Fanetti who called?"

Marta gave Steven a poisonous stare. "He's the bandleader. You know, the orchestra guy..."

"Daddy doesn't want you singing with them, Marta."

She sighed. "Mom, for God's sake!"

"Don't aggravate him, Marta. Your father has enough to worry about. And so do I," she added with a deep sigh.

Marta didn't answer but she was aware of her mother's

brooding eyes on her as she took the paper and went to read it in the front room. They needn't worry. She was off guys altogether. She couldn't go through another session like the one last night with Lou Morrow.

She found herself staring out the window into the swaying trees beyond, lining her street. There was a cool north wind blowing today. Fall was here for real. It was a marvelous day for a football game, the first game of the season, a big one, with Hillcrest's main rival, West Philly High. Everybody was going. The girls had planned to meet at Doris's house and all troop over the bridge and down the hollow together to root for their team. Bobby Goldin and Al Rosenberg were ends. Lou Morrow was their stolid center, and Vince Fanetti was the starting quarterback, the guy with the big arm, the long-ball heaver.

She decided not to go and immediately had such a letdown feeling that she went back into the kitchen looking for a hot Danish. Steven was still piling food into his mouth. She looked at him and walked out again without the cake.

"I'm going for a walk, Ma," and out she went into the bright October morning. The trees were just starting to turn color, and the sky was high and a deep bottle blue with little strips of clouds stretched here and there. Her hair blew about her shoulders and she kept sighing while all kinds of funny yearnings and sensations wobbled around in her chest.

What she had done to Fanetti was wrong. He had invited her to sing, had rehearsed her for the Friday-night dance, had shared his own secret creation with her. And she hadn't had the decency even to call him and tell him she wouldn't come. He must think she was a brat. A spoiled fancy princess, that's what her kind were called.

Rightfully! She hadn't been fair to him. Her own feelings had alarmed her to the point where she had lost her head and run like a scared rabbit. And she was still running. Why not go this afternoon? She had never been to a football game. It was her team. It was her school. Fanetti was her friend.

That was it! They were friends. Why not? They had something very strong in common. They both loved, craved, needed music. Why couldn't a guy and a girl be friends? Just friends. She laughed out loud to herself and ran all the way home. She knew exactly which tweed blazer and flannel skirt she'd wear.

The stands were filled, all of West on one side and Hillcrest on the other. Marta and five of her girl friends were packed into three seats on the forty-yard line. Everybody was babbling, kids up and down the stands yelling back and forth to one another. They all had Hillcrest pennants and the marching band had just come onto the field to play their school anthem. Standing up, waving her little flag over her head, Marta sang with all her power: "O Hillcrest High, O Alma Mater," while the girl cheerleaders in whirly skirts and the boys in white sweaters and pants did flips and twirled their batons in fancy patterns before the stands.

From the far side the West Philly players ran onto the field. The Hillcrest spectators booed and razzed them while their band tooted and drummed. And then, there they were, in the blazing afternoon sun, their own guys, trotting onto the field like warriors, big and polished in their neat blue-and-white uniforms and helmets. The kids in the Hillcrest stands rose as if they were one person; encouraging their team with a deafening roar. Marta watched the players toss the ball to one another, spotting Lou

Morrow, who looked like the Hunchback of Notre Dame with his big 25 printed on his back, going up and down on his haunches out of sprint position.

And then, before she could see his number, before she even realized that she had been searching the group for him, she saw Fanetti. More graceful than the others, taller, leaner, even with all the clumsy-looking pads. When he turned to toss the ball off, she saw the 10 emblazoned on his back. Without wanting to, without willing it, she was riveted on that 10 all afternoon.

The cultivated grass was brilliant green on the field and the yard lines had been carefully marked in white and numbered. Marta tried to remember everything Steven had explained to her before she left the house. But when the whistle blew and Fanetti kicked off the ball, their guys coming on down the field like the Roman army, smashing into the line of West players who formed a wedge in front of their ball carrier, Marta couldn't figure out any of it. She pushed forward on the edge of her bench, half-under Phyllis's behind, and half-over Doris's, peering into the jumble below, trying to see the plays unfold. Steven said watch the ball, watch the line, watch the backfield, watch the opposition. She needed four pairs of eyes. West had two more downs to try to get their ten yards to keep the ball, but they couldn't budge through the Hillcrest line. Lou Morrow was all over them, his big head bobbing, his face protected under a nose shield.

There was a measurement; the tape was stretched; it was Hillcrest's ball. Their guys were in the huddle, and then as the lines re-formed for the play, she saw Fanetti step back and heave the ball high up in the air. Down the field it sailed, and Bob Goldin, running like a bandit for it, leaped up, caught it on the edge of its spin, almost lost it, and collapsed under a heap of West players who seemed to

131

have materialized down the field out of nowhere. They were all on their feet in the stands shrieking. One by one the gang on the bright green turf unpiled and Bob Goldin picked himself up from the bottom, shook himself a little, and trotted back to the huddle for the next play. They were already deep in West territory, on the twenty-yard line. Would they make a touchdown in the first five minutes of the game?

They tried three straight running plays, two around the ends and one right through the center, and still couldn't make their down. On the fourth, Fanetti stepped back once more and just as he raised his arm to toss, a West back broke through the right side of the line and made a lunge for him. The ball wobbled, Fanetti spun around, elbowed the West player, recovered the ball, and saw an opening on the same side where the opposition had pulverized their guard. He went through that hole like a train in a tunnel. When the West team woke up, Fanetti was over the goal line. The Hillcrest stands went nuts! The kicker made the point after touchdown, and the kids never stopped screaming for a second. When Hillcrest kicked off again, the ball went spiraling down the field like a comet, and the team went charging after it. The clock was moving relentlessly toward the half, and West tried everything they knew to score. But it was Hillcrest all the way with West losing the ball on downs. They couldn't make a dent in the Hillcrest line. Those guards were like tanks. And the coach kept most of the first team in when he saw that the combinations were clicking. He had pulled out all the stops for this game. There were some fancy single-wing plays and some sharp stuff out of the T. Of course, Marta didn't get any of it. But she heard all the kids in the stands talking about their smart offense and she kept looking for the patterns, meanwhile trying not to lose the movement of the ball.

She began to realize that there was more to the game than smashing headlong into the nearest body. But the contacts were so violent that even yards away in the stands, separated by the band and cheerleaders and sunshine distance, she could almost hear the thuds. It was too rough a game. She wondered how Fanetti could protect his hands. He kept getting rushed. Really badly. And not because he was hanging onto the ball. He was throwing it straight, right down the field to his receivers. But West had marked him as the most valuable Hillcrest asset, and Marta was sure they were trying to put him out of the way.

Hillcrest scored again and the score was thirteen to zero at the half. "In the bag," Solly Grayeboys said to his buddies as everybody stood up to stretch. They were seated right behind Marta and her friends. When Phyllis and Doris were on their feet, backs to the playing field, looking over the stands to see and be seen, Marta began to move out of the row.

"Where you goin', Mart?" Phyllis was right behind her.

Marta shrugged. "Just want to stretch my legs."

Doris pushed out of the row after them. "You won't be able to see any of the guys," she said. "They don't let 'em out at the half."

Marta didn't know why she wanted to walk around. She just couldn't sit still. The air was electric. Her school was winning. Their team was the best. A couple of the boys in her class came over to her. Kids, she thought. Messing around, trying to hold her attention. Everybody had caught the excitement. They weren't all just school grinds today. Today they were guys and gals out for fun, and Marta stood up as tall as she could, feeling slender and golden with the sun glowing on her petal skin and lighting up her green eyes.

Wandering around, Phyllis and Doris found the hot-dog

vendor and, after buying one each, tried to talk Marta into sharing another with them. She laughed them away and climbed back to her seat just as the cheerleaders were coming onto the field followed by the band. There were school songs and cheers, and the half was over. As the players ran onto the field, team by team, the students on both sides shouted encouragement to them.

Something had happened to West during the break. They didn't look like the losers of the first half. They zoomed onto the field like a bunch of gladiators. They were thirteen points behind in the biggest game of the season, but it was clear to everybody sitting out there in the afternoon sun that they weren't out of it yet. Hillcrest kicked off, West received, and their star back ran the ball up to the fifty-yard line. They dug through the Hillcrest line on the second play for a gain of six yards, and then on the third play, when everybody really expected them to push it up the field again for the four yards to the down, damned if they didn't get off a long spiraling pass that swished deep into Hillcrest territory.

In the West stands, the cheers were wild. The Hillcrest kids first moaned, a long deep sigh that swept their side, then the cheerleaders went to work. They put some pep into their yelling and tried to encourage their players. The game got close. West scored and made the point after touchdown. Thirteen to seven.

Solly Grayboyes, sitting behind Marta, groaned as the ball kicked off by West was picked up by Al Rosenberg, who was promptly tackled. When the pileup cleared, man by man, Al was on the bottom, hugging the pigskin, and they were way down on Hillcrest's fifteen-yard line.

It was Hillcrest's ball. The stands went quiet. The West team was hugging their line, down on their heavy knees, and when Hillcrest came out of their huddle you could have heard a pin drop.

The coach took Fanetti out and sent in a substitute.

They couldn't move it past the twenty. And when they tried to kick on the fourth down, a West player rushed the kicker, grabbed the ball, and ran for the second touchdown. They made the conversion and the score was fourteen to thirteen, favor West Philly High School.

"I don't believe this." Solly groaned. "What the hay's happening here?" The clock was moving like a pinwheel, and first the Hillcrest coach called a time out, then the West coach called one a couple of plays later. They were all on edge now, but Marta couldn't understand why Fanetti wasn't in the game.

"Where's the quarterback?" she asked Solly over her shoulder.

"Fanetti?"

"Why'd they take him out?"

"I dunno. Maybe the coach thought that fancy play would work and he sent it in with the substitute. Anyway, there's Fanetti coming back in."

When the tall figure jogged onto the field, the cheerleaders did a rousing, "Yay Vince, yay Vince! Vince! Vince!"

Marta was on her feet screaming with everybody else. When the Hillcrest team came out of the huddle, with just four minutes left to play, she knew she was going to see theatrics like she'd never seen before. The team was in a fever to win. The kids in the stands could feel it, and bellowed, "Go! Go! Go!"

Fanetti tossed the ball to Goldin, who ran the ball to the West ten-yard line as the second hand of the clock was sweeping toward the closing gun. They had time for one play. They raced out of the huddle and history repeated itself. Neatly, as if it had been planned by a loving fate, the last minute of the game was a perfect replay of the first few minutes. Fanetti went back and raised his arm high for the toss. A Hillcrest end went out and down into the end zone to catch it. But the West defense broke through and Fanetti was being rushed by both guards at the same time. He spun on his heel, twisted, shoved, and snaked his way through the dirt, running the ball on the bare edges of the field for the touchdown. He was buried under the goal post by the whole West Philly team.

It took a full minute for the umpires to unroll them. Fanetti stood up, tossed the ball to Baxter for the kick, and the gun went off. The game was over. Hillcrest High, twenty; West Philly, fourteen.

They didn't know it then, any of them shrieking with joy in the stands, nor the big guys down there on the field, but it would be a watershed afternoon. This would be their toughest game in a victorious season, and the last important season for high-school football for five years to come. The schools in the city would try to keep organizing athletics in the war years, but the spirit just wouldn't be there, with all the ex-heroes carrying packs in basic training in Louisiana and Georgia and sitting in mud all over Europe and the South Pacific.

Marta's throat ached so much that she knew she must have been screaming for the last five minutes of the game. The kids were jumping up and down and hugging one another. The players had surrounded Fanetti and were pounding his shoulders, half-carrying him.

He looked neither left nor right, nor up nor down, and they all left the field. A cool autumn wind had come up from the north. The sun was sinking behind the stands and the shadows stretched purple across the field now. Marta and her friends climbed the path and started back across the bridge to Woodlyn. Phyllis and Doris suggested going right to Eddie's luncheonette for their usual sandwiches and french fries before the sorority meeting. But Marta had to get off by herself.

"I can't," she said when they urged her, and she headed home alone.

The next day she ran all the way to school through a heavy gray downpour, while her girl friends trudged behind in their reluctant Monday-morning path under dripping umbrellas. Leaning against the heavy entrance door to hold it open, she pulled off her wet rain hat, the scarf she had tied under her chin, and her dripping slicker, and shook her long blond hair out over her shoulders. Rather than stopping to put her wet clothes away in the locker, she rolled everything up in a ball on top of her books and hurried directly to the gym. She heard the music before she entered. Vince was playing the piano, a section of "New Love." It was a terrific song, and he had made some interesting changes. For an instant she stood listening to the lift of the melody in the verse, then shoved open the door and walked toward the bandstand. He never looked up but continued playing, every once in a while glancing over his shoulder at the band to instruct them in their parts. Russ Jones, the trumpet player, leaned toward him, gesturing with his chin, and Fanetti turned, saw her, then bent over the keyboard again. Just as if she weren't there. She felt like a simpleton, standing with her wet things in her arms, gawking. When he continued to ignore her, her impulse was to get out quickly.

But she decided to swallow her pride. She had rehearsed over and over in her mind while she ran through the rain how she would apologize to him for not showing up to sing Friday night. She had decided to do it right in front of the band if necessary.

He was giving her the treatment. And inwardly she made a small salute of recognition to a pride at least as fierce as her own. So be it. She sat down on a folding chair near the stage and continued to listen to the new song as sharply and unemotionally as she knew how. The changes were right, unexpected, but original and fresh. She realized she was nodding her head when he suddenly looked up and caught her eye.

"You're a little late," he said. "Four days to be exact."

"I'm sorry." She got up and came over beside the stage, looking up at him. She hated the humble pose but there was nothing else to do. He was planted up there at the piano and wasn't about to make it any easier for her.

"Don't worry about it," he said, and motioning to the band went into a fast "Blues in the Night."

She had been dismissed. Dismally she turned and left the gym, not understanding at all why she suddenly wanted to cry. She kept swallowing hard, all the way to her locker, where Phyllis Cooper was shaking out her umbrella and coat. When Phyllis asked Marta why she'd been in such a hurry to get to school, Marta had trouble answering her.

"What's the matter?" Phyllis stared at her over a pile of books.

Marta shook her head and muttered, "See you in math." She headed for her homeroom, still trying to make sense out of her feelings. The best thing to do was to skip the lunchtime dance. Whatever was between them, Fanetti and her, would end right there. What was the point anyway? She had made her apology. He hadn't accepted it gracefully. Neither of them ever seemed to act like particularly graceful people.

While Little Preston was going over the new algebra at

the board she kept replaying like slow-motion film the way the meeting in the gym had gone. Or hadn't gone. Well, there wasn't anyplace to go. They couldn't be friends and that was all she had planned on. She shook her head dolefully as Mr. Preston said, staring at her, "Not clear, Marta?"

"Uh . . . not quite." God! The whole episode was taking up too much of her time and energy. She made an effort to sweep it all out of her mind that instant, Fanetti and his music and his song and his band. And his eyes . . .

The trouble was, he wasn't a kid, like the other guys. She had been mistaken in thinking about him as if he were one of the boys she was used to going out with. Even big Lou Morrow had a more or less familiar reaction to things. But Fanetti was different. He had a sureness, a certainty about his work and himself that was more grown-up. He was on some kind of a track and he didn't like being hampered. Mixed in with her embarrassment at having behaved like a brat, and then at being treated like a nobody, was a kind of awe at his composure.

He was tough to know. Everything about him spoke of a different world, another set of reference points. He was almost a man, with a man's sensibilities, and he wasn't to be toyed with. Alarm at this conclusion made her suddenly sit bolt upright. Once more Preston's eyes were riveted on her, and she slumped back down in her seat, staring at the now-meaningless jumble of letters and numbers on the algebra paper in front of her. I've got to stay away from Fanetti, she thought. For the first time in her life she was confused by the information reported by her own senses and her own thought processes. Scribbling and doodling on the paper instead of figuring out the new problems, she decided that in spite of everything, her weepy, dopey, hurt pride, her fear of the unknown, and her knowledge of what was acceptable in her world, she was going to go to that dance after lunch. If she wondered why, the answer hit her hard just as the bell rang for the change of classes and she stood up with her books and papers carelessly under her arm. She was going back down to the gym to see him. And she couldn't stop herself.

The dancing had already started when she walked in. The music was good. Vince had rehearsed the band until they sounded clean, sharp, and professional. He stood with his back to the dancers, as usual. Then he turned and casually took the mike. "Hope you like this," he said. That was all. He sat down at the piano and began the opening chords of "New Love." The arrangement was completed. As she stood against the far wall of the gym watching him play, listening, she suddenly felt his eyes on her. All the way across the room. Without knowing exactly why or how, she began to walk toward the bandstand. When she was standing beside the stage he nodded to her, and with a lift of his chin and a sideways tilt of his head he motioned her up on the stage. She climbed the little flight of steps, and Russ, the trumpet player, lowered the mike for her. With her hand cupping the cold metal, she sang Fanetti's song: "Hello, new love. / Won't you say my name? / We hardly know each other, but we're really just the same. / Our eyes will tell us what we cannot say. / You'll call me your love, I know, one day. / Look, new love, at the moonlight shining through the tree. / We need no words to tell us it's for you and me. / Let me touch your hand, your lips, your cheek. / Let me hold you close / And you'll hear it speak, this new love."

The dancers had stopped, couple by couple, and were clustering in front of the stage. She tried to keep her sound quiet and breathy, the way he liked it. Even though she hadn't rehearsed the new lyric or gone over the intricate rhythm change, the music came easily to her. It was right, it was logical. The song just seemed to grow out of the opening bars. Somewhere between the verses, Marta's heart took off for the metal-beamed dome of the gymnasium and went sailing around among the tied-back climbing ropes and rings.

The applause was wild when she finished. But she knew it was for Fanetti's music, so she said into the microphone, "That song was written by Hillcrest's own composer, Vince Fanetti."

The kids screamed and stamped their feet. Without looking at him, she knew Vince was smiling. He jumped up from the piano, touched her shoulder, and said, "Green Eyes," leading the band right into it, two slow choruses and then a rackety fast finish. The kids were still all ganged up around the foot of the stage.

She did two more songs, feeling her way, trying to pick up on his rhythm changes and the instrumental switches and solos. She did "Dancing in the Dark" and was in the middle of "Jim" when the bell rang.

Standing absolutely still for a minute on the stage, her heart still doing the rumba, she watched everybody begin to push out through the doors, listening to their calls of "Okay, Marty!" and "Terrific!" and "Loved it, Marta!"

Fanetti was busy with the band, standing among them, giving them last-minute instructions as they put their instruments away, commenting on the performances, making arrangements for their next rehearsal. She waited a second or two, then called to him, "See ya..." and started down the steps.

"Hold it a minute." He picked up his books and some music and came after her.

"Thanks," she said.

He shrugged. "What for?"

"Giving me another shot."

"I was anxious to hear it sung."

"It's a terrific song."

"You did it well."

"Thanks..." She laughed with embarrassment. "I enjoyed it."

"You're a natural."

Her laughter became joyful. "If you mean I'm untaught, untutored, and unrehearsed, you're right!"

"I mean you have natural skill. A real solid voice! Good range, musical intelligence...and your style is coming along."

"Yeah?" She was grinning like a jack-o'-lantern and tried to stop herself.

"You've got a future. If you want it, that is."

"I think it takes a little more than carrying a tune."

"Nothing's easy."

"But show business is the roughest," she said.

"Most good things are rough, to get, to hang on to. A career in music is like anything else. You've got to want it and work for it."

"Is that what you're going to do?"

"Me? Well, I'm going to be a little detoured, I think." They were standing by the gym door. The large room was empty and strangely quiet. He was looking down into her eyes. For the first time since they had met she didn't look away.

"What kind of a detour?"

"The bang-bang kind. Uncle Sam wants me." He smiled. "And three million others, of course."

"The draft?"

"They're starting the registration this week."

"But you're not old enough."

"I will be."

"You still have time."

He nodded. "I may enlist."

"For God's sake! Why? They'll get you soon enough."

He shrugged. "I don't know. I just thought I might."

She started to push open the swinging gym door and he reached over her head to shove it for her. His arm rested for a split second on her shoulder and she felt his warmth against her back. The contact was like an electric shock. She moved quickly through the doorway and started up the steps.

"Hey, Marta?" He was standing three steps down and their eyes were almost level.

"Yes?"

"Would you be able to sing Saturday night for me?"

"Saturday night? Where?"

"We play at a little spot in West Philly. It's called Nino's. From nine to one."

"Gee. I don't know. How would I get there? Where is it?"

"I could pick you up."

"No!" She caught her breath. "I mean, I don't know if I can, Vince."

"Why not?"

"Well, I don't know. I'm just not sure that I can."

"Well, let me come by for you and you can see what the place is like. If you don't want to sing, you don't have to."

"It's not that I don't want to sing. . . ."

"So okay. You'll see what it's all about and then you can decide."

He came up one step and his face was so close to hers that she could see the black outlines encircling the amber-flecked irises of his eyes, and the dark areas of his jaw line where his beard had been closely shaved that morning.

She panicked. "I think I have a date for Saturday night."

"Break it."

"I don't know. . . ."

"Yes you do."

She took a breath. "Give me the address. If I can, I'll come."

He shrugged and started up the steps. "Just like Friday night."

"No! Not like Friday night. I want . . . to be friends," she said softly.

He was now standing above her and she had to look up into his face. His expression altered slightly but she couldn't read it. "You like being friends, huh?"

"Yeah. Why not?"

"Okay, Marta. We're friends." He scribbled the address on a piece of loose-leaf paper and handed it to her. "Wait. Here's the telephone number. Just in case you want to call and tell me why you're not coming." He smiled wryly and in an instant was gone.

When she got home after school, Mom and Uncle Hank were sitting in the front room talking, their faces serious. "Hi, sugar!" Uncle Hank kissed her gently but he didn't jump up and horse around like he usually did. Steven stuck his head out of the kitchen. "Mart!" he called to her.

"Go help Steven," her mother said. "You can cut into the apple strudel now. It's cool enough." Mrs. Resnick turned to her brother, her eyes focused on his face. He was leaning forward and speaking to her in a low, somber voice, unlike his usual tone.

Marta took one glance over her shoulder as she went into the kitchen, where Steven had already mauled the strudel with a blunt knife and a heavy hand.

"Let me do it," she said and cut him a big piece. She poured them each a glass of milk and sat down at the kitchen table to read the Debby Deb column in the *Evening Bulletin*. Steven had the sports page spread all over in front of him on the table. "Penn's got a great football team," he said, chomping on the cake.

The voices from the sun porch made a low buzzing murmur, but all at once, because the house was so quiet, Marta and Steven caught the words. Uncle Hank was saying, "Look, Lil, I have to live my life my way."

"I know that, dear," Mrs. Resnick replied.

"I love Kathy, Lil."

"I think it's a mistake, Hank."

"How can you say that? You've never even met her."

"It'll hurt Mom and Dad. Her background is too different."

"Too different for what? Not for me. She's a fine person, Lil. . . . She understands about my going into the army. She wants me to go if it's what I want."

Mom raised her voice, and both Marta and Steven looked up suddenly from their newspapers. Steven had stopped chewing. They didn't mean to listen. They understood they were purposely excluded. But they couldn't ignore the urgency and stridence in their mother's tone.

Mrs. Resnick said, "In the first place, there's no reason to enlist. You'll be drafted soon enough. And in the second place, Hank, she's not for you."

"How can you say that? Will you at least meet her?"

"Why are you going to enlist?"

"Because I'm getting nowhere in the real-estate business. I can't stand it, to tell you the truth! If I enlist I can pick the kind of service I want. It's better this way, Lil. Kathy understands. She may go in herself. They're going to need nurses."

It was the way Uncle Hank was arguing back that arrested their attention in the kitchen. Steven said to Marta, "What's it all about?"

"Sh," she said.

"She's not for you," Mom repeated. And then there

was some exchange that was lost as her mother and uncle lowered their voices.

Marta shook her head. "It's serious," she whispered.

Steven said, "Boy, I'd enlist if I was old enough."

"Yeah? Well, thank heavens you're not!"

"Why doesn't Mom like this Kathy girl? Who is she? What does Mom mean?"

"Steven! I'll talk to you about it later. Just be still!"

Mrs. Resnick's voice had risen again. The words rang clearly back to the kitchen.

"I just don't approve, Hank."

"Lil, I'm a big boy now. You've got to try and understand. Mom and Pop have got to let me alone!"

"But why pick right now to make such a test case? I don't understand your timing. What's the urgency?"

"This war's going to be no picnic. I want to marry her before I go."

Silence. Marta strained to hear. Steven was half out of his seat leaning toward the doorway.

Mrs. Resnick said, "If it's love, Hank, it will keep. When you come out of the service you can marry her. . . ."

"It's going to be a long war. . . ."

"God forbid!"

"Look . . ." They heard him striding around in the living room and back to the sun porch. "I hope I'm wrong. I hope it's over in six months or that we never get in it! But I'm not going to wait for my happiness."

"You're twenty-eight years old. You waited this long to find your . . . happiness. What's so terrible if you—"

"We're going to do it, Lil. With or without your blessing. I hope you'll meet Kathy soon. Right away if possible, and I hope you'll talk to Mom and Pop."

"Now look, Hank . . ." The following words were lost. Then, "If this war is as terrible as you say, and will last as long as you think, that's even more reason to wait to get married. Is it fair to the girl?''

Uncle Hank's voice was strangely bitter. ''Would you say that if she were a nice Jewish girl from Woodlyn?''

''Honey . . .''

''Be honest, Lil!''

''I think two things, Hank: one, your timing is all wrong, and two, the girl doesn't fit in.''

''Fit in? Where? With whom?''

''With your family. With your mother and your father and your sisters.''

''I see.'' Steven later told Marta with surprising adult sensitivity that Uncle Hank sounded sad. Marta heard it too and it made her feel terrible.

When he left, Mrs. Resnick bustled cheerfully as usual in and out of the kitchen getting things ready for their regular six-o'clock dinner, making chitchat about school with Marta and Steven and never once referring to the ominous conversation with Hank. Neither Marta nor Steven opened the subject.

Marta pulled the phone into her room, lifted the receiver for a few seconds, and listened to make sure nobody was on the line downstairs. Doris answered the phone after three rings.

''Dor . . . listen, there's something I want to do . . . Saturday. I wondered if you could . . . do it with me.''

''Saturday afternoon? I thought we were going into town. Blum's has a sale. My mom said I could pick up a new cashmere. Hey, Marta, did you see Sandy Lopersteen's gray cashmere today? My God . . . it was the most gorgeous—''

"Doris, I don't know about Saturday afternoon. What I'm talking about is Saturday night."

"What's up?"

"Fanetti asked me to sing at his club."

There was total silence. She could hear Doris breathing into the phone.

"Dor?"

"Marta, are you for real?"

"I just want to go and take a look. . . . What's wrong with that?"

"You want to go to some nightclub? Alone? The two of us? An Italian nightclub?"

"It's for young people."

"What kind of nightclub is for young people? They serve liquor?"

"I don't know. It's probably just a . . . luncheonette, or something. It's in West Philly. At Fifty-fifth and Market."

"How would we get there?"

"We'll take the bus. Big deal! We can go about nine-thirty, take a look, and get back to Woodlyn by ten-thirty."

Doris said softly, "Mart, I really don't understand you. What's Fanetti to you all of a sudden? I mean, it's crazy. You know that. You're the smart one. For God's sake. You're the brain. How can you . . . ?"

"Oh nuts, Doris! The 'brain' has to do everything right. I know it all. I'm always where I'm supposed to be and I never wander where I'm not allowed. Right? Okay. I'm the perfect little goody-two-shoes."

"I didn't say that, Mart. But you know that you're lookin' for trouble. . . ."

"Why? A guy whose background is different from ours, admittedly, asks me to sing, and I want to see what goes on in that professional world."

148

"You planning on being a professional singer all of a sudden? I mean I know you're good at it . . . but how 'bout college and—"

"I am not planning anything. For once in my life, I'm really planning nothing. It's just something I want to do. It's an impulse. Don't you ever give in to an impulse?"

There was a pause and then Doris said softly, "Yeah. I do. But you don't. Not usually. What's so special about this guy, Mart? I mean I know he's good-looking. But . . . he's not . . . our type. I mean he's typical . . . with the black hair and the style and the name. . . ."

"That's just it, Doris. I resent the fact that somehow I'm not allowed to mix with him. I think that's lousy. And un-American. And there's a war coming. What kind of world is it?" She knew she sounded agitated. Maybe a little loony.

"Boy, I don't know what you're talkin' about, Mart! I just know your parents would have birds! My God, if they ever found out! You said your dad really didn't like it when you sang at the first senior dance. You deliberately didn't go to the big Friday-night hop. I mean, all of a sudden now, you change your mind. You were good singing today. Is that what it is? You got the bug . . . and he's talkin' you into going to some joint on Market Street?"

Marta sighed. "Okay. You're right. Forget it."

"No. I'm worried about you."

"Oh great! That's what I need is for you to lecture me now. . . ."

"Well . . ."

"I'm not gonna do it. Okay? I just won't go. The world doesn't need one more Jewish-girl singer. The world doesn't need one more fence to be broken down. It's better to keep the fences up. And we'll all stay safely and nicely

149

in our own little pens. And if the walls get higher, that's not our problem. . . ."

"I don't understand you all of a sudden. I really hope you won't go."

Marta sighed. "I won't."

There was another long silence. Doris sighed. She said, "If you do, I'll go with you."

Marta said softly into the phone. "Gosh! You're really a friend!"

"If it means so much to you . . . I just don't think you ought to go there alone."

"We'll come back almost right away."

"Are you sure, Marta?"

"No. I might change my weak little mind again. But right now, it seems like . . . well, sort of brave and . . . the thing for me to do. Not according to my parents' rules. That's true. But some other rules, Dor. But anyway, thanks for offering."

Mussolini invaded Greece. When Marta mentioned it to Phyllis the next day, Phyllis said, "Thank heavens it's not here!"

"How do we know it couldn't happen here?"

"Oh, don't overdramatize it, Marty! It's bad enough."

"No. I mean it!"

Stanley Baum, the smartest boy in the tenth grade, was standing next to them at the door to their classroom, and he stuck his skinny head into their conversation. "There's a lot of miscalculation going on! I agree with you, Marta. There's a lot to be worried about. Right here!"

But nobody else was concerned. The kids were focused on winning the football pennant for the season. And they were concerned about the curtailing of certain after-lunch privileges, such as being able to sit outside and buy food from the vendors. The seniors were making out their applications to the universities. Most of the top kids applied to the University of Pennsylvania and the others were divided between City U. and State. The jocks all wanted to go up to State, where sports were emphasized and there were parties every weekend. If it occurred to any of the boys that they weren't going to be able to get much schooling because of the draft, unless they qualified for ROTC or some other special program, they didn't mention it. They were all concentrating on sports and dances and battling over the policies of the *Hillcrest Literary Forum,* their school magazine.

Marta pushed the war out of her mind as well as she could. She guessed that her father, with his special superconsciousness, unlike the other kids' parents, had made it such a living issue that the war had become a steady presence in their household. What she couldn't push out of her head was her concern about her brother Steven's eyes. Their father had examined him and had mentioned quietly, but somewhat grimly, to them after dinner one night that he wanted to talk to one of his doctor friends at the university, a well-known ophthalmologist, about Steven's problem.

"He just needs corrective lenses," said Mrs. Resnick.

Dr. Resnick answered quietly, "Let's hope that's all there is to it."

Knowing that her father was a chronic worrier didn't prevent Marta from having a deep unease every time she looked into the open, brilliant blue of her brother's eyes. How could anything serious be wrong in there? He was so . . . normal, such a good kid! She found herself observing him as he read the paper or the comic books he collected by the hundreds. (Her mother had not allowed her father to confiscate them.) She was reassured when she stood on the back porch and watched him moving with speed and grace, dribbling the ball, closing in on the basket, and shooting some absolutely perfect beauties. He could see all right, she told herself. But when he came up into the kitchen sweaty and hungry as usual, he said to her, "I could hit the basket blindfolded."

She studied his regular, fine features. "What do you mean blindfolded? Are you having difficulty seeing the rim?"

He shrugged, grabbed his books, and took off for Stan Kowalsky's house, where he was supposed to study for a geometry test.

Her impulse was to call after him, to pin him down, to try to ease, with assurances from him, the rising concern in her breast. But she bit her lip and kept silent. His appointment with the eye doctor was next week. They would know soon enough.

Saturday night at quarter to nine Marta and Doris sat on the bus giggling. Everything struck Marta as funny and her laughter was instantly echoed by Doris's nervous hilarity.

"Girl singer bombs on Market Street," wisecracked Marta.

"Girl singer's best friend drinks Manhattans with the Mafia," Doris said, and then hiccuped.

"We're out of our minds...." Marta looked out the window.

"Let's get off the bus." They were already at Girard Avenue. Doris poked her with an elbow.

Marta sat up very straight and was all at once sober and quiet. "No," she said.

"Uhh..." Doris sighed and settled back into her seat.

They went through the black section of West Philadelphia, watching people in their Saturday-night finery getting into big cars parked in front of small, rundown row houses, past saloons on the corners where the doors swung open and they could see people crowded around the bar. Two young black men got on the bus, and both eyed Marta and Doris before taking a seat in the back. The girls moved closer together. "We're almost there," Marta said, more to reassure herself than Doris.

They located the club almost as soon as they got off the bus and began to walk down Market toward Fifty-fifth. There was a flashing red neon sign that was unmistakable: NINO's on and off, turning the sidewalk bright crimson.

"They're certainly not hiding anything!" said Doris. "You could see this sign in Camden."

"It's legit. I told you."

"I hope so."

They stopped in front of the heavy door and stood hesitantly, listening to the faint rhythmic sounds inside. When the Market Street elevated train suddenly shot by overhead, they both jumped and grabbed each other. After the train passed, they could hear the music from within again. Marta pushed at the door, and Doris, holding her by the elbow, said softly in her ear, "Look, I'm willing to stay for about an hour, Mart. But I don't want to make . . . you know . . . a whole long thing out of it."

"Absolutely . . . Agreed!"

As they came from the brightly lighted exterior into the dim light, they almost missed the man standing in the hall and the girl in the cocktail waitress's uniform beside him. There were twenty or thirty tables in the room, some seating four and some for bigger groups. Only a few of the tables were filled. The band was playing on the stage, which was half the size of the school bandstand. The guys were packed together around Fanetti, who sat at a small console, head down over the keyboard. Just as the man in the entrance asked her, "Table for two?" Fanetti glanced up and saw her. He jumped down from the stage.

"Hi." He nodded to the man. "This is the singer I told you about, Fabio. Marta Resnick, George Fabio." The man nodded and retreated back to his post in the little entrance.

Marta said, "Vince, this is my friend Doris Molner."

"Hi, Doris."

"How do you do." Doris was suddenly very formal and she hung back as Vince led them in.

Marta appeared to have forgotten her, and Doris, pursing her lips agitatedly, hurried after them. Fanetti showed them to a small table back against the wall, to the side of the bandstand, pulled out chairs, and sat down with them. Meanwhile, the band was playing a soft and slow version of "Perfidia."

"They seem to go on without you," Doris said nervously, pushing her chair flush against the wall so that she could view the whole room.

Fanetti shrugged. "For a while, anyway," he said. He was dressed in a white shirt, striped tie, and a navy sport jacket. His hair was combed back and he looked very grown-up. The other musicians were similarly groomed. It was apparent to both girls that this was professional business.

Edging around on her chair, Doris asked, "So where's Nino?"

Fanetti glanced her way only briefly. "It's just a name. The owner is that guy I introduced you to, Fabio." His eyes were riveted on Marta's face as she scanned the small room, trying to get her bearings. "The place doesn't fill up till after eleven," he said.

"Oh we can't . . ." Doris began.

154

Marta interrupted her, swinging her glance back to him, getting tangled at once in his fixed star. "I'm ... not going to stay ... not that late, Vince. I told you I couldn't. ..."

He shrugged again. "It's up to you." He looked around the small room as some more people were being shown to tables. "I just want you to know it's not going to be a full house."

"For my maiden voyage," she said, taking a deep breath to try to calm herself, "believe me, it's okay."

"There's a lot of action here from about eleven till two in the morning. That's the way this business is. ..." He focused back on her again with that intense expression she had come to recognize, his eyes unblinking on hers. "It's up to you," he said. "They're usually a good bunch here. They listen."

Doris leaned toward him. "Yeah? What else could they do?" she asked, her voice betraying the fact that she was very uncomfortable.

Vince laughed, and she grinned nervously with him. "I mean they're not gonna throw things are they?" she asked.

"They better not throw things at me!" Marta giggled.

"They drink. They talk. They laugh. Some audiences are better than others. You really can't predict with a certainty." He was speaking quietly to Marta again. She realized he was instructing her, and she paid attention to the low, authoritative tone. "You just do your job. You go on singing no matter what you see or hear in the audience. Most of the time the crowd that comes in here is young and they really want to listen and dance."

Marta was carefully attentive. "There's a 'but' in there, I think," she said.

"The 'but' is that sometimes there's noise, sometimes there's ... disturbance from the floor. If you're a pro, you keep going and ignore it. Do you understand?"

She nodded. "When do I go on?"

He glanced at his wristwatch. "We'll do a couple more numbers to warm 'em up, and then I'll give you a signal and you just get up . . . come up these steps." He pointed to the side of the small stage. "We'll do 'Green Eyes' and then we'll try 'New Love.'"

"That's a terrific song," Doris said.

"Yeah . . ." His eyes had not left Marta's.

"Okay," she said.

He got up. "Oh, by the way, what would you like to drink?"

The girls looked at each other. "What've they got?"

"Beer . . . wine . . . you can have whatever you want."

"I don't drink," Marta said.

"Cokes?" When they nodded, he motioned to a waiter who had been sitting back near the bar. "Two Cokes, Mike." And he jumped up on the stage without using the steps.

Marta sat stiffly at her table while Doris drew noisily on the straw in her glass. "You nervous?" she asked when she noticed that Marta hadn't even touched her drink.

Marta shook her head.

"Don't worry. You'll do fine."

"I'm not worried. I'm just . . . you know . . . keyed up!"

When he gave her the signal she jumped up and mounted the steps to the stage. Avoiding the faces at the tables before her, she sang to an exit sign, brightly illuminated high over a door in the side wall. The first two minutes were all studied posturing, thinking about the timing, thinking about the breathing and phrasing he liked, concentrating on her back being straight, her hands being still, her face free of contortion. And then, with the music pounding around her, Conti's drum lying solid under her melody like a scaffolding, Buster Mackie's sax sweet and winey, right beside her on the chorus, and all the while, in

156

and out, Fanetti's rippling keys, teasing over the tune, she just became a part of the band, one more instrument, responding to his presence and the little signals he gave them, so undramatic that nobody in the audience could possibly have noticed.

She knew she did all right. When he went into the first bars of "New Love" she stopped thinking altogether and let reflex take over. She was lifted high on the clear melodic line, reined in and then released with a rush by the rhythmic tension. It was music that kneaded the heart. She wasn't surprised when they finished, soft and easy, that for five seconds there was absolute silence in the room. Then the small audience clapped for a full twenty-five seconds, which was really great because they hardly had responded at all up to that point; and Marta had been sure that this group would just sit on their hands all night.

There was a chair on the edge of the stage behind the piano. He motioned her to it and she sat quietly during the next two numbers, observing again the meshed, ensemble playing of the group, how they watched him, how he controlled them, kept on top of the volume and the tempo, moving them up and down seemingly without doing anything. The sound was different from up there. It was tougher, harsher; she could hear their breathing, their feet moving. She could hear the separate sounds. It was less perfect but somehow more marvelous, the way they fitted it together, rubbed onto one another, slid off one another, layered over and under. She knew his arrangements were being followed to the note, and she was impressed as never before by his technique. He had an instinct for the finished product that placed him automatically, she felt, in the ranks of the professionals. He had analyzed that instinct, made it functional, and put it at the service of the whole sound so that his presentation never had any ragged edges, no loose dragging instrumentation. He had them all under control, all the time. And if now and then, as she supposed, somebody got a spot of virtuosity going, couldn't hang on to the urge to let it go wild, Fanetti would know how to make use of it, how to turn it into another interesting integer in the finished song.

His source was deep in his head and it exited through his hands as skill on the keyboard. His eye caught hers momentarily as he lifted his head, and she nodded. She knew that talent. It sprang from his soul.

At the break Doris threw her arms around Marta. "Egads, girl! You were terrific!"

"Really sounded okay from down here?"

"Fabulous, Mart!"

The musicians had disappeared, Fanetti along with them. The two girls sat at their table, Doris periodically and ostentatiously looking at her wristwatch.

Finally she said, "I really think—"

"Yeah," Marta interrupted. "As soon as he comes back in. He knows I have to leave."

"He's going to try and persuade you."

Marta shrugged. She knew she had to go, but her whole being wanted to stay. Her feelings were so confused that the thought of leaving was almost painful to her.

"Marty?" Doris was pressing her. "Kid, you really shouldn't stay. And listen, I don't want to go home alone on that bus. . . . Mart? You're not gonna stay, are you?"

"No. No. I can't stay either." She got to her feet and just at that moment Fanetti came back into the room and headed toward their table.

"You did fine," he said.

"Thanks."

"So . . . can you do a couple more?"

"I told you . . ."

"I'll take you home if Doris has to leave. . . ."

"I have to leave too."

"There's another song I want you to look at." He handed her a piece of paper, just a scrap like the first time. It had the music written out, the top staff with the lyric written in over it.

"I'll try it at home."

"What's your hurry? You were just getting warmed up. . . ."

"I have to go. . . ."

He shrugged. "All right." He began to turn away. Was he angry again? He could turn so cold so suddenly, so indifferent. She couldn't rely on his feelings from one minute to the next. What the heck, she didn't owe him anything.

She picked up her pocketbook, shoved Doris gently, and moved toward the entrance, where a steady stream of young people was coming in now. "Good night," she said. He reached for her arm and again she wondered if she would ever understand him, because it wasn't anger that she saw inscribed on his features when she turned to face him. There was an intensity about him that almost shocked her. She had never known anyone like him.

"I'll call you tomorrow," he said.

She caught her breath. "I won't be home."

"In the morning?"

"I'm . . . going . . . away . . . with my family early." And in a rush: "I'll see you in school on Monday."

If he was disappointed, he didn't reveal it. His face was a closed window, his light eyes flat and opaque, his mouth neither grim nor pleased. He raised a brow just a little. "Sure," he said. "See ya . . ." and turned away toward the bandstand.

All the way home on the bus she stared out the window,

her emotions in a heap at the base of her throat, unable to think straight. Each time Doris said something, she asked, "What?" And still didn't hear. Doris abandoned the effort, and as her stop approached she got up to leave the bus. Marta suddenly turned to her and looked up, while Doris hung on precariously to the seat handle, the bus swaying and rocking through the darkening night. "Dor? Don't tell . . ."

"Are you kidding?"

"I mean it."

"Honey, I give you my word."

"I'm in serious trouble if anybody . . . anybody finds out!"

Doris shook her head. "You were wonderful tonight. Okay? You got it out of your system. You're through with it. Keep a cool head, Mart! I'll talk to you tomorrow." And she hopped off the bus.

Walking home rapidly from her bus stop through the cool October evening, Marta tried to pull her chaotic feelings into some orderly pattern. There must be no repeat of the evening. It was a mad thing she had done. Her parents would explode if they knew. It was dumb. It was chancy. She didn't need it!

As she went up the steps to her house, the moon was sailing fast through a cloud-tossed, purple-streaked sky. She stood still for a minute staring up into the heavens. The north wind tugged at her collar, whipping her hair around her cheeks. Winter was coming. She could feel it in the new sharpness of the air and see it in the high night sky. Why were her pulses running crazy rhythms like Conti's drum? Why did her chest fill up with melody instead of air so that her lungs felt loaded with unsung songs? Where was the old control, the lady on top, the girl who knew how? She touched the piece of paper in her pocket, the new one he had honored her with. Because that's what he was doing. He was offering her the tribute of his mind and his heart. The best part of himself.

The wind blew hard and the moon suddenly disappeared behind a cloud, leaving a lingering glow overhead so that the outline of her house was a clear and sharp black against the sky. She shoved at the front door and from upstairs her father called, "Marta?"

"It's me," she answered, turning out the lamp, standing stock still in the front room. She peered out once more through the venetian blind into the night. "It's me," she said softly to herself. And without meaning to, wanting to, or understanding why, she said, "It's Vince."

CHAPTER 8

November 1981

HE DIDN'T SAY WHO IT WAS AND DIDN'T HAVE TO. SHE probably knew even as she reached for the ringing phone. She hadn't stopped thinking about him since she had seen him at the charity dance a few days before. Holding the receiver in one hand, with the other agitatedly ruffling her hair, she stretched out the long kitchen cord, tensely prowling the short space between the counter and the kitchen table.

"How are you, Vince?"

"All right. Why haven't you called?"

She didn't reply. Then, "Are you staying or going?"

"I don't know yet."

"What's it depend on?" and was instantly wary, trying to intercept his answer by adding quickly, "Your wife wants to go back?"

"It depends on whether I like it here or not," he said shortly, as if he hadn't heard the interruption.

"Are you going into the hospital?"

"Yes. Every day. Still looking around, spending the time. To see what it adds up to . . ."

"What does that mean?"

"What's the difference? Can you meet me this evening?"

"No. No! How could I do that?"

"This afternoon, then . . ." His voice was low, as if he had to shield the mouthpiece.

"It's insane, Vince!"

"No, not insane. I won't make you do anything you don't want to do, Marta. I don't think I ever did."

"I did too many things you wanted me to do."

"Things *you* wanted to do."

"I was a kid. . . ."

"And now you're a woman."

There was a long silence between them; the telephone wire crackled with static.

"Where?" She drew a deep breath. "Where should I meet you?"

"Pull your car into the hospital garage. Then walk across the street to the hotel. On the side of the building behind a garden is the hotel parking lot. I'll wait for you there. I have a dark blue Porsche."

Her heart was jumping in her chest. "How ritzy."

"It's not mine." He laughed out loud, right into the phone so that she had to move the receiver away from her ear.

"Neither am I," she said.

"What a fresh kid you were!" He was still laughing. "Be there at noon," he said and hung up.

The telephone buzzed and sputtered and still she hung on to it, standing first on one foot and then the other, staring off into space. His timing was inspired, as it had always been. It was nine o'clock in the morning of a gray, depressing fall day, and in the preceding days her husband had somehow failed her. She was feeling lousy, sorry for herself, unable to go back to the new song. She hadn't been able to call Steven in New York and say either, Brother, I can't do it, even for you, even though I want to more than anything else in the world; or, Brother, I'm doing it! For me, for myself as well as you, even though my husband may never forgive me.

Dan's patient explanation of his problems at the bank had been patronizing, as if she were a slow-witted child—a beloved child to be sure, but what was it exactly that Dan loved? The fresh kid that Vince remembered had been only too quick to bury herself in devoted domesticity, to accept being tamed by the strong and loving man she had married. Dan handled her like her father had, with respect, tenderness, and with a good strong yoke. The yoke's on me, she thought. Or was. She paid great attention to her dressing, much more than she had in a long time. Among other things, being a woman, as he had reminded her, meant doing what she wanted to do. She knew she still wore clothes well. She was tall enough, still slim enough, curved enough for a simple black wool suit to cling at all the right places without making her look like a chorus girl. That was an image she had avoided all her life, although it was tempting because she knew she could get away with it. The men in her generation, unlike their contemporary counterparts, appreciated powder and paint and the sensuality it expressed. Illusion it may have been, but Dan liked her all dressed up and in makeup. He always praised her appearance, her choices, no matter what. He approved of her. She was the perfect, model wife.

Things tended to slip through her fingers all morning as she straightened up the house. Everything she did was nervy, hasty, incomplete. As she was on her way out, the phone began to ring. She let it ring and ring without

165

answering it until a sudden concern that it might be her kids made her dash back and reach for it. It was Doris, calling to tell her that she was getting ready to go into the hospital. Doris wanted to chat, wanted support, wanted to be joshed and kidded in the way they always helped each other. But Marta couldn't rise to it. "Call me when you're all settled in there," she said finally. "I'll come down and sit with you."

"Please not before, Mart," Doris answered. "Afterward."

"Whenever you want me."

When she got to Municipal Hospital she couldn't find the garage entrance that Vince had told her to locate. She sat in thickening traffic with taxis blowing their horns at her, searching the front of the building, trying to see around to the side portals, and still couldn't find any entrance. She knew she couldn't park in the hotel lot without an entrance card to cross the barrier. Vince had tried to plan ahead for her, and stubbornly she went around the block once more, spotted the steep driveway before she got anywhere near the hospital entrance, and quickly went down it. When she had parked and was crossing the street, she looked up at the hotel in front of her. It was fairly new, done in space-modern, all prefabricated modules, glass, and plants. People were rushing in and out of it as if it were Thirtieth Street Station. If he had any immediate plans for her, this overcrowded, anonymous beehive would be a natural. But she doubted that he had picked this uninviting place for a serious reunion. She thought she knew him better than that. Walking around to the side of the hotel past the lavish plantings, she came to the parking lot and almost at once spotted the blue Porsche.

He was leaning down on the steering wheel, reading something spread in front of him. She approached the car and opened the door on the opposite side. "Waiting long?" she asked, and he looked up and smiled.

"That's okay." He started the motor.

"I couldn't find the garage over there at the hospital."

He turned his head briefly, grinning at her. "That's my Marta!"

"It's hidden!"

"So where did you park? There's no damned place down around here. . . ."

"Oh, I found it, Doctor! Finally . . ."

He nodded, still grinning. "I knew you would. You like things to be difficult. . . ."

"Oh," she said, sighing. "Are you ever wrong! I was the princess, remember. I like it all easy. Handed to me. That's what you always said, anyway."

As he drove toward the Benjamin Franklin Bridge, she stole sideways glances at his profile, until, conscious of her eyes on him, he swung his gaze to her.

"Well, Marta princess," he said softly, "I'm glad to see you."

She smiled in return.

"And you? How do you feel about seeing me, Mart?"

"I'm overwhelmed, Vince, to tell the truth!"

In Jersey he drove fast, California style, and she hoped they wouldn't be flagged down by the state cops. "We'll get arrested for speeding," she said.

"I keep forgetting I'm back east." He slowed down and glanced her way again, lifting his right hand from the wheel and reaching over to touch her hair. "You're still beautiful. You had hair like my grandmother's polished brass."

"I remember your grandmother. She lived with you."

"Of course. That was my mother's mother. You didn't

167

know my father's mother. She came to live with us too . . . later, after the war. My mother had a houseful.''

"Is your mother living?''

"No.''

"Nor mine . . .''

"My mother approved of you,'' he said. "And my grandmother thought that once we taught you a little Italian and a little catechism, you'd be just fine!''

She didn't answer. There was no way to account for that world. It was gone. And the bits and pieces remaining, the leftover conformities and niceties and expectations, were daily being ground down by other styles, more-abrasive modes, tougher realities.

She said, "New world a-comin'.''

And he had followed her train of thought. "It's here. . . .'' Smiling at her again. "My son is engaged to a nice Jewish girl from Pasadena. Her family approves of him.''

She stared out the side window. "Talk about something else,'' she said.

"What can't you stand . . . kids of today or yesterday's pain?''

"Both,'' she said. "Neither . . .''

"You're not so blissfully happy. . . .''

When she didn't answer, he insisted, "Are you?''

"I'm okay,'' she said.

"But less than happy . . .''

"I'm less than gorgeous! I'm less than young; I've got all the classic burdens and doubts. I'm certainly no smarter. . . .''

"You got exactly what you went after.''

"So did you. . . . Are we going to spend this whole afternoon saying, 'I told you so'?''

He reached for her hand and held on to it. "We're going to talk about it all. There isn't any other way, you know.

We went smashing into each other's lives. We left the pieces lying there. And then we went sailing on past each other. Now we have to back up, Mart. I have to. There's a lot to look at.''

She sighed. "I don't know what that will accomplish."

"I don't know either. It's just something I have to do. You meant . . . something to me. It was very deep and very important. I think I meant something to you, too. . . ."

"Yes," she said softly. "You did."

As they drove into the flat, open Jersey countryside, the leaden cloud cover began to lift. The November sun broke through and the raggedy corn fields were washed with a bright golden sheen. He turned unexpectedly into a small, paved side road, and a couple of hundred yards later, in a large grove of pine trees, she saw a big rambling structure made of half-hewn logs and pale bricks. The sign in the front said BONZIO'S INN. Smoke was slowly curling from a large chimney. In the back where he pulled to park, there was a long, low motel made in the same architectural rural style.

She said, "At first I thought you were taking me to the new hotel across from Municipal Hospital. That's really what I thought."

He sat back after he turned off the motor and smiled at her. "I never tried to take you to any hotel."

"You never had the money."

"Oh yes I did! I was a working kid, don't forget!"

"You didn't know that that was how it was done."

"What a superiority complex!" He shook his head mockingly.

She insisted, "Did you take girls to hotels in 1941? Tell the truth!"

"No."

"Okay . . ."

He came around, helped her out, and took her arm. He didn't say, as he might have, Who needed fancy hotels or motels? There was the backseat of the old Ford.

Given the out-of-the-way location of the inn, she was surprised to see that there were already people seated at the scattered tables. The hostess smiled and led them to a table near a big fieldstone fireplace, where a fire was burning brightly. In spite of the filled tables, the restaurant was hushed and music floated softly in the air. "I've Got You . . ." he held the chair for her, ". . . Under my Skin."

"Nice place," she said. "They're playing the right songs." She smiled at him as they sat down next to each other in padded chairs. She felt their legs touching under the table.

"That's our music," he said, looking into her eyes.

"Don't you like the new stuff?"

He shrugged. "Who's got time?"

"I don't know . . . car radios, offices, whatever. You never listen?"

He shook his head. "Only to the old songs. And I listen to classical music. I learned that from you."

"We never listened to classical music together."

"I knew you did, alone."

"I still do. . . ."

"What else do you do?"

She shrugged. "What does your wife do?"

"My wife? She lives a middle-class lady's type of life. Tennis and volunteer work."

"There you are." She laughed. "Me all over!"

"She doesn't hate it."

"Oh, Vincent, I don't either!" She drew a breath. "I'm giving all the wrong signals."

He shook his head. "Not by my standards."

"Our standards were always different."

"That's what you thought. I never agreed."

"You have a different vision then. I'm afraid to ask what you see."

"I see a restless girl, a beautiful woman who thinks she's missing something."

"What's so new and different about that?" she said. "Those feelings probably existed when you were in kindergarten and I was playing on a blanket on the back porch."

"I have a picture of you on your blanket on the back porch." He grinned. "In a sun bonnet."

"Are you kidding?"

"No. I copped it once from an album in your living room."

"The album under the coffee table..."

"Before I was unwelcome in your home," he said.

Her breath got stuck in her chest. He was caressing her palm, and with her free hand she covered his. "I never knew how to get them to welcome you. Ever."

The expression on his lean face altered, his jaw muscles working, but he held her hand tighter. "I know you tried."

"I couldn't figure it out," she said softly.

"It wasn't your fault."

"Oh no? Whose fault then, Vincent?"

The waitress interrupted them and they moved apart to scan the menu. They ordered their lunch and he asked for a bottle of white wine to be brought immediately. "If I were working I'd have to eat lightly and skip the booze," he said, laughing.

"Do you like your work?"

"Yes." He let go of her hand and leaned back in his chair as the waitress offered him the wine to taste. Holding the glass up to hers, he clinked and said, "To us."

She hesitated barely a second and replied, "To us."

"Do you like being a housewife?" he asked.

She considered the question, trying to be accurate. "I did like it." She searched her memory. "I chose it. I know that even then there were some few regrets. I expected that. . . ."

"Regrets . . ." he repeated. He was staring into the pale wine, gently tilting the glass so that the clear meniscus moved up and down.

"I did know what I was doing," she insisted. "I always liked to be in control. Always. But then it gets hard . . . to stay in control. . . ."

"In control of what?"

"I thought maybe you knew," she said wistfully.

He leaned close to her again. "But you were such a little know-it-all . . . how could I tell you anything?"

"I'm not now," she said. "Maybe you could tell me now. . . ."

"It's unfinished business," he said softly.

But she wasn't looking at him. Her eyes were on the fire burning brightly in the stone hearth nearby. "There's something in the air," she tried to explain to him. It was important that she clarify it. Her gaze swung back to his. "You were right about my being restless. It's all the old promises that I didn't keep."

"Yes," he said. "They come back to haunt you. I know that song too well. . . ."

She was looking at him intently. "You compromised too."

"If you mean my career, Marta, I wouldn't agree at all!" He shook his head. "I cannot regret any of that now. It was too tough, too much of a strain, too demanding to have any regrets about it now. It took the best I had to offer. I'm always aware of that."

"But your music . . ."

"I wasn't good enough."

"Oh my God, Vincent! What a lie!"

He shrugged. "It's like you said before. We had different standards. I would have called it a different view. I wasn't good enough."

"I thought you were good enough. I told you so."

"You told me it would probably be a second-rate career, with a third-rate life attached."

"Yes." She sighed. "That is what I thought."

"And now you want yours back," he said. "You want to test it all again."

"Whatever the talent was," she said, "it never had its chance. How will I ever rest if it doesn't have its chance?"

"So that's all?" He was searching her face. "That's all you want?"

She didn't answer, shifting back in her chair as the waitress served her lunch.

They picked at their platters and were almost at the bottom of the wine bottle. He emptied the remainder into their glasses. She was fascinated by his long fingers, wrapped loosely around the stem of the glass, his surgeon's fingers, piano-player's fingers. "Did you love your wife when you married her?"

He said, "She reminded me of you."

"That's a dumb answer, Fanetti!" she snapped.

"What would be a bright answer, Marta?"

"Try yes or no."

He shrugged once more. "I was in love a hundred times. I was in love only once."

"That doesn't make sense. . . ." ·

"Being in love has to do with being wide awake . . . being wide open . . . taking the big whirl. It has to do with feeling in complete control while you're completely letting go."

"Pretty good lyric," she said.

"You always came up with a wisecrack when it got near the heart."

"Can't we leave my heart out of this?"

"You didn't leave mine out of it," he said.

"You keep making me responsible."

"Not I," he said softly, shaking his head. "You made yourself responsible. That was the best part of it. That was the best part of you. You were a miracle to me. You were a heroine. You were the brave new social conscience that I used to hear about from those few, ill-assorted intellectuals I knew."

"My God, Vincent, cut it out! You make us sound like a musical Sidney and Beatrice Webb. We were just two dumb kids."

"I was impressed with you."

"You were impressed with a pretty face, a nice figure, and an interest in music that matched yours."

"Sure," he said.

"And that was that!" When he didn't answer right away, she prodded him with her elbow and he grimaced. Looking into each other's eyes, they burst into sudden, gay laughter.

"It was the best!" he said. "For all the hundreds of reasons you already know. And I couldn't get over you," he said. He put his arm around her and drew her as close as he could. The arm of the chair was between them. "I want you."

"There's always the back of the Porsche," she said.

He leaned away, grinning. "There isn't any back. It's the new style. Remember. Everything is the new style. But not for you. You were right about being a princess. That's how I see you still."

"And how about all the . . ." she motioned with both hands, "between us. Pretty royal behavior, right. In the back of a Ford yet!"

"That's right," he said. "All the . . ." He mimicked her motion, "was loving. In case you forgot the word."

"It wasn't the word I was thinking of."

"What was the word?" he asked softly, leaning toward her.

"How about fucking?" she said just as the waitress came up to the table with their bill. Without looking at either of them, she dropped the check on the edge of the cloth and scurried away.

"I didn't see her." Marta felt her face flush and she began hurriedly to gather up her things.

"I have a witness now." He was laughing out loud. "She thinks you're propositioning me." He held her chair as she stood up and slid into her coat.

"You don't need any witnesses, Vincent. I'll admit to everything."

It crossed her mind as they sauntered back to the parking lot that he had paid the bill, taken her arm, and steered her back to the Porsche without a moment's hesitation. He had never once looked in the direction of the motel rooms.

On the way back to the city he chatted with her as if they were just old friends, the moment of intimacy gone. He seemed to find the exact light tone without making an effort. "I like Philadelphia," he said. "I had forgotten the special quality of the gloom in fall." The sun had disappeared again, gone for the day.

"I like the city too," she said. "There's nothing worse than feeling lousy in the bright sunshine." She expected, as before, that he would pick up on it and turn the talk toward them again. But he didn't. His entire manner had become casual. The intensity she had sensed during lunch was gone.

"I see very little of the weather anyway, in my work,"

he said. They were on their way back across the Whitman Bridge and the traffic, heavy in the late-afternoon rush, was inching its way into the city.

"Yes," she murmured. "I know doctors work very hard." She turned toward him. "Don't you ever take vacations?"

He returned her glance. "No . . . rarely."

"No need to get away?"

"I used to take my son skiing . . . or swimming."

"And your wife?"

He shrugged. "She likes to stay home. Do you take vacations?"

"Yes," she laughed, "as many as possible. We love the change of scene."

"I like my scene," he said.

"How rigid!" She stared out the side window.

"Mm-hm," he answered, "I remember that line."

"It was no line then and it's no line now."

"It was just your device to get your own way. Admit it, Marta!" He touched her cheek.

She turned back to face him, grinning. "I admit it."

He laughed heartily. "What a great broken-field runner you would have made!"

"I hate football."

They were approaching the area of the hospital. "What do you think about working here?" she asked.

"I haven't made up my mind yet."

"But what do you think of the hospital?"

He shook his head. "I think they have themselves one helluva problem."

"What does that have to do with you? I mean if you were to come onto the staff."

He smiled in her general direction. "Quite a bit. Their

176

problems would become my problems. They've invited me to join the board.''

"Well," she said, "that's an honor!"

"If you're in the market for honors . . ."

"Who isn't?"

He laughed aloud. "Somewhere there must be somebody. . . .''

"But it's not you!"

"Well, it's a great substitute . . . for whatever is missing."

"What's missing, Vincent?" She knew she was pressing him back into intimacy and she couldn't stop herself. It was all ending too quickly.

But he failed to reply. The radio had been playing softly. She recognized James Ingraham singing and turned up the volume. It was a good song, "Just Once." Asking the lingering questions about the way it was and if it could be as it should be, just once . . . ?

He was paying no attention to the music and the lyric that was timed for the moment. His mind seemed miles away. Pulling into the hospital garage, he turned the Porsche around and motioned the attendant away. They sat in the subterranean gloom for several seconds, and then she began to rummage around in her bag for her parking ticket.

"Thanks for lunch," she said and opened the door.

He grabbed her arm and held her back. "When you know," he said, "call me at that number I gave you."

She swung back to face him. "You're still handing it all to me to decide, is that it?"

He shrugged.

She sank back against the seat, sighing and looking out the windshield before her. "How much longer?"

"A month. I'd have to go back to the coast in any case at that time."

"And when would you start here . . . if you did?"

"After the first of the year."

"But you don't know yet?" She held her breath.

"No." He reached over and smoothed her hair off her brow. He made no move to pull her into his arms or to kiss her. "If you tell me to call you," he said softly, "I will."

She opened the door and stretched her long legs out of the low-slung car. James's voice was soft and plaintive. "Just once," he asked, will there ever be a way . . . ?

"Okay," she said. "You do that."

CHAPTER 9

November 1940

"MELANCHOLY BABY," CROONED RAY EBERLE.

"Turn it up," Steven said as they were sitting at the kitchen table listening to the radio after school. "I can't hear it."

"You just like it deafening!" Marta snapped at him, and then seeing the astonishment in his face, in the wide wide blue eyes, over her shortness of temper, she reached to the counter and turned the volume louder... "My Melancholy..."

"Great number," he mumbled, focusing back on his comic book, holding the page up close to his face. There was still a question of whether he needed eye surgery. He had had several appointments with opthomologists, and the next one would be decisive. Each time that Marta lost patience with him she berated herself. He didn't seem worried about his eyesight, and he rarely expressed the kind of temper she let fly. Whatever strong feelings he had, he vented in the pounding he gave his basketball against the hoop above the garage in the back of the house.

Or by banging out some new boogie-woogie he had picked up on the piano, loud and ferocious, fingers digging into the keys, feet thumping the floor and pedal, his entire body swaying. The percussive sound made his mother tight-lipped, and his father always left the room.

Marta pointed to his Flash Gordon magazine, which was right beneath his nose. "You better put that rag away before Dad gets home." But he only shrugged and went on chewing chocolate pinwheel cookies three at a time, and reading.

"Melancholy . . . " he hummed, with his mouth stuffed, of sad moments and how to cure them.

The music stopped abruptly and they looked up at each other in surprise. "We interrupt this broadcast for a news bulletin," intoned the nasal voice on the radio. The station switched overseas and there was sharp static crackling in the background. Another voice continued, "Rumania has joined the Axis and the Germans have taken possession of the Ploesti oil fields."

That evening the war was discussed as usual. There was a thundering inexorability about the German advance, observed Dr. Resnick with a worried shake of his gray head. They were sitting at dinner in the kitchen and Steven had asked him about this latest development that provided the Germans with a fresh supply of oil. "It may well be the apocalypse," said Dr. Resnick while they all stared at him uncomprehendingly. What followed was the usual twenty-minute question-and-answer session between Steven and his father, with Steven pushing more and more complicated queries until Mrs. Resnick said impatiently, "Enough already! Please! Let's eat dinner in peace. I can't take any more war talk."

Marta had already tuned out. Her mind was always on the same things these days, the same person. She thought

180

about Vince Fanetti when she got up in the morning and thought about him the last thing at night. He called her now a couple of times a week in the evenings. Their conversations were easy, picking up each time right where they had left off the last, reading each other's minds, clicking. But then when they met in the gym to go over a song that she was going to do with the band at a school dance, they could hardly look at each other, had almost nothing to say, exchanging information so briefly and formally that anyone looking on would think they were the most casual strangers.

They were too conscious of each other. She kept trying to put him off because he wanted to date her, to come to her house.

Her girl friends were privy to part of it. But she didn't want to tell them about the calls at night. It was hard to keep it to herself, but the girls thought she was wrong in doing the lunch dances. They tried to persuade her to end it quickly. Before it was too late, they said. She thought they were acting like babies and she ignored them.

At the next Friday-afternoon dance Marta sang three songs, two of them written by Vince. When the dance was over and she was on her way to her next class, Marilyn Kaufman said, "Do your parents know?"

Marta stared at her coldly. "Know what?"

"That you're doing all this singing! Didn't your father say he didn't like it?"

Marta shrugged without answering and, waving so-long, ran up the steps. "See ya."

Glancing down before she turned off the landing into the hallway, she saw the girls down below, joined by Phyllis, with their heads together, yakking it up. Now she regretted ever telling them anything. She regretted that they didn't understand. But above all, she regretted that she didn't have anyone to talk to about the whole situation.

Doris and Phyllis were standing by their lockers after school, doing their end-of-week collection haul, when Marta came down to drag out her own accumulation.

"Friday, Friday, Friday!" She almost screamed with joy.

"What're we doin' tonight?" asked Doris. She was looking at Marta, who was tugging at scarves, hats, books, and a dirty gym suit.

Phyllis said, "Want to go up to Eddie's?" It was the local luncheonette, the meeting place, and something and somebody were always there Friday evenings. They were both waiting for Marta to answer.

"I don't know yet," she said.

"Something up?"

"No," she answered.

"So what do you think?" Phyllis persisted as they climbed the stairs toward their exit, burdened by their belongings.

"Call me after dinner," Marta said to Doris. "Make any plans you want; if I can, I'll go along."

Phyllis pushed open the heavy door in front of them, then suddenly let it slam back closed and wheeled around so abruptly that Marta and Doris, who were right behind her, collided into her.

"What's with you?" complained Doris, stooping to pick up dropped books.

"He's out there, Mart." Phyllis was staring through the small glass section of the door.

Marta peered out the window over her shoulder and saw Vince standing by himself near the curb. The Woodlyn kids were trailing past on their way home across the bridge. It was a raw November day, just starting to rain. But Fanetti wore no hat, no gloves, and just a lightweight windbreaker. He rocked from foot to foot to keep warm and made no effort to talk to anyone.

"You go ahead," Marta said to the girls. She stood inside the doorway waiting for the homeward-bound throng to thin out.

Phyllis and Doris exchanged glances and, hugging all their belongings and books, went down the steps. Marta peered through the window. She saw them make some comment to him before they turned toward the bridge. He nodded and answered briefly. When she finally walked out she could feel the fine drizzle on her face. Pulling her beret down on her head, she shifted her books about, everything piled on top of them ·in her arms.

"Hi," he said.

"Hi, Vince."

"I have my car here. I'll take you home."

"Look. It's not necessary."

"It's starting to rain."

"I won't melt."

"So . . . I'll take you home. Come on, Marta. Don't be dumb."

"I beg your pardon!"

"You're acting ridiculous."

"Boy, talk about dumb! You're the one who doesn't understand!"

He had taken her arm and was propelling her away from the bridge. She allowed herself to be led to his car, which was parked on the lot on the Hillcrest side of the school. The rain was coming down steadily when he unlocked the door of the Ford for her· and she climbed in. They sat inside and she waited for him to start the motor. But he put the key in the ignition and sat there, staring down at it, making no move and saying nothing. The rain was pelting the windshield with little pinging sounds that kept getting louder and more explosive.

"It's hailing," she said. "We better get going."

He turned to face her. "What is it I don't understand?"

She sighed and tried to avoid his eyes. "It's no good, Vince."

"Why not?"

"Because . . ."

He reached for her and she pulled back away from him. But he got his right arm tightly around her and with his left hand was forcing her head around toward him. Their faces were so close that she couldn't help but stare into his eyes. He brought his lips down on hers hard and for a second she almost cried out. Then his mouth softened, the kiss deepened, and he began to open his lips. This time she did pull away from him before he could stop her. "Please," she said softly.

"Tell me you don't feel anything!" he said.

When she didn't answer he tried to kiss her again. "I feel exactly what you feel," she said quickly and moved into the angle formed by the edge of the seat and the car door, leaning against it and staring straight ahead. "Please take me home." She drew a deep breath and when he didn't move she said, "Or let me get out and walk."

"What's the big deal, Marta?"

"I can't, Vince. . . ."

"Can't what?"

"I can't . . . have a . . . thing . . . with you," she said lamely.

His mouth twisted. "Christ, you don't even have the guts to call it what it is . . . a love affair. You can feel it all right, but you're scared to death of it. Tell me something, Miss Woodlyn princess, how many times in your life have you been kissed like this?" And he grabbed her again and wrapped his arms around her, his mouth all over her face and neck, and finally finding her lips, forcing her to open her mouth, his tongue probing and warm.

The dampness outside had penetrated the car and she felt herself trembling from nerves and the cold. She pushed him away. "Please, Vince," she said. "Try to understand. We're so different. I just can't . . . get involved with you. . . . For me . . . it's impossible. It's wrong."

He sat back against the car seat and gripped the steering wheel in front of him. "That Neanderthal minibrain Morrow is okay and I'm off limits, is that it? It doesn't matter how we feel together, what we know together, the way we . . . fit! None of that counts. What matters is to come from the right neighborhood and have the right . . . birth certificate? Is that how you're going to live your life? Get all the credentials in order first? And then think about the feelings later. Is that it?"

She couldn't answer. She was huddled, shaking, on the far corner of the seat, her books and surplus hats and gloves on the floor at her feet.

His tone changed. "Marta?" His voice had a pleading note in it.

"I don't know how I'm going to live my life. I haven't decided yet."

His hands were gripping the steering wheel so hard that his knuckles had turned white. "Don't trouble!" His voice was a growl from the back of his throat. "It's been decided for you, baby! It's a big boat and you're not strong enough to steer it!" He shoved in the clutch and angrily yanked at the gear, dragging it groaning into first. He drove across the wet bridge at top speed. "You're just a passenger!"

Although as far as she knew he had never been to her home, he somehow knew exactly where to turn, where to pull up, and where to stop. They sat in silence for an awkward few moments in front of her house. He had turned off the motor and the rain tattooed on the roof of the car. It was streaming down the front steps, rushing in rivulets down the curbs, carrying dead leaves and twigs toward the sewers at the bottom of the street corner.

"I'm sorry, Vincent." Clumsily laden with her belongings, she tried to tug at the car handle, but the door was stuck.

He reached across her, leaned on the metal, and the door eased open. "Forget it." He didn't look at her.

She sat back on the seat again for a second. "Why can't we be . . . friends?"

"Goodbye." He sat staring straight ahead through the foggy, rain-spattered windshield.

She began to climb out of the car when Steven suddenly appeared, loping up the hill, his blond hair plastered wetly against his head, his books dripping.

"Hey, Mart!" He stood by the open car door. Then leaning down and peering inside, squinting his eyes, his face suddenly broke into a grin. "Hi ya, Vince!"

She heard Fanetti say softly, "Ho, Steve."

"Hey, you comin' in, Vince?" Steven turned to her as she started toward the house. "Mart, I want to show Vince some music I'm doin'."

She turned around to face her brother. "You're soaked, Steven. And I'm getting drenched through and through. Come on now!"

Steven just stood by the open door, not moving. "Well, I want Vince to hear this song. Maybe his band can play it." He bent down again and stuck his head in the car. "Hey, Vince. Why don't you come in for just a few minutes?"

She couldn't hear Fanetti's answer, but Steven was

persistent. They were both dripping now as the rain got heavier. "I'm going in," she said. "You suit yourself."

"Well...can't Vince...?" Steven, who was never embarrassed, suddenly seemed to know that he was in the middle of something peculiar.

"Vince can do whatever he wants," she said clearly. The car door on the driver's side opened and Fanetti jumped out, following them up the steps to the house.

When they pushed open the front door, the warm air and sweet aroma of baking hit them immediately.

"Hello," Mrs. Resnick called from the kitchen. "Hot brownies. Right out of the oven." She stuck her head around the kitchen door. "Oh," she said when she saw Fanetti with them, filling up the doorway between the sun porch and the living room.

Without looking at her mother, Marta said, "Mom, this is Vince Fanetti."

"How do you do," her mother said softly.

The moment was engraved in Marta's mind. She would never forget it, the three of them wet and uncomfortable, standing awkwardly fixed in the living tableau that they couldn't break.

But then Steven, still dripping, impetuously slammed his books down on the floor beside the piano, plunked himself down on the bench, and began to play his new song.

"Get your clothes off, Steven," his mother said.

"I'll be right down," Marta mumbled and escaped up to her bedroom, where she stood for a minute looking into her eyes in the mirror, not understanding herself. And then shaking her head as if at a stranger, she ripped off her wet shoes and jacket, piled her belongings on the radiator to dry, took a breath, and went back downstairs.

Her mother had gone back into the kitchen; Vince stood beside Steven, watching his hands on the keyboard, listening.

Mrs. Resnick was pouring milk into three tall glasses at the table when Marta walked into the kitchen. Her mother looked at her quizzically for a second, then turned back to the oven, where she was tending to another batch of brownies.

"It's teeming out there," Marta said, putting paper napkins on the table at each place. "Vince Fanetti gave me a lift home."

Mrs. Resnick nodded but didn't answer. When Marta went back into the living room, Vince was seated beside Steven, playing the same music, Steven's song. His long fingers moved quietly over the keys as he talked in a low tone to Steven about the melody. "You can modulate right in here. Have I got the tune right?"

Steven was peering closely over the keyboard, following Fanetti's hands. "Yes," he said. "But I don't know what you're doing now. Did you change the key or something?"

Fanetti hit two chords. "Yes. From here to here. It feels like a key shift to me. Right there." He went over it again. "I don't want to alter your melody, but it was too . . . sweet the other way. Listen." He repeated it with the shift. "Isn't it more interesting like this?"

Steven was rapt. "Oh yeah! That's terrific! I really like that. How about the beginning, the first eight bars? What's wrong there?"

Marta touched her brother's shoulder. "Mom's gonna be sore if you don't get out of those wet clothes." He looked up at her, his blue eyes wide with surprise. He had almost forgotten where he was.

"I'll be right back, Vince," he said. "I really appreciate your showing me these things. I mean, I can hear the melody. But sometimes it just doesn't come out the way I want it. You know?"

Fanetti nodded. "Sure," he said. "That's the way it usually is the first time you try something. You have to work it out."

Steven dashed up the steps and Marta stood beside Vince, watching him noodle around, his fingers brushing lightly over the keys. He glanced up at her. "Your brother's a natural," he said.

She leaned down and whispered, "Sh. My parents ... don't ... really ... like it!"

He whispered back, grinning, "Too bad!"

She jabbed him with her elbow and was about to argue back when he started the opening chords of "New Love." She got caught in the melody and began to hum along with him. "It's a terrific song," she said. He varied the tempo, first upbeat, then slowing it down and adding embellishments, little trills and grace notes. "I wrote it for you," he said, looking up at her over his shoulder.

A sudden sound from the back of the house made her turn guiltily toward the kitchen. Her mother was standing in the doorway, drying a plate, watching them. "The brownies are ready," Mrs. Resnick said.

Steven came leaping down three steps at a time and beat them into the kitchen. They sat at the table and Mrs. Resnick handed around the plate of brownies. Indicating a bowl of fruit in the center, she said, "Help yourselves, children," and then disappeared from the room. Usually she hovered there over them or nearby, starting her preparations for their early dinner.

Marta sat stiffly across from Vince, sipping her milk, pushing her brownie around on her plate. He took a long gulp and shook his head when she handed him the plate again. Only Steven was completely at ease. He gabbed on and on about the top ten songs of the week, praising the Pied Pipers, who were coming the following week to the King Theater, the number-one showplace in Philadelphia for live appearances of the big bands.

"You goin', Vince? I really am crazy about Tommy Dorsey."

Vincent said, looking at Marta, "I might go Friday or Saturday night."

"I thought you play at your club Saturday nights?" Steven asked, his mouth full of brownie.

"Every other week," Vincent answered Steven, but he was talking directly to Marta. "I can't do it every weekend anymore. Fabio got another combo, three guys, when I can't play."

When they finished, the three of them went back into the living room, Steven shoving Vince toward the piano again. Marta wondered if her mother was upstairs phoning her father. She thought she heard her voice from behind the closed bedroom door. It angered her that her mother had showed so little interest in Vincent, just short of being rude. But she knew it was alarm she had seen in Mrs. Resnick's eyes.

Steven monopolized Vince, watching everything he was doing at the piano, asking endless questions. Finally Vince said to him, "I want to talk to your sister," as he got up from the piano bench.

Steven looked puzzled, but he nodded and got up too. "Boy, Vince, I really like your music!" He started back to the kitchen. "And I really like the way you fixed up my song."

"We'll play it at the next junior-high concert."

"Jeez, you mean it? Can I sit in on trumpet?"

Vincent laughed. "Why not?" He came out into the enclosed front porch, where Marta was reading the paper, and looked through the recordings piled carelessly under the player. "You'll ruin your records like this," he said.

"They're Steven's," she said. She opened a small cabinet beside the sofa. "These are mine. What do you want to hear?"

"What do you want to hear?" he asked, reaching for her hand.

"Vince!" she whispered, pulling away from him and glancing hastily toward the other room. She put on "Autumn Nocturne."

"I've never danced with you," he said and took her in his arms, holding her firmly. Despite her frantic gestures and her attempt to get away, he wouldn't release his grip. "It's dance or get caught!" he teased.

"You're terrible!" She laughed and floated into the music with him. They moved together to the sound of the rippling piano as if they had practiced for years. She could anticipate his every step, the held beats, the hesitations, the swaying in time to the music. He had her very close against his chest, his chin against her temple. Each time she tried to back off, he grasped her tighter to him so that their bodies were locked together. She had no choice but to keep moving. She could smell the mixture of aftershave and cigarettes, the mysterious male aroma of his sweater. Her left arm was up around his shoulder and as they danced her hand brushed the back of his neck, her fingertips touching his thick hair. He moved his head to look into her eyes and pressed her close again, his palm flattened against her back, synchronized with her as if they were permanently attached. Her heart was pounding so loudly that she could still hear it when the music stopped; he moved back and she realized that the record had ended.

"That's nice piano," he said, letting her go and turning back to the record player. "Mind if I hear how he did it?"

"Go ahead," she said, and he started the needle again. This time he didn't come near her, but sat down on the opposite side of the room, listening to Claude Thornhill put the melody together. She wondered if he had forgotten her, and then he swung his gaze back, riveted it on her eyes, and never blinked until the song was over.

Mrs. Resnick came downstairs, glanced quickly toward the porch, and hurried back into the kitchen, where Marta heard her speaking softly to Steven.

"Want to go to the King with me tomorrow night?" Vince asked her.

"I can't."

"Why not?" He indicated the other room. "They know now."

"Know what?" She jumped up. "What is there to know? You drove me home from school! I sing a few songs at the dances. Big deal!"

"You're transparent, Marta!"

"And you're opaque! You're thick, that's what you are. I won't start a war here in my house for you or anybody else."

He stood up. "You're overstating the case," he said quietly. He pulled her toward the front door, out of the line of vision from the kitchen. He kissed her tenderly on the mouth and she was too surprised to move. His lips lingered on hers as he held her face between the palms of his big hands, his mouth brushing her eyelids, her nose, and her cheeks.

"Just a little war," he said, laughing.

"You're insane, Fanetti. The whole world's gone nuts."

"I want to see you tonight. I'll pick you up at eight."

"No!" She jumped back, away from him.

"Okay, where should we meet?"

"I can't. . . ."

192

"I'll come by at eight. . . ."

"Oh God! . . . I'll meet you at Eddie's on Fifty-fourth
. . . . Outside . . . Just wait near the corner for me."

Doris called right after dinner. "I'm stuck," she said.
"I have to go to my aunt's tonight. Want to go into town
tomorrow?"

"I'll call you in the morning." Marta hung up and
hurried upstairs to put on her makeup.

As she was leaving, her father looked up from his
newspaper. "Where are you going, sweetheart?"

"Just up to Fifty-fourth Street, Daddy."

"With Phyllis and Doris?"

"Doris is going to her family's . . . I'll see Phyllis and
Marilyn."

"Don't stay out late, Marta!" her mother said.

"Be home by ten . . . ten-thirty at the latest, Mom."

She ran up the hill until she was almost out of breath.
The wind was coming down from the north with the
persistence of winter, but she was warm inside her gabardine coat and tan skirt. The girls all wore casual clothes on
Friday nights; it wasn't smart to be overdressed. Eddie
Gilbert, the man who owned the luncheonette, allowed the
kids to gather at his place over the weekend. They could
kill two hours or so there, sipping Cokes, smoking, eating
peanut-butter crackers, and Eddie never asked them to
leave. It was pretty much the same high-school crowd all
the time, and they came and went sometimes two or three
times during the evening. The guys who could get their
fathers' cars were parked outside on Fifty-fourth, and if it
were warm a lot of the kids would be leaning against the
cars, kidding around. Even on this cold, damp night there
was a group around a car in front of Eddie's when Marta
walked up. Some inside, some outside. Louis Morrow

called to her from the backseat of the big Buick . . . Bob Goldin's family's car. "Hey, Mart! Hop in!" Lou Morrow beckoned. "We're going bowling."

"Thanks," she said. "But I can't. Have to be home real early tonight." Before they could ask any more questions, she went inside Eddie's. Marilyn and Phyllis were in a booth with two other girls when she came up to them.

"Don't bother," she said as the girls began to slide together to make a spot for her in the booth. "I'm going bowling with Lou Morrow. He's outside."

She went back to the entrance, standing just inside the store until she saw Bob Goldin drive the Buick away. Taking her time about picking out gum and Life Savers, she suddenly spotted Vince's Ford pull up in front and then slowly move to the corner. She paid for the candy and left quickly. He had the radio on and was leaning back smoking when she opened the door and got in. "Go!" she commanded.

"Who's after us?" He laughed and leisurely started the motor, driving to the center of the street.

"Just move it! You don't understand!"

He immediately pulled the car back to the curb. "Yes I do," he said, and he wasn't laughing now. Gesturing behind him with his thumb back toward Eddie's, he said, "You don't want any of them to see you with me. I don't need a *Bulletin* to get the news, kid."

She drew a deep breath. "Vince . . . I told you. . . ."

"What? What exactly have you told me?"

She hesitated, then sighed as she turned to face him. He was freshly shaven, his black hair combed and smooth. His eyes were glittering in the light from the lamppost at the corner. "Don't make it hard for me, Vince."

He reached in her direction. "Want to see how . . . ?" He had taken her hand and pulled it down toward his lap.

.''God!'' She pulled her hand away and tried to open the car door.

He was laughing. ''I'm only kidding you, Marta. I wouldn't force you to do anything. Anything! Do you understand? I wouldn't waste two minutes of my time on you if I weren't so sure you wanted to see me just like I want to see you!''

She stopped jiggling the stubborn door handle and moved back to the center of her seat. ''I'm all mixed up. And it's your fault, Fanetti! You're messing me up. . . .''

He reached for her again and held her chin gently in his big palm, pulling her face toward his. ''What're you so afraid of, Marta? What has you so scared to death?''

''You know as well as I do.''

He started up the motor and didn't answer.

''Where are we going?'' she asked as he went over the bridge past the high school. When he failed to reply she said, ''I absolutely have to be home by ten-thirty.''

''You're in charge of the time,'' he said. ''We'll get you back.''

He drove through Hillcrest and turned into a small street where he parked in front of a row house with a flight of steep concrete steps in front.

''What's here?'' she asked.

''Come on.'' He got out, opened her door, and held her hand as they went up to the front door. It was unlocked and he pushed it open.

There was a sweet aroma in the air . . . like licorice, and there was music coming from a record player in the living room. She thought it was Puccini and was about to ask him when she realized that the living room was full of people sitting around listening. She hung back until he pushed her in front of him.

''My sister Lizabetta.'' He indicated a little girl on the

floor. "My sister Flora." A slender, dark-haired girl of about fourteen. "My brother Mark, my brother Angie." The two boys glanced up at her shyly. "My grandmother." He indicated the elderly lady in black sitting in a rocking chair near the record player. "Nonna . . . this is Marta."

The old lady raised her brows and nodded. At that moment a stout, dark-haired woman came into the room wiping her hands on a kitchen towel. "Hello . . ." She took Marta's hand. Vince said, "Mom, Marta."

"Vincent told me about your lovely voice, Marta. Maybe you can sing for us sometime," she said.

"Thank you. Sure," Marta said. She was bewildered and stood in the middle of the room with them all staring at her until Vincent said, "Give me your coat." She slid her arms out and he took it from her. She sat down on the couch next to Flora, who said, "I know your brother. He's a terrific musician."

"Are you in his class?"

"Yes," said Flora. "I'm in his geom class . . . we're in the same section."

"Do you play the trumpet?" asked Marta.

Lizabetta jumped up and came over to Marta. "I can play the trumpet."

"You can?" Marta looked into the little girl's large gray eyes, which reminded her immediately of Vince.

"I play trumpet," said Flora shyly.

"Flora's a violinist," said Mrs. Fanetti. "That's her number-one instrument."

"Do your other children play?" Marta asked.

"Everybody . . . everybody plays. Anthony, the oldest, plays the cello. . . ."

The girls began to laugh. "Mom!" they cried. "You know he won't play that anymore!"

"Sure," said Mrs. Fanetti. "He'll start again. You wait

and see." She turned to Marta. "Anthony works hard all day. He doesn't have much time anymore. And Stella... my older daughter, she works now too. But she plays viola. Everybody plays." The front door suddenly shot open and there was a draft of cold wind and the door slammed shut. A heavyset, gray-haired man in a windbreaker came into the room.

"Pop," said Vincent, pointing to the couch. "I want you to meet Marta Resnick."

Mr. Fanetti said, "Pleased to meet you, young lady," and walked off to the kitchen with Mrs. Fanetti trailing right behind him.

There were six pairs of eyes focused on her and Marta picked a spot to stare at on the wall where there was a crucifix set with colored stones and a picture of Jesus underneath. She looked right in between until Vincent came and sat down beside her on the couch and casually put his arm around her.

"What do you think, Nonna?" he asked his grandmother. "Isn't she pretty?" The little kids all snickered. Marta tried to move away from him, but he held her shoulder firmly with his big hand. The old lady nodded.

"*Bellissima*? Nonna?" he insisted, and the old lady nodded again.

At that moment Mrs. Fanetti came back into the room with a plateful of warm cookies. "You'll like these," she said to Marta, holding the plate down for her. "I make them with anisette. They're delicious."

Marta took one and ate it. "That's really good," she said, and Mrs. Fanetti, who had put down the plate, picked it up and came right back to Marta with it. "Come on, have a couple more. Here, take a napkin." She handed her a paper napkin from her apron pocket.

Mrs. Fanetti never sat down. She moved among them,

197

offering the cookies until they were all gone. "Now I'll make some tea and get out the panetone," she said. And then looking at Marta, "You'll like it. It's full of fruit. Maybe you'd rather have cocoa with it?"

"No, thank you, Mrs. Fanetti, neither," said Marta. She added quickly, "I had a big supper."

"We're going out, Mom," Vincent said. "Don't make anything." He stood up and called, "Hey, Pop?"

"Don't shout, Vincent," said his mother.

Vince took Marta by the arm and pushed her toward the kitchen. Mr. Fanetti was seated at the kitchen table, drinking beer from a can and eating some of the anisette cookies. His eyes were riveted on the sports page of the newspaper in front of him. The radio was buzzing the news on a small elevated shelf beside the table.

"Pop?" Vincent had shoved Marta in front of him and she stood nervously shifting her weight from foot to foot until Mr. Fanetti looked up.

"You goin'?" He put down his beer and half-rose out of his seat. "Come over again," he said and smiled. In the lopsided grin and the squareness of the jaw, Marta instantly saw his son. But where Vincent was tall and lean, his father was thick and stocky. He had large square hands and heavy, ropy forearms that bulged out from his rolled-up shirtsleeves.

The radio was blaring, "A small British force has attacked the Italian army in North Africa...."

Mr. Fanetti cocked his ear. "Bad," he said.

The tinny voice on the radio continued, "A limited number of British soldiers is repeatedly attacking an Italian army of over two hundred thousand men, pushing back tanks and fighting off aircraft and artillery fire."

Mr. Fanetti reached over and shut off the radio. "Very bad," he said, nodding his head. He looked up at Vincent suddenly, thrusting out both his arms and shaking them up and down from the elbow. "The Italians don't want to fight. That Mussolini is nuts! Hitler got to him all right!"

Vince put his hand on his father's shoulder. "Don't worry about it, Pop. We'll go in after 'em soon."

His father shook his head. "Don't be so anxious!" he said and went back to his sports page. "Saint Joe's is doing good in basketball," he muttered, and Vince tapped him goodbye on his shoulder.

When they were seated in the car, Marta said, "Your family's very nice, Vince."

He was relaxed, his arm on the back of the seat behind her, but not touching her. "I told them all about you. Did you like my grandmother?"

"Oh yes. She reminds me of my grandmother."

"She doesn't say much. But she knows everything that's going on."

"Does she speak English?"

He started to laugh. "We're not sure. She understands everything . . . but if you ask her a question in English, she'll answer you in Italian."

"I liked them all. Your sisters are very pretty and so nice. . . ."

"Okay . . . so I pass. Right?"

He started the car and she stared at his profile, sharp and clean in the reflected light from the lampposts. "What's to pass?" she said. "I'm no board of examiners!"

He was driving fast in the way that pleased him, through the streets of West Philly that were almost empty of traffic in the early evening. "We have to try to understand, Marta."

"Understand what?"

He shook his head. "You're not ready to come to grips with it . . . or you wouldn't ask silly questions. . . ."

"Silly or not, I don't want to play twenty questions!"

"How about the one big question? How about the one that demands that you grow up and face a few ugly facts? . . . Like why are these walls there between people?" He drew a breath. "And okay . . . a couple more to go along. Who put them there? And how do you get them down?"

She said impatiently, "All right, Socrates. . . ."

"He was Greek."

"And I'm Serbo-Croatian . . ." she said.

"And this is America!"

"America goniff," she giggled suddenly.

He glanced at her questioningly. "*My* grandmother," she said. "That's her wisdom for you! It means thief, but don't ask me to translate it!"

There was silence between them, unbroken except for the multiple knocks in the motor of his old car, and the slapping of his almost-bald tires on the asphalt. The narrow streets of West Philadelphia spun past as she stared out the side window, telling herself she wouldn't ask where he was taking her now. He turned on Market and, weaving around the poles of the elevated train, found a place to park a few doors from Nino's. Waiting for him to open the stubborn door on her side, she watched the brilliant red neon sign flash on and off, washing the sidewalk in its red glow. He took her hand as she stepped out of the car and kept hold of it as they entered Nino's. Fabio, the owner, greeted them in the little foyer and took her coat, tossing it to the hat-check girl behind the counter of the closetlike cloak room.

"Pretty good crowd for an early Friday night," Vince said to him.

"Not bad. I got a table near the music and one over there in the back." He stood beside them, waiting, while Vincent looked around through the smoky gray haze suspended in the room.

"We'll take the small one back there against the wall." He steered Marta in front of him toward the table. When the waiter came he ordered a beer for himself and a Coke for her. The table was so tiny that their knees touched underneath, and if he wanted to he could reach across, past the rickety lamp lighted on the edge, and outline her mouth with his fingertip. She thought he was going to do that when he raised his arm, but instead he handed her a cigarette, placing it between her lips, and lit his own, searched her face through the spiraling smoke and held the flickering match for her as she inhaled, his narrowed eyes never leaving their target, his chin lowered. She could feel the power of his focus on her, but she couldn't return it and stared at the glowing end of her cigarette. She stirred the ice in her Coke when it came, and head tilted down sipped through the straw.

"Mart?" He said it quietly.

She looked up and sighed. "Okay, Fanetti." She felt as if a double set of gears had shifted inside, everything falling into place, not necessarily where she willed it, but where it seemed to will itself. "You're a terrific guy. You're talented. And you're clever. And you're right. I'm afraid of tough questions. I don't want to know about them."

He shook his head. "I don't believe that. I watch you up there on the bandstand, singing your little lungs empty. You're not the kind that scares easy. And you're smart. . . ."

"Not so smart, Vince."

He laughed. "I know a lot about you, Marta Portia Resnick.... You're plenty smart!"

"Oh God!" She giggled. "I thought I buried that middle name!"

"It's on your junior-high transcript."

"Fanetti! You went and looked me up! You have your nerve!"

"I just wanted to know exactly what I was dealing with."

"In the first place, those records are private. How did you get into the student-association office? How did you know where the files were? My God, what else was on there?" She laughed.

"All those A's you got. You must be number one in your class!"

She was surprised at the flush she felt starting at her neck and rising around her ears, a surge of pleasure and embarrassment. "You could have gotten into real trouble poking around in that SA office," she said.

"You've spent all your time studying, haven't you?"

She looked at him shyly. "Quite a bit ..."

"You like to use your head. That's what that record says. Loud and clear."

She said softly, "It says a few other things too, Vince. It says my family thinks it's important that I get good grades. They want me to be a top student. They want me to go to college and get ... maybe more than one degree. It matters very much to my parents that I learn and study and do well in school. Do you see? That's part of it ... part of the way I am ... part of what keeps me ... going on my track."

He reached across the table and took both her hands in his and held them tightly. "That's great! That's fine! But now ... you've got to start putting it together for yourself.

ALL SHE WANTS

Now you have to stop making A's for Pop and start doing it for Marta! That's what I was talking about before...."

She withdrew her hands and gripped her drink. "What you were talking about before, Vince, those walls? I didn't make those walls. They were there a long time before me." She glanced up at him quickly and the intensity of his focus was too strong for her. She lowered her eyes and sighed. "I'm not a one-woman army. I can't go ramming into something I don't even understand!"

He leaned farther across the table, his face not far from hers. He said softly, "Just answer me this...what the hell's the difference between us, Marty? What is so peculiar about a guy and a girl caring about each other and wanting to be together?"

"There's no difference between us," she said. "I know that. And there's nothing odd about...any of the things ...we feel."

He drew a deep breath. "So what's odd and peculiar is the wall...isn't that so? What's bad is the barrier. It's artificial. It's rotten!"

"Yes," she said softly. "It's wrong...."

He reared back in his chair and laughed triumphantly. "You understand! I knew you did! Nobody could taste the music like you do, and give it out like you do. If you were some little phony...!"

The combo was a piano, bass, and growling saxophone, and they held together with a soft blend of voices, keeping the lyrics quiet and buzzing in the background. "That's a nice sound," she said, watching the black pianist as he hummed into the mike bent sideways over the keyboard. "Easy to dance to..."

Vince stood up and reached for her. She pushed back her chair and slipped into his arms. They were the only ones on the floor. Moving together, hips joined, hands held tightly: "You Go to My Head." Melodies intoxicated, like love. He sang the words in her ear and she pulled away to smile up at him. "I like your voice. . . . Why don't you ever sing with . . . ?" She didn't finish the sentence because he brought his mouth down on hers and silenced her. She couldn't move away from him; his arms were vises encircling her. She felt that the eyes of the whole room were on them, but when he took his lips away and she turned her head just enough so that his mouth moved to her cheek, and she could stare over his shoulder, she realized that no one in the room had so much as glanced their way. Alone, clinging to each other, the brain reeling, feelings rising like bubbles in champagne . . .

"I'll buy you champagne," he murmured.

"I had it once," she said, "at a wedding. I liked it!"

"I'll get you everything. Everything you want!"

"Okay, Rockefeller . . ." She laughed happily; her heart was a soap bubble floating in her chest, and her feet were off the floor.

They danced three numbers, reluctant to move apart, and only stopped when the group took a break. When they were seated back at the table he said suddenly, "We could do a record together. We're ready for it. Any of our new songs." He was staring off into space, puffing on a cigarette, concentrating on his own thoughts.

"You could," she said at once. "Not me!"

"Why not you?"

She shrugged. "I'm not good enough. . . ."

"That's how you get good enough. . . . The only difference between the pro and the amateur is that check you get . . . for doing the same damn thing we do twice a week in the gym and once every other week here. We're good enough!"

She looked into his face and saw the intense dream

modeled in his jaw, fixed in his mouth, which was pulled to one side in a tough grimace. "That's not for me," she said, "that life. . . . You want it. You love it. But it's not for me."

"How do you know?"

She tapped her skull. "Secret messages!" She broke into laughter.

But he was sober and serious. "How do you know?" he insisted.

"I know I don't want to spend my life in smoky cabarets. I don't want to spend my life with an audience staring at me! I don't want it!"

"You love an audience," he said.

"I love a lot of things. . . . I could eat my way through Eddie's candy counter, too . . . and dance my way through the next ten years making believe I'm Eleanor Powell . . . but I won't."

"It's not that bad a life. You have to be successful. I can do it. I can turn my band into big time. I could do it right now. . . ."

She looked at him curiously. "You have no plans to go on? To go to college?"

He shrugged. "I don't know. The war is coming."

"Maybe not," she said. "But you could get started. . . ."

"You sound like my mom."

"It would make sense," she said.

"Security and safety, playin' it close to the form. That's how it is with women."

"That's the way I am, Vince. I've never lied."

"I'll give you that!" he said.

There was a long moment of no talking between them, staring unblinking into each other's eyes. "I'll never lie to you," she said.

205

"You never have to, Mart. Whatever you are, whatever you do, it will always be okay with me."

"Some things . . . you may not like. Some things you may . . . hate. . . ."

"Things!" he said. "You . . ." He took a breath. "You, I love." He said it softly but it rang in her head like a gong. She looked down at the table.

"We're too young . . ." she muttered.

"Oh sweet Jesus! . . . You've got the most complete collection of . . . of . . ." He hunted for the word.

"Clichés." She laughed.

He smiled. "I love you," he said. He pointed his finger at her. "Put that away with all your A's and all your scary caveats!"

She raised her brows at the last word. "Very impressive, Fanetti! Latin yet!"

"Omnia Gallia est mia Italia."

"What?"

"My dialect is closer to your big-deal Latin than any little text on Caesar's wars. Believe me!"

She reached across the table, her fingers brushing the back of his hand. "Don't be touchy," she said.

"I don't like being excluded on the grounds of ethnic differences," he said quietly. "But what I really can't stand is being thought ignorant."

Years later she would remember that it was from Vincent Fanetti's lips that she had first heard the word *ethnic*. She thought about it and said it softly out loud, "Ethnic . . . differences." She glanced up at him. "Look, you said you'd never get angry . . . and already you're burned up because you think that I think you're ignorant."

"Does telling no lies mean always telling the exact truth, Marta? Are you going to be our special court stenographer and read back everything . . . all the baloney too?''

"Probably," she said and puffed on her cigarette.

He grinned and tilted his beer, draining the glass. "Then, holy Christ, I better get used to it!"

The combo came back and the pianist stopped at their table. "How you doin', man?" he said.

Vince stood up and shook his extended hand. "How's it goin', Marcus? I really liked that little medley there. . . ." He turned to Marta. "This is Marta Resnick. Marcus Appleby, the best jazz pianist in Philadelphia!"

"You not so bad youself, man! And you're the vocalist? You want to do a number, you two?"

Vince looked at Marta questioningly. "Want to do 'New Love'?"

"Sure." She stood up and walked up on the bandstand ahead of the two men. Marcus Appleby adjusted the floor mike for her and said into the mouthpiece, "This here's Mizz Marty and Doc Fanetti. . . . They gonna play you their new one. It's called 'New Love.' And that's nice . . . when it's all brand new. . . ." He grinned a wide, white smile and went to the back of the little stage, pulling over an empty chair and picking up a trumpet that had been lying on the floor.

The room had filled completely, but one by one the tables quieted down as Vince, at the keyboard, hit the opening chords. She began to sing. He was doing remarkable things with runs and trills under her vocal, and then in the second chorus he nodded to Marcus, who came in softly on the trumpet, wailing as if the voice in the horn were human. She sang the chorus a second time through with the trumpet in honey harmony and was so mad for the new sound of it, the different texture in her ears, that she couldn't stop herself from

207

shifting her glance away from the audience, sideways to Vince at the piano. He was looking back at her with his heart in his eyes.

When they finished, she thanked Appleby and the two of them went down the little steps. "Hey, wait there!" Appleby came after them, bending down on his haunches at the rim of the stage. "Why don't we cut that, man? That might go!"

Vince turned around to face him. "You think so?"

"I do! I do! You call me on it, man, when you got time. You hear? We got ourselves a number there! That's a top ten!"

"You got somebody to record us?"

"I got a guy in town here. I cut a few already. We partners. Okay?"

"Absolutely!" Vince shook his hand on it. "Call you," he said as Marcus Appleby sat down at the piano and went into a soft "Blues in the Night."

"You might be a famous singer in spite of yourself," Vince said. He was holding the back of her chair, waiting for her to be seated at their little table.

"I have to go now, Vince."

He glanced at his wristwatch. "It's only a quarter to ten."

"Please," she said softly.

He paid their check, told Fabio he would see him the following weekend for their performance, and they left Nino's. The wind was rushing down Market Street, tossing bits of trash across the sidewalk into the gutters. Marta turned up her collar and lowered her head against the stiff breeze. She said, "I can't get involved in cutting a record, Vince."

He laughed and put his arm around her as they made their way to the car. "Don't worry about it! It won't happen that easy. Anyway,'' he looked down at her and the wind whipped her long hair up across his face, "I can always find another girl singer.''

She pulled away from him. "Oh really?'' she bridled. "Who?''

He laughed out loud. "There's a long line of 'em, honey.''

"God, what a big shot! Fine! Okay, Fanetti, as long as you don't bother me about it!''

When they were in the car and on their way back to Woodlyn, he said softly, "Nobody can sing my stuff like you, Marta. How could they?'' He turned to look at her. "Those songs were written for you.''

As they approached her street, the rows of houses were mostly dark, telling of cold evenings and early bedtimes. He suddenly made a turn and headed in the opposite direction. She saw what he was doing but said nothing. He went three, then four blocks past until the street widened and the large single homes appeared. He turned abruptly into a narrow, darkened road, and parked under an arch of half-leafless trees, in front of a house without lights that was set far back from the street.

"It's late,'' she said, but he pulled her toward him and she melted into his arms and stopped thinking altogether.

His lips were light and gentle as they moved back and forth across her mouth. His tongue began to probe hers. He drew her even tighter against his chest and she wasn't sure whose heart was pounding like a tom-tom until hers gave one more lurch and sent the blood pummeling into her temples and into the rapid pulse at the base of her throat. Her arms trembled and a great, heavy, rich weight settled across her pelvis and began to work its path down into her thighs. A sudden rush of wetness between her legs made her draw back away from him, and she leaned shaking against the car seat. Catching her shallow, uneven breath, she said, "We better go."

He didn't answer. He leaned toward her and reached for her again, softly kissing her forehead and the smooth skin over the bones of her cheeks and then her chin. Her mouth, its own needs too strong to speak the fears forming at the back of her mind, surprisingly sought his. And with a groan of pleasure and victory, he pressed his lips on hers once more.

His hands were moving over her shoulders and back, gently kneading, pressing. Her arms had entwined themselves around his neck of their own volition. As she held on to him, his free hand, the large palm flattened, slowly caressed her side and underarm, touching the edge of her swelling breast where it rose from her rib cage. She moved. He withdrew his hand, his lips. He murmured in her ear, "I love you, Marta. I always will. No matter what happens. You're in my blood." And allowing herself to be kissed again, her fingertips felt the thickness of his hair above his collar, and his scent was strong in her nostrils. His hands returned gently to her breast, but now she didn't move away. His fingers found the stiffening nipple and he squeezed it through her sweater while wild tremors traced their way like machine-gun bullets furiously up and down the length of her frame.

His hands were all over her and she couldn't stop him or even try. He took her arm from his neck and slowly moved her hand to his rigid flesh swelling inside his flannel trousers. He tightened her fingers around it, then tugging at his fly he pulled down the zipper and his warm hard flesh was in her hand. It felt strange and unexpected to her touch, but she wasn't frightened; it was as if she had known it all before somewhere, and memory bit by bit supplied the next step.

210

His fingers were touching the bare skin of her thigh between her stocking top and her panties. He moved his hand and gently, firmly pressed her crotch, which was running with wetness, and pressed again and again, then slowly moved his fingers inside her panties. And as he touched the springy hair and separated the tender lips, she suddenly cried aloud, and all the colors of the spectrum exploded in her head, reds and purples and greens running together like dye down some mysterious hill. His flesh leaped in her hand and she felt his thick juice flowing into her palm, shooting off on the seat.

As suddenly and crazily as it had begun, it was all over, almost as if they had been in a sound tunnel with the music set at the highest decibel and had all at once emerged into the quiet of the night. Only his ragged breathing, verging on sobs, broke the silence. Her pulses still faintly echoed the charge she had experienced as she opened her eyes. His gray eyes were shining close to hers, and she thought momentarily that she saw herself reflected in their deep light. He put his cheek against hers and as he rubbed gently, the beginnings of his beard scratched at her soft skin.

"Marta," he said. He expected no answer. "Marta." He breathed her name.

"What happened?" she whispered, closing her eyes again. "What was it?"

"Don't you know?" He moved back and held her chin in his hand and she heard that winning roar of laughter. "Well . . . you're not a baby anymore!"

"I didn't know . . ." she said softly, "it could happen . . . just like that!"

"When you care for somebody it can. Just like that!"

She searched for tissues in her pocketbook and he retrieved a rag from the floor of the car, helping her wipe her skirt and the car seat. He smoothed her hair and whispered, "I love you."

She sighed in his arms and closed her eyes.

He said softly in her ear, "Now you tell me. . . ."

Her lids flew open. She smiled and moved her lips. But there was no sound.

"Tell me!" he commanded.

She wrinkled her nose at him and moved over to her side of the seat. "I love you, I love you, I love you," she sang.

He looked at her soberly for a long moment but asked no more. Her head was back and her hair was a bright fan against the dark leather. Still humming, she laughed happily as he started the motor and drove her home.

There were lights on all over the first floor of the house. "Looks like my family's still up," she said, pulling out her compact and lipstick. She didn't try to stop him as he came around and opened the door for her. Together, arm in arm, they walked up the front steps. Just as she moved away to push at the unlocked door, he held her back a second, his lips lightly brushing her cheek. She looked up at him, and with her fingers moistened by her own saliva, wiped at some tiny traces of pink above his mouth. She turned and he followed her inside.

Dr. and Mrs. Resnick were sitting in the living room and Uncle Hank and a young woman Marta had never seen before were seated together on the couch opposite.

"Well, look who's here! How are you, sugar?" Uncle Hank jumped up and hugged her. He looked over her shoulder when he became aware of Vince standing there in the space between the sun porch and the living room.

She said, "Hi, Uncle Hank. I didn't know you were coming over." Turning about, she said, "This is Vince. . . ."

Uncle Hank moved around her and the two men shook

hands. "And this is Kathy, Mart. Kath, this is the princess I've been telling you about. Got all the family brains and beauty. Well, almost..." He blew a kiss at his sister. But Mrs. Resnick didn't smile. She was staring down at her folded hands.

Vincent was still standing behind Marta in the doorway. She looked toward her father.

"Daddy, this is Vincent Fanetti. He's a friend of mine... from school." Dr. Resnick said, "How do you do," and nodded but didn't make any move to get up. His face was calm and his eyes met the younger man's casually. "I heard your band play... the night Marta sang at a school dance. It was quite good."

Uncle Hank had reseated himself next to Kathy. "Musician?" he asked eagerly.

"I have a little band," Vince answered. Nobody had asked him to sit down and he remained where he was, half in and half out of the room.

"He's a pianist," said Marta. "And a very good songwriter..."

"My God! How marvelous! Kathy, isn't that fabulous? Boy, I wish I could do that!" Uncle Hank said.

Kathy was a small girl with a pale pretty face and large brown eyes. Her mouth was carefully shaped in tomato-red lipstick and on each cheek were two bright patches of rouge that further emphasized her pallor. Her fair hair was held to one side with a barrette like a child's. She was delicate and small-boned and was all dressed up in an elaborate black silk dress with a low V front. Pinned upside down on one shoulder was a bunch of artificial violets with tiny green velvet leaves. Her hands tugged at each other and moved shiny metal bracelets with little clinks up and down her slender arms. Her feet, in spindle-high-heel black patent sandals, crossed and uncrossed as she moved about on the soft sofa. She looked up shyly as Hank addressed her, and speaking to the room at large, she said, "Hank loves music. I think he could have been some kind of musician." Her face flushed suddenly with the effort of speaking out.

Hank took her hand and held it tightly. "I wouldn't practice," he said, laughing.

"Like Steven," said Marta. Without looking at them, she felt her parents exchange glances.

"Steven's a real musician," said Vince. "He's got natural talent." He was speaking to Mrs. Resnick, but after the initial greeting she had not once glanced his way. Dr. Resnick was looking at him with measuring eyes. "It's just a hobby for Steven," he said.

Mrs. Resnick added, addressing the room in general, "He practices. And he's doing all right with the new Bach his teacher gave him."

Thick silence like a fog hung in the room. Marta could hear the sharp ticking of the mantle clock over the buffet in the dining room. She thought she heard the sudden swish of the oil burner going on in the basement. Still no one said a word. Fixed in their positions, they were all locked in discomfort, and nobody tried to break through it.

It was Vincent, legs spread, feet planted, his hands in his trouser pockets, who said at last from his midway spot in the arch, "Well. I think I'll say good night." He glanced at Hank and Kathy. "Nice to have met you..."

There were murmurs of goodbye and Marta turned automatically and followed him to the front door. Angry words and burning tears were crowding into her throat but she couldn't even say she was sorry. Her chest was filled with anguish and she was afraid that if she uttered one word she would begin to cry. She held the door open for

214

him, leaning on the handle, the cold night air flowing in around her. He touched her cheek with his fingertips.

"Don't keep that door open, Marta," her mother called.

He said softly to her, leaning down a little, "Will you go with me to the King tomorrow night to hear Tommy Dorsey?"

"Yes," she answered at once.

"I'll pick you up at seven-thirty."

"Yes. Good night," she said. Their hands brushed and she closed the door behind him.

The four adults were still sitting in their awkward charade in the living room. She wanted to tear through the room and rush upstairs to be alone. But she forced herself to stand quietly in front of Kathy and Uncle Hank.

"I hear you're a nurse," she said to the young woman.

Kathy glanced up and Marta saw understanding in her deep brown eyes. "Yes," she said, "I am."

"It must be very hard work. . . ."

"Well, you get used to it. . . ."

Her mother and father made no move, and after several more unrelieved seconds she said, "Will you excuse me? I'm going up now." As if magically released, Uncle Hank took Kathy's arm and they stood up together.

"We're going now too. Kathy's on duty in the morning."

Marta didn't wait for the front door to close after them. She ran up the steps, saw that Steven's light was out behind his closed door, and hurried into her bedroom. She locked the door behind her, something new for her, and without lighting her lamp, took off her clothes in the dark. Naked, she stretched out on her bed, overwhelmed by the mixture of emotions assaulting her. But beneath the anger and resentment there was something else coursing through her blood—the memory of his hands on her.

CHAPTER 10

November 1981

MARTA PICKED UP THE AFTERNOON NEWSPAPER ON HER way into the house and the headline added to the gloom of the late, raw afternoon. SOLIDARITY IN TROUBLE. POLISH GOVERNMENT APPLYING PRESSURE. The phone was ringing as she unlocked the door, and tossing her things onto the table, she hurried into the den to answer it. It was Steven calling from New York. "I like the song sketches you sent," he said. "Are you working on them? I'd like to see them developed. . . ."

"Well," she said, "I'm sort of working." She wanted to say, Yes, and I love doing it; but she felt she had to move cautiously. Nothing was certain. It might all be left right were it was, unfinished, up in the air, just sketches. She sat down and cradled the telephone against her shoulder. On the couch beside her was the portfolio containing the new lyrics and ideas for other songs. With one hand she opened it and rifled through the papers, surprised and pleased at how much she had gotten done.

He was waiting for her explanation and when she didn't respond he said, "So what's the problem, Mart?"

She sighed into the phone. This was the one person in the whole world who could not, would not, be fooled. "Dan doesn't like it."

"Why not?"

She said thoughtfully, "He's afraid of it, Steve. . . ."

"Oh come on, Mart! Don't overdramatize!"

She laughed grimly. "Yeah. I wish! You really want to know? He hates it! He literally hates the idea of my doing work that takes me away. . . ."

"Takes you away? Away from what? What are you talking about?"

"Steven, would you mind if Maureen went back to work?"

He answered so promptly that there could be no doubt about his feelings. "No, I don't mind. She will go back to work . . . as soon as the kids are out of the house. Look, Mart, do you want me to talk to Daniel?"

"No," she answered quickly. "No, I don't. I simply have to decide whether it's important enough for me to buck him on this one."

"What's the big deal?"

"That I have to come up to New York. That I'll probably have to stay over there . . ."

"You'll stay with us . . . when it's necessary."

"That's not the point."

"I don't get it!" There was a long silence and then suddenly, because she couldn't stop herself, she said, "Vincent Fanetti's in town."

"Is that so? What's he doin' there?"

"He may go onto the staff at Municipal Hospital. He's been invited."

"I hear they're having problems. Is Dan involved? Is that what's worrying you?"

"Well . . . everything's worrying me. Fanetti doesn't seem to mind at all, Steve, that he gave up his music."

Steven said thoughtfully, "He was a real talent. But you have to want it, Mart. Talent is all over the board up here. You don't last six months without it. But to stay the course, you gotta drive it like a truck."

"Yes," she said.

"Let me call Dan this evening and talk to him."

"No! No! Please, Steven. I can handle this myself. I do want to do it. Do you like the lyrics I sent?"

"I loved them. There's nothing like lost loves to knock you out!"

"Are they too sad?"

"Well . . . I wouldn't want more than two . . . maybe three numbers like that. This is a big special . . . upbeat is the modus! You understand. I'm not being paid to tell the TV audience that it's a crappy world out there."

"Why not?" She was curious and not trying to provoke him.

"Our sponsors think the audience already knows all about the limits. They think we should shoot over the walls. . . ."

"Yes," she said, "or what's a heaven for. . . ."

"The TV heaven has gotta look reachable, hon. They pay me in attainable dollars."

"Sure," she said. "I'll get to work."

"You have to make a trip up here, Mart! We need to sit down together in the studio. I want you to see how this is produced. It will help with ideas."

"I don't know, Steve. . . . But it's true, I am working in sort of a vacuum."

He said impatiently, "Marty dear, that's because you

219

won't get out of that rut and get yourself to New York. You're making excuses...."

"I know it looks like that to you. It's a much bigger problem."

There was a moment's silence on the line. "There always is, sweetie. Please let me talk to Dan....He knows we'll take care of you."

"Oh, Steve, it has nothing to do with you. He thinks you're wonderful and sane and stable et cetera, et cetera. But, darling, he's an old-fashioned guy. He's worried about my getting involved in that world up there."

"I think you're telling me that Dan doesn't really trust you, Mart. And I won't buy that. He's a little ... crusty ... and rusty, maybe. That's from being an establishment type for so long. But he's a wonderful guy ... and he loves you...."

"Steven, for Christ's sake, all we need is 'Hearts and Flowers'!"

"You're the silly worried one, sister, not me!"

"Okay ... what's the point of arguing it. I'm doing my best...."

"Just let me say, quite honestly, Mart, that if you can't work at least part of the time in the next three months up here with me ... we'd better let it go altogether."

She stared out the window at the smudgy fall sky and swung around to avoid the grayness, the gloom. "You mean it won't work this way ... with my sending stuff on ... just that and no more?"

He said firmly. "Will not! If you can see your way to spend time in the studio with me in the next month or so and we can work right up to the week before the special, fine! If not, well, I think you'll have to forget about it ... at least on this go-round. We have most of the program planned already, and the slots I've allocated for myself . . . that is for you and me, have got to be done soon.''

''Yes,'' she said softly, ''I understand.''

When she hung up the phone she sat bemused, wondering how to take the next step, what it was, where it would lead. What was it she wanted? Why were there always needs so frightening, so demanding that they remained just around the bend? Maybe the not-so-smart ones were the lucky ones, the ones who didn't bother looking down the road and therefore could take brave and foolish plunges. But what did Carole Moyers or Phyllis Bogin have to lose or gain that she didn't? They had gotten themselves into jobs they thought would please them, make them useful and therefore satisfied. Like Carole, she had done her bit for home and school and God and country and . . . for cryin' out loud! What else was necessary!

She wondered if Carole or Phyllis had lovers or were tempted. Were there old loves who had come back or new ones appearing? Marta and her friends were part of a generation that didn't tell. They had never told. Not sinful, they had enough guilts, God knows, but it wasn't evil they feared. It was breaking the rules; toppling the traditions; altering well-established self-images, as if the image one showed the world were ever complete anyway! But what happened when one went to extremes to avoid egregious behavior? It often seeped out, overflowing those tightly corked compartments.

She dialed Carole's number.

Carole's voice sounded far away, as if she were talking out a window. ''I called Herb. The operation's over. It doesn't look good for Doris.''

Marta stared regretfully at the phone. Not wanting to

know. "What is it?" Her own voice sounded solemn and portentous to her.

"It's the worst. . . ."

"But the surgery . . . ?"

"Well . . . that went okay, Herb says. . . . That's not the point. Are you going down to see her tomorrow?"

"Is it all right to go?"

Carole sighed tremulously. "Well . . . it's not all right for me. I'm terrified, you see. I hate hospitals. I have to wait till she gets home."

Marta said softly, "Yes, I understand, Carole. I'll go." She had forgotten now why she had called. She hung up the phone as the front door opened and Dan came in. He stuck his head in the den, nodded, and went off to put away his things. "Eating out?" he called.

She sighed deeply. "No. Just about to get it together . . . whatever the hell it is!" she murmured under her breath, again feeling resentment against him rise in her stomach like a small siege of nausea. Dragging things out of the freezer, she plunged the neat frozen packages into the microwave oven and went looking for him, spoiling for a fight.

He was sitting half-undressed in their bedroom, staring blankly out the window. His stillness and the sag of his heavy shoulders suddenly alarmed her. In that instant all her anger disappeared. "What's the matter?"

He turned around but his face couldn't be read. "Oh . . . nothing really . . ." He smiled and stood up, changing into his old corduroys and a sweater.

She came up in front of him. "Hey, boyfriend . . ." She put her arms around his broad chest, her hands just meeting across his back. "What's up? Awful world out there?"

"Well . . ." He had never admitted that.

"Okay, hero." She dropped her arms and started to walk out of the room.

"Mart?" Something in his voice stopped her. She came back apprehensively and sat down at the foot of their bed, watching him change his shoes.

"I resigned from the hospital board today," he said quietly, glancing up at her.

"Oh, Dan! I'm sorry. Was there pressure?"

"Not from them. From the bank . . ."

"What's their problem, for God's sake? You're the best man they've got! You helped build up that blasted institution . . . it's the number-one bank in the city today because of you!"

He gestured vaguely, deprecating himself. "I don't know about that. The point is, there are all sorts of problems right now. We're in other building projects that are on the verge of bankruptcy."

"So what are you supposed to do, Dan? What's it all mean?"

"I have to sit tight. I just wanted to warn you. . . ."

"About what? Money? What the heck . . . !"

"No. No. Money's the least of it. You'll hear a lot of talk. Try to ignore it."

"What kind of talk?"

"Dirt. Mudslinging . . ."

"Aimed at you?"

He nodded. "I'll get through it. I just don't want you involved."

The look she tossed in his direction was sharp. "Why not? Have I been so fragile then, over the years? Are you worried about my ability to take it?"

He gestured again, as if to push it all away as quickly as he could. "I don't like anything like this to touch you. It has nothing to do with weakness or strength."

"Maybe that's our problem, Dan. Maybe that's always been my problem. There's always been somebody who wanted to protect me. I don't know that I need protection. Maybe we'd both be better off if I faced everything without you as a buffer."

"I don't want my home life interfered with, Marta." He knotted his shoes calmly. "And that's what husbands are for . . . protection."

"I'm not sure about that. . . ."

"All right." He turned away wearily.

She trailed around in front of him, forcing him to look into her face. "Dan, I never believed that everything had to be perfect and beautiful all the time."

"But it has been, Mart." There was an earnestness in his voice, almost an appeal.

She saw instantly the shield that covered the doubt that covered the time that had passed between them. If only by millimeters, the shield moved. If only for an instant they both could look at themselves. And then it moved back into place; the moment revealed nothing useful. The lyrics she was working on, that she was especially troubled by because she wasn't sure what they were supposed to mean, line by line ran through her mind: Would I know if it were over? / Would I know if it's not okay? / And the lights go down with the sound of the hit parade / Would I know not to play / This game forever in our fun charade?

Dan finished tying his sneakers and began to shuffle papers, going over his projects for the next day, straightening his bureau as she sat watching him. The second chorus was a headache: Baby, is it all over but the shouting? / Are you lettin' me know something's not so sweet? / Is the perfect love all set for a routing? / Would I know, from your tone, from your eyes, from the way you touch me / That it's over, done, complete? / Oh baby, would I know?

She smelled the food sizzling in the microwave down in the kitchen. She jumped up and hurried out of the room.

They were both quiet during dinner, sitting across from each other, separated by the expanse of shiny teak. Every once in a while he put down his fork and looked over at her, frowning as if he wanted to know what it was all about too. But the words were never uttered.

"Well . . . it's a neat joke!" she said to herself as she ran hot water over the knives and forks in the stainless-steel sink before dropping them into the dishwasher. He was right behind her carrying the dirty dishes. "What's the joke?" he asked softly, and then she realized that she had spoken aloud. He put down the china with a clatter and turned her around so that her back was pressed against the sink and he was half-leaning on her.

"There seem to be blank patches in my brilliant brain," she said. "But don't worry about it, Dan. It's my problem."

"I love you, Marta. That's no joke!" He kissed her gently. "And no problem."

"And I love you. I have always loved you, Daniel! And I never thought it was either a joke or a problem!"

"I want you to be happy."

She pushed him away gently. "No," she said. "You want me to behave and not bother you, not upset your apple cart any more than it is already."

"That's right," he said immediately. "I want the kind of happiness that we've had all during these years; I'll do every damned thing I can to keep the apple cart right side up."

"Keep your eye on the truth, Dan," she said at once. "Dump the platitudes! Along with the apple cart! It will make everything easier for both of us."

"What are you talking about?"

"I'm not sure. I love you. You love me. That's something to hang on to, isn't it?"

He had turned away. He said softly, "I thought so. I don't know anymore."

"Are you going to hand me an ultimatum? Are you going to tell me that if I don't do what you want, it's all over for us? What are we arguing about here, Daniel?"

"Don't be childish!" he said at once. "What nonsense! You're just upset."

She finished piling the dishes in the washer as he went into his den. The phone rang and when she picked it up she heard Dan saying hello and then Herb Brenner's voice on the other end. He was weeping. She hung up the phone. A minute later Dan came back into the kitchen.

"Were you on the line?" he asked.

She nodded. "I heard."

"She might be okay."

"Is that why Herb was crying?"

"Nobody can predict the course of these things, Marta. You have to be hopeful. Because there's always a chance."

With a sudden shudder, she came into his arms and they held on to each other. The tears spilled down her face and were hot on her chin. "Poor Doris! It's so sad," she said. "And so rotten."

"Yes." He looked down at her. "I think you've known, haven't you?"

"I tried not to. . . ."

They spent the rest of the evening sitting near each other, reading, listening to records, glancing up and over at each other many times until they wearily went off to bed.

The next morning she found Doris's room at Municipal Hospital, but the door was closed. She went looking for a nurse at the information station in the hall.

She found one working behind the counter, her head down. The woman looked up Doris's chart when Marta questioned her.

"She's pretty weak," the nurse reported. "She just came down from intensive care. That's why the door's shut." She looked up. "A private nurse is ordered for her."

"Can I go in, just for a few minutes? I'm her best friend."

When she got permission, Marta walked slowly back and pushed open the door. Doris was ashen, her eyes dark-rimmed and tightly shut, her face small and shrunken on the pillow. She had tubes in her nose and arms and Marta felt her knees go weak. But she smoothed Doris's disheveled hair, seeing how gray it had suddenly gone at the roots; Doris, who was so meticulous about everything, with her weekly hair and manicure appointments, hadn't been able to concentrate on such details in recent weeks. Everything had collapsed for her at once. She stirred and opened her eyes as Marta touched her forehead.

"Hi, Mart. It's over . . . but I'm in pain."

"Oh, Dor, I'm sorry. I won't stay long."

"S'okay." She managed a feeble, familiar grin. "I'm gonna be fine. The doctor was here when they moved me down this morning. They got me clean as a whistle. It's just this damned pain. . . ."

"You will be fine, Dor, as good as new! I'll go talk to the nurse about giving you something to relieve you. You just need rest now. I'll be back tomorrow or the next day . . . when you're stronger."

Doris's eyes had already drifted shut and Marta quietly left the room. She went back to the nursing station and found the same nurse she had talked with before.

"My friend seems to be in pain," she said. "Is there something you can do?"

The nurse nodded. "She was sedated before they brought her down. She'll get something soon."

"Thank you," said Marta. She began to leave but on a sudden impulse turned back to the station, where the nurse had her head down once more over her work.

"I wonder if it would be possible for you to locate a nurse who works here?" She thought for a moment. "She's in the surgical service. I'm not sure about her present shift. . . ."

The nurse reached for a large ledger. "What's her name?"

"Kathryn Caplan."

The woman leafed through the large notebook, then picked up the telephone. She swung around with her back to the counter as another nurse came in with reports for her. In a minute she swung back to Marta and hung up.

"She's down on the third floor. B wing, nursing-station two. She's on duty now."

Marta thanked her and went to the elevator.

She found a group of nurses at the station on the third floor and asked them about Kathryn Caplan. Again one of them telephoned, then said to Marta, "She'll be here in a few minutes. She was in surgery all morning." She indicated a bench in the hall. "You can wait right there."

In about five minutes she saw the slight, gray-haired figure of her aunt-by-marriage hurrying toward her. She was still in her operating-room greens. She had a broad smile on her thin face and her arms were outstretched as she came toward Marta.

"Marta dear! What a super surprise!"

"How are you, Kath? Gosh, you look great! Not a day older. How do you do it?"

"Look who's talking! You're gorgeous as usual. The family beauty, as Hank used to say."

"Have you got a few minutes free?"

"Sure. Let's get some coffee." She took Marta's arm and led her toward the service cafeteria. "What are you doing here today, Mart? Volunteering again?"

"No. I came down to see a sick friend, Kath. Do you remember Doris Brenner?"

"Oh yes," said Kathy. "She's the one you were best friends with as a youngster. I know who you mean."

"She had surgery yesterday." Marta peered into Kathy's brown eyes. They were kind and placid as she remembered them from their first meeting in her own living room. Marta said softly, "I think she's very sick, Kath. She thinks she's okay, but her husband said . . . they couldn't get it all. It had spread."

Kathy shook her head, lips pursed. "I'm sorry to hear that. Would you like me to look in on her, Marta?" She added, "Not that she won't get good attention there. The floor care is excellent."

Marta gestured vaguely. "I'm not concerned about that. She has private nurses starting this afternoon. It's all been arranged. But . . . a friendly visit would be nice, Kath. I'm sure she'll remember you. Along with all my little girl friends, she was madly in love with Hank."

They exchanged smiles and held arms as they went into the cafeteria. They got their coffee, located an empty table, and sat down opposite each other. Marta sighed, nodding to Kathy. "I really wanted to see you. . . ."

Kathy reached across the table and squeezed Marta's hand. "We don't get together often enough, do we? Now that the kids are grown . . ." She smiled. "I miss them. I know you do too. Diane does give me a call now and then.

She seems to like graduate school and I think she's doing well. . . ."

Marta nodded. "She's okay. My kids are both really attached to you, Kath. Just the way Steve and I were crazy about Uncle Hank. . . ." She looked out over the bustling restaurant. "Poor Uncle Hank . . ."

Kathy said, "You're feeling blue. That happens when we see our friends get sick."

Marta stirred her coffee, not sure about her sudden impulse to confide all her problems to Kathy, although there had always been deep understanding between them. Right from the beginning, Marta had had special tender feelings for Uncle Hank's young wife, who was unwelcomed by the family; the little blond outsider who "didn't know how to dress with class," according to Lilly Resnick and her sisters, who "unfortunately could never be one of us," according to Grandma Caplan, the "nice, earnest girl, who simply had too different a background," according to Dr. Resnick. It was, as Marta remembered, the only comment her normally taciturn father had ever made about Uncle Hank's unusual choice of a wife. Everything, from Kathryn Ryan's fancy black silk dresses and stiletto-heeled shoes, to her Saint Mark's Parish Philadelphia accent, was too much for them. Not one of the adults in the family found a way to love her. But to Marta and Steven, with no effort, the road was unblocked. Kathy was their friend. And the three of them clung together, after her young soldier husband was killed in Italy in 1943, as much as Aunt Kath ever clung to anyone other than Hank.

Marta remembered it all too clearly. She could recall moments from the past as if they were on a big movie screen in front of her, seeing herself, seeing the others, hearing the music on the radio at the time, feeling the shock and pain again. They had all followed the course of the war closely, Dr. Resnick clicking on the radio as soon as dinner was over every evening. She could see him shaking his shaggy head pessimistically, while her mother sat sewing in the living room, frowning over the bad news on the Russian front, the bad news in the Pacific theater, and the bad news from Italy. Their own bad news came in a telegram to both Grandma Caplan and Kathy.

The exact daily events leading up to Uncle Hank's death were not known until after the war when Steven and Marta read accounts of the beginning of the Italian campaign and pieced it all together. The Seventh Army under General George Patton had landed in Sicily after the success of the fighting in Tunisia. Uncle Hank, an infantry seargant, along with his buddies from the States, had captured Palermo. It was bloody and costly, but an important victory. It was after this battle that Uncle Hank wrote his last letter home to his wife: "My Dearest Little Love: It's going great! The tide is turning!" That was the part that Aunt Kath had read them. The rest she kept for herself. But Marta never forgot those words.

Shortly after, during the first hot week in August, the Seventh Army broke northward. A wild and terrible clash took place on the slopes of Mount Etna, where Hank Caplan was hit by artillery fire early in the afternoon. The battle was won and the Sicilian campaign was declared a total success. The British army, under General Sir Bernard Montgomery, forced the Germans to carry out a general withdrawal.

The death knell of the Fascist regime in Italy was sounded! It was the end of Mussolini. And Uncle Hank, with his shining black eyes and a whistle on his red lips, never came back to his dearest little love.

The family mourned the loss of the darling son, the beloved younger brother, the light of everybody's eyes, and they commiserated with his young widow. But relations with her grew stiffer and the attitudes more distant than ever when Kathy, grieving privately in her own quiet way, enlisted in the army and went overseas right after D Day in 1944 as the war moved into France. Her act of independence was the final break with the rest of the family. Unapplauded and undiscussed went the love and loyalty of the young wife during the couple's two previous years together. Kathy had never left Hank once during his training until he had to go overseas.

At the end of the war Kathryn Caplan came home a captain, left the service, and went right back to nursing at Municipal Hospital, the largest medical center in the area. She never married again. Long after the older members of the critical Resnick and Caplan clans were gone, Kathy and Marta remained close. Over the years Kathy developed a special devotion to Marta's children, Allen and Diane. There was even one point when the aunt executed what Dan and Marta considered a vital rescue. Their rebellious sixteen-year-old daughter, Diane, fighting with her father, ignoring her mother, left home in a huff and went to stay with Aunt Kath. She was tended and loved and talked with as an equal all weekend long and sent home promptly on Sunday night in order to make school on Monday morning. Diane came back not quite apologetic, but at least willing to discuss her difficulties with her parents once more.

Marta, remembering her own painful adolescent years, was grateful to Kathy for giving Diane her time and her love, for providing neutral ground for all of them and allowing heated emotions a chance to cool down. Diane, from that point on, stayed very closely in touch with her aunt, a special circuit of kindness and support circling between the headstrong young girl and the childless woman.

Even Allen Reiter, the solid, easygoing elder brother,

turned to Kathy when his moment of anxiety and separation arrived. Somehow he had had fewer problems growing up than his younger sister. His breaking-away difficulties began later on, when he was already through college and law school. He had passed the bar and was about to take an offer from a top Philadelphia law firm, when he suddenly decided that he wasn't sure about his future. With his grim father asking him terse, puzzled questions, and then giving him equally short commands, and his adoring mother pleading for time and level-headedness, Allen walked out. He went west, leaving his job commitment dangling in the Philadelphia summer, while his father struggled to make rational, holding-type excuses to the law partners who were among his bank's top customers. Before Allen left he found time to see Aunt Kath, and she played her usual role of nonadviser. She was that rarest of birds, a good listener. Knowing that he had at least one staunch friend (she never told him she was an ally), Allen took off, reveling in the sudden burst of freedom he had gained for himself. He kept in touch with his parents and Aunt Kath on a casual basis. His letters were filled with the light and openness of the West. Only occasionally, and only to Aunt Kath, did he confide his down moments and his fears. Marta thought about him and tried not to discuss him with Dan. When the need arose to reassure herself that her son was well and reasonably happy, she talked to Kath. As was to be expected, Kath didn't think that Allen's world was coming to an end and was sure that he would make reasonable choices for himself. She frequently, and with no irony intended, congratulated Marta on having produced two strong and independent people who would always be able to take care of themselves. Marta didn't report these conversations back to Dan.

For herself, Kathryn expected little from any of the

Reiters. She seemed to have no need to unburden, to lean, to complain, to confide. There were some men in her life. She made no secret of their presence. And Marta always knew that the arrangements were not permanent. Kathy clung to her work. And her solitude.

Marta's own impulse to confide, sitting at the small table in the noisy cafeteria, suddenly passed. "A little blue," she repeated with a smile. "It's a tough game as soon as you're really aware of the rules. Die young or grow old painfully. Not fun! Anyway, Kath, we've still got our looks!"

Kathy said at once, "God knows you've got yours!" She patted Marta's arm again. "So what else is new? The last letter from Allen was terrific. He likes working in that little bookstore. . . . He loves hiking around the countryside on weekends. And," she added, smiling, "you know, Marta, I think he may be in love."

Marta nodded. "I sort of picked up the same vibrations from the last note. But he didn't say so right out. Keep me posted, Kath, if he tells you the details."

Kathy was glancing at her wristwatch and Marta began to gather up her things. "Time to get going," she said. "Oh, you asked what else I was doing . . . I'm working on some music and lyrics for Steve . . . for a spring TV special!"

"Sensational, Mart! Gosh, how exciting!"

Both women stood up. "If I can bring it off, Kath." Marta was buttoning her coat. "Dan is pretty much opposed. . . ."

There was no surprise in Kathy's smooth, oval face. "Yes," she said softly. "That would disturb Dan, I suppose."

They were walking out of the noisy cafeteria arm in arm. "I don't know what I'm going to do," Marta said.

"What do you want to do?"

"Oh, I want to do it! I don't have the slightest doubt about that!"

Kathy laughed. "That's the Marta I remember. Never in doubt! I have a lot of confidence in you, honey. You'll work it out."

They kissed goodbye, and just as Marta was turning to leave, Kathy suddenly grabbed her arm and said, "I forgot to ask you. Did you know that Vincent Fanetti might come onto the surgical staff?"

Marta avoided her eyes. "I heard," she said. "We ran into him at the hospital charity ball. He's not sure, though. I gather his wife prefers California."

"He has a super reputation, Mart. He must have worked very hard during all these years. . . . I only met him once when you were both kids . . . but who would've guessed he had this kind of career ahead of him."

On the way home, Marta switched on the radio, thinking about the smallness of her world, how quickly information got around, personal as well as political, as well as social . . . good news, bad news. . . . The voice on the radio said, "Martial law is being threatened in Poland. Solidarity is in trouble . . . strikes in key industries. Reports of Soviet tanks on the border . . ."

And on and on, she thought with a sigh. She switched the station and found music. Kathy Caplan knew details of her romance with Vince all those years ago that no one else knew. Marta herself had confided in Kath. When there was nobody to talk to, even before Kath had married Uncle Hank, Marta had called her and told her about the problems that were too confusing to work out. And Kathy had dealt with her just as a generation later she had dealt with Marta's daughter. "Think about it! And talk to your family, Marta," she had urged. And when Marta insisted that she couldn't because they simply couldn't understand, she had repeated quietly, "They're the only ones who can understand, and who will help you through this. . . ."

But Kathy was only half-right. Marta's family had helped her through, but they had never understood. And she had stopped trying to make it clear to them.

Spinning along the River Drive in the darkening afternoon, she heard the Boston Philharmonic doing Beethoven's Ninth. She turned the volume up high, hoping that the sound and fury of the music would drown out her own thoughts and doubts. Just as the choral section began in the last movement, she pulled into her driveway and was sitting in the car, absorbed in the voices singing the "Ode to Joy," when there was a sudden knock on her side window that made her jump. Dan was standing in the driveway, leaning down and peering at her through the car window. "I couldn't imagine what the heck you were doing in there," he said, as she opened the door and he heard the music booming inside the car.

He had picked up the late-afternoon newspaper from the drive, and instead of putting it down as he usually did when he came in, he carried it upstairs with him. She didn't think about it until he came down again, having changed clothes, and went to the bar with the paper still rolled under his arm.

"You may put that down if you like," she said, laughing.

He placed it on the kitchen counter, but when she reached for it he stopped her, his hand over hers. "The story's in there."

"What story?"

"About the bank. About me . . ." He made no further comment but handed her the paper and turned to fix himself a drink. He poured wine for her and picking up both glasses began to walk out of the kitchen. The headline read, BANKER IN SHAKEUP AT PHILADELPHIA HOSPI-

TAL. She continued to read, her expression grim. "What a pack of lies!" she cried.

He had turned and was watching her.

"What a monstrous distortion this is, Dan!"

"Let's go sit down, Mart. In the den." He carried their drinks and handed hers to her as she sat on the couch. She took it distractedly, still reading, her glasses sliding off the end of her nose, her brows drawn in a frown. "They say you sold the hospital on the idea of the expansion. That you engineered the building program. That you were involved in the bank's other bad real-estate deals! What the hell is this?"

"It's baloney," he said quietly. "You'll have to ignore it. Remember, I told you there would be mudslinging."

"But, Dan . . . this is terrible . . . your reputation."

"That's why they love it. Quite a boon for the local press when a businessman has troubles . . ."

She pushed aside the paper and took a long swallow of her wine. "Isn't there any way to fight back?" she asked.

He shook his head. "Only by indirection. Right in here we have to keep quiet. To mind our own business and hope they'll tire of the dirt . . ."

"And the board at the bank?"

"Everybody understands what's happening. We all have to keep our heads down. It will blow over."

"But they want you off the hospital board, just the same."

"It was a joint decision. . . ."

"But you didn't plan that building program!"

He took a deep breath. "No," he said softly, and then he got up and came over to her, sitting close beside her on the couch. "We've been lucky, Mart. Life has been kind to us. We've had our health, our kids, luck in business, plenty of energy . . . and each other. Now we have a rough one. . . . We'll get through it!''

She took his hand and pressed it hard. ''Okay. No point in going on about it anymore. We'll get through it!''

But lying in bed that night, the window undraped, a perfect full moon rising in the autumn sky beyond and laying a brilliant pathway of light along the carpeting, she thought about the risks one took just by holding up one's head. If you burrowed in the ground like a small careful mole, you reduced the hazard of getting trapped by the big-game hunters. If you took the wide road, the moonlit path, the spotlit way, you exposed every aspect of your action as well as every nerve in your body.

For the thousandth time she remembered the foolish wonderful things she had done as a sheltered young girl. All the silly risks she had taken and the price she had paid. And she knew, lying there beside her besieged husband, whose hand was gripping hers even in his deepest sleep, that if you've got the guts, you do it!

She sat with Doris again for a brief time the next morning. But Doris kept drifting off into heavy slumber, and Marta, her portfolio under her arm, left the hospital earlier than she had planned. She had hoped to keep her friend company all morning and had brought her material along to work on. After a productive spell at the piano, she was moving again on another new song. In the first flush of work, everything seemed right. It all came together and was creating for her the kind of big bang she wanted to make happen for the listeners. There was no question in her mind that later on, looking over the material in a quiet, critical mood, getting it ready for other, less-emotional eyes, she would see many little cracks in the wall. She'd have to plug and patch and in some cases tear down and start again. For the moment, it all seemed to be constructing itself, and the sad little lyrics had turned joyful out of creative excitement. A celebration of the exercise of skills, a toast to the talent itself. She heard the music that would go with the words echoing in her head and made sketches of melodies for Steven. He would understand. They always heard things the same way...their talents interhooked. He was the musician, no doubt about it, but she sensed the music as he did, right along with him.

Instead of the depression she had braced herself for on the visit to Doris, she had a sudden mad rising of spirits as she left the hospital. The sun had come out after a gray morning, one more in an interminable string of gray mornings. Terrors seemed to shrink; the concern for her sick friend, the terrible national and international news, the shock of the local bad news for Dan, all took flight. How can I feel so crazy good, she wondered, when things are so shitty bad?... and laughed out loud as she crossed the huge marble foyer of Municipal Hospital and went out onto the sidewalk in the brilliant fall sunshine. She entertained the possibility of spending a couple of hours wandering around the campus of the university nearby, enjoying the sun, which had turned unexpectedly warm. And then, euphoric because she was remembering all kinds of things, she thought about those sunny afternoons, fall and spring, when she would spot Vincent waiting for her after school, standing by the side of the battered old Ford, leaning against it as if he had all the time in the world, as if no force on earth could drag him away before she came running out of the building. Making believe she hadn't seen him first. She turned around and went back into the hospital.

In the entrance hall, she rooted through her handbag until she located the card he had given her. She had taken it out of her calendar one morning, planning to toss it into the trash, and instead had tucked it into the bottom of her pocketbook, saying aloud to herself, "Tell the truth, Marta Portia, you don't know what the hell you're going to do about him!"

She found a phone booth off the lobby, closed the door carefully, and dialed the number he had given her. The voice that answered was incurious and businesslike. "I'll try to locate him. . . . Whom should I say is calling?"

She thought about lying. She said, "Tell him Marty. . . ."

In minutes he was on the line. "Where are you?"

"Downstairs . . . in the lobby."

"Don't move. . . ." He hung up.

Sitting back on the little seat inside the booth, she saw her smile reflected in the glass of the folding door. "Damn fool!" she said and came out to wait for him.

When the elevator opened he was the tallest man and she watched him with remembered pleasure towering over the others as he came striding out, his windbreaker open, no tie, and his graying hair across his forehead as if he had just combed through it with his impatient fingers.

Someone observing them would have thought they had parted only minutes before. They barely greeted each other. He took her arm, entwining his fingers with hers, and never let go until they were down in the gloom of the hospital garage, waiting for his car to be delivered.

"So . . ." He looked at her hand as he released it.

"I came to see Doris Brenner."

"I know," he said.

"You're having me watched." She laughed. "Private Eyes are Watching You . . ." singing the lyric from the Hall and Oates popular song.

He echoed the tag line, right in tune. And they laughed together.

"Aha!" she said. "You do listen to the new stuff on the radio!"

"I have to find out what you're thinking. . . ."

"How did you know I was here today?"

"I didn't know you were here today . . . I guessed you might be. You told Kathy Caplan yesterday that you were coming back . . . I looked for you all morning, on and off. . . ."

"What did you say to Kathy?"

"Nothing much. She approached me . . . reintroduced herself. I had no memory of ever having met her . . . but I do remember your uncle. . . ."

"You met him more than once . . . Kathy you met only one night. She was being given the third degree in my living room. You came into it like an unwanted witness. It was awful . . ."

"Ah . . . yes . . . that was the night . . . that was our first time together."

"Yes . . ." she said, but couldn't look at him.

He turned her face toward his. "Are you embarrassed to remember?"

"No." She smiled. "Well . . . not very . . ."

They brought his car, and she thought he would head again for New Jersey, but instead he turned deeper into West Philly, going south beyond the university into a new neighborhood being carved from a rotting older one. Burned-out houses and boarded-up stores stood side by side with newly painted, plastered, reconstructed façades. He pulled into a narrow street where a few already-wind-denuded poplar trees lined the curb and parked in front of a brick-front restaurant with a sign that read MIKKO'S . . . GOOD FOOD.

"Well," she said, "you did the impossible."

He came around to help her out of the car.

241

Stepping out, she said, "You found the one place in the city where no one will ever find us . . . as we lie dying of ptomaine poisoning."

He grinned at her. "I'll save you."

"I won't need a chest surgeon," she said. "A gastroenterologist is more like it!"

She knew the second they walked through the doorway that she was mistaken about the place. The small room faced a high-walled garden in the back, and even in the pale November light, with just a glass wall separating them from the outdoors, the tiny paved terrace with its evergreen bushes and pieces of statuary and fountain was charming, a delight to the eye.

No customers had arrived yet. It was early for lunch, but the air was full of good smells. The white linens were crisp, and a single fresh chrysanthemum stood on each table. There was a tiny bar, a piano in the opposite corner, and music coming softly over the speaker system.

"Hi ya, Mikko." Vince shook hands with a heavyset, stocky man who turned and gestured as his wife appeared in the doorway to the kitchen. She was wearing a large white apron and a chef's toque.

"This is Marta," said Vince. "Mikko and Sally . . . great cooks, both of them!"

"How you been, Vince?"

It was apparent to Marta that they were old friends. "This is nice," she said.

"I thought you'd like it. It'll begin to fill up after twelve-thirty. But we have it to ourselves for a while."

A clear female voice was coming in and out softly from the speakers in the corners of the room, telling of lonely nights and long empty days.

"Do you like that song?" she asked as he handed her a small menu.

He shrugged. "It's all right."

"You're not listening."

He looked at her over the menu. "No," he said. "I gave up on that."

Barbra sang, Going In and Out of Your Life . . . and the song was a question. How can I free you, when I see you . . .

Marta said, "I don't know why but I'm feeling crazy good! I mean, everything is falling apart all around me . . . Can you imagine that?"

He grinned at her. "Feeling free!"

"But why? With poor Doris lying there . . . and Dan's got all kinds of lousy problems . . . and I'm not at all sure I can bring off the work I'm trying to do. What happened to me, do you think?" He started to answer and she interrupted, "Oh yes, you're going to take credit for it, aren't you?"

"Of course! You're glad to see me, Marta. That's what it is!"

The melody rose and fell. Love that's strong makes you remember. They were holding hands as Mikko stood beside the table to take their order.

The music became tender, coming in and out of lives . . .

She pulled away her hand and they ordered. When Mikko left for the kitchen, she said, "I *am* glad to see you. But I think there must be some wild gene that gets loose in me every so often. There's something in me, Vincent, that wants to fly away . . ."

"With me . . ."

"A little trip in the ether. Not for long! A little voyage with my feet off the ground . . ."

"Is that all there is, Mart?"

"For us? I don't know if there's anything. . . ."

"Tell me you don't care!"

"It would be a lie . . . but some things just won't add up!"

The lunch was small but appetizing. "This is marvelous food," she said to Mikko when he came up to the table. "Please tell your wife."

"What is it you're working on?" Vincent asked as they sipped their coffee.

She opened the portfolio and handed him the lyrics. There were just five bars of single staff notes along with the words. He hummed to himself. "It's nice. You're going to do the music too. . . ."

"No," she said. "I just thought it might be an idea for Steven . . . a few musical notations."

"Let's hear it," he said, and pushing back his chair, he walked over to the small upright against the wall in the corner. "Hey, Mik," he called to the owner. "Turn off the sound, will you!" Barbra faded, remembering.

Marta trailed Vince to the piano. He had the lyrics in front of him, and standing up, with his right hand only, he played the simple melodic line she had suggested. He carried it on, developed it, sat down and began to put accompaniment to it. He was singing the lyric softly, and she joined in with him. He grinned at her over his shoulder. "It's good. It's good."

Sally had come out of the kitchen and was standing beside Mikko listening as Vince and Marta sang together. They turned away only when customers began to come in and had to be seated.

Marta sat down on the piano bench beside Vince. When he finished the verse he continued to run his right hand up and down the keyboard as if the keys felt good under his fingers. "How about this?" He began to play "New Love."

She listened but couldn't bring herself to sing it. "It's a lovely song."

He looked up at her as he played. "A little dated maybe."

"Who cares?"

"I thought we had a hit," he said.

"So did Marcus Appleby. . . ."

"Old Marcus baby! He made it okay. . . ."

"You could have gone right along with him! Past him, if you wanted . . ."

"So could you. . . ."

She sighed. "I didn't know what I wanted then."

He began to play, "All she wants is what she wants, / A great big slice of everything."

She leaned against his shoulder. "That's a nice one too." And moving away slightly she gazed at his profile until his eyes turned to hers. "Why did you stop writing music, Vince?" she asked softly.

Not answering, he looked back down at the keyboard, playing the bridge. "What are the answers I seek alone? / Searching old hangouts for leads . . ." Still not lifting his eyes, he said, "I lost interest in it . . . when I lost you."

"Oh, Vincent," she said softly and leaned her head on his shoulder. "You never lost me."

"I never had you." He was staring down at the keys. "It was a dream of a girl I had. She was the perfect girl-woman. She had beauty and class. She had brains and sex and joy and talent. She was perfection."

"That wasn't me," she said.

"No." He took his hands off the keyboard. "No, it wasn't. So . . ." he stood up, "I went after other things."

She looked up at him, tall, straight, his jaw line stubborn. "You tackled the toughest things you could find, Vincent."

His eyes narrowed as he looked down at her. "Yes," he said. "But what I wanted to do was to smash up the world!" He took a deep breath. "I wanted to rip open your smug little life and take it apart, person by person and object by object. Do you know what really propelled me through courses that I didn't understand, through work I wasn't prepared for, through hours of exhaustion, and feelings of inadequacy that grew like a mountain . . . ? You want to know, Mart? I wanted to be better than you and your family at that game you were all playing. I wanted to beat you at your own game."

She stood beside him, looking up into his scowling eyes. "You did," she said. She got her things from the table, and together, soberly, not talking, they left the restaurant.

CHAPTER 11

Spring 1941

IN DECEMBER, PRESIDENT ROOSEVELT TOLD A RELUCTANT America that he would keep them out of war, but that their security depended on supplying the British with tanks, guns, aircraft, and munitions. "We will be the arsenal of the free world," he said, and sent Congress the Lend-Lease Bill.

In December, Marta's father said to her openly for the first time, "I really think it is a mistake for you to encourage that boy, Marta."

"Vince is just a friend, Daddy," she lied.

Her father shrugged, looked pensive, but said nothing else.

All winter long the U.S. Navy convoyed ships for the British through the North Atlantic. There were attacks and several sinkings. Still the American people hoped their leaders would keep them out of the conflagration in Europe.

Vincent came infrequently to her house. Most of the time she insisted that he meet her outside. When he said angrily that it wasn't his style to sneak around that way, she answered soberly, "If they forbid me to see you, I'll have to obey. Please understand, Vince." For the first time in her life she flunked an algebra test, hid the returned paper, and couldn't work up the interest to go in and see Little Preston about her problems. She vowed to spend the entire weekend studying. She was having difficulties in Latin and history too. But Vince wanted her to sing new music at Nino's on Saturday night and she sneaked out of the house unnoticed, to be with him. She had gotten the cold shoulder at her sorority meeting the month before when Sandy Lopersteen had taken her aside, saying with mock concern, "The girls are really shocked that you're seeing that dago, Marta." Marta felt her skin crawl. She wanted to hit Sandy hard on her beautifully painted, Revlon mouth, but she looked down at the floor and said nothing. Afterward, she hated herself for not speaking up, but swore that she was through with them. From then on, she went to meetings only when Doris worriedly urged her to attend. "Don't burn all your bridges, Marta. Your parents will find out!" When she did show up at a meeting on a Sunday night in January, none of the older sorors welcomed her, and her girl friends were all uncomfortable.

In March, Bulgaria joined the Axis. But that didn't stop the Germans from crossing the Danube and occupying the country. The eyes of the German high command were turned toward the east. There followed a rapid coup d'etat in Yugoslavia, which was always, so the newspapers said, a severely divided country, with the Chets against the Slavs and the partisans identifying themselves openly with the Communists.

There was a late snow storm in March; and coming home from Nino's one Saturday night after they had performed, Marta said to Vince, "Better take me right home tonight." He was letting her off these days at the corner instead of directly in front of her house. But he ignored her words. With the snow squishing under the wipers on the windshield, he turned toward the wide streets, away from the row houses, and parked in "their spot," on Woodside Road, where the big house on the big lot seemed permanently unoccupied, and the streetlights were spaced far apart.

When he stopped the car he leaned over and opened her door. "Let's get in the back," he said.

"Vince . . . It's really starting to snow heavy. . . ."

"I'll take you home in five minutes."

She climbed in the back with him. Letting him kiss her, being held and kissing him back. It happened the same way all the time now; the hunger came on unbidden even as her hunger for food and everything else disappeared. It rose up in giant waves just on seeing him across the room, watching him at the piano, walking toward him after school when he hadn't yet seen her. And when she touched him and smelled his skin her desire for him almost suffocated her. Her young body responded instantly to his touch each time they were alone together, and with her back arched, her bra stuffed in her pocketbook, she would allow him to fondle her and bring her to climax just as she would squeeze him and rub him until his breathing was ragged and he exploded too.

The snow had quickly covered all the windows and their heated breath steamed and warmed the interior of the old car. "Marta," he murmured in her ear, tugging at her panties. "Take them off," he whispered. She helped him and edged them over her shoes as he leaned down on her, his heavy body moving, his mouth on hers, on her neck, all over her face. She felt him pushing her thighs apart, his hard flesh hot between her legs. "Don't put it in!" she warned. He held it between her legs and together, as always, they rocked to rhythms that were tides in their blood. His hands moved down between her legs, opening her up. "Just the tip," he said. Slowly he eased it, swollen and rigid, into her running, throbbing openness. There was no pain, no discomfort, only a wild need to push harder than she ever had before. Almost at once she crashed down with a loud moan and sob, and he pulled out of her, spraying up and down her legs.

"Oh God!" she said.

He sat back staring blindly, breathing hard, as if he were numb. "What is it?" she asked, sitting up.

"I don't know," he said. "It was like the end of the world."

"End-of-the-world good or bad?" she whispered, moving into his arms.

"No. No!" he repeated, shaking his head.

"What is it, Vince?" She moved away and stared at him.

"It's no good like that. To come out of you like that is . . . like . . . pulling my heart out of me."

"Oh, Vincent." She began to cry. "We have to end this. . . . This can't go on!"

But the next time he had a rubber and he didn't come out of her; and the time after that, and after that. . . . It was a deep habit that moved in on them both and took complete possession.

In April, Yugoslavia was bombed. After eleven days of fighting, it passed under German control. The press reported large concentrations of German troops, all being moved eastward by rail. Then came the expected attack on Greece. The fighting was vicious, the casualties high. In the final hours the Royal Navy evacuated the remaining imperial forces and the independent foreign units that were battling there. The losses were severe on both sides as the Allies retreated to Crete.

America believed it could stay neutral. But Uncle Hank thought for sure the big one was on the way. Everybody urged him to stay cool and not to enlist, except Kathy, who told him to do what he wanted to do. He stayed on at the real-estate office, hating every minute of it, barely eking out a living, trying to figure out how to reconcile his family to his forthcoming marriage.

The political speculation, still not in the press or on the radio, but flying around among the population, was that the Germans were eyeing Russia. Stalin, Hitler's erstwhile partner, took steps: he occupied three Baltic states to cover his flanks. Still no one really believed Hitler would do it. Britain, after an entire winter of night bombings, was almost on its knees. Only the Channel separated Britain from the victorious German Wehrmacht. All Europe was now under the power of the Axis. The common wisdom was that although the Russian front was long and had always defeated aggressors, the Russians were poor fighters and ill prepared.

When Marta's mother saw her third-quarter report card, she sat down, pale and speechless.

"I don't know what happened," Marta said, unable to look at her mother's face.

Mrs. Resnick was swallowing and shaking her head. Marta suddenly threw herself into her mother's arms and began to cry. "I'm sorry. I'm sorry," she said, sobbing.

"All right. All right," her mother said, her own voice shaky with unshed tears. "It's not the end of the world. You'll be a professor a year later. Come. Stop crying. Have a piece of cake. It has pecans. I just made it. You don't eat anymore. That worries me more than anything else."

That night, after they had finished their dinner in the kitchen, Dr. Resnick sat down at the dining-room table beside Marta. She was studying for an important history test.

"Marta," he said. He seemed to be hunting for words as she looked into his sad eyes. "Doing well," he said finally, "is an expression of . . . of the joy of life! Doing well means one is using one's power. One's inner resources. There is no pleasure quite like that. You have experienced it. And no one has ever needed to push you. Because you discovered it for yourself. By yourself. It is an enduring pleasure. Where most good things fade away, that kind of achievement remains. You know the exultation of using your own skills to their optimum."

"Oh, Daddy," she said, and the tears began to well up at the back of her throat again. Her mother sat stiffly in her chair by the radio in the living room, reading but somehow never turning a page of her book. Their disappointment was almost too much for Marta to bear. Steven, who was in his usual place across the table from her, his face bent down close over his paper, carefully ignored the exchange between her and her father.

"I'll do better." She managed to get the words out without tears. "I promise I will."

Her father stroked her head. "Don't make promises to us, Marta sweetheart. It isn't necessary to make promises to me. Or to your mother. Make them to yourself. Remember the joy of succeeding. And how quickly one can lose the knack."

She nodded unhappily. "I understand, Daddy," she said.

It wasn't any lack of understanding when the skid began, and it wasn't any lack of comprehension on her part when the skid continued. The words on the pages of her textbooks had ceased to have any meaning for her. They were emptied of all content and all reference. She was constantly being pulled between desire and anger. And she couldn't discuss either. With anyone. She tried to tell Vince. He understood the desire but was so caught up in it too that language failed him, and neither one could come up with any suggestion to dislodge the hold it had on them.

One morning in April her father stayed home, lingering in the kitchen in an unusual change of routine for him. Steven was gulping hot oatmeal as Marta came down to the table. He said to his father, who had already lit his first morning cigarette and was sitting sipping his second cup of coffee, "I'll be ready to go when you are, Dad."

"Where're you going?" Marta asked, apprehension gripping her as she saw her mother and father exchange quick glances.

"Gotta see this doctor," Steven said, not stopping his breakfast.

She looked at her father, unable to mask the fear she felt tightening her face. "What's this for?"

He said softly, "This is the best eye man in town. We want his opinion."

"But I thought you had a final opinion. . . ."

He shrugged. "One more . . ."

Steven wiped his mouth on the paper napkin. "Look, I'll go to ten more," he said so firmly, in such an adult way, that Marta looked at him in amazement. "I'd like to avoid surgery if I can."

"Of course," she mumbled. And for her that was the end of that day. She could barely hear anything that was said in class, and when she saw Vince in the hall, for the first time she openly clung to his hand as he moved into a corner with her, away from the thronging mob passing to their classes. "What is it, Mart?"

"Oh, poor Steven!"

"What did they decide?"

"We'll know today. . . ."

"It'll be okay, Mart. You'll see. Keep your chin up."

She rushed home after school and the house was fragrant with the aroma of freshly baked cinnamon buns, her mother's single greatest culinary achievement, fat, high, light wonders filled with honey and nuts, currants, and cinnamon.

"Well?" Marta held her breath.

"Thank God! It's all right."

And for the second time that week the two women clung to each other, this time in relief.

Mrs. Resnick said weepily, "Just thick glasses. That's all. He doesn't mind!"

"No. I don't think he will."

When they sat at dinner that night, as usual two feet from the kitchen stove, with Mrs. Resnick at least half the time on her feet, moving back and forth, serving them before they themselves knew they needed anything more, they all smiled to one another and congratulated Steven. "I wasn't worried," he said, shrugging, but he gave his sister a sly, surreptitious look, to see if she believed him, and she beamed back at him with her whole heart.

She wasn't even bothered when her father began talking about the newly formed Office of Price Administration, going on and on, as Steven asked his nightly dopey questions about "price spirals" and "rising costs of living" and "profiteering" and the possibility of rationing.

Marta just tuned out as usual. The war, which her family insisted on observing daily and feeling personally, had been largely blocked out by her of late. There was one moment in school when somebody said that the Jews now had to wear yellow stars in Vichy France, and she felt some strange panic beat for a second or two in her breast.

But spring was coming, was almost upon them. The air was clean and fresh after the long cold winter and the tips of the irises were pushing through the soil by the side of the steps leading to her house.

Vince went out for track as he had for three years. His graduation was only two months away. To Marta's surprise, he had decided to apply to City University, though he wasn't sure just what he wanted to study there. He never would have told her, but senior year had been an academic triumph for him. She found out by accident from his buddy Mike Conti one morning when she had come down to the gym before school to rehearse for a big Saturday-night dance.

"Where's Vince?" she asked. He was usually the first one there in the mornings.

"He's up in the main office."

"What for?" she asked, leery; trouble always seemed ready to leap out at them.

But Conti was grinning. "He made honor roll for the third consecutive time. How 'bout old Doc Fanetti! Turned out to be a goddamn hot shot with the books!"

She took a breath and stared at Conti. "Well, that's marvelous! So what do they want to see him about?"

"I think he wants to talk to them. . . . He's gonna try to get a scholarship. . . ."

"An academic?"

Conti shrugged. "I'm not sure about all this. I think it's to play ball . . . you know, an athletic scholarship. . . ." He jerked his thumb toward the entrance. Long-striding, straight as a rifle, Vincent was just coming across the gym floor. His expression betrayed nothing.

Marta and Conti and the others were looking at him expectantly.

But he made no reference to it. "Let's go," he said shortly, jumping up on the bandstand and going into "String of Pearls," real fast. Afterward, walking up to class together, she said, "No chance?"

He looked at her sheepishly, grinning. "I got it," he said.

She stopped in her tracks. "What do you mean you got it? Vincent, for cryin' out loud!" Careless of the others around them, she grabbed his arm.

"No big deal!" he said, but his lopsided grin and the sheen in his eyes, focused directly on hers, told her otherwise.

"That's marvelous! Wonderful! Four years? What do you have to do for it?"

He shrugged. "Get a little dirty . . . No problem."

"Not football?"

"Why not? I'm good at it. And baseball and track . . . three sports . . . And they pay my way."

There was no opportunity to talk any more about it. After school she saw the Hillcrest track-and-field team down by the stadium in the hollow, working out. She thought it was Vincent who was jumping over the hurdles, his legs flying, his head high. He could do it, skim the markers, make it at CU; he could do it all. Still she wondered why he had made his decision and what he planned to study. How could he square it with his hopes for a band career?

She wanted to share her elation with someone and couldn't with her parents. So she broke her own rule and told Doris Molner. Locked in her bedroom after dinner, listening to Doris gab away on the phone, Marta suddenly interrupted. "Vince Fanetti got a scholarship to City U."

"Really? Gee, Marta, isn't he lucky?"

"Lucky?" She stared restlessly around her bedroom, which was still not quite a grown-up boudoir despite her attempts to get rid of the silly little-girl lamps and pictures and gimcracks. Mrs. Resnick was fighting it every inch of the way, reluctant to see the mementos of Marta's childhood discarded. Marta nevertheless kept quietly whisking them out of sight one by one: the faded dolls, the stuffed animals, the kids' books with bright jackets. Over her desk she had hung a Matisse print and over her bed she had replaced a picture of a basket of plump kittens with a pale pinkish Picasso.

Irritated at Doris, at herself for discussing it, at the room that dragged her unwillingly back to her childhood, she said shortly, "I don't think luck had a damn thing to do with it."

"Well, you know what I mean." Doris had no desire to argue with her.

"He's earned it," Marta insisted, knowing that she was fighting the right war, but the wrong enemy.

"Sure," Doris agreed. "That's terrific. Do your parents know?"

Marta frowned at herself in the mirror over her dressing table. "No," she said shortly.

"They don't know . . . anything . . . do they, Mart?"

"Know what? For God's sake."

"Well . . . you know . . . that you're singing. . . ."

"We don't talk about it. . . ."

"Oh . . ."

"Are you going to the track-and-field meet Sunday?" Marta asked.

"Sure. We'll all go together. Phyllis said she and Marilyn are definite. . . ."

*　　*　　*

257

Spring beat a temporary retreat over the weekend, and Sunday was gray, cool, and dampish.

"I don't think you should sit out there, Marta," her mother said as she was getting her things on to go to the meet.

"It won't be bad," she said.

"It's supposed to rain."

"Mom, I'll be okay. Please . . ."

"Is your . . . friend in it?" It was the first time her mother had ever asked her a direct question concerning him.

"Yes," she said, wrapping a scarf around her neck.

Mrs. Resnick took Marta's face in her hands. "Marta lovebird, please . . ." But she didn't go on.

Marta waited. But she wouldn't help. Her feelings were too sharp, too tight.

"Daddy and I are very concerned. You know we've tried never to interfere with you. We trust you and believe in you. We . . ."

"Oh for Christ's sake, Mom!" she exploded. Her anger was a flash fire in the living room. And her mother jumped back as if she had been burned.

"You don't interfere . . . oh no!" she screamed at her terrified mother. "You just walk around with sad long faces like I committed murder. That's all! If I *had* committed murder, you'd rush to my side . . . but no—no—all you care about is . . . is how it looks!"

"That's not true, Marta. I care about what happens to you."

"What's happening to me is I'm not a little child anymore. Now you let me go! Do you hear me . . . both of you . . . you let me go!" And she flung out the front door, going down the steps two at a time, her face flaming, the tears coursing down her cheeks. Still shaky, she stopped at the drugstore to get a Coke and cigarettes, trying to collect herself before she picked up the girls. She knew she had to figure it out alone. There wasn't anyone who could do anything for her.

Shivering in the stands hunched with her girl friends, a fine rain falling on their umbrellas, she couldn't work up any enthusiasm for the action down on the field. Then she saw Vince walk out from the crowd of Hillcrest athletes on the benches. He didn't look into the stands for her. He had his mind centered on the business at hand. That was his way, she knew; he could compartmentalize his preoccupations. She had forgotten how to do that. Sometimes she felt the stirrings of resentment, that she was paying a higher price, much higher, than he, for their entanglement. But those feelings were fleeting. When they came together, he brought that same intense focus on her. She knew she was important to him. She still couldn't settle herself down enough to figure out where their future lay . . . if there even was a future.

At the moments when she realized that she had muffed her chance for the mayor's scholarship by getting a D in Algebra and a C in Latin, and that no amount of hard work in the next two years would erase those two rotten grades that put her behind the real achievers in her class, she told herself that she must be out of her mind to be so involved with him. She thought herself bewitched, and she had said as much to him. "We're under a spell." He had agreed. With pleasure and delight. He was riding the crest of the tidal wave, but she was frightened that she was going to be swallowed up somewhere along the way.

Nevertheless, her heart started to spin up and down like a yo-yo when she saw him drop his zipper jacket on the bench, jog to the starting line, and do the hundred-yard dash with his head up and his body arched against the wind, a super athlete, lithe, graceful, flying down there on the muddy field in the drizzle.

"He's really good!" Doris said in her ear.

It was going to be another routine meet between West Philly and Hillcrest, with the scores close. But in the middle of the pole-vaulting competition, a black boy from West Philly accidentally, or purposely, nobody ever was able to say, bumped Dominic Perrina, a Hillcrest boy, just as he was taking off. It threw off Dom's timing, or so he said, and he failed to clear the bar. He came trotting back to the referees, wanting to take it over. But they hadn't seen anything and wouldn't permit it. He loped over to the black kid who, he said, had jostled him and began to yell at him. A general shouting match developed, with other black athletes joining in. There were ten Italian boys on the Hillcrest team and they suddenly came forward like a phalanx. The black boys on the West team stood their ground. There was some pushing and shoving, but the coaches from both sides intervened and broke it up.

They all thought the trouble had been contained, but a squabble broke out again during the lineup for the hurdle race that was the final event. Again it would have been impossible to say who started what, but there was another general rush from the benches on both sides and a lot of shouting. Once more it was settled and the race was run, Vince hurtling over the barriers as if he had wings. Hillcrest won and Marta saw him pick up his jacket, as his friends congratulated him and start off the field with his buddy Nick Genardo. Suddenly Marta's eyes were drawn back to the center of the field where several black boys and two of the Hillcrest guys again were coming at one another, throwing punches, lashing out angrily, and name-calling. The coaches tried to break it up as before but the fracas was shooting rapidly out of control. The other kids began to get into it, pushing, shoving, and bellowing so loudly that the girls could hear it all the way up in the stands.

"Let's get out of here!" Phyllis Cooper said to the others.

"Wait a minute!" Marta wanted to see where Vince had gone.

There were boys from both schools running down the steps of the stands and a free-for-all had developed on the field.

"Get the niggers!" screamed an Italian boy who was usually a quiet, conscientious student in Marta's class. He was leaping down the rows of wooden seats, not waiting to use the blocked aisles.

The girls hurried up the path away from the field, but Marta, ignoring their warnings, pushed down toward the action. There was a small group of Hillcrest athletes still standing on the sidelines. She recognized Lou Morrow and ran up to him. She couldn't see Vincent anywhere. But there seemed to be dozens of guys wrestling and cursing all over the muddy field.

"Lou," she shouted, "what is this?"

"You better beat it, Marta!"

"What happened?"

Bob Goldin answered, not looking at her, "The wops and the shines are after one another."

Suddenly she saw Vince running back toward the field with his teammate Nick Genardo. Both boys headed right for the thick of it.

"Vincent," she called, coming after him onto the field.

"Hey, Marta," called Lou Morrow, rushing after her and grabbing at her arm. "Don't be a jerk. Get away from there!"

She pulled away from Lou. "Leave me alone," she

cried, going after Vince, who was up ahead wading into the rumble. There seemed to be a hundred bodies piling into one another, pummeling, reeling, kicking, cursing. Somebody threw a direct punch at Lou, who was running alongside Marta, still trying to persuade her to back out. The blow landed right on his nose and as she looked at him, Lou's nose began to bleed. "You stupid bastard!" Lou shouted, and hit out wildly at the big black boy who had caught him by surprise. The two boys were instantly locked in a struggle. Marta saw Vince in front of her, trying to drag a colored kid off Dom Perrina, who was rocking in pain down on the ground. Dom had his arms clasped over his stomach. His eye was cut and blood was running down his brow into his ear.

Marta screamed, "Vincent!" He turned at the sound of her voice and the kid who was over Dom reached up and swung at Vince's head. It was a light blow, just grazing Vince's cheek. Vincent, startled by Marta's sudden appearance on the field, dropped his hands momentarily. The black kid, who got to his feet like lightning when Vince turned away, moved in and landed a second punch with a heavy thud, this time directly to the side of Vince's face. Staggering under the blow, Vince reached for the kid, grabbed him by the shirt and shook him, swinging him around like a sack, and sent him hurtling off into the back of another black boy a few yards away.

"Please, please," she heard herself sobbing, not knowing what she was saying or why.

Vince reached down and helped Perrina up. He couldn't see the two other black boys coming up behind him, buddies of the kid whom Vince had knocked around. Putting his arm around Marta, Vince shouted to her, "Let's go!" One of the black kids reached them before they were able to get away and pounded Vince on his back. He stumbled under the force of the blows, and Marta, hanging on to his arm, almost went down with him. But they didn't fall, and Vince spun around in his tracks and started after the guy who had hit him. The kid was loping off already with his pal. Marta grabbed once more at Vince's arm. "No! No!" she cried. He stopped again and together, his arm around her, they ran toward the path by the stands.

When they made it up to the street, they both stood panting, the rain pelting their flushed faces. Down below, the field was a jumble of muddied, scrambling bodies. The coaches were futilely blowing their whistles from the sidelines. Suddenly up at the corner where the bridge began on the Woodlyn side, Marta saw red cars approaching.

"It's the police!" she said. With his arm around her shoulders, Vince pulled her along, back toward the school, away from the corner where several red cars were now converging. Policemen began jumping out and rushing down the hill. There was a large bruise turning blue on the side of Vince's face. She stared at it miserably as they ran for his car.

They sat inside, still out of breath, confused, both of them looking straight ahead out the rain-spattered windshield.

"My God!" she said. "How awful! I don't understand it!"

He didn't answer. He zipped up his jacket and started the car, heading toward her house.

"Vince?"

"What's to understand?" he said, his voice hoarse with bitterness.

"What started it?"

"What the hell difference does that make?" he said angrily, driving fast past the red cars, across the bridge to Woodlyn.

She was alarmed at his anger and sank back into the corner near the door.

He glanced over at her. "The animals just can't wait to join in with that kind of thing. . . ."

"You joined in," she said.

"I went back to get Dominic."

"If it hadn't been him it would've been for somebody else."

Vince shrugged. "I couldn't run away from my friends."

"Your friends were animals too, you know!"

"Look! Shut up! You don't know what you're talking about. Don't be stupid!"

She looked at him sadly. "The brave thing would've been to walk away, Vince. . . ."

"Oh Jesus, Marta! I don't want to hear any crap from you now! You weren't exactly smart getting down there in the middle of it."

"I was worried about you," she said softly.

"I can take care of me," he said. But he pulled her over toward him and drove the rest of the way to her house with one arm around her.

She kept the incident from her parents but it was all over the junior high school the next day and Steven came home from school yapping about it. "Be quiet!" she admonished.

"It's in the paper," he said. "Hey, Mart, did you see the guys gettin' hit?"

"Yes, I did. It was disgusting."

"They said some of the kids had to go to the hospital. They were bleeding. . . . Did you see . . . ?"

"Steven!" she hissed. Her mother had been upstairs and was just coming back down. But Marta realized that her parents knew, because they disappeared together upstairs immediately after dinner, with the *Bulletin*. She went up to her bedroom, and her father, coming out of his room, stopped her just as she was about to close her door.

He pointed to the article. "Were you there?" His face was stiff.

"Yes . . ."

"I want you to stay away from that riffraff." He said it softly but there was a note of iron in his voice.

She turned to go back into her bedroom.

"Did you hear me?" he repeated.

"What riffraff is that?" she said, her throat constricting.

"You stick to your own kind, young woman. Or you're in serious trouble! I don't want you to do the following things, Marta . . . I don't want you to sing any more at school dances . . . or anywhere else. Until further notice!" He was leveling a stubby, nicotined finger at her, shaking it under her nose. "I expect you to stay away from that boy . . . and I don't want him here. I don't want you to go out with him or socialize with him in any way. Don't try to find loopholes. You know what I'm saying to you. Stop it! Now! And no more telephone calls! You tell him. Because if you don't, I will. Do you understand me?"

She nodded, her head lowered, chewing on her lips. "Yes," she murmured.

"Are these yours?" He handed her a pack of Chesterfields.

"I don't know. . . ."

"Your mother found them in your desk drawer. No more smoking, either!"

"What the hell was she doing in my desk drawer?"

"You watch your language, young lady."

Her anger exploded. "I don't want anyone—anyone! —rummaging around in my drawers. That's the biggest nerve I ever heard!"

Dr. Resnick ignored her fury and started down the stairs. But he turned on the top step. "You were seen down on that field yesterday, Marta. You could have been hurt. It was no place to be. Your sense of propriety and discrimination are all mixed up. Now you set your life in order!"

"Discrimination!" she screamed from her bedroom doorway. "Discrimination! That's a laugh! There's a war going on . . . over issues just like that. Oh, that word is clear all right! It's discrimination when it's against us . . . but against somebody else it's okay." She sobbed suddenly. "Well, it isn't! It isn't right! It's all wrong! What difference does it make if his religion is different? What do you care?"

Dr. Resnick slowly turned and came back up on the landing. He looked sick and exhausted and through the fog of her anger she saw him as old. Her heart was a lump of lead.

He said quietly, "You are a good, respectable, intelligent girl, Marta. You come from a long and honorable tradition. You have fine instincts, but I can tell you, you wouldn't be the first good person to wind up on the trash heap. I've seen it happen a thousand times. If I've spared you the ugly news that the world is a divided place, it was just for that . . . to spare you! To give you and Steven a sense of security and stability and identity! Perhaps I was wrong. You should have been better warned about the kinds of risks you're taking. You've made a series of very foolish mistakes. We gave you all winter to work things out for yourself, to come to your senses. And you're in deeper than before. Now . . . we're not fools, your mother and I. We can't lock you up. I won't try to be your jailer. You are still very much your own person." He came up close to her and she thought he was going to put his hands on her shoulders, but he didn't. His arms hung heavily by his sides and his shoulders drooped. "But now there are firm rules. And you will obey them. Because I am still your father, and your mother and I are in charge of your life. Until such time as you are ready to be in charge yourself, you will do what I tell you to do. You will stop seeing that boy. You will stop singing in school. You will begin to go to your sorority meetings again...oh yes! I know all about that. All about the whole thing! And you'll either go out with the boys from the community, or you'll stay home." He paused and tried to smile. "I am not worried about my sixteen-year-old daughter being an old maid."

She stood looking down at her feet as he finished and shuffled off wearily down the steps.

A few minutes later she heard happy sounds coming from the radio as they sat listening to Fred Allen. She heard her father's quiet chuckle and her mother's careful laughter.

What did it mean to them? How could they understand what they were doing to her? But somewhere in her yet-to-come adult mind was the knowledge that what was done was long-since done.

It was a lovely spring afternoon, and Marta and Vince sat in the old Ford on a tiny road in Fairmount Park. They were apart on the seat. She wouldn't let him near her. "What can I do?" She wasn't really asking him. She was telling him. But he couldn't accept it. "You can grow up," he said quietly.

"Does growing up mean stepping on the people I love?"

"They don't seem to mind stepping on you," he said.

"They don't realize. . . ."

"So what else is new. . . ."

"Vincent, please . . ."

"It's the same old shit road to hell. And all the good intentions are still in place, Marta. I don't question your parents' love for you.'' He took a deep breath that quivered as he exhaled. ''Okay . . .'' he said softly. ''Maybe you're just not strong enough. You can't cope with it.''

''The problem is, Vincent, I don't know what 'it' is. I can't define what I have to cope with. . . . I'm in a bind. I can't see my way out! We have to wait. . . .''

''What do you mean wait?''

''I have to do what they say . . . not see you for a while.''

He answered at once. ''All right.'' He turned the motor over and started back to Woodlyn, silent, his jaw rigid.

''I can't sing at the dances anymore.''

''I understand.''

''You can't call me.''

He nodded.

''Please, please,'' she said, moving closer to him. ''Please try to help me. Don't let anger come between us now.''

He pulled over to the curb, but he didn't take her in his arms. ''You must think I'm jolly old Saint Nicholas!'' he said and his voice was deep in his chest. ''I'm no self-sacrificing saint, sweetheart! I can't solve your problems. And I'll tell you something else, Miss Woodlyn Princess of 1941, you really don't have a clue as to what the world is all about. You really are in a bind! And what's more, you're never gonna get out! So good luck! But don't wait around for Vincent Fanetti! I'm not going into the grocery cupboard, Marta, to wait for other times and other suppers. We're through. It was fun. And it's . . . over.'' He took her home.

As she walked up to the front door of her house she saw that the forsythia bush was covered with golden flowers and that the tulips her mother had planted in the fall were almost ready to open, smooth, dark red and orange. The

April world was filled with bloomings and murmurings of hope and renewal. And for her it had almost come to an end. She didn't turn around as he pulled away, but she heard him gun the Ford's motor as if his foot would go through the floorboard. All she could think about, crazily, was his saying to her the week before, "I'll buy you the most stupendous orchid I can find for the senior dance. And you'll be the most beautiful Woodlyn Princess. . . ."

CHAPTER 12

December 1981

DAN REITER WAS NOT THE KIND OF PERSON ANYONE could feel sorry for because he never felt sorry for himself. Marta was grateful for his strength and his equilibrium in the face of the lying newspaper stories, and the questioning looks from their friends and the questions from their acquaintances. She had always accused him, during their arguments, of "silly stoicism," wishing at those moments of tension and conflict that he would loosen up and let go. But she understood in the deepest and best stratum of herself that he did what he had to, that his stability was based on staying private, cool, and keeping himself in hand.

As winter approached, he went about his business with his sense of humor intact, a little quieter than usual, asking for no special considerations from her or from anyone else. And the story began to subside just as he had said it would, like a medium-high tide that had nowhere to go but back to sea. The bank stood behind him. The problem had been theirs from the start; Reiter was a careful man and had conferred with the other officers before advancing Municipal Hospital the building funds; he had consulted all along the way. Notwithstanding the fact that the original program was a fiasco, that the hospital board had mismanaged the budget right from the start, and that the entire construction industry was in the doldrums, the bank still supported the idea of going forward with the hospital's new plans. Within several weeks of Dan's leaving the board, negotiations started with a new contractor and Dan remained, as he told Marta, "no longer ex-officio, but very much ex-parte," consulting on every move, watching now where the pennies as well as the dollars were headed. The federal and state money was coming through after the first of the year. Dan assured her that 1982 would be better.

She had two wonderful days of euphoria when she saw that the situation had turned around for him. But her good spirits didn't last because she couldn't see things getting any better for her. His fight had never been hers, and the anger she had felt at the treatment given him more or less evaporated. He accepted his situation. And she accepted what he accepted.

It was something else that swamped her as she watched the holidays approach, the stores turn bright with decorations, and the streets and people begin to jolly up for the coming season. It was melancholy. Her kids had told her that they weren't coming home. They knew that she and Dad would understand. Diane was going skiing with her new boyfriend, and Allen, shy and, as always, careful not to reveal too much to them, hinted that he was involved with a new romance too. He planned to spend the week camping out somewhere in the desert.

Marta spent a lot of time alone, longer hours every day, working out the patterns of her lyrics and the possibilities for the music, losing herself for whole chunks of time, surprised at her absorption, pleased at her rediscovered facility at the keyboard. Steven had kept his word and had not pushed her or spoken to Dan. She was still not quite sure what she was going to do. She had given herself one week to make the decision.

She had another decision. Vincent was in her dreams. One night she awoke trembling, wondering if she had called his name aloud. In the nightmare she had been up on the Hillcrest–Woodlyn Bridge and was looking down into the hollow. She saw him but he was walking away; he was following the train tracks and a train was coming. Marta remembered the sounds of the trains clearly from her childhood, and the emptiness of the night that those sounds evoked. She had grown up with the clatter and chug and lonely whistle echoing, but she couldn't ever remember watching the trains go past.

In her dream, she was riveted to the concrete overpass, watching a train that was coming on too fast, and Vincent, a tiny undefended spot yards away and below, was walking right into it! She called out to him again and again!

When she sat up in bed, her heart was pounding and she was covered with cold sweat. She looked to see if Dan was awake, but he was sleeping peacefully. She moved over to his side of the bed, and he held her in his sleep, grunting with comfort and pleasure as his arms went around her.

The next day as she sat at the piano playing around with notes that might go with her lyrics, she remembered the dream and stared disconsolately out the window into the bleak December morning. She sighed and turned back to her work, picking up the paper she was working on, and was startled to see that she had written his name all over the top margin, like a schoolgirl, without realizing she was doing it. Guiltily, looking around the room as if she might be caught, she scratched out: VINCE, VINCENT, VINCE, V . . .

She reached for the phone and left a message at his service. Yet, it was with a small shock that she heard his voice when he called back a half-hour later. There seemed to be two of her, and the adult, married, sensible Marta couldn't be sure what that sixteen-year-old, gambling Marta would do.

"It'll have to be after two," he said.

"All right . . ."

"Do you know where Mikko's place is?"

And for the first time she laughed into the phone, her heart lightening again, as some hidden happiness insisted on surfacing and some young, joyful sense of fun and adventure pushed its way into her life.

"No! You really think I'm dumb, don't you, Fanetti!"

"Pretty dumb," he agreed.

"Well, maybe I'll get lost and you'll just sit there and wait. . . ."

"I've done that before. . . ."

She said softly, "I'll be there on time."

They stared at each other across the table but didn't touch. They sipped their wine and talked about the kinds of things they had known together.

She asked him abruptly, "What did we give up?" She added quickly, "When we sacrificed the music, I mean."

He looked at her thoughtfully and answered the whole question anyway. "Exactly the same thing we gave up when we gave up each other: problems, difficulties, risks, unpleasant moments, rejections, pain . . . you name it."

"Well," she laughed, "now I know why, as well as what!"

"Oh, you knew then," he said.

"I can't remember. . . ."

"Yes, you can," he said. "And along with all that mess, an enormous amount of happiness, maybe even ecstasy . . ."

"The music never left me."

"If being only an observer and a rememberer will do . . ."

She said, "At least nothing grows old. Nothing grows ugly. Nothing gets mean."

"So why the sudden urge to get back into it again? What do you need it for?"

"Do you think it's a bad idea, then?" She waited for his answer.

He shrugged. "Not me. I'm the great believer in bad ideas. Remember? I always tested them out before all the others . . . if only to get them out of the way."

"It doesn't seem like such a big deal, does it?" she asked wistfully.

"You've kept to very little circles, Marta. Anything outside the chalk line is going to seem dangerous now."

"I have no fear of it, Vince. Absolutely none! No fear of failure. No fear of looking like a jackass. I'm all for it!"

"So?"

She sighed. "Dan is very threatened by it. He doesn't want me up in New York."

Vincent laughed. "Christ! It all sounds so . . . ridiculous!"

"Don't be a rat, Fanetti!"

He was laughing hard at her, and instantly they were transported back to all the times when puncturing pretensions was common sport between them. Relaxed and happy with him, she didn't ask the question that was in her heart: Would you let me, if I were yours? But it hung there in the space between them. His face changed, some different attitude filmed over it. And was instantly gone.

275

He sat back in his chair, tilted his glass, and finished his wine. I wouldn't want you to either, he would say. And she would smile an I-told-you-so, and he would add, But I'd let you go anyway . . . to the music. . . .

She said, "I hear music all the time now." She sighed. "Even when I don't expect it. I don't want it to stop!"

"That's what happens. You always had the makings of an addict."

"Yes," she said. "Things grab at me. The music is a narcotic. It hits my veins with a super rush. If I were X-rayed you could see my veins all filled up with it."

He laughed. "Well, maybe."

"It's there. Going in or out. No difference. My veins, my arteries, both would be transparent and empty without it."

"You always had a nice sense for the dramatic line."

"I'm not coming on, Fanetti!"

He waved his hand. "And I'm not knocking it! Jesus, you are the dramatic line! You always were. I thought it was fantastic! There you were, to both of us, right at the center of the universe!"

"Woodlyn anyway . . ."

"Mom's and Pop's universe," he said slyly.

She said softly, "That's another story."

He shook his head. "No. It's exactly and precisely the same story."

She handed him a sheet of paper. He read, "Go easy on my heart / There's crystal in my soul." He got up, reading it, and took it to Mikko's upright piano against the wall. He ran over the melody, saying the words as he played, "Go easy / Go easy / There's crystal in my soul. / To leave me is to break me / And I never will be whole." He added the chords and embellished it. She stood beside him, grinning with embarrassment and pleasure when he looked up at her admiringly.

"It's good! Steven has to be pleased with this . . . with everything you've done. . . ."

Standing together in Mikko's doorway at four o'clock before going in opposite directions to their parked cars, he suddenly pulled her to him. It was the first time since they had met again. He bent and kissed her gently on the mouth, and then released her at once. He said nothing and was waiting for her to tell him. But she said, "I'll have to call you. . . ."

And once more she drove away confused, happy one second, miserable the next.

She spent the next afternoon with Doris, who had come home and seemed to be so much better that Marta thought, Well, Dan's right and I'm a lousy crepe hanger! She'll make it!

But after a half-hour of sitting together in the overheated bedroom, Doris closed her eyes, put her head back against the easy chair, and seemed to drift off. Marta sat looking at her, gloom regathering in her chest. Doris was frail and her color was faded, as if the illness had drained the brightness from her blood. She opened her eyes after a minute and said, "I get a little tired."

"Should I beat it? Be honest!"

But Doris reached out for her. "Oh please, Mart! Stay with me for a while!"

Marta settled back and searched her mind for gossip and nonsense that would amuse Doris and not weary her. But in the middle of talking about friends, Doris interrupted suddenly, "Are you seeing Fanetti?" And taken off guard, Marta sat silent.

"You don't have to tell me." Doris pressed her hand

again. "Wasn't I the only one who knew about the adventures at Nino's famous café! I never told, Mart. I never told a soul." She winked. "Quite a feat for a bigmouth like me!"

"I always trusted you completely, Dor. You were my best friend. Through all that mess . . ."

Doris smiled at her. "I envied you your guts!"

Marta waved away the compliment. "For God's sake . . . I was an idiot! I never knew what I was doing!"

But Doris insisted, "Yes, you did! You wouldn't accept the rules. The rest of us never would have questioned them! Or . . . we might have privately, but we could never have acted on it like you did."

"Well . . . it doesn't matter," Marta said.

"Sure it matters."

"I behaved. Eventually."

"But you tested the system. . . ."

"And found that it was too tough for me."

Doris sighed. "It's changed. A lot." She closed her eyes again. "My kids won't listen."

Marta shrugged again. "It doesn't matter."

Doris's eyes flew open. "Oh, but it does!" she said, and Marta was surprised at how much energy she was able to muster in support of her own beliefs. Marta decided to drop it, but Doris was insistent. "You have to keep telling them, Mart . . . explaining to them how important it is. They don't understand."

"Why is it important, Dor?" Then she regretted the rebuttal when Doris sighed wearily and moved around on her pillow in obvious discomfort.

"It's an obligation we have. . . ."

Marta didn't ask to whom. She took Doris's hand and tried to rub some warmth into it. "I'm cold all the time now," Doris said, "for some reason. . . ."

When Marta left the sickroom and the nurse let her out the front door, the melancholy that had been trailing her all day came roaring back. The brief pleasure of the meeting with Vince had disappeared. The days were growing shorter, and it was dark when she pulled into her driveway. She was about to switch off the radio and the ignition when she was suddenly held by a news break that interrupted the music. "Martial law has been imposed in Poland. General Jaruzelski has taken over. Solidarity officials have been arrested and the union activists interned."

As she unlocked the front door she was transported back many years to a September afternoon, opening the door to Aunt Moll and Aunt Min's house. She was meeting Mom and Dad and Steven there for Sunday dinner and she had pushed at the unlocked door, gone in, and instantly been shushed. They were all crowded around the radio, and a crackly voice was telling the world that Hitler had marched into Poland.

The players had changed on the world scene, but some things were still the same. Everywhere somebody was coming down hard on somebody else. And even Doris believed, sick as she was, that she still had a mission to come down on the kids, to steer them back to the tried-and-true path: stay with your own kind; our way is the right way.

How certain everyone was! How easy it was to follow the yellow line right down the center of the highway. Doris said she was obligated, still in debt somehow to Mr. and Mrs. Molner, long gone. And Marta remained obligated too . . . to the universe that Vince mockingly said was Mom's and Pop's.

When Dan came in shortly after her, she could see at once that his spirits had picked up. "What a nifty, tough fella," she said as he reached for her and kissed her lightly on the cheek. "You're right on top again, Daniel Reiter!"

He shook his head. "Not quite!" He smiled. "However . . . it's all right!"

"Oh, Dan . . ." she said, sighing.

"Did you go to see Doris?"

"I just came from there."

He started up the steps. And then stopped. "How 'bout going out to eat? We need a break, Marta." He came back down and kissed her again. "I hate to see you so low. It really isn't like you. What can I do?"

"Let's look in the paper," she said, "and see what's exciting in this drab old city. Let's go out for dinner and have some fun. Let's go dancing, let's . . ."

"Whoa, whoa," he said. "We'll do whatever you want to do. Just don't plan too much, please. It's been a long day."

"We used to dance the night away."

"We had nothing else on our minds. . . ."

She was rifling through the newspaper when the telephone rang. Dan answered it. Holding his hand over the mouthpiece, he said, "Do you want to have dinner with the Moyerses?"

Marta looked up and nodded. "Is that Carole?"

He handed her the phone. "Make any plans that please you. I'm going to change. And have me a martini! You too?"

"Sure." She swiveled around and said into the phone, "How you doin', Carole?"

"Oh, so-so. You went to see Doris, didn't you?" asked Carole.

"Yes. I was there this afternoon."

She heard Carole sigh. "I called and spoke to Herb. He had just gotten home. God, he's upset!"

"She's doing all right," Marta said stubbornly.

"He's very pessimistic." Carole sighed again into the phone. "Listen, Mart, I'm having difficulties getting myself over there. Do you know what I mean?"

Marta frowned, pulling her feet up and tucking them under her on the couch, trying to get comfortable. "It's really not that bad, Carole. She's just a little thin and washed-out–looking. That's all."

"Oh, it's me! It's awful that I don't go! Isn't it, Mart?"

Marta shifted about restlessly on the soft couch. "Do what you want to do." After a second she said, "We're going out to eat and we'd love you to come with us. We can all use some cheering up. There's a rock concert I see here in the paper. It looks really exciting. Mike likes that kind of music, doesn't he?"

There was a second's silence. "A rock concert? Oh, I don't think so, Marta. We would like to eat with you. And then we'll just come on home. I have to go to work in the morning, kiddo." Carole drew another deep breath that whistled in Marta's ear. "Maybe I'll still get over to Doris's. I don't know. . . ."

When Marta hung up, she had a long moment of irritation. Why the hell did a grown woman have to ask her permission not to make a sick call that she didn't want to make? To whom was she obligated? Stretching all around them, obligations were a fine network trapping people in a sticky spiderweb of complications. And Carole Moyers was one of the strong ones who had "worked her way," to use the current lingo, "back into the world." The goofy euphemism meant that she had managed to convince her stubborn mate that it was all right for her to get a job. Each one had his own little war to wage, and the scene of the skirmishes shifted periodically. If you were like Diane, twenty-three and beautiful, with the world wide open before you, a job was the normal "next step." And the scene of the battle shifted to home and laundry and cleaning and babies. And so on . . .

Marta had said to Doris that it didn't matter. It was the same old refrain: long views versus short views, business as usual. But of course when it was your career, or your dirty dishes, it mattered! Or your young love . . .

The younger guys Allen's age seemed to want their wives out there earning. Bled by life in the twentieth century, did they need all the help they could get? Allen had two degrees and a hot-shot job with a first-rate law firm, and somehow he didn't want that either. He thought he was better off selling books on the edge of the desert a thousand miles from home.

For all she knew, maybe he was! Why bother judging whether he was too weak or too strong? Mart smiled involuntarily, as she always did when she thought of her good-looking, tender-hearted son. She had told Vincent that Allen resembled Dan. And he did, strikingly. But the one he reminded her of over and over was his uncle Steven. Those quiet, smiling, stubborn ones . . .

When she went upstairs, Dan was tying his shoes, getting ready for a casual evening.

"Good," she said, eyeing his sweater and corduroys. "We're going to a rock concert."

He looked up in surprise. "Is that what the Moyerses are doing?"

"As a matter of fact, no. They'll have dinner with us and you and I are going on alone. . . . Just you and me, babe . . ." she sang.

"Where is it? What kind of rock concert? That music is too loud for me. . . ."

"Starting from the rear: no, it is no longer overamplified so it won't be too loud. It's a black rock group . . . and it's up in North Philly."

He sat back and stared at her. "You're kidding, aren't you?"

She felt the nub of irritation begin to push into her chest again. "I'm not kidding. Why would I kid? This is one of the best groups around today. They have a wonderful sound."

He took a breath, his shoulders stiffening. "Not for me, Marta."

"You don't want to go?"

"I definitely don't want to go."

"Why not?" The irritation had sprouted and she could feel the familiar tug of petulance pulling at her features, dragging in her voice.

He said, "Don't be silly."

She jumped up like a shot from the edge of the bed. "Oh damn it, Daniel! Anything you don't want to do is silly! What do you mean silly?"

He stood up too, fixing his sweater, hooking his belt, and then started for the doorway. "Let's have a drink and we'll have dinner with the Moyerses. If you want to do a movie afterward that's fine."

"Don't put me off! I want to go to that rock concert!"

He left the room. Slamming things around, she changed into slacks and a sweater. As she came back downstairs she saw the Moyerses' car pulling up at the front door. Before he could reach to open it, she touched his arm. "Do this for me," she said softly.

They heard the car door slam in the driveway. He looked down at her. "I don't understand any of this," he said, his voice flat.

She nodded. "I know you don't. Can't you just do what I want? For me. No matter how foolish. Just for me." She couldn't keep the wistfulness out of her tone.

He said slowly, "It's very dangerous to go marching

around in North Philadelphia. We'll be the only white people in the audience. It's chance-taking. For no good reason. Except to satisfy some whim.''

"I don't often ask you to satisfy my whims, do I?"

The Moyerses were at the front step. They rang the bell and the chimes sounded through the house. Dan reached for the doorknob.

"Dan?"

"We'll decide after dinner. . . ."

"I will not have a debate in front of the Moyerses!"

"All right, Marta." He opened the door.

"Very cold for December," Carole said as she came in, her pale fox zipper jacket drifting Joy, her matching fluffy fox hat pulled down around her face. She was dressed for a casual evening in Gucci boots and Saint Laurent gabardine pants.

"We're dreamin' of a White Christmas," said Mike Moyers.

"We may get it." Dan closed the door and led them into the den. "Drinks?"

"Sure thing!" said Carole. "Exhausted," she lamented, flopping on the couch with her jacket unzipped.

"Stay awhile," Marta said with a laugh, helping her take off the jacket. "Why so tired?"

"Work, lovey!" Carole took the wine that Dan was handing her. "Don't let 'em kid you. It's hard to get out there and earn!"

"So they tell me," Marta answered, avoiding Dan's glance, which flashed briefly her way.

Mike said, "My Carole loves to work. She also loves to complain. She always loved to complain! At least now the complaints are followed by a nice pay check."

"Which you claim adds to your tax burden," Carole said accusingly to her husband.

"Doesn't it?" he shot back. "I showed you . . . you saw the figures. . . ."

"We're coming into bad times, Mike." Carole shook her finger at her husband, then turned to Dan and said, "Tell him! There's going to be a real first-rate depression! Right, Dan?" Turning back to Mike, "And you'll be glad I have a job!"

Dan smiled. "Well . . . I don't know."

Carole insisted, "You think things will pick up right away? Gosh, I don't!"

Dan shrugged. Marta knew he would resist being pulled into a discussion of economics. He avoided it like the plague when he was with friends. Anyone who wanted to talk business with him had to get him from nine to five at the bank.

Marta said, "I think the point is being lost there somewhere." She spoke directly to Carole. "You work because you want to. It's good for you. It makes you happy. You like being paid, being out in the world, exercising your skills."

Carole nodded. "Yes to everything!"

Mike said, "Look, I'm not against it. Don't turn me into the enemy. If you want to be out there battling the tides every day, go ahead!"

Standing together while Dan got their car, Carole said, "I don't know why we tend to keep on fighting the same battles over and over. . . ."

Marta shrugged. "Because you know they're never completely won."

Mike came toward them. "We can bring you home after dinner. Why is Dan getting the car?"

"We're going on to a rock concert," Marta said.

Mike looked interested. "Oh . . . who?"

"They're called The Smoke. They're very big right now," Marta explained.

Mike nodded. "I know who they are. We handle the accounts for two of them." He was a CPA. "They make a pile!"

"I sort of thought you might be interested."

Mike shook his head. "Well, I don't know. Where are they performing?"

"At the Gateway. Up on north Broad."

"God, that's terrible up there, Marta!" Mike shook his head again. "You better think twice about that!"

But the consensus of fear irritated her, and she didn't answer. After dinner they said good night to the Moyerses and got into their own car. Dan began to back out of the parking spot.

"Well?" She looked at him.

He stopped where he was, staring out the windshield. "I want you to reconsider," he said softly.

Her anger mounted. "I want to go!"

He nodded. "All right, Marta."

They drove all the way in silence. As they approached the dismal, grim section of the city where houses were burned out or boarded up or falling down, where the remaining businesses, small stores and taverns, had iron gratings across their doors and windows, she repressed her own sudden flutter of fear and kept her thoughts to herself. He wasn't interested in explanations anyway: how important it was for her work to hear live music now and then, to be present at the scene, to get the nuances and overtones, and any suggestions of new styles. He walked out of the room when she tuned in rock stations on the radio or tried to beam in on the current top ten. Damn! If his business was to follow interest rates and the fluctuations of the dollar, then hers was to track musical trends and performers! She glanced at him, saw him frown. He drove around, passing empty spots between other parked cars, but not taking them, looking for a lot where he could pay and have his car watched for the evening.

"There must be a parking garage around here somewhere, connected with the theater," she said.

He shrugged and drove up one narrow dark street after another. Half the streetlights were out. Trash piled at the sidewalks in many places spilled into the street, making passage difficult. Back on Broad, one block farther from the Gateway, she spotted an open parking lot with attendants and pointed to it. "Okay," he said.

Walking back in the raw December air, she saw several groups of young white kids walking toward the theater. "There," she said, "we won't be the only ones." He only tightened his hold on her arm.

Not wanting to be conspicuous, she had dressed in her duffle coat and knit hat, her old pants and flat shoes. But entering the theater she saw that it was fancy night for the young black population. They wore mink coats and lots of glitter, the men as well as the girls. Cadillacs were pulling up every second, letting out high-style people, laughing, buzzing, ready for a big evening.

Dan bought the best seats that were left, high up in the second balcony of the old theater.

"We're in heaven . . ." Marta sang as they climbed the steep steps.

"I asked for seats downstairs. This is all they had left."

"Because The Smoke is so terrific!"

When they were seated, her eyes roamed around the balcony and down into the first rows of the orchestra, just visible if she craned her neck. There were a few white faces in the audience. They all seemed young. Nobody had paid much attention to Marta and Dan when they entered the theater, and after a curious stare or two from the people seated around them in the balcony, they were ignored. Sitting shoulder to shoulder, they waited for the show to begin. Marta slipped her arm through Dan's, but he didn't turn as he usually did and smile at her. He was uncomfortable, wary, and unwilling to relax. He stared straight ahead until the house lights began to lower and then he leaned back stiffly in his seat and closed his eyes. He was trying to take a nap. She moved over in her seat as far away from him as she could.

A young singer came out onto the stage with a guitar. There were two other minor acts and Marta watched them with limited interest, although they were professionally competent and their style wasn't bad. When the last of them had left the stage, the lights went completely out and there was a second of total darkness and silence. A drum roll started in the pit and as it grew in volume, colored beams from strategically placed spotlights zoomed around the audience, up and down at such a dizzying speed that Marta was forced to close her eyes for a moment to avoid a sudden wave of vertigo. A young black man dressed in red satin came out and announced the appearance of The Smoke.

Screams began downstairs and were rapidly picked up by the balcony, building into a roar. Feet stamped and metal whistles purchased beforehand in the lobby shrilly capped the wild noise. Just as the sound was approaching its crescendo peak, the group appeared. The entire audience got to its feet. Dan, wide awake now, stayed in his seat but Marta jumped up to try to see over the bobbing heads in front of her. The group, bearded and mustached with high-polished Afro hair arrangements, was not as young as Marta would have expected. They were dressed all in white, silk shirts open down the front, neckpieces, wrist

chains, and gold medallion-link belts glinting in the flashing strobes. As they smiled and bowed and hip swiveled in
a prechoreographed introduction, their white shoes moved
together magically to an unplayed beat. The din of the
applause and shouting reached upward to a new ear-shattering
decibel. Dan stirred miserably in his seat. Then the noise
began to subside. A brief silence descended as The Smoke
took their places front center stage behind their instruments, five of them glittering at their audience. As the
guitars began and the electric piano came rippling in, the
audience sat back down, buzzing to one another.

The lights were playing on the group more slowly now,
more sensuously, rolling over them and their instruments.
Each man had a small mike hidden someplace on his
clothing, and the individual sounds of their instruments
came through clearly, starting small and neat, then beginning to mingle together in their famous smooth ensemble
playing. After about ten bars as their volume built, pan-
demonium broke out once more at exactly the same moment all over the theater. The audience had recognized
"Warm Up Girl," The Smoke's big hit number, and was
saluting them again with shrieks and rhythmic stamping.
The music rose above the din, contrary to what Marta had
assured Dan, the entire performance was to be as loud, as
hard, and as amplified as she had ever heard rock played.
Dan retreated even farther into his seat, his chin on his
chest, as Marta leaned forward, trying not to pay any
attention to him.

The Smoke had been around for a good while. Marta
had heard their records on and off during the past years.
They had moved easily from tough rock and early soul into
the new disco of the late seventies and were now back into
hard rock again. Their driving beat was as fresh as if it had
just been invented. She was astonished by the immediate

excitement and tension generating inside the music itself. The lead singer had a clear silky voice. He was reputed to be the group's arranger too, and as Marta listened to the open-throated ease of his range, she was impressed by the harmonies in the background, the modulations, the sophisticated ideas incorporated into the body of the sound.

They were good all right! She was caught up in the music, song after song. Only once was she diverted, when Dan looked around, frowning, his nose twitching, his mouth tightening, and she became aware of the ripe smell of pot filling the balcony, mingling with the odors of hot dogs and popcorn. The audience never stopped smoking, drinking, eating, commenting, and humming until the intermission came. But Marta tried to ignore them too. The music was engrossing.

She was surprised when the house lights began to go back up. The first part of the program had flown for her. The group took their bows, coming back five times for the applause and the cheers.

Marta stood up, stretching. "God, they're good!"

Dan rose too. "Let's go!" he said.

She raised her brows. "To the lobby?"

"Home."

"Why?"

He sighed. "You proved your point."

"What does that mean?"

All around them in the balcony people were scrunching up their empty packages of food, corking their booze, tossing the trash right and left, laughing, and singing the last number.

Dan never got around to answering her question because there was a sudden rush down the aisles of the balcony that surprised them both. Some peculiar shift was taking place in the crowd downstairs, a tremor, a concerted movement of heads. The steps of the balcony were steep and the audience had been moving slowly down for the break. The pace had suddenly increased and the balcony people were draped over the brass, velvet-curtained railing, trying to see down below. Over the shoulders of the group ganging in front of her, Marta could see agitation down in the orchestra. A general rush had begun all over the theater and they could hear and feel the thud of feet starting to move fast.

Dan turned to her at once. "Something's going on down there!" He went first, gripping her arm and pulling her after him. They finally made it through the horde into the mezzanine lobby. An usherette in pink satin was trying to get out of the crush of the mob that was milling around, shouting, and pushing toward the steps that led down to the main lobby. Dan called to the girl, who had flattened herself against a wall, "What is it? What happened?"

"Fight down there." The girl looked at them, worried. They were the only whites in a sea of black faces and they could see the alarm reflected in her face. "You'd better stay put!" She touched Marta's arm. "Go over there near the water fountain. Keep out of this crowd!" She whispered as Marta and Dan pushed past her. "This is big trouble!"

Later, when she was trying to review the evening, remembering details one by one as they flashed past her, Marta realized that she was not yet frightened at that time. It had all happened too fast. She said to Dan, "Should we just wait over there till everybody gets out?"

But Dan never stopped moving, pulling her hard behind him. He gave no explanations. His face was tight as a drum, his jaw rigid.

She tried to press up beside him. "Honey?" She tugged at his jacket.

He turned to her briefly. "We're going to try to get the hell out of here!" he said under his breath. "If we can!"

It was when they were five steps above the lobby and she could see the mass of humanity shoving and screaming at the center that she became scared. She said to a man trying to get down the steps beside them, "Do you know what happened?"

He looked at her with raised brows, and gestured, pointing with his chin. "Fight over there. Two guys over that there girl." Never stopping, elbowing his way ahead of them now, he said over his shoulder, "Trouble here, lady! White girl in that fight!"

A young black teenager squeezing along on Marta's other side said to a friend beside her, "Guy got cut!"

At that point Dan pushed himself directly in front of Marta and, never letting go of her forearm, yanked her behind him, trying to stay close to the wall. The entire lobby had become a sea of punching, shoving bodies, with arms raised and flailing at one another. Women's screams mingled with men's curses and shouts of demented anger.

It was impossible to get to the entrance. The doors had been blocked and couldn't be opened because of the press of the mob against them, inside and outside. As they tried to move forward, a tall black boy raised his arm over Dan's head and Marta screamed, "Dan!" He whirled, saw the blow coming, and leaned to one side, almost toppling back on her. The punch went wild. Just to her right she spotted a flight of steps going down to the lower-level restrooms. She pulled hard on Dan's hand. "Down there!" she shouted, then turned around and made her way toward the stairs. Dan shoved after her, still trying to avoid the blows of the boy who had continued hitting him about the shoulders. The steps were already filled with people trying to get up and others trying to get down. But when they finally came down to the bottom, the crowd was less dense. People were milling around the center and every once in a while somebody came rushing in or out of the bathrooms. A white boy and girl were huddled near the ladies' room behind a large urn of artificial plants. Dan pulled Marta toward them, and they flattened themselves next to the young couple.

"Oh God, I'm scared!" the girl whispered. Marta nodded.

"All we want to do is get out!" The young man was pale.

"It's impossible to try up there!" Dan said.

"Where are the police?" the girl wailed.

"They couldn't get in anyhow," Marta said. "The whole front of the theater is blocked. People are going crazy all over here!"

Dan looked around. "There must be some way out from down here." He moved out a bit from their spot. "There should be a fire exit."

Marta came after him. The lower lobby was filling now and fighting had developed on the steps midway. There was no chance of pushing back up through there.

He said to her, "Stay here, please."

"Oh no!" She hung on to his arm.

The young couple came after them as Dan skirted around the edges of the large lobby, peering over heads, searching for an exit. Near the men's room there was a break in the wall and he made for it, snaking between people. It was a small foyer and in the right-angle walls were two doors with signs on them. One was marked Manager's Office; Dan headed toward the other, which was marked No Admittance, with Marta and the young couple right behind him. As they opened the door they heard shouts behind them, and a quick backward glance showed them that the fight was now in the lower area. Two men were wrestling each other, rolling together on the floor, knocking into people.

Dan pulled at the door in front of him and they felt a sudden blast of cool air. They were in a dim corridor that smelled of dampness and rot. They had to inch their way along because when the door closed behind them, the hall got darker toward the far end.

"I feel fresh air," the young man said behind Marta. "There's gotta be a door out of here somewhere."

As they approached the end it was almost impossible to see. Dan stopped so suddenly that they gasped, piling into his back. "There's a door here," he said. On the right was the faint outline. He pushed at the door but it wouldn't budge. He said over Marta's head to the young man, "Come here next to me. We'll try to shove together." The door was solid metal around the edges. There was a cool draft of air coming under the bottom crack. Marta prayed that they could move it as Dan and the younger man leaned their shoulders against the center and heaved. The door groaned and moved.

"It's an old fire door," the young man said. "It's not locked. But the hinges must be rusty. We gotta push together."

The two of them, grunting and breathing heavily, leaned into the door once more. It creaked and slowly yielded. They managed to pry it open about a foot.

"Can we get through there?" Marta asked. It was dark on the other side. They couldn't tell if they were outdoors or in another part of the building.

Dan reached for her arm again. "That's as much as it will go. Turn sideways and ease through after me," he said. Then he said to the young couple, "Be very quiet.

We don't know where we are. Or who might be out there.''

One by one they squeezed through, and feeling around them realized that they were inside still another corridor. Dan, going first, tripped over something on the ground and fell against the stone wall.

"Dan!" Marta cried. He had let go of her hand. She was frantic as she grabbed for him.

He straightened up and grasped her hand again. "Be very careful. There's debris, wood or something, all over the flooring here. Go slow!"

At that second a black shape scurried out of the darkness and rushed past them toward the iron door that they had come through. The young girl screamed and began to cry. Her boyfriend tried to calm her. "We'll be out soon. Please. It's okay."

Still sobbing, she came behind him. Again Dan tripped, and as he steadied himself something else shot out of the trash on the floor and went past their feet.

"Oh God!" the young girl moaned.

They groped their way forward and into a small hallway. It was lighter than the corridor behind them and it had a window and a door. They could see a streetlight beyond the window, which had no glass but was covered with a metal grille.

"Okay," Dan said to the young man, as he leaned on the door. "Let's try this baby. It has a busted bolt. If we're lucky, we're out!"

The two men pushed together and the heavy old door began to swing open. They pushed through out into an alley that in turn led to a small side street behind the theater. Dan stopped and the others stood beside him under the only streetlamp still working in the whole neighborhood. "We better think before we run," he said.

Marta pointed. "That must be Broad Street," she said. "There's noise coming from that direction and the sky is brighter over there."

The four of them, still keeping close together, followed the narrow alley, past empty houses and boarded-up stores. They shuffled through bottles and bags in the middle of the little street, clattering into old cans, until they reached the corner and were out on Broad. They could see down the block to the front of the theater with mobs still pressing around the entrance. The traffic on Broad had been stopped by people piling into the middle of the street and cars halting to gape at the disturbance. Blue-and-white police cars and wagons were ten deep up and down Broad, their red-and-blue top lights flashing wildly into the night sky. Dodging cars that were stuck and were blowing their horns, the four of them crossed over Broad, then Marta and Dan headed for their parking lot two streets away. The young couple was still with them, following close behind.

The young man, his arm protectively around the girl's shoulders, pointed toward the corner. "I'm parked right on the street. I thought I was lucky to find the spot, but I don't know if we'll be able to get out of here now!"

Dan said, "Get in your car and stay there. The police will clear the street very soon. Lock your doors!" he called over his shoulder as he and Marta ran toward the lot. Because they had arrived late, their car was on an outside lane. Drivers who were blocked were sitting in their parked cars, waiting for others to come and move so they could get out. Dan located the attendant locked inside his little shack and picked up his key, which he had worried about all evening. He sighed out loud with relief when they opened the car door and got in at last.

"I was so afraid to leave that damn key!" he said

between his teeth. "And now I'm not sure we can get out!"

The attendant was gesturing to him from the doorway of his shack. Dan put down his window. The kid called, "Out the back! Out the other way! Don't block the aisle!" He was pointing toward the rear of the lot. Dan pulled around several parked cars up a narrow lane and found the exit, in an L angle leading to one more narrow, dark, dilapidated, semi-inhabited street. Muttering to himself, he drove several blocks down the deserted way until he could see that at the corner Broad was cleared of traffic. Neither of them spoke until they were out on the expressway speeding home.

He was driving fast, like a man who was being chased, and she said, "Take it easy, Dan!"

"Sorry," he mumbled, but he remained hunched over the wheel as if someone were going to try to pry him loose.

Marta stared out the side window, watching the empty hills of the park fly past, cold and bare in the winter night. Shivering, she pushed the heat higher. She knew she should beg his forgiveness. She knew she had been a fool. Still, she huddled silently in the corner of her seat, her heart hanging like a sodden old plant in her chest.

He paid no attention to her all the way home. She accepted his anger, if that was what he was feeling. He was entitled. But when they stopped at their garage and he waited for her to get out before putting away the car, he suddenly reached for her hand. He was grinning. "We made it, baby!"

She sank back on the seat. "Dan." She sighed. "It was awful!" And peering at him through the darkness, trying to see into his eyes. "What a terrible thing to do to you!"

"All over," he said. "Forget it!"

She swung her legs out of the car. "I'll never forget it!" she said. "Never!" As they came up the path toward the front door he suddenly stopped her. He pointed up at the sky. "Look!" he said. There were a series of brilliant streaks flashing right over their heads through the blackness.

"What is it?" She stood with her head thrown back, enthralled by the continuing display.

"Some fireworks, courtesy of nature herself!" he said. "I was going to tell you about this earlier this evening. But we got a little . . . sidetracked."

"What are they, comets?"

"It's called the Quarantid meteor showers. . . . Oh look at that!"

A dozen new flashes ripped through the heavens directly over their heads, small rounded light balls followed by dazzling tails, burning like explosives somewhere out in the atmosphere.

"Where will they go?" she asked softly.

"I don't know. Some of them just burn out . . . some of them fall to earth. Maybe in the Antarctic."

Dan stood behind her, his arms around her, pressing her against him in the damp night air, watching the magic overhead. He leaned down and said in her ear, "I love you. I arranged this for you."

"You are the most clever fellow!" She swung around into his arms. The bulk of their duffle coats got in their way, but his lips were warm on her cold cheeks and his mouth was sweet on hers. She threw her arms up around his neck. She wanted to say, and he wanted to hear, how much better to be alone together and watching these faraway performers than sitting in that terrible theater, watching.

But she didn't say that. She whispered, "What a bother for you to have to cope with me."

"Yes," he said and kissed her again, deeply lingering on her lips. Arm in arm they went into their house.

CHAPTER 13

Summer 1941

THE TIDE OF THE WAR WAS RUNNING AGAINST THE English. There were repeated sinkings of ships transporting materiel to Europe from the U.S. On the island of Crete, the Germans kicked the hell out of the imperial forces, which included Australian and New Zealand brigades. The capture of Crete was strategic for the Germans after their occupation of Greece. It enabled them to secure sea communications in the Aegean and to provide airfields for action against the Middle East and Mediterranean shipping routes. Continual German bombings and intense land fighting on Crete forced the British finally to evacuate toward the end of May. There were more than twenty-seven thousand Allied troops involved in the Crete action. Only fourteen thousand were able to get out. The Germans, trying to keep their own losses quiet, themselves lost fifteen thousand men. It was the largest operation of its kind ever attempted and its scale would never be repeated in any of the campaigns yet to come.

Marta did not see Vince again. She stopped going to

school dances or anywhere that they might meet. Each was consciously and conspicuously avoiding the other. On Sunday nights she had started once more to attend her sorority meetings, accepting the raised eyebrows and smirks as well as she could, trying not to hear the mocking laughter and snide remarks. She had begun to date the boys she had known from Woodlyn before Vincent. Her close girl friends were sympathetic and that attitude offended her more than her older sorors' obvious condescension.

"Oh can it!" she said nastily to Marilyn Kaufman, who had told her how really lousy it was that "the older girls have it in for you!"

"The hell with 'em!" Marta added. "Save yourself the trouble, Marilyn! Don't tell me!"

"Look, Marta," Marilyn retorted, hurt that Marta wouldn't share her problems, "don't blame me! You knew what would happen!"

After that exchange Marta refused to hang around with Marilyn. Doris Molner said, "She's so dumb, she thinks if you're sexy when you pee, you get pregnant! Like a rabbit! Ignore her, Mart!"

"Oh I'll ignore her all right!" Marta bristled and stopped talking to Marilyn altogether.

Until one night when Marilyn called on the phone, her voice thick with tears. "I'm sorry, Marty, I didn't mean to make you mad at me."

"Forget it," Marta said. They remained in the same girl pack but their friendship was never the same. Phyllis Cooper and Doris Molner were treating Marta like someone who has barely recovered from a life-threatening illness. On one hand they showed a silly kind of guarded carefulness, and on the other a hearty, phony camaraderie. The combination quickly got on her nerves.

Bob Goldin asked her out to a movie on a Friday night

in the most beautiful and blooming spring anyone ever remembered. The lilacs were huge and heavy with fragrance; the azaleas were masses of pink and fuchsia. All up and down the streets of Woodlyn the grass had turned bright green before the holidays and the air was soft with summer's promise. She didn't care one way or the other about Bob Goldin but went out with him anyway. After an indifferent movie and a hamburger at the Hot·Shoppe, he brought her home and proceeded to try everything he knew with her on the living-room couch. She couldn't stop his crazy wandering hands and had to dig her nails into his wrists to get his grip off her bare thigh. She was black and blue for days with his fingerprints tattooed on her soft, pale flesh. When she pushed him out the front door, he snarled, "Too bad I don't smell of garlic like a wop. I know that's what gets you hot, baby!" She slammed the door so hard that her mother, who never got up at night to check on her, came to the top of the stairs to see what had happened.

She spent most of her time studying and her marks began to pick up again. But there was no joy in it for her. She knew that she had changed. There was a calculated objectivity in her conquering of difficult subjects now. She was using the best part of her brain and none of her emotions. Her feelings were locked away. They went deeper and deeper underground, and even in the sanctuary of her bedroom, she kept busy, fixing, checking, reading, exercising. She never thought about falling in love again. It was off limits for her even as a dream. There was no more idle lounging on her bed, the radio softly accompanying her swinging, tender feelings with the latest number from the hit parade. Action was the key and she never stopped moving.

One day a small vulnerable spot opened and was exposed before she could defend herself. She had walked in late from school, having been detained at the *Hillcrest Lit.*, going over the proofs for the graduation issue. Steven had gotten home before her and was fully absorbed at the piano. The music was instantly familiar. He was playing the song he had written, and it brought back, with an unbidden rush of feeling, the first day Vince had come to her house and had worked on the song with Steven. The beating of her heart seemed to come to a halt. The pain hit her hard in the middle of her chest, and she wondered for a second if she were going to die. And then her pulses began again, pumping so wildly that her breath came in rapid harsh bursts and she had to sit down on the steps. She tried not to listen but the music was too magnetic. Steven had worked on it, lengthening the line of the melody, shifting the key in the middle, incorporating all of Vince's suggestions.

Pushing herself to her feet, Marta dragged upstairs and closed her door to shut out the song as Steven began to play it through once more. But the music penetrated. It entered where all other feelings had been locked out.

From then on, whenever Steven went near the piano, she beat it fast. She had put herself on a rigid, fast-paced schedule, entering again into all the school activities with energy and a grim determination to excel. The orchestra was playing difficult music; and fighting her way from the back, she fiddled in competition with three other second violins and moved up close to the first-chair people. With her mind riveted on the notes, she tried to get a purer intonation and to develop her technique beyond the point where it had languished for so long. She was even practicing alone in her room at night now when her other work was finished. There was no more family learning hour around the dining-room table. Nobody said anything. They all accepted that it was part of the past. Even Steven did his homework in his room, although, unlike Marta, he never touched his fiddle at home. The orchestra in the high school was preparing music for the graduation and there were rehearsals almost every day. Finally there was an announcement that the orchestra would practice one afternoon after school with the senior class as they marched down the aisle and then marched back out. With the music from *Aida* on her stand, Marta practiced at home. She was determined not to lift her eyes from the pit when Vince walked in, and not to pay any attention when he walked out up the auditorium aisle.

But there were circumstances she hadn't foreseen. One afternoon the orchestra was having difficulty with the marching rhythm and the seniors were not coming in quickly enough. They all practiced over and over until the teachers told them to take a break and be back in ten minutes for another go. The seniors went whooping out of the auditorium with the usual noise and horseplay. Nobody tried to stop them. It was end-of-the-term entitlement time and the faculty was indulgent. The seniors stood around in the hall, kidding, laughing, hilarious with their new freedom, reveling in the hiatus between graduation and the next step, whatever it was to be. The students in the orchestra quietly, a little wearily, left their instruments and came out in the hall after them. Marta, whose back was stiff from sitting and playing for such a protracted period, stood next to one of the kids who played the cello, and stretched herself, trying to work out the kinks. Suddenly she looked up and saw Vincent with a group of his friends who were laughing and joking loudly. Marie DiVito was right next to him, her arm linked possessively through his, while Mike Conti and Dominic Perrina were saying something that made Marie rock back and forth, laughing gaily up into Vince's face. Marta stared. Vince glanced up and in that second their eyes meshed. Marta said to the guy next to her, "See you back inside," and escaped into the bathroom.

There were two girls primping at the blurry old mirror over the battered sinks. They gave her a quick eye-sliding once-over as she walked in. She took one look at them and hurriedly went into a toilet booth. She recognized them; one of them was Alice DiVito, Marie's younger sister. They were both in her class although they never acknowledged one another. Occasionally Marta had wondered during the preceding term what would happen if she were stuck on a desert island by herself and some of these kids from her class stumbled onto her lonely beach. Would they still obey some unwritten social directive and make believe they were total strangers?

Waiting in the smelly little cubicle for Alice DiVito and her girl friend to leave the bathroom, Marta heard one of them say in a loud, distinct voice, "Marie is really the most beautiful girl in the senior class. They put it in the senior book!"

The other voice said, "My sister Marie is not only the prettiest but the most popular! Everybody knows it! She had ten invitations to the prom, but the way Vince Fanetti hounded her, she had to accept him!"

Marta flushed the toilet noisily, shuffling around in the cramped space, hoping they would leave. When it was quiet in the bathroom for several seconds she pushed open the booth door, thinking that they must have gone. But the two girls were still there, talking very softly to each other's reflections in the mirror as they reapplied their already-heavy makeup, drawing and redrawing their Lana Turner lips, rouging their cheeks, and smoothing violet-blue eyeshadow on their lids.

Marta rinsed her hands, trying not to look into their faces in the mirror. The girl friend said, "Oh, I know Vince has always been crazy about Marie!"

Alice DiVito walked around Marta, reaching for a paper towel. "Gad, how that guy hung around our house!" She tossed the crumpled paper on the floor near Marta's feet. "You know, when they first got to Hillcrest High they were together all the time. Now he's going to City U. and believe it or not he's already invited Marie to his freshman hop!"

"Boy, he really must go for her!" answered the other girl.

Marta let the door swing shut with a snap as she went out into the hall. Head down, she hurried back into the auditorium and took her seat with the orchestra in front of the stage. She tuned her violin, trying to quiet the tumult inside herself. Her hands busy, her eyes riveted on the music in front of her, she ignored the seniors who had resumed their trek down the aisle. She was trying to concentrate but her mind wandered as the music, which had become easy and mechanical for her, rang out the triumphal march. Her problem was, as it always had been, to reconcile all the separate conflicts she was going through. As she bowed in cadence with the other violins, she mused on her father's belief that the difference between right and wrong was obvious, apparent, and entirely related to the truth. As if the truth were permanently situated like a mailbox at the corner and events presented themselves like letters. No problem if they were correctly addressed and stamped. Maybe that was how it was for her father. But for her the effort had become strange and quixotic. Her parents couldn't understand why certain emotions would not fit into the nice little envelopes they had supplied for her. She didn't know why either. It was her burden to have discovered, or created, or imposed those emotions on herself.

Among her friends she seemed to be the only one who had difficulty locating the truth. All the others marched toward it like the seniors headed down the aisle, each to his assigned place. The notion had grown in her mind all during the past year that the truth was a shifting, ephemeral shape out in undefined space, not some point fixed for all time in clean, safe, pretty Woodlyn.

The rehearsal finally came to an end. The seniors and the musicians got up, stretching, and left. She carefully covered her violin, placing it back in its case. Now, for the first time in an hour, she glanced around the emptied auditorium, staring for a few seconds at the section where he had been sitting. He had made no effort to talk to her. Marta-Portia-know-it-all had been properly ignored. She could almost feel the presence of her parents right behind her as she trudged out of the hall, loaded with her books and her instrument, her papers and her music. Mother and father were guiding her, leaning lightly on her back, indicating the correct direction. But she still wasn't sure where she was going.

She carried her things to the school's Woodlyn exit and out of habit glanced first through the little windows to see if he was waiting for her. But the sidewalk in front of the school was empty. Her shoulders and spine still felt stiff as she pushed open the doors, and she knew that she had been holding herself together all afternoon, tight, straight, hardly breathing. Had she been afraid that he would come to her? Or that he would ignore her, as he had?

Dragging home slowly, she could feel his gaze on her, his strong body striding beside her, his big hand holding hers. With no center and no core, she thought she might be beginning to unravel. Eyes cast down on the endless walk across the bridge, she never noticed the blooming, bright afternoon all around her.

On June 23 the headlines in the *Philadelphia Inquirer* were banners two inches high streaming across the face of the front page: HITLER INVADES SOVIET UNION.

At dinner around the kitchen table, Dr. Resnick said, "How fitting! June 23rd was the date of Napoleon's invasion of Russia!"

Steven said, "Gee, they say the Russians aren't prepared, Pop."

Dr. Resnick shrugged. "They're a stubborn people," he said. "And this will at least give the British a chance to breathe."

"It's good for us, Dad," Marta said. "I mean it has to be better to have them as allies than as enemies."

Her father gave her a long look. "Yes," he said. "That's the truth."

Steven was biting on a lamb chop bone. "I don't know," he said. "They almost got beat in Finland."

Dr. Resnick sighed and Mrs. Resnick said, "It's going to be a beautiful summer. Do you all mind if I start enjoying it?"

Dr. Resnick patted her plump shoulder and Steven shut up.

At Hillcrest High the whole week had been taken up with graduation activities, culminating in the senior prom on Saturday night. Marta stuck close to the house, reading, talking to her girl friends on the phone, and trying to decide whether to accompany Aunts Molly and Min to the seashore for the summer. They had rented a little house on the bay in Ramsgate for July and August. She had spent many seashore summers with them, happy, free, idle times that always came back to her in winter as gauzy, golden, magic hours. She told them she would think about it for the coming months. Her father was urging her to go.

"But I thought I'd get a job, Daddy," she said.

He gestured broadly, hands waving no. "You go to the shore. You'll enjoy it."

"Oh, I always enjoy it!" And she decided to spend one more lazy summer lolling on the beach, swimming in the hard-moving Jersey surf, and doing exactly what she wanted to all day long. Dr. Resnick further sanctified the arrangement by adding, "The aunts love to have you, Marta. It's good for them to have company."

The two maiden aunts, Dr. Resnick's only relatives, who spent their busy year teaching elementary school, made it apparent that they enjoyed having their niece and nephew with them. They treated Marta as one of their grown-up intellectual friends, including her, if she wanted, in their evenings out, spending time with her discussing books and music and politics, and taking long walks in the salt air, with Aunt Min in her charming light soprano voice marking time for them with arias from operas and songs out of their childhood. Many a memory would center forever for Marta and Steve on the melodies of "Juanita," or the "Pilgrim's Chorus from Tannhauser," with Aunt Moll and Marta supplying harmony and Steven doing rhythm oom-pah-pahs for them as accompaniment.

She was free to join them, free to be alone, or free to be with her friends. They had never asked her any questions; they made no demands. They tolerated, better than her parents, her protracted periods of lazy thoughtfulness, and asked for no accounting of her time away from home. Those summers with the aunts had always been a special kind of paradise. The two elderly ladies treated Steven

308

exactly the same way, and he adored them just as Marta did. He spent his time zipping around on his bicycle with a pack of local kids, watching and imitating the lifeguards on the beach, endlessly swimming, diving, and playing touch football or basketball long into the evenings after the sun had dipped down beyond the bay.

The first hint that Marta had that her mother and father had given the aunts some particular information, and perhaps special directions about her summer, came one Sunday afternoon in early June when the family was together at the aunts' house for dinner. Aunt Moll, not quite looking at her, said, "Marta darling, you must invite some of your good friends to visit this summer at the shore. We have some interesting things planned and we hope you'll do them with us. We . . ." She rambled on for another few minutes while Marta stared at her in surprise. Right before her eyes, Aunt Moll turned a bright pink. Mrs. Resnick and Aunt Min quickly joined in to change the subject. The remarks themselves had been innocuous, but Aunt Molly's constraint and embarrassment put Marta on guard. Saying nothing more, she resolved to think long and hard about the summer before going away. A job would keep her busy and out of the house and would avoid all the painful possibilities of empty time.

At home the next day while she was helping her mother camphor the winter clothes, get ready to change the rugs, and put on the slipcovers, the yearly summer ritual, her mother began to talk about the summer once more. "You'll probably need a new bathing suit," she said.

Marta answered shortly, "I'm still thinking about it. I still might stay home and work."

Her mother said softly, "Suit yourself. The aunts will be disappointed, but I'm sure they'll understand."

Marta and Doris made a trip into the center of the city,

stopping in various shops to see if there were any summer sales jobs for them. They left their names and on the way home Marta said, "I'm pretty sure we'll get something."

Doris looked at her wryly. "Do you really want to do it?"

Marta shrugged. "Are your parents taking those rooms in Brighton again?"

The Molners always stayed at the same old wooden boardinghouse every summer, with its wide rocker-filled verandas, and the perpetual smell of chicken soup cooking somewhere deep within the building.

"Well, I think so."

It was left there. All the unasked questions about who could afford what and whether jobs were a real necessity for these young women who loved clothes, makeup, and fripperies—all allusions to economic problems—were deliberately avoided.

In the end, both girls went to the seashore. The aunts were overjoyed and made a marked effort to stay out of Marta's affairs. Her suspicions about being watched subsided as the old summer routine with its simple pleasures began to take over.

Some days the war came closer. On the beach she ran into three guys who had just graduated from Hillcrest High, and one of them said he had enlisted in the Merchant Marine. He had never been a very good student, and Marta wasn't surprised that he had decided not to go on to college. But when both of the other boys talked about being drafted and wondered how much college they were likely to get in first, whether or not in fact it was even worth the effort, Marta felt the conflict in Europe beginning to loom over them.

One evening she met Doris and Phyllis uptown for a walk on the boards, and as they wandered giggling and gawking, they met several French sailors. Their ship had just docked and they were girl-hungry and ready for adventure. They pursued the girls down the boardwalk, laughing and trying to pick them up, using pidgin English and hand signs. Only Phyllis had studied French, and she wasn't good enough to get a real conversation going. But the girls were sufficiently intrigued to stop, stand against the rail, and try to communicate in the universal language of youth.

"So where are you from?" Marta asked one little guy with bright blue eyes whose pom-pom beret was tilted jauntily. He seemed to know more English than the others.

"Eh?" he said, and then when Phyllis said, *"Votre maison, votre ville?"* he grinned and said, "Toulouse." He then rattled off something that Phyllis missed. She made him repeat it and finally she said, "He says, I think, that he hasn't been home in over a year. . . . *Un an? Oui? Pas a la maison . . . oui?"*

And he nodded sadly. The sailors all shook their heads, their faces turning serious.

Marta asked, "Why did France fall?"

The short boy chewed his lips for a second, nodding to show he understood. He raised his eyebrows and gave a typical Gallic shrug. *"Qui sait?"* And then said in his halting English, "Don't know."

His buddy, who had been listening over his shoulder, said to Marta, *"La politique,"* and then added, "Soon Amerique in war!"

"Oh no!" cried Doris.

"Ah yess! Yess!" the sailors said in unison.

But they were all too lighthearted to stay sober and sad for very long. The night was warm and filled with laughing people and fireflies, and the stars were shining out over the inky sea. The sailors kept trying to make dates for the evening with the girls. "You come. You come weet us!"

Doris said to Marta, "You wanna?"

"No, I don't," Marta answered softly.

Doris whispered in Phyllis's ear, "Tell 'em so long and good luck."

Phyllis, whose vocabulary fortunately included farewells, was eager to escape the strain of her role as translator. *'Au revoir et bonne chance!''* she said.

The sailors protested and tried to hold them back but the three girls took off, hurrying away down the crowded, brightly lit boardwalk. When they finally slowed to a stroll, Marta looked around, struck with a sudden prescience. "This may be the last summer . . . like this . . ." she said softly.

"Oh come on!" answered Doris. "Don't be such a lousy, sour lemon!"

The aunts had a small Emerson radio that stood on a battered cabinet in the little living room of the cottage, and they all listened to the news twice a day, first thing in the morning and then in the evening after dinner. The situation on the Russian front seemed to be worsening as July wore on, but the seashore season was going full blast. The beach was loaded every weekend with kids and families and ice-cream men; the hot-dog stands were bursting with hungry, thirsty people; the skies over the Atlantic were hot blue and filled with puff-ball clouds; the sand was so sizzly that Marta had to run like a hop-toad over it to keep from burning the soles of her feet. It was a clear, rainless summer, and all over the golden beach carefree souls were playing, tossing balls or quoits, reading, with their feet stretched out into the water, talking, kidding, eating lunches and popsicles, while little kids made drip castles and big kids made time with girls in tight bathing suits and sun-bleached hair.

One evening Steven and Marta were seated at the table in the cramped dining room, having dinner with the aunts. The windows overlooking the bay were wide open, and the evening breeze had come up off the water to cool the hot interior of the stuffy little house. Aunt Moll said, "According to today's paper, the Germans are terribly close to Moscow."

"Do you think it's accurate?" asked Marta.

Aunt Min said, "They censor everything. It's probably much worse. I met our friend Rafe Hyman in the market this morning, and he said that General Budenny's defenses in front of the city of Kiev have been broken through. He heard it at a union meeting up in the city this week." Both worried ladies shook their gray heads in unison.

Steven had his mouth full of food and while chewing he said, "At least it's giving the British some time to pull themselves together."

Aunt Moll didn't agree. "According to Lowell Thomas last night, the bombing has gone right on!"

"And there's still talk that the Germans will cross the Channel this summer," added Aunt Min.

"Churchill wants us to come in," Aunt Moll said softly. "That's what he talks to Roosevelt about all the time."

"I don't think Roosevelt dares," answered Aunt Min. "There's still such strong sentiment against going to war."

Aunt Moll sighed. "Ohhh. God help us all!" She piled Steven's plate high once more with mashed potatoes and meat loaf.

The bad news that continued to come in over the Emerson, or via the aunts concerned, intellectual friends, or from reading *The Evening Bulletin*, most of the time could be folded up, clicked off, set aside. Marta's preoccupation with her own feelings was stronger than any news, good or bad. For the first time since she and Vince had said goodbye, there were long stretches of empty time filled with thinking and remembering. She had taken to getting up very early in the morning and wandering along the bayfront, watching the sun glint and glitter on the smooth water, or on gray days observing the fog rolling in damp and briny. Fair or gloomy, her desire for him went on unabated. She had stopped crying. She would take a lungful of sweet wet air and dash as fast as she could along the bankheads of the bay, watching the gulls wheel and dip for food, their screams ripping the quiet air as they skimmed the surface. The wailing of the birds echoed the unuttered sounds inside her. She thought she saw him walking toward her every now and then, tall and straight, and she wondered when the space that held his face and his presence would fill up with someone else.

Doris and Phyllis fell in love with someone new every other week. They all dated, but Marta seemed removed from the boys she went out with. She couldn't stand the thought of any of them touching her, even holding her arm. She went along on the dates, but Phyllis told Doris, who repeated it to Marta, that she was acting like a "wet blanket."

"Okay. Count me out then," Marta said to Doris the next time a sixsome came up for them all to go dancing at Steel Pier.

Doris shook her head. "I'm not gonna go without you. I know these guys are nothin', but what the hay, Mart! It's better than wandering around on the boardwalk again tonight. Maybe we'll meet somebody exciting there."

Doris and Phyllis continued to meet "exciting some-bodies," but to Marta they were blank faces with empty eyes.

Some days she thought she was recovering. She woke up feeling happy and well, full of energy and hungry for breakfast. But as the day wore on, her euphoria would die out, and by evening her resolve to get out and have fun would disappear. The aunts had returned to their former technique of laissez-faire; and as the summer slowly passed, she spent more and more time with them, reading, dozing on a beach chair out on the little front patio, or practicing her violin. She went out with their friends for casual suppers and sat quietly in their houses with the aunts while books, art, and the war, always the war, were endlessly discussed.

In the middle of August, with only three weeks before the season ended at Labor Day and all the summer people headed back to the city, she decided to shop for a few new fall things uptown on the boardwalk. School resumed in the middle of September and the shops were filled with plaid skirts and tweed jackets, bright sweaters and shirts. Her mother had given her money one Sunday when the Resnicks had come down for the weekend. They were not fond of the seashore, and Marta always sensed that her mother was eager to get back home.

On the day she picked to go shopping, Marta was halfway out of the little cottage after lunch when Aunt Moll handed her an envelope. "A little extra to get something pretty, dear."

Thinking about the generosity of her family, who spent very little on themselves, she tried to enjoy the bright afternoon as she walked to the car line and hopped on an open trolley. As the rickety car rocked its way up Atlantic Avenue, she caught glimpses of the beach with its colored umbrellas and the ocean, green and rough beyond. When she got uptown on the wide boardwalk, foreign flags were fluttering and snapping in the fresh breeze from the tops of the light poles, and people dressed in their summer finery were strolling leisurely along. Marta selected the shops that had the most colorful displays in their windows, some of them in the huge and elegant beachfront hotels. She wandered in and out comparing prices, examining the quality of the wools, trying things on, pleased with her slim, brown reflection in the fitting-room mirrors. She finally bought herself a new skirt, a sweater, and two shirts. Loaded with her packages, she thought about going quickly back now on the trolley to take a late-afternoon dip. She loved the beach as the light turned coppery and the crowds dispersed.

Instead she decided to walk on down the boardwalk watching the people, enjoying the warm winds that tossed her hair and flapped at her skirt. As she approached Convention Hall, she saw that the small spaghetti parlors all around were doing a thriving business. They had open-front stands where people could come up from the beach and eat outside in their bathing suits. A bunch of dark-haired little kids ran up with sandy feet, their hands clutching nickles and dimes, excited about buying water-ice. Crowding in at the stands that were decorated with oversized illustrations of Italian hoagies and subs, the children waved their hands for attention. Right after them came a grandmother and two mothers warning, "Watch out for splinters!" "Hold on to your money!" "Just buy water-ice!"

Going past the luncheonettes, one by one, Marta suddenly spied straight ahead of her, in front of another little place with an open counter, a group of guys in bathing suits, their hair still wet and plastered down from their last swim. They were drinking soda from cans and eating big sandwiches. She was sure it was a group from Hillcrest High and her heart began to pound. Her first impulse was to turn and go back up the boardwalk, but she kept on walking, trying to keep her eyes straight in front. She heard a voice call, "Hey there, Mart! 'Zat you, Marta Resnick?"

When she glanced in the direction of the voice she saw instantly that Vincent was not in the group. She walked over to them. Nick Genardo said, "Wow, whatta tan! You been here all summer?"

She made small talk with them for several minutes, all of them avoiding any reference to Vincent. "Hey, you doin' any singin'?" asked Dom Perrina, the clarinet player from Vince's band.

She shook her head. "Just relaxing down in Ramsgate."

"Where's that?"

She stared at him to see if he was kidding. Then she realized they probably only knew these three or four blocks of the city. She often wondered why the Italian families all seemed to cluster on these few beaches. There was a small, contained Irish section as well. And when you walked down the few streets, you passed taprooms with names like O'Shaughnessy, and Paddy's Tavern, where the ripe smell of beer bloomed out onto the sidewalk from the propped-open doors. These people, too, apparently never spread beyond the rooming houses, apartments, and beaches of their immediate area. All the circles were magically, invisibly demarcated.

One of the guys answered Dom's question. "Ramsgate is where that big elephant is, right?"

"Yes," she said. "Sort of. It's in Seaport. We stay not too far from there."

Laughing and joking, tossing away their soda cans and napkins, the group began gradually to move toward the steps to the beach. "So, you gonna be around for the next couple of weekends?" Dominic Perrina asked her.

She felt her throat begin to tighten, unsure where his question would lead. "Well, I guess so. I don't know. I may go home sooner."

As the others waved so long and went flying and jostling down the steps, Dominic looked at Marta directly. "Vince gets down weekends," he said.

She had known in advance that the name was coming but still couldn't stop the flare of heat in her face as the blush spread up her neck and jaw. She turned her head away. "Oh yeah?"

"Dr. DiBuono took a place for Vince's grandmother and he and Vince both come down on Friday nights."

"Who?"

"You know. His uncle, the family hero!" Dom laughed out loud.

"I don't know him," she said.

"Michael DiBuono, Mrs. Fanetti's youngest brother. The professor, they call him. He's a stomach doctor."

She didn't answer. She knew she should say goodbye, but instead she stood rooted to the hot boardwalk, leaning against the railing, staring out at the bobbing heads in the indigo sea, and hoping Dom would tell her more.

"Vince is at school full-time. The whole goddamned summer!"

She nodded but still had no answer.

"He wants to get in as much college as he can before the army gets him."

"Yes." She gestured vaguely. "It's going to be a problem for everybody."

"Not for me!" Dom laughed. "I got a job in a band. Not as good as Vince's, but anyway it's a job!"

"Oh, have you?" she asked. "Where are you playing?"

"Back at Nino's. You know, where we all performed together. Vince had to break up the band after graduation.

He's got no time now. In the fall he's supposed to play ball for this scholarship. But you knew that.''

She sighed. "Sure . . . well . . ."

He had more to tell her. "And now he wants to be a doctor like Uncle Michael."

"What?" She turned and stared Dominic Perrina in the eye for the first time, to see if he was telling the truth. "How do you know that?"

Dom shrugged. "It's all he talks about, Vince! And Dr. DiBuono is helping. So Vince says. I don't know. With his talent for playing and writing music, what a waste!"

"I gotta get going," she said at last. "Be seeing you, Dom. Good luck!"

He touched her arm as she turned to leave. "Hey, Mart, you want me to tell Vince your address? You know, down in Ramsgate."

She smiled weakly but didn't hesitate. "I don't think so. Thanks anyway, Dom."

"Well . . . maybe we'll see you on the beach this weekend."

"Well . . . maybe . . . I don't usually come up this far . . . to this beach."

"So maybe we'll walk down. You know, just amble down on the beach on Saturday. Anyway, I'll mention it to Vince. . . ."

"I have to go now. So long, Dom." She ran down the ramp that led from the boardwalk at the next street and hopped a trolley on Atlantic. Her heart continued to race all the way home, but not from the jog to the trolley car. Vince could locate her now if he wanted to. Even though he didn't know exactly where she was, he could see her during the weekend . . . if he wanted. She could have told Dominic exactly where she would be. But it was better that she didn't. Whatever happened would happen without too much planning from her.

Nevertheless, when she went for a walk on the boards in Brighton with the aunts Friday evening, she found herself searching the heavens to see if the clouds that had been threatening rain all day would blow away and leave a clear and sunny Saturday, a beach day . . . a day for long walks along the water's edge . . . up the beach, down the beach.

"Feels like rain again," said Aunt Moll. "But you never know. The wind may whisk it away by tomorrow."

And by early morning when Marta woke, the hot sun was pouring in her bedroom window. She glanced out at the bay and it was calm, reflecting the summer sky, high, wide, and almost a September blue. Doris called her just as she was finishing breakfast. "What time are you walking up the beach today? I'll meet you."

Marta answered slowly, deliberately. "No, I can't," she lied. "I think my parents are coming down. I'm going to hang around."

"Should I come down there? To your beach?"

"Well . . . I may not get on the beach today, Dor."

"Gad! It's gonna be a scorcher, Mart! This is a big vacation week coming up."

"I'll call you later," she said. "If you don't hear from me, just go ahead and I'll call you when I can."

Marta puttered around the cottage all morning, helping the aunts straighten, vacuum, and put away the groceries brought back from the market by Aunt Min, who made her trip up to the avenue with her shopping cart three times a week.

After lunch Marta got into her best red bathing suit and tied a white shirt around her middle. She brushed her hair, which was streaked and yellow from the weeks of sunbathing and swimming, and put on lipstick and eyeshadow. She never allowed herself to think about where she was going or what she would do. She was moving like a person following a script, making believe it was all spontaneous.

At two o'clock she was walking slowly up the beach toward Selsey, near the water's edge, stepping over little children who played in puddles, ducking footballs, base-balls, and beachballs that flew through the air like hail-stones until the lifeguards spotted the throwers and stopped them.

Behind her dark glasses, Marta's eyes combed the beach and the people coming and going. Everybody walked in the shallow water or on the hard sand where the little wavelets slapped at the clam-strewn shore. She saw dozens of kids she knew from school, and she lingered to chat, but her glance was never still for a second. She had decided to walk most of the way up to the center of town, telling herself it was great for the figure and that the jog back would take a fraction of the time; not giving full conscious voice to the nagging, who're-you-kiddin'-Marta-Portia? Because if once she had framed the words, You're out here looking for him, she would have turned around and located Phyllis and Doris and skipped it.

But she never had to frame the words because she saw him coming in her direction. And this time she knew it wasn't some trick of the sun, or her imagination, or her willful optic nerves, but that he was walking toward her at a purposeful gait, long-striding, bare-chested, in a pair of navy trunks that had a college emblem on them. Even at the distance she knew every detail, because her mind supplied what her eyes couldn't see. His eyes were roaming the beach and ocean as hers had done. A second later he saw her. They met with water burbling around their ankles and the sun in their faces, neither smiling, both accepting the fact that each had been looking for the other.

"Hi, Vince..." Her voice sounded fuzzy in her own ears.

"This can't be your beach."

And she smiled, knowing how he had rehearsed a dozen greetings and wound up saying the first silly thing that came to mind. "No," she said and pointed toward Seaport. "That way."

"Let's sit down," he said.

"It's terribly hot."

"There must be someplace. . . ."

"Up there . . . if we can find a spot under the boardwalk . . . near the street."

He didn't make a joke out of the under-the-boardwalk bit as he might have done months before, but moving with her through the crowd spread all over the hot beach, they found a place, shaded by the boards overhead. "Take the glasses off," he ordered as they sat down together.

She stuck the sunglasses up on her head. "How you doin'?" she asked and added quickly, "at City?"

He shrugged. "All right."

"So what's this stuff with Uncle Michael?"

He started to laugh and stretched out on his back beside her, his head resting on his folded arms. "You certainly picked up a lot of information quick. Leave it to Perrina!"

"Looks like you listened to him too."

"You paid attention! You didn't miss a trick!"

"Wanta fight, Fanetti?" She got to her knees, brushing the sand from her legs. "Because I don't." She started to get to her feet.

He reached up and easily pulled her back down. He rolled over on his stomach, still holding her arm, dragging her down beside him. "Come here," he said softly.

Without looking around to see who was snooping, not caring, she felt his big arm across her back and his hand gripping her arm. She stretched out beside him, her face close to his, her hair hanging in the sand. He pulled her tightly against him. "I missed you."

"Yes," she said. "I know."

His mouth was on her cheek. "You've changed your mind." It was not a question.

"About what?"

"Us. Everything."

She pulled away from him and sat up again. "Oh, Vince." She sighed. "Not a thing has changed for me. My family would have conniptions if they knew I was seeing you."

"What do they think? I'm some fuckin' mafia member? What the hell have they got against me?" He sat up beside her, jamming his fist again and again into a hole left by some little kid's shovel.

"It's nothing personal," she said, and it sounded so stupid that she started to laugh.

"I'm glad you think it's funny." His face was cold.

"It's dumb." She sighed. "The whole business is nonsense." She stretched out her slender legs. They were bronzed from the sun, long and firm with tiny golden hairs glinting on her thighs. His hand moved slowly toward her and she didn't stop him. He tenderly caressed the smooth skin at the top of her inner leg, and her breathing quickened and goose bumps began to pop out all over. But she put her hand over his, took it from near her crotch, where it was headed, holding it, pressing her palm into his.

"Time will help everything," she said softly, leaning against him, smelling the sun-heated sweat on his chest, rubbing her cheek against his shoulder. "Please try to be patient with me. I'm doing my best."

He took her chin with his other hand and turned her head so that their eyes were inches apart. "I know you are. I'm an impatient guy. Especially where things don't add up.'' He kissed her lips. She bit him.

''You took Marie DiVito to the prom,'' she hissed.

''That hurt, you little cur!'' He pushed her down flat on her back and held her arms, leaning over her.

''You couldn't wait to take out somebody else, could you, Fanetti?''

''Don't big-shot me, Miss Woodlyn Princess,'' he said, grinning, his teeth white and even in his suntanned face, close over her face. ''You've been dating regularly . . . I know all about it!''

''You don't know anything,'' she said, wrinkling her nose, laughing up at him.

''You better behave!'' He started to climb onto her, and she squealed, ''Vincent, for Christ's sake. We'll get arrested.''

''If they put us in the same cell, I don't care,'' he said.

''God! You're impulsive. That's what scares me.''

He let her go and she sat up.

''Everything scares you,'' he said.

She shrugged. ''You wouldn't try to change the color of my eyes, would you?''

''The color of your eyes suits me,'' he said. ''Your fears I don't like.''

''No,'' she said slowly. ''I don't either.'' She turned and looked at him earnestly. ''But I can't change them. You must accept me as I am. I accept you.'' She stared, squinting out into the hot sun, the beach blindingly white in the glare.

Now he shrugged. ''There's a war coming,'' he said flatly. ''Everything will change. Nothing will ever be the same.''

''Why do you say that?''

He raised his brows and pulled his mouth to one side in a thoughtful grimace. ''It's just something I know. I can feel it. It's going to hit us one day, full force. You want something to be scared of? Consider that!" He turned to her and looked directly into her eyes. "You have to grab at life, Marta. I've been seeing people all around me not taking their shot! And they wind up with empty hands. I don't want that to happen to me!"

"It won't," she said. "You'll get everything you want."

They climbed to their feet and started walking down to the water, the sand hot under their soles. "Nobody ever gets everything he wants," he said soberly. "But you sure as hell have to try!"

Arm in arm, they strolled together at the water's edge toward Ramsgate. They noticed neither the people they passed nor the sea beside them, intent only on themselves and each other. "You still haven't told me about Uncle Michael," Marta said.

"He thinks he can get me into medical school. If I can complete three years of college . . ."

"But how can you . . . ?"

"I'll go summers."

"Playing ball?"

"No. I'm paying my way this summer. If the athletics interfere, I'll let the scholarship go and borrow the money."

She stopped to stare at him. "I don't understand. Why medicine of all things? You're a musician! You're a fabulous musician!"

"That's a hobby," he said.

"Since when?"

He shrugged. "We all change our minds about things. I have a lot of heavy studying to do in the next couple of years . . . assuming that the army will let me!"

When they parted he said, "I'll pick you up tonight. About seven-thirty."

"I better meet you."

His expression remained unaltered, but she could feel his mind rumbling. After a second he said, "You better at least give me your telephone number."

On the way home, swinging down the edge of the beach, now unseeing, uninterested in the people remaining, she thought about what the aunts would have said if Vincent had simply come by for her with no fanfare, and if she had quietly introduced him and then just as quietly left with him. The aunts would have been polite. And embarrassed and upset. It wasn't their problem, after all, to monitor her. But knowing them, in loco parentis as they accepted the role, they would have been devastated! No, she couldn't lay it on them. So the sneaking around had to continue.

The sun was a burning crimson as it got lower on the horizon, but a breeze had come up from the sea. The walk home was a wonder! The glow within her matched the brilliant clear light all around. When she got to the cottage the aunts were in the kitchen fixing dinner. Steven sprawled in the living room with the radio on quietly for a change, and the small rooms were flooded with the rays of the sunset. The water in the bay beyond the open windows was green-gold, and the curtains moved gently in the twilight breeze. Marta was alive with joy. She shut the door of her bedroom and lay on the bed dreaming of the evening ahead.

They met on the boardwalk at Selsey Avenue in front of one of the big, old-fashioned hotels. It was a popular rendezvous with hordes of young people hanging around on both sides of the walk. He was there first, and she spotted him at once in spite of the crowd. He was standing against the railing, lean and sun-dark in his pale summer sport coat. His eyes were full of her as she came toward him. She had worn white because she knew the contrast with her tanned skin, pale hair, and bright makeup would knock him out. He was smiling like a large pleased Cheshire and continued to grin as he kissed her and held her around the shoulders. "You're all . . . lit up!" he said, and she laughed aloud with pleasure. Ambling together, their arms entwined, they were oblivious to the Saturday-night mobs shifting around them, the hawkers of kitchen wares, the weight guessers, the arcade games, and the busy food stands. As usual he did not ask her what she wanted to do, but turning to a side avenue led her off the boardwalk. The street was filled with one bar after the other, noise, laughter, and the smell of beer coming from them all. He finally stopped at a café in the middle of the block, and as he held the door open for her, she heard good jazz, live music inside.

It was dim in the entrance with the usual bar in the front. He seemed to know half the people sitting or standing and drinking there. The musicians up on the small bandstand were all his friends, and he saluted them as they walked to a table. She spotted Buster Mackie on the stand and waved. He motioned back with his sax.

"Well," she said, "you seem to know everybody here!" They sat down at a small table at the side of the dance floor.

"Not everybody," he answered casually.

"You must hang out here a lot."

He shrugged. "Not much."

"You know, Fanetti, you have the silliest way of denying things!"

He reached for her hand. "Let's dance."

"You do come here often," she said again as he held her in his arms. The combo was playing soft and slow. "That Old Feeling." They were doing it jazz style, syncopated with spots of improvisation . . . All it takes is looking

327

at you. Marta and Vince moved together to the music like one person. They didn't want to stop, and they danced one number after the other, not talking, breathing quietly in each other's arms. She lost track of time, and when they were sitting back at their tiny table while the musicians took a break, she was surprised to hear him say, "It's time to go."

"What time is it?"

"Let's go," he said and steered her out. They picked up his Ford, and he headed back down toward Ramsgate. But he passed right through it and went straight for the most deserted stretch of bay in Seaport at the southernmost tip of the island. The only lights were pinpoints across the water coming from other little towns down the coast, and the sharp glitter of the stars and moon overhead. He pulled the car in on the grassy edge and held her close in his arms.

She couldn't resist questioning him again. "You've spent a lot of time locating places here at the shore, haven't you?"

"I've been coming down since I was a kid."

"You never told me."

"I don't tell you everything." His lips on hers stopped her answer.

She pushed him away. "Your buddies all stay put up there! But you've been all over the board, with hundreds of different girls."

"I visit my grandmother! I stay weekends and vacations up there at my grandmother's apartment." He gestured uptown toward the city. "The family always gets her a place for the summer. What difference does it make, Marta? Who cares who was with who?"

"I don't know," she said softly. "I hate being a number in a long series."

He leaned across her and opened the temperamental door. "You have the world's greatest talent for making little things into big things. Come on. Let's get out and look at the moon on the water."

Though the air was warm, it was a fall moon riding the clear sky, full, luminous, cutting a wide spangled swath through the dark still waters of the bay. Every now and then a fish broke the smooth surface, leaping into the air to catch the light in a brief flash and then falling back into the water with a tiny splash.

"Look at them," she whispered. "Jumping for joy!"

"Lots of life going on down there," he said. "A whole other world."

"Let's never go home, Vincent. Let's float around in the ocean and drift around on the beach all day long, and wander around all night. Together. I don't ever want to have to think seriously about anything!"

He walked back to the car and opened the back door.

"Please," she said. "Let's not."

"Get in." And she did. Right up to the minute when he took off her clothes and they made love, she was still softly protesting. And though he ignored her words, his hands were easy and gentle on her. And then her mind clicked off. Only her pulses, her plunging bloodstream, her young body, were wide awake.

When he drove her back to the cottage, she saw that the usual lamp was left on somewhere in the living room. They sat together planning softly what they would do the next day, the next weekend, the next month, parting reluctantly. "It's late," she said at last.

"I'll call you in the morning, early," he said. "I don't want to miss any of the day." He came around and yanked open her door. Holding on to each other, they walked awkwardly up the short, shallow flight of steps. She pushed first at the creaky screen door and then opened the glass front door that was as always unlocked. They were standing in the semidarkness of the narrow front porch when she suddenly saw Aunt Molly in the doorway to the living room, the lamplight outlining her small figure. She was fully dressed.

"Marta?"

"Oh, Aunt Moll. I didn't know you were there! This is . . . Vince."

She couldn't make out Aunt Molly's features, but she knew that her aunt was very disturbed. Gently pushing Vincent back toward the door, she said softly, "Good night. Talk to you in the morning," and clicked the front door shut, turning the lock. Surprisingly, Aunt Molly came forward and put her arm tenderly around Marta's shoulders, walking her into the living room. There on the couch sat Aunt Min, her feet up, her head back, resting but not asleep. Something was happening! Marta knew it at once. "What is it?" Her nerves were alerted, sensing trouble.

Aunt Min stirred and sighed. "Oh, thank God you're back!"

And then Marta realized that Aunt Molly was crying silently, the tears large and regular as they coursed down her wrinkled face. "It's your father, Marta. It's Aaron. He's very sick!"

"Sick? What do you mean? What happened? How do you know?"

"Your mother called," answered Aunt Min. "She took Aaron to the hospital."

"But what is it?"

"Lilly says it's his heart." Aunt Min's mouth was shaking and Marta stared fascinated at the pale lips trembling out of control. Aunt Molly was sobbing noisily now. "He's very low. It was a massive attack!"

"Oh!" Marta stood in the dimly lit little room, staring wildly around. While she was out there ... her poor father ... while she was ... "We gotta go back to the city, Aunt Min! I want to go now!"

Aunt Min got wearily to her feet. "There's a train at seven in the morning. Nothing until then. We have to wait. We've already ordered a cab to pick us up at six-fifteen."

Aunt Molly was hanging on to Marta's hand. "Just stay dressed, dear. And lie down and try to sleep a little, if you can. It's two-thirty now. ... We'll call you when it's time."

"Where's Steven?" Marta suddenly wanted her brother and started toward his room. Aunt Min stopped her. "Oh honey, I think you should let him sleep! He was exhausted. He took your mother's first call and was very agitated. But it was already too late to make a train up to Philadelphia."

Aunt Moll was trying to control her sobs. "She ... called twice, poor Lilly; the first time, when they got to the hospital sometime after twelve. And then later when he took a turn for the worse ..." She couldn't finish.

Aunt Min said, "She just wanted to talk to us ... to Steven. ..."

Aunt Moll said, "She knows we'll be there as soon as we can."

Marta stared blindly at her aunts. There was nothing else to say. Her mother had wanted to talk to her and she hadn't been available. She was slopping it up in the back of his old Ford, mindless, wallowing. She turned away, toward her small bedroom behind the kitchen. She could feel her shoulders sagging and she thought she would fall asleep instantly. But she lay there on the narrow bed in the darkness, numb, eyes half-shut, until finally they called to her that the cab was waiting.

*   *   *

The trip to the city was a blur. Things, scenes, people rushed past. Afterward she remembered flashes and not much else. She sat curled next to Steven, who was pale under his suntan, his lips almost blue. They were silent, rocking on the beat-up old train, the windows open to the warm morning wind, the soot whirling in on the sills and gathering on their hands and clothes. Her white dress was wrinkled and had turned gray. She couldn't, in retrospect, fix the morning's chronology, but somehow they got to Philadelphia, found a cab, and went to the hospital where Mrs. Resnick was waiting on a bench in the hall outside the sickroom. The minute they saw her, despite her strained, blanched face, they knew things were better. "It's hopeful," she managed to say as they fell into one another's arms. All afternoon they sat together like a small frightened tribe under attack, Steven holding his mother's right hand and Marta her left, while the sisters-in-law pressed as close as they could, chairs pulled up facing, knees touching, all needing contact and comfort.

At three in the afternoon the cardiologist came out of the sickroom as they were all dozing again on the hall bench and told them that Dr. Resnick was out of immediate danger. They were permitted in to see him in two groups. Marta and Steven and Mrs. Resnick went first and stayed just a few minutes, kissing his hands as he opened leaden lids under the oxygen tent. He tried a feeble smile.

When they came out, Mrs. Resnick motioned to Aunt Min. "Go ahead. He's awake."

"Try not to cry, Aunt," said Steven to Aunt Molly, whose face was swollen and red.

"Yes, yes," said the old lady, stiffening her back, and balling her wet handkerchief into her palm. She took Aunt Min's arm and together the two sisters went in for the brief visit with their brother.

*   *   *

All summer long, three German armies had relentlessly pushed the Russian offensive, searching out weaknesses in the Soviet defense. The attacks turned not on infantry masses but on armed forces. The Germans hoped to obliterate the Russian armies holding out at the Dnieper, and from there to have a clear path forward into the heart of Soviet territory. The Russians fought back stubbornly, outsupplied and outmaneuvered though they were. In July the Germans crossed the Dnieper and reached the city of Smolensk. It was a German victory all the way. Large parts of the Russian army were trapped, and more than six hundred thousand prisoners were taken. In October the Germans began their renewed thrust toward Moscow. But the Russian winter came on early, and with it the Soviet army started their counteroffensive.

In December 1941, as the Russians were battling for their lives, trying to keep Hitler from his stated goal of entering the "gateway to the Caucasas," the world situation took a sudden turn, altering history. The Japanese attacked Pearl Harbor on December 7, and within a few days the United States was at war with Germany as well as Japan.

Dr. Resnick's convalescence was hastened by great quantities of devotion and chicken soup from his wife and by attentive love from his children. There was no keeping the war news from him, and by the time he came home from the hospital he was back at his usual routine of listening to the radio and reading the papers from cover to cover every day. In the middle of October he returned to his office, frail and more silent than ever. With Lilly's urging, he worked a shortened day and an abbreviated week.

If the aunts had ever said anything to her parents about her date at the shore with Vince, Marta never knew it. She

333

thought they would try to spare her mother and hoped they understood that for her it had been the final blow-off. She was back in the fold, trying to blot his image from her memory, trying to erase lingering traces of him in her autonomic nervous system, trying to bring adult perspective to her own behavior. Nobody ever mentioned Vincent Fanetti's name, including her brother. That fateful summer night when Dr. Resnick almost died, Steven had undergone his own metamorphosis. He seemed more thoughtful, less inclined to share himself. Marta sensed him moving away from them, even as he petted his mother, sat with his father, and listened attentively to his sister. Even as he had grown less bound to the family, she had felt her own connections becoming stronger and more demanding. She had not spoken to Vince again after that last night together. Whether he tried to reach her, whether he found out from her friends what had happened, whether he understood, she didn't know. But some strong sense told her he had all the facts. She struggled to put him out of her life.

In the beginning, the war in the Pacific was a series of disasters for the United States. Japan, which had been battling constantly with China through the thirties, had one major objective: to reconstruct the so-called Greater East Asia Co-Prosperity Sphere, and to do it by taking, one by one, the islands in the Pacific. In short, they wanted to reestablish the Japanese empire as it had existed before the first Manchurian invasion. At Pearl Harbor they had badly damaged the U.S. Pacific fleet, and they hoped that the quick occupation of the islands from the Marianas and Wake to the Marshalls and Gilberts would ultimately lead to a negotiated peace. They made the mistake of thinking they were sure winners and would net all their gains. But it was to be a long and bloody war.

In Woodlyn guys were going into the service now at an

ever-increasing rate. Some enlisted; some were drafted; some hung on to their status as college students. All knew that they would eventually have to serve if they were physically able. Still, the war talk at Hillcrest High was limited. Marta had her nose to the grindstone. She was after top grades. She was doing great. Her social life was under control. She kept her mouth shut and picked her dates with care. She could've gone out every Saturday night, but she didn't. She sat in on the usual girl talk after weekends, laughing and listening but rarely participating. She felt removed from her friends. She tried to separate herself as well from the music around her, but that proved more difficult. Steven had thrown himself into composing, playing, planning songs. He kept urging her, and she began once again to sit by him at the piano to do lyrics for him, to add musical ideas of her own to his stuff. They wrote song after song together, but she never heard them performed outside of her home. Her mother and father, who listened quietly while Steven played and Marta sang in their living room, never really encouraged him, never went to his school to hear his more and more frequent performances. Nevertheless, they were silent about his becoming a doctor. He was playing piano in school and Marta suspected in other places too. She discouraged him when he started to talk about it, and finally he ceased mentioning it altogether. She was moving steadily toward the university, with top scholarship her goal. She knew her brother had given his heart and soul to music. Whether it was concern over his poor eyesight or exhaustion, Dr. and Mrs. Resnick were resigned and never pressed him anymore. They seemed old, tired, and perpetually worried.

In the spring of her sophomore year, when she was waiting to hear if once again she had made the honor roll, and Mrs. Resnick had finally hung up the blackout curtains, when the rationing of cigarettes made it tough to get Chesterfields, and Dr. Resnick was lamenting that now there was no way either to buy a new car or to replace his old, bald tires, when her own world was as regulated and on course as it had been in her childhood, Marta heard from Vince again.

The family, listening to the radio after dinner, had just heard the first reports about the surrender of Corregidor. With it went all hopes of holding the Philippines. Her parents had settled into their nightly postures, each in his own chair, Dr. Resnick reading a new biography of Rembrandt, Mrs. Resnick leafing through a bestseller by John O'Hara. Neither Marta nor Steven had any intention of hanging around the living room, but as usual Steven had stopped at the piano, bending his long frame over the instrument to run through a new song he was constructing. Marta stood for a moment beside him, watching his strong, tapering fingers on the keys.

Dr. Resnick looked up when the phone rang. "It's probably for one of you," he said, and then sighing, he got heavily to his feet. "I better take it. I have a couple of sick patients who may need some help." He walked off into the kitchen to answer it, dragging his feet. They could hear his voice, muffled, but Marta made no effort to make out the words. When he came back into the living room, he looked at her strangely. "It's for you," he said. "It's a man."

As she went upstairs to take it in her bedroom, she thought how peculiar it was that some "man" would be calling her and assumed as she flopped on her bed, holding the long cord from the hall, that it was one of the teachers from school, the adviser of the *Hillcrest Lit.* probably. Carelessly she picked up the receiver and heard Vincent's voice. For a second she sat up straight on her bed, staring at herself in the mirror over her dressing table. As she heard her name come over the wire, the phone clicked downstairs; somebody had hung it up.

"Marta?" he repeated..

"Yes . . . How are you, Vince?"

"I'm okay. . . . How about you?"

"Well, I'm okay too."

"Listen," he said, "I wanted to tell you something."

Silence stretched between them, taut and vibrating like the wire itself, so separated that they might have been on different continents.

He said, "The army is sending me back to school in Boston. . . . I wanted you to know."

"That's fine, Vince. What does it mean exactly?"

"If I can finish up by next winter, get all my credits, they'll send me on to medical school."

She nodded to herself in the mirror; and as if it belonged to a stranger, she saw the pale oval face, the lips being chewed, the eyes full of indescribable signs and signals. "Hey," she said at last, pushing herself, "that's really incredible! I mean . . . how could you get in all those credits?" .

There was a mental shrug. She knew him so well. The eyes in the mirror said he would play down the whole deal, the whole impossible, rigorous, demanding . . .

"Trimesters, heavy schedules, whatever they say to do. Anyway, my uncle introduced me to a general. . . ."

She tried to laugh. "Well, that always helps!"

"I never minded a little help."

"Well, of course not." She sounded like the school guidance counselor, so objective, so removed and clever. "Jeez," she breathed, trying to let it go a little. "I hope you do great! I hope you knock 'em dead! How marvelous for you!"

"I thought . . ." and how careful he had become too, "maybe we could meet tomorrow . . . for lunch or something. Whatever you say."

For the first time indignation came to her rescue. That he could continue to do this to her! Self-pity, the functional device. "You know that's not possible!"

And silence again. "Yeah. Well. Okay. Take it easy, Mart."

And once more, accumulating at the base of her throat, the old painful clump of reasons and feelings that had been, with great effort, spread around the nervous system, circulated in the blood with the hope of some final dissolution of pain. Finding it almost impossible to swallow, her voice came weakly through the obstruction. "I will always think . . . well of you, Vince."

"Sure," he said and was gone. Somewhere into the ether; somewhere back into his world of grinding work.

In the late winter of 1943, Dr. Resnick gave Marta and Steven permission to perform together at the canteen for soldiers in town. She wanted to do it and her father saw her determination. And then there was patriotism and all that went with it. Anyway, she seized the opportunity. She was a senior, and Steven was in tenth in high school now. They worked up a routine, Steven over the keys as usual, Marta on her feet in silver high heels and fancy gown, leaning into the curve of a big old Baldwin, happy, with her hand around the mike, belting it out, or crooning it over, or whispering it, all of Steven's music and her lyrics, and of course the pop songs that the soldiers and sailors wanted to hear: "Don't Sit Under the Apple Tree," and "Kalamazoo" and "Blues in the Night," which always made her sad, and made the noncoms cheer for more. She thought for sure that all the receptors used in the process of falling and making love had been destroyed, blunted, or too well hidden. But one night after they performed, a tall, good-looking young soldier came up to her as she was leaving the stage and said, "I'm Daniel Reiter. Can I buy you a Coke?" And the world that had been flowerless, loveless, and devoted to the Resnick work ethic for two years suddenly burst into bloom again.

In the Pacific in the winter and spring of 1943, the tide was turning for the Americans fighting in the island jungles. There was an Allied victory at Guadalcanal, and then, the real turning point, success at Midway. A big military conference was held in Washington and an entire new schedule was worked out, more optimistic, bolder, with long-range strategy included for the first time. The Allies were at last on the move in the Pacific theater.

The war against Germany turned around too in the winter of 1943, and operation "Torch" was a success; the Axis was on the defensive in North Africa. After an important meeting at Casablanca, the Allied leaders decided that "Project Overlord," the long-hoped-for, full-scale invasion of Europe, would take place in June 1944. Churchill was pushing; Stalin was pressing; Roosevelt was planning. The Germans had launched the V-1, a pilotless plane, and the V-2, an unmanned rocket, and were devastating Britain. The Allies stepped up the bombing of Germany until it reached new and record proportions.

Marta had put Vincent Fanetti out of her mind when she had put him out of her life the preceding year. And when he called her for the last time in the spring of 1943, she probably would have been able to talk to him with no emotional residue. She certainly would never have arranged to see him again. But Dan Reiter, with whom she was in love, had pulled rank on her, infuriated her, disappointed her, knocked her out! He had come home for a short leave after officer-candidate school, stalwart and overwhelming in his new lieutenant's role and uniform. Before being reassigned to a unit in North Carolina, he had told her, out of the blue, that they ought to cool their romance a bit and perhaps date other people.

She handled it typically: at first she was controlled and quiet (stunned really!), and then when they said goodbye at the end of the leave, she cried, argued, reasoned, and protested passionately. Whatever his problem had been, he got over it fast. The day after he arrived at his new post, he called her to apologize and to tell her he had made an awful mistake, that he loved her and always would. She refused to take that call and the others after it. She read his letters, tore them up, and didn't answer them. Her mother urged her to reconsider, and her father told her she was high-handed and unpatriotic. They very much approved of Dan.

Vincent called on a Friday evening right before dinner. She answered the phone herself. Her mother, father, and brother were wandering around in the small kitchen, chatting, getting set for dinner. As soon as she heard Vince's voice she said, "I have to have some privacy for this call. Hang up for me in a minute," and took off for the upstairs phone. Her mother trailed her out of the kitchen. "Dan?" she called hopefully after her. Marta stopped on the stairs and looked down at her mother's face. "Why no," she said. "As a matter of fact, it's Vince Fanetti."

"I'm being sent to Texas," he said with almost no preamble.

"When?"

"After a short leave."

"You're in the army then?"

"Yes. I'm being sent to medical school in Texas. I

won't have any more time off. This is it. I want to see you. I want . . . to talk to you, Marta.''

She had not closed her bedroom door and she suddenly realized how quiet it was downstairs. As if they were all holding their breath in the kitchen. The radio that had been playing soft music had been turned off.

"All right," she said.

Thirtieth Street Station was full of soldiers and sailors the next afternoon. She supposed that everyone knew what he was doing, but there was a desultory randomness about the shifting crowds that made her wonder if trains would ever run on time again, if the war would ever end, if everything would ever be as it had been before.

I'll never find him in this mess, she thought, standing in the middle of the station near the information booth, watching the throngs push and shove their way across the marble floor. But the second he came up from the lower level where the trains from New England came in, she saw him. He looked thinner in his khakis. He had a duffle bag in his hand with an overseas cap hooked onto it and a raincoat over his shoulder. She stood very still watching him look all around for her. Then without any effort, he spotted her and pushed his way through the Wacs and Waves and Marines who had come up the stairs with him from the arrival tracks below. They looked at each other for a second or two, and then he put his bag and coat on the floor. He reached for her and she was in his arms before she could stop him. She pulled away after the hard kiss. Her mouth hurt and his fingers were digging into her arm.

"Where should we go?" she asked. They were the first words exchanged between them.

"Over there," he said and steered her toward the station

drugstore, where there was a luncheonette counter and booths. He found one unoccupied in the back, and they sat down across from each other.

They might have been meeting after a week's separation instead of two years. The only change she saw in him was something in his eyes, a crystal glint that had not been there before, or maybe it was his new trick of narrowing them so that the gray irises glittered behind the dark lashes and tiny lines, burned in from the sun, formed at the corners. Everything else was the same.

He was taking the same inventory of her. "You look beautiful," he said. "Thinner."

"And you're thinner."

He laughed. "If we meet only every two years and we keep getting thinner . . ."

She echoed his laughter. "There'll be nothing left but our smiles. . . ."

"There'll always be something left. You must know that, Marta."

She sat back in her seat, holding back a sigh, scanned the room vaguely, out of focus, breathless, like somebody coming up for air. Conscious for the first time of the buzz of activity in the lunchroom, she searched her bag for a cigarette, located a match, lit up, sipped her coffee, and then at last returned his gaze, which had never left her face. He handed her some papers. She took them, not understanding, not able to decipher them.

"My orders," he said.

"Oh." She looked at them blindly and then handed them back.

"I'm starting medical school. Next week."

Now she drew the deep breath that her lungs had been waiting for and it turned at once into the sigh she had wanted to avoid. "Well . . . you really packed it in! While I've still been dallying through high school."

He shrugged. "First things first."

"Has it been hard?"

"I guess so. I don't weigh it like that."

"How do you weigh it?" But she knew his answer already.

"The same way," he said, "as always. What does it add up to?"

"You're a very constant person, Vincent. That's a great gift!"

"You're the same kind of person, Marta."

"I don't know what I am. I never had as certain a picture of myself as you do."

"I have a very clear picture of you."

"That's not what I meant."

"I know what you meant."

"I see your sister in school," she said.

"You try to avoid my sister from what she tells me." Marta stared up at the ceiling. "I don't really. It just seems more . . . sensible . . . that's all."

"Still doing what's 'sensible.'"

She nodded.

He said, "And what comes next for you?"

"The university . . . in September . . . or this summer. I'm not sure if I'm in a hurry or not. I don't have your ambition."

"You have other ambitions," he said softly. "Are you singing and writing songs?"

She smiled. "Yes. With my brother. He's really good, Vince. You'd be amazed!"

"I know that talent."

"Yes . . ." She knew they could go on shooting the breeze indefinitely. They had always had a lot to talk

343

about. He wanted her to know about his plans. He kept trying to tell her, and she kept changing the subject. "You'll do great!" she said three or four times, and at last he stopped. For the first time between them there was a silence that couldn't be filled, or ended. His eyes were still narrowed. He snubbed out his second cigarette and his jaw was moving as if he was grinding his teeth. She didn't want to look into his eyes, but his gaze was riveting and held hers. He said at last, "Will you write to me?"

She didn't hesitate. "Sure."

He drew an uneven breath. "I don't believe you."

She shook her head and the tears that had been collecting since the minute she saw him came sliding down her cheeks and fell on her fingers. She stared at them as if they had come from some mysterious source other than her scalding eyes. The words she had to say stuck in her throat.

He said them for her. "Goodbye, Marta." When she looked up she saw his tall form in khaki, toting his bag and coat, disappearing through the doorway into the rush of people beyond. A waitress came over to her booth. "Somethin' else, sis?"

"No . . . no," she said. "Just the check please."

The waitress jerked her thumb in the direction of the doorway. "That guy in uniform paid already."

Marta jumped to her feet and ran out of the station.

CHAPTER 14

December 1981

DAN PUT DOWN HIS NEWSPAPER. MARTA LEANED FORWARD, dropping her copy of *Billboard*. Their eyes had been instantly riveted by the frenzied action erupting on the seven-o'clock news. The television screen swarmed with men rushing, pushing, and shoving. There was a fuzzy photograph of Lech Walesa in the upper left corner, while in the center, live from Poland, eleven truckloads of riot police were raiding Solidarity's Warsaw headquarters. A photo of the Communist party leader Jaruzelski appeared in the upper right-hand corner. His voice was heard in the background declaring a state of emergency, while a voiceover translated into English. Poland was under military rule.

At that moment the TV set buzzed. The picture wobbled, zigzagged, and quickly disappeared. An announcement of problems at the source of transmission printed across the screen. Marta, her elbows resting on her knees, chin in hands, waited for the news from Poland to continue. Nothing happened.

"The police state in action," she said. "They jammed it!"

"Not necessarily," Dan said. "The satellite might be giving them trouble. It'll come back on."

"The Polish government doesn't want the whole world to see the police destroying the last little bit of freedom over there!"

"Possible." He picked up his paper and put on his glasses again to read.

The news resumed, this time from Washington, with no further reference to the interruption. Marta shook her head, got up, and turned off the set. "Daniel?" She stood beside his chair. On impulse she reached out and smoothed his curly gray hair. He looked up and smiled over his paper.

She touched his cheek. It was rough with the day's growth of beard. "Do we have to go tonight?"

He raised his brows, shrugged, and pulled off his glasses again. "You don't feel like going?"

"Oh . . . I don't know."

"It's your kind of evening . . . two hours or so of chamber music, with first-class musicians. The DiStephanos are terrific!"

"I know, I know."

"And to hear them in a living room will be a treat. The Rowans went to a lot of trouble to get them."

Marta sighed. "The Rowans are so . . . precious."

He stared at her. "What?"

She grinned suddenly. "Their style gets on my nerves! They're old hippies. It's obnoxious!"

He folded his paper on his lap. "You accepted their invitation."

She shrugged. "Well, I knew you wanted to. I mean, I know George is the young hotshot at the bank these days. I thought it was good for you . . . to be there."

He nodded. "You were right. It is. And you'll enjoy it."

"She'll have on jeans and no makeup and sandals on bare feet as if it were July! Her hair will be swooshing around down her back. And he'll have on jeans and a patched flannel shirt!"

"So what? You don't care how people look. What's bothering you?"

Sighing, she went back and sat down opposite him on the couch again. "It's that superannuated façade. For cryin' out loud! They're both past forty! They'll serve cheap red wine and doughnuts. And all five kids will be squirming all over the place. And their house is freezing!"

Dan threw back his head and laughed. "What a list! I think they must have trouble heating that old Victorian barn! But the living room is big and comfortable and there will be a fire in the fireplace. It's perfect for chamber music. George remarked to me this week on the special quality of the acoustics. And nobody will disturb anybody! George may look like a hippie, but he's tough minded and intelligent."

"Oh I'm sure," she agreed. "Beard and boots and all! And Nina is smart and very well educated. It's just that they're so...so..." She hunted for the word. "Precious!" she said and broke into self-derisive laughter. "Okay...I'll go." She turned the news back on, stood looking at the set for a minute, switched it off, and started to leave the room. "I'll get dressed." In the doorway she stopped and swung around to face him, hands on her narrow hips. She cocked her head to one side. "Do you think she's pretty?"

He never lifted his eyes from his paper. "Who?"

"Nina Rowan."

He looked up at her, puzzlement and surprise on his face. "No. Of course not. I think she's funny-looking."

It was a cold gray night. December had landed ferociously. It had snowed, briefly thawed, and the landscape then quickly refroze. Marta stood at her bedroom window holding back the heavy drapery. Through the rigid branches of the tall empty trees she could see up into the red, starless sky. It could snow again tonight. She didn't want to analyze why she didn't feel like sitting in the Rowans' living room. But the truth seeped through anyway: she was too restless, too unsettled. They reminded her of how fast time went! It was their joint clutch at youth that she couldn't abide. Not now anyway, with her head going in one direction and her heart flying off in the other. And in between her conscience, superego, whatever the hell it was, bouncing back and forth, giving her no peace. She had to try to relax, to listen to the music. She knew that the DiStephanos were good. They were quartet-in-residence at a suburban college and several of them taught at Philadelphia's most prestigious music school. She had heard them perform as members of the Main Line Symphony Orchestra, which was earning recognition in local music circles. It ought to be pleasant to sit close to the musicians, watching them, observing the nuances. If she could concentrate!

As far as the Rowans themselves were concerned, she had tried to be friendly with them and found it almost impossible. Nina Rowan was on her own kick, and you had to lend yourself to her values and routine to make any connection. George was probably a good guy. No doubt, as Dan said, he was sharp. He certainly liked women and had always been warm and attentive to Marta, the compliment he didn't pay her aloud shining nevertheless in his eyes. For half a second Marta thought about showing up in jeans and an old turtleneck. But what difference did it make after all? She had nothing to prove. It was just one more evening out. She slid into a pair of Givenchy gray gabardine trousers, slim, elegant, and well creased.

When they pulled into the Rowans' driveway it was already after eight o'clock. The tires crunched menacingly on the ice-slicked surface. "Don't go all the way!" Marta warned Daniel.

"We're a little late," he said.

"Too bad! We could get stuck down there!"

He stopped right where he was, close to the top of the drive. "Anyway," he laughed, coming around for her, "we can be the first ones out." He held her elbow as they made their way down the long slippery driveway.

She skidded suddenly on her boot heel and clutched at his arm for support. "They might at least have salted it!" she complained.

"Old hippies don't salt!" Dan said as he rang the bell. The door opened instantly, and the laughter on Marta's lips spilled into the greeting to George Rowan. He kissed her cheek and shook Dan's hand. As she had predicted, he was in his faded jeans and a red flannel shirt. Two little boys were on either side of him, staring up at the newcomers.

"Welcome. We're just about ready to begin!" He handed their coats to two older girls who scurried upstairs to put them away while a younger sister sat on the steps watching out of large, unblinking eyes. All the children were in pajamas and robes as always at the Rowans' parties. They would roam around until exhausted; then one by one they would fall asleep on the hook rugs here and there around the room. George would quietly collect them and bear them aloft to their beds like small trophies. Marta thought

349

the whole process represented the victory of some principle to the Rowans. She couldn't imagine what it was.

As Dan had predicted, there was a fire roaring in the big hearth in the living room. It had to be the warmest place in the big old house. Taking her arm, he headed right for it. "This is fine," he said, and left her standing in a space between two easy chairs that were taken by other guests. "I'll get chairs for us," he said.

The musicians were already seated opposite in a large bay-window area, tuning their instruments. Drafty over there, thought Marta, looking to see if the café curtains behind them were moving. There were several temperature zones in the room and you could feel the alternating rise and drop if you wandered about. The lead violin, a stocky gray-haired man with large graceful hands, bowed the A string and the others in the quartet followed suit. There were three men and a woman, two violins, a viola, and a cello. Marta's attention was suddenly drawn by the profile of the woman who played second violin. There was something very familiar about her. But Marta couldn't place her and wondered if perhaps she just remembered her from one of the Main Line Symphony concerts. Dan had pulled two canvas sling chairs near the fire for them and she sat down still staring at the woman violinist. She had smooth black hair, with two white streaks at the temples that winged up into a high chignon held by pearl combs on the crown of her small, rather regal head. Slender and simply dressed in a long plaid skirt and dark sweater, she seemed younger than the gray hair suggested. Placing her instrument in her lap, she was turning to confer with the lead. As she faced about in Marta's direction, the delicate beauty of her features, the fine bones and arching brows stirred deeper chords in Marta's memory.

"Who is she?" she asked Daniel, who was moving about in the wobbly chair, trying to get his big frame placed comfortably.

He followed her glance. "I don't know. One of the DiStephanos obviously. A wife, I think I read somewhere."

"How do we know her?"

He shook his head. "I don't know her," he said positively.

Two men, acquaintances of Dan's from the bank and the hospital board, came over to shake hands. Marta greeted them, remaining seated as Dan got to his feet. The three men stood together talking. Marta's eyes restlessly roamed the room. She had not yet greeted the hostess, Nina Rowan, who seemed to be nowhere about. Suddenly Marta spotted her deep in conversation at the far side of the room. Nina had paid no attention to any of the newcomers, including two couples who had followed right after the Reiters. Her back was to Marta, but over her head Marta recognized, with a sudden jolt, the man on whom Nina was concentrating. It was Vincent Fanetti.

Marta felt the blood drain from her face. She took a quick breath as a flush started on her neck and mounted relentlessly up her cheeks. In that instant, with her skin blazing, his eyes met hers. She looked away quickly, not sure what to do, fighting the impulse to leap up and leave. He made no move to come over. He was listening to Nina Rowan, occasionally nodding his head and smiling while Nina continued to gaze intently up at him. From the back, her small neat figure was youthful in its tight casing of blue jeans and rib-hugging sweater. George Rowan called to her across the room as the musicians appeared ready. But Nina ignored him, shifting slightly so that her back was turned to him. People carrying wine pushed past her and Vincent on their way from the dining room, where a table served as the bar. Marta watched in astonishment as

351

Nina pressed herself closer to Vince to make room for them to pass. Leaning against him, she tossed her long brown hair over her narrow back and set her dangly earrings jiggling on her shoulders. She was tiny and moved with quick, dancelike steps on small sandaled feet. At that moment all of Marta's vague dislikes suddenly crystallized. What a terrible woman! Then, embarrassed by her choking burst of antipathy, Marta jumped up and tried to join in with Dan's conversation. The words went sailing over her head. "Budgets and cash flows and restructured loans . . ." She couldn't make any sense out of it. She felt someone behind her, touching her shoulder, brushing her arm. Turning her head, she looked up into Vincent Fanetti's eyes.

"Good evening," he said.

"Hello."

One of the board members said to Daniel, "You know Dr. Fanetti?"

Daniel nodded and reached out. "We have met," he said as the two men shook hands.

Nina Rowan had followed Vincent across the room, still ignoring her husband, who was waving his hands and calling to her. She inched herself between Marta and Vince, leaning on his arm for support, and kissed Marta lightly on the cheek. "Why, sweetie," the soft southern drawl interspersed with current lingo, "like I never did see you come in!"

"Good evening, Nina," Marta answered in a voice that she knew was stiff and formal. Marta caught the heavy pungence of Nina's musk perfume.

The men had picked up their interrupted discussion of the hospital's renewed building program and Vincent, with apparent reluctance, was drawn into it. Moving slightly to her left, Marta tried to disengage from the group. Nina stayed right beside Vincent, her head barely reaching his shoulder. Marta couldn't help glancing at her. From up close the little-girl illusion dissipated. With augmenting pleasure, Marta stared at the network of lines on Nina's forehead and around and under her eyes. The lower lids were small puffs and two deep parentheses cut from the tiny round nose to the cupid's-bow mouth. There was another loud summons from George across the room, points of irritation pricking at his words. Nina turned her head, her features reflecting her annoyance, as he called, "Listen, we're ready to begin, Nina! Now let's go! Please get everybody seated over there. There are more chairs in the dining room."

Vincent stepped back at once, breaking the circle, and moved toward Marta. He was looking directly at her, his focus a beacon on the side of her face. Nina was forced to back out of the way. "How are you?" he said softly to Marta, as she turned to face him. There was urgency in his voice.

"Well," she answered, her voice low, "I'm all right, I guess." She read the comprehension in his eyes. His dark brows drew briefly into a quick frown.

She smiled to relieve the tension, trying to ignore Nina's eyes riveted on them. "I see you found the local music scene," Marta said, aware that Nina was listening to every word.

He seemed oblivious to everyone else. "My wife went back to California for the holidays. I had to stay here." He gestured over his shoulder. "That's my sister, Lizabetta DiStephano. You don't remember her." It was a flat statement. No disappointment in it.

Marta sighed. "Yes, I thought she seemed familiar." She looked across once more at the violinist, who had her instrument under her chin and was intently playing over a difficult passage. George Rowan, shifting impatiently from foot to foot, was in front of the quartet, facing the room, still trying to get the large noisy crowd settled.

Marta said softly, "It's been such a long time, you know . . . since I saw her."

Nina Rowan had never taken her eyes off the two of them. Marta was uncomfortable but Vincent still ignored her. Suddenly Nina spoke up, coming up directly next to them again. "Hey, we really must get started. Marta, you and Daniel have your seats here, don't you?" And turning to Vincent, "There are some more chairs back there; like, if you wouldn't mind helping me, Vince?" The voice cooing.

He hesitated a second, but when Daniel took Marta's arm and led her to their seats, Vincent turned and followed Nina. As people finally settled down around the room, the quartet began the Schubert no. 7. It was a lilting, romantic work that Marta knew and especially loved. She tried to fix her thoughts on the music but her eyes kept straying to the farthest corner of the room, where Nina had pushed two chairs together. For herself and Vincent.

Marta felt her irritation rising again and shook her head to clear it. Who the hell cared anyway! She tried to focus on the musicians, watching Lizabetta DiStephano. She was a graceful and elegant performer, sensitive to the group, using her instrument, as did the others, to create a total sound. They were top notch! Despite her inner turmoil, Marta found herself admiring the quality of the ensemble playing. She relaxed into the music, growing more and more involved, hearing bits of musical complexity that she had never noticed before. During the brief break between movements, while the musicians tuned, Dan leaned toward her. "Aren't they wonderful!"

She nodded, and as she turned to face him, she unwillingly

caught sight again of Nina and Vincent. Nina was leaning toward him, her long hair brushing his sleeve, animation moving the little-girl features. Her children, scattered as usual around the room, might have been invisible to her. She never glanced their way as one by one they dozed off on the rugs like puppies at the guests' feet. Toward the end of the second movement of the Schubert, George Rowan began quietly circling the room collecting them. Holding one up in his arms, with a second dragging sleepily at his side, he took them upstairs. Nina turned around, concentrating again on Vincent, thrusting her small chin upward, moving in close to him to whisper something. He nodded but never budged. Each time Marta involuntarily glanced back at them, their eyes met across the room.

The second the quartet was finished, Marta was on her feet. Dan looked up at her in surprise and rose too. "Didn't you like it?"

"Oh yes," she said. "I want to use the bathroom." She started to leave the room, then turned back. "Listen, why don't you get us some of that crappy wine," she said softly. He nodded, grinning, and started toward the dining room. Marta went out into the large cold entrance hall, where there was, she was sure, no heat at all. She shivered, trying to remember the exact location of the powder room. When she finally found it down the hall near the kitchen and tried the door, it was in use. The guests were wandering around chatting during the intermission, holding plastic glasses of wine, munching doughnuts in paper napkins. Marta waited outside the door for several minutes, and when the bathroom remained locked, she decided to go upstairs. Halfway up she overtook George Rowan, who was carrying kid number three while number four crept sleepily up step by step, her bathrobe catching under her feet. George said over his shoulder to Marta, "Enjoying the music?"

"Yes," she said, taking the little girl's hand and helping her up the stairs. "They're a splendid group of musicians!"

George stood holding the children in the hall near an open bedroom door. "I hear you're a pretty fine musician too," he said. "So Dan tells me."

"I used to play," she said. "Not too much anymore though." And looking down the hall, "Point me toward the bathroom, George."

He indicated a door near the end of the hall, calling after her as she walked away, "Would you be interested in joining a new chamber group I've got organized? I play cello. We'll need a good pianist. Just for fun, you know."

"Thanks for asking," she said. "But not me. I gave up performing some time ago."

When she came out of the bathroom, the hall was dim and quiet. She could hear voices still conversing downstairs. The upper story of the old house creaked suddenly. She could hear the wind sighing around the corners from up there in the hallway. The building ticked, rocked, and settled. Rickety old barn! But, Marta conceded, if Victorian was your inclination, this house probably had its charm. Right next to the bathroom, running the entire width at the end, was a paneled den. There was no light on in there, but she could just make out the interior from the hall illumination. Slowly she wandered in and stood still in the middle of the room until her eyes grew accustomed to the darkness. A pale light filtered in from the curtained windows. In the center of one wall was an oversized brick fireplace surrounded by filled, floor-to-ceiling bookcases. She made a hesitant tour of the room, bumping into easy chairs; there was a large sofa and coffee table at the far end.

Vincent came up behind her, softly saying her name. He turned her around. She wasn't frightened. It was expected. "One second," she whispered. "That's all."

He pulled her into his arms. "Oh my God," she moaned. His mouth came down hard. Then his face was rubbing hers and his skin was warm and rough. She inhaled his scent, her heart pounding. His hands kneaded her back and shoulders, pressing her close and finally holding her so tightly that she could barely breathe.

"I hoped you'd be here tonight," he whispered in her ear.

"And I almost didn't come. Oh, Vince . . ."

"I want you, Marta." He kissed her again, gently now, lingeringly.

With a sigh she pulled away from him. "Please . . ." She touched his face. "Please . . ." And wetting her fingertip with her tongue, she rubbed the lipstick from his mouth.

He began to pull her toward the couch across the fireplace. "They won't miss us. . . ."

She touched the strong angled bones of his face, remembering, her fingers finding the familiar surfaces and textures. How many times in the last months she had wanted to do this! Still she resisted his urging her toward the couch. "Dan will come looking for me."

Still holding her arms, he stood peering through the dimness into her eyes. Then he said slowly, "Does he always go looking for you?"

"Yes," she whispered. She wanted to touch the thick hair near the back of his neck, the memory in her fingertips alive and compelling. She wanted to touch his chest and shoulders beneath his coat, beneath his shirt. . . .

He had released her and she kept her arms rigidly by her sides. "We must go back down now."

But he reached for her again and smoothed her hair back from her face gently with both hands, the familiar hunger in him too. He cupped her chin with his large palm and then ran his fingers up her neck. "I want you," he said again so softly it was like breathing.

"Please . . ."

He still didn't move away from her but he dropped his hands. "Will you meet me tomorrow?"

She hesitated.

"Marta . . ."

She nodded.

"Mikko's at noon," he said.

She watched him straighten his tie, adjust his collar, and walk away, tall, square shouldered, his step light.

She waited in the murky hallway. A child was crying and she listened for a few seconds to see where the wailing was coming from. Then, locating the closed bedroom door, she entered quietly. The room was bitter cold. One little boy was fast asleep, buried under his blankets, but the other was sitting upright in his narrow bed, his eyes closed, sobbing. A small lamp burned on a chest in the corner. The window shades rustled against the windows, which were rattling in their frames. The room was an igloo! "What's the matter, love?" she crooned softly, sitting down on the bed beside the child, covering his shoulders and holding him in her arms. She felt the small warm body relax against her. "Wanna drink!" the baby voice lisped.

Marta went back into the hall and to the bathroom. From downstairs she heard the musicians starting to tune up for the second half of the program. Bringing back the drink, she felt goose bumps rising on her arms under her sweater sleeves as the chill in the room assaulted her. It had direction and a current swirled around her ankles as she leaned over the thirsty child. She held the glass for him and he drank deeply, his eyes still closed. He sighed, burped, and put his little head back on the pillow. She smoothed his hair and covered him. "Poor little guy," she said, not sure why, and bending over, kissed him on the forehead. Searching for the source of the cool wind in the room, she found that both windows were open several inches. Mad, these Rowans! She shut the windows, pulled the shades down almost to the sills, tugged the cotton curtains closed, and tiptoed out of the room.

As she started down the stairs she heard the music. The quartet had begun playing a chamber piece by Samuel Barber. Marta had heard it only a few times on record, never live, and had always been curious about it. If she could muster the will now to concentrate! If she could make believe he wasn't there! If Daniel wouldn't wonder . . . Looking neither right nor left, conscious of everyone's eyes on her, she slipped into her seat again next to Dan. He turned his head and gazed at her for a long minute as she tried to get comfortable on the narrow canvas chair. She looked up and smiled at him. He nodded, reaching toward a small table to retrieve a glass of wine for her.

"Thank you."

He said under his breath, "Everything all right?"

She nodded. "One of the kids . . . the little boy . . . Jeremy? . . . was crying. I got him some water and sat with him."

How easy to tell the truth. By half. Daniel patted her arm, starting to comment, when the woman in the easy chair beside him touched her lips to quiet them. Once again Marta shifted about on the wooden frame. It creaked and the man on the other side of her stared up at her with irritation.

The truth! She had learned its uncertain nature long ago. That it had its own logic, its own shape, its own sense of time. That above all it resisted being told by halves. Because the mathematics of choice was working against you, half becoming automatically a minus quantity, less than an out-and-out lie. Sighing, unable to monitor herself, she glanced at her watch. Dan caught her and mouthed, "Soon . . ."

Vincent had changed his seat for the second part of the program, sitting close by the musicians, his eyes focused on them. Without wanting to, Marta observed him innocently in her discreet line of vision. He was still so damnably handsome! All the wild flash and promise of his youth had been realized. As she stared, he turned his head; she glanced away, then back, and in that split second their eyes meshed. They both looked quickly back at the players. She saw clearly in that instant that he had never lost his capacity for disappointment. He was still, like her, hurtable. Like Daniel . . .

As the thought shot through her head, igniting feelings, it transmuted simple cases into complicated aches in the chest and ragged breathing. The music had suddenly turned harsh. Pain and pleasure mingled within Marta. The violins were abrasive and the cello's part was dissonant. Program music for a deep-sea epic of buried giants and sunken treasure. The half of the truth that wouldn't stay drowned.

She sighed deeply, moved restlessly, shuffled her feet, and felt Daniel glancing her way again. Across the room Nina Rowan was watching her too. No amateur malcontent herself, Nina perceived Vincent's power, had gone to work at once, casting her line at him. She was a pretty able angler. But she wouldn't make a catch this time. And now that she had so obviously failed, Marta could regard her with more charity. And more objectivity. Nina sat by herself, Vincent's vacated chair beside her. There was nobody else that interested her tonight. In the middle of the Barber, sometime after George Rowan had deposited the last drowsy child upstairs, he sat down next to his wife. He whispered in her ear. Nina tossed her head, shaking the long silver earrings, evaded his eyes, and the small, pale mouth drew up in a peach-pit pout. There was too much tension between them. George was struggling upstream to her, and she paddled away from him. He tried again, leaning toward her, his hand lightly on her arm. She moved herself to the opposite corner of her sling chair. Marta made a mental note to avoid them henceforth at all costs.

The Barber ended the way it had begun, with a tentative question about its own nature. This kind of music was the hallmark of the twentieth century. It disquieted the audience. They never knew what to make of it. The group in the Rowans' living room uneasily moved about on their uncomfortable chairs, coughing behind their hands and endlessly clearing their throats. Audiences wanted answers, not questions. Marta shrugged. Art had no answers. At best, the music clarified the questions. You still had to supply your own conclusions. As in everything else.

The crowd began to break up. The musicians wiped their foreheads and their instruments, placing them carefully covered in their cases, then all of them stood up to stretch. Vincent was conversing with them, his arm around Lizabetta. The brother and sister turned to face each other, chatting quietly, smiling in response to some remark or other. Getting to her feet alongside Daniel, Marta couldn't help watching them, fascinated by their resemblance to each other. Both were tall and slender with profiles like Roman medallions, straight noses and chiseled mouths. As if he felt Marta's eyes on him, Vincent suddenly turned toward her. Gently pulling his sister by the hand, he brought her across the room to them.

"Mr. and Mrs. Reiter, my sister Liza."

They might have been meeting for the first time. And Marta could have let it go like that, but Lizabetta reached out immediately to take Marta's hands in hers. Holding them, she leaned forward and kissed Marta's cheek. "I'm so glad to see you," she said. "How have you been, Marta?" There was no concealing the fact that she at least remembered.

Marta could feel Daniel's eyes on her. "Lizabetta! I knew you were familiar. At first I couldn't place you."

"It's been a very long time," the musician answered. "But I think I would have known you."

"You were wonderful," Marta said. "All of you. It was fine ensemble playing!"

Lizabetta smiled with pleasure. "I'm glad you enjoyed it." Her smile was so like Vincent's that Marta registered a small jolt.

Daniel said, "We've heard you play with the Main Line Symphony, Mrs. DiStephano."

"Call me Lizabetta, please! Marta and I knew each other as . . . children." How carefully she phrased it for him. "But you must let me know the next time you attend! Perhaps we could have coffee together afterward."

"I'd like that, Liza," said Marta. The two women found themselves shoulder to shoulder as Vincent and Daniel were joined by one of the doctors. Marta turned to face Lizabetta. Smiling, she said, "Tell me, whatever happened to the trumpet?"

The musician looked confused for a moment, then broke into gay laughter. "Oh my! I gave it up! I was never too good at it. The strings were for me!"

Marta said softly, "Mama knew best."

Lizabetta's laughter faded. She looked at Marta gravely through long dark lashes, the gray eyes wide and clear. "I often wonder. Families had terribly old-fashioned ideas in those days. Anyway, I was the only one who went on with the music. One by one they all . . . found something else." She glanced at her brother, who caught her eyes on him and reached over for her, draping his arm again affectionately around her slender shoulders. She said directly to Daniel, "I would like to introduce my husband, Joseph, to you . . . and to Marta."

They followed her back across the room where a small, enthusiastic group had collected around the DiStephano brothers. "Joe!" Lizabetta tugged him from the circle. He stepped back and then came forward to face the Reiters. He was stocky, with a large head, a strong face, and a thick shock of tousled gray hair. He reminded Marta immediately of Vincent's father. Shaking hands with both of them, DiStephano said to Dan, "I believe you're an executive with Philadelphia Federal?"

Daniel nodded and Marta felt the usual twinge of concern. How Dan hated shop talk on a night out! But he was nodding and seemed interested in what the musician was saying. "Lending any money to music schools these days?" DiStephano was holding tightly to his wife's arm. Both he and Lizabetta were intent on Dan's answer.

Daniel said evenly, "Sure. That's our business, lending money. Whose school is it?"

"Ours," said Lizabetta softly.

"I thought you were on the faculty of the Eustace Academy." Daniel was referring to the city's largest, most prestigious music school, which had an international reputation.

"We were . . . but we left last year and started our own."

"With your own funds?"

DiStephano nodded. "Mainly." He gestured toward his brothers. "We're all more or less in it together. My brothers are still connected with the academy though. They couldn't afford to make the full-time switch . . . yet!" He smiled at his wife. "With us, it was now or never!"

"We'd really like to buy our building," said Lizabetta. "It's just perfect for our needs. And we're a little afraid it will be sold out from under us."

"Is it on the market?" asked Dan.

"Not officially, but we hear rumors," said DiStephano.

"It's owned by an estate," said Lizabetta.

Daniel took a business card out of his breast pocket and handed it to Joseph DiStephano. "Give me a call," he said. "We'll make an appointment and see what we can arrange for you."

"Thank you very much," said Joseph. "George Rowan said you were the key man to talk to about this. . . ."

They were speaking quietly but the others were listening to the exchange, Vincent standing next to Marta, their arms side by side. She accidentally brushed against him and felt the current whip sharply between them. He started to turn his head. She moved quickly away from him.

Minutes later he beat them to goodbyes. "Nice seeing you again," he said formally to them both, not meeting either's eyes. He kissed his sister and reached out to shake his brother-in-law's hand. "Great concert, Joe . . . worth the trip to Philadephia! Good night . . . everybody." Then he turned and walked into the hall to get his coat.

Dan had murmured, "Good night," as Marta stared at Vincent's disappearing broad back. She wanted to get out of there too, but just then George Rowan came up to them, gesturing toward the DiStephanos. "Did Joe talk to you about a loan?"

Dan nodded. "He's coming into the bank next week."

Rowan said, "They're good people. Ambitious . . . I was hoping you'd see them!"

He accompanied them out into the hall, going upstairs with Daniel to get the coats while Marta stood waiting in the chilly entryway. Nina Rowan had just closed the door behind Vincent, the tail end of her tinkly laughter trailing as she turned and came back toward Marta. "Way out!" she bubbled. "Like wasn't it an interesting evening?" The wise little face was upturned, smiling, the blue eyes with their puffy lids appraising, measuring. Marta saw again, but with no special pleasure now, that Nina would go directly from extended adolescence to faded middle-age.

The interior of their car was icy. "Little hippie prune," Marta muttered, shivering against the cold upholstery.

Daniel raced the motor, trying to warm the cold engine, and backed the car out of the glassy drive. He ignored her comment, if he heard it, never asking who or what. He remained self-absorbed all the way home. Once the car skidded at an intersection, and he didn't seem to notice. "Hey!" she cried.

"Hm?"

"Take it slow, honey! These streets have bad patches."

Home, in an enveloping silence, mincing carefully up their own drive, which had been cleaned but was still slippery in spots, and into the blessed warmth of their house. "Am I ever glad to be back here!" she said, sighing, as he followed her upstairs.

He was always the first in bed. He lay quietly, his arms tucked behind his head, his eyes already shut.

"Asleep?" she said softly, circling the room, picking up, putting away, brushing her hair, creaming her hands, fixing her pillow and the quilt on their bed.

In a wide-awake voice he said, "You haven't changed, Marta. She knew you right away."

Marta stopped beside the bed. "What?"

"Lizabetta DiStephano. She remembered you. Because you're still so young . . . and so lovely."

Marta drew a long quivery breath. "That's very flattering, Daniel. But we could hardly remember each other. I think she was just seven years old. It was too long ago to remember anything." She fell exhaustedly into bed. "To remember anything, Dan," she added softly.

She heard his breathing growing deeper. He reached for her hand and held it lightly for a second. Then he was asleep. "Sweet dreams, Daniel," she said. She leaned over and switched off her table light. "You deserve sweet dreams."

CHAPTER 15

May 1947

THE MUSIC PIPED IN OVER THE LOUDSPEAKER SYSTEM IN the department store was meant to be innocuous, to fade into the scene, a muted rhythmic presence designed to soothe. But it was a good song and Nat Cole was doing it, as usual, smooth and easy. From long habit and reflex, Marta listened as "The King" crooned "For Sentimental Reasons..." How do you not listen when you've been trained from the age of six to mark it, examine it, judge it; when you're entirely wired into it! It had nice lyrics, hoping for belief, offering the whole heart.

The saleslady brought out still another pattern of silver flatware, by Gorham this time. Marta and her mother were seated on high stools before a velvet-covered glass counter, with different manufacturers' samples in front of them. All the silver had begun to look alike to her. Two hours of hanging over teaspoons and forks! Stealing a look at her mother's intense face, she tried to get a clue. Mrs. Resnick was handling the pieces tenderly. She had always wanted sterling, and all she ever had had was Community plate.

367

Mrs. Resnick squinted closely at the tablespoon she was holding, weighing it in her hand, and then gave it to Marta. "Feel this!" She nodded encouragingly. "Isn't this heavier than the others? There's a lot of weight here, dear!"

On the convex surface of the big spoon, Marta saw her slender oval face staring back at her, distorted and swollen cheeked. "Really lovely," she said. The pattern was elaborate, lots of little scrolls and whirls.

Her mother glanced at her sharply. "You really like this?"

"I really do."

"You like the La Scala better than the Reed and Barton Spanish Baroque?" Mrs. Resnick picked up the more ornate knife and fork from the crowded square of royal-blue velvet on the counter before them. They had looked at thirty different patterns by five different silversmiths.

"I love it!" Marta said firmly, standing up to stretch.

Mrs. Resnick glanced up at her over her glasses. "Which one now? This one, the Gorham, do you mean? Are you sure?"

"Yes. I love it!" Marta said again. "For Sentimental Reasons..." The lyric asked for belief... she believed everything Daniel said. And all the things he didn't say. It didn't matter, what Dan didn't say. The song declared the gift of the heart. And Dan had given her his heart! Daniel! She sat back down, sighing, and picked up the shiny tablespoon again, smiling this time into the concave side, seeing herself upside down. But right-side up about Daniel! How lovely that it was Daniel! Thinking of his love every morning, Nat Cole serenaded her, dreaming of his love every night....

They had to register her so that any wedding guest

inquiring in the department store would be told that Marta Resnick, soon to be Reiter, was collecting La Scala.

"Maybe we should show Daniel first?" Mrs. Resnick hesitated once more before handing Marta the pen to sign the book.

"Mom, he'll love it!" Marta said as she printed her name, knowing that Dan wouldn't care one way or the other. Picky, unimportant stuff, this business of china and silver, the wife's province. Her big serious-minded fiancé had his dark eyes on longer-range objectives. He was working for a local bank during the day and studying at night for his master's degree in business. He saw himself as a future bank officer, with his present position as just the beginning. He was trying to prepare for what he called "the coming revolution in credit."

"What does that mean?" Marta had stared at him when she heard his comment the first time. "I haven't studied any econ. . . ."

He had just come out of the service and was trying to decide what job to take. "I don't know that studying classical economics would tell you much about this situation anyway," he had answered thoughtfully. "Since it's all so new. What I mean is, I think we're about to enter a period of wild spending, enormous consumption." He spoke quietly, his expression intense. "It's a result of the pile-up of capital from the war years. There's a whole fresh technology out there. New businesses will be starting up and old ones will be expanding. A slew of products are going to hit the market. And real estate, Marta! There's a big, big demand coming! The public will need financing. A lot of it! That's where I see my future!"

By the time they had discussed these ideas, Dan Reiter had already made up his mind about what he wanted. Still in uniform, he had been offered two positions, one with

the Wheat-Exchange Bank, the other with Keystone Fideli-
ty, a local mortgage company. Keystone Fi was staffed by
ambitious Jewish businessmen, all friends of Daniel's
father, Nathan. The bank, well, "It's a WASP enterprise,"
Dan had said to her, holding her in his arms on the porch
couch late one winter night the preceding year. He was on
leave before being mustered out of the army. "It's strictly
a low-pressure outfit. I like it, Marta." He had stood up,
walked to the front window, and thoughtfully gazed into
the icy January night. Thinking out loud, he had added,
"It's a slower beginning. But I can go farther. I like this
kind of operation." He had turned around, rubbing his
strong chin with its deep cleft. Then he had come back and
sat down close to her again, arms around her. She had
waited for him to ask her what she thought. He never had.

And he never would. Daniel Reiter neither sought nor
gave advice, keeping his opinions mostly to himself. He
dismissed as trivia matters that didn't immediately concern
him, and on those affairs that did pertain to him he acted
decisively and alone. It was more than a mere matter of
style. Deep in the contours of his personality was the
conviction that his best interest lay within his own thinking
processes. It was that solitary toughness that had made him
so magnetically attractive to her.

And he had chosen her! With her mother peering
encouragingly over her shoulder and Nat Cole telling her
what she wanted to hear, Marta picked up the pen to sign
the register. Her two-carat, blue-white diamond engagement ring glittered on her finger as she held down the page
with her left hand. The store now had a record of her silver
pattern, to go along with the record of her Wedgwood
china pattern and her Bavarian crystal pattern. As her
name fit neatly on the line after the signature of some other
happy bride, Marta thought once more how remarkable it

was that she and Dan were so similar. Each needed room. Each needed autonomy. Each needed privacy.

As she and her mother came out into the warm spring afternoon, Mrs. Resnick had the perpetual frown on her forehead that had appeared when she first began to make the wedding plans. It was all only one month away: hotel, music, caterer, liquor, rabbi, flowers, attendants, gowns, gifts. . . . "For Sentimental Reasons . . ." Marta hummed to herself, the song pleading for her loving heart, telling her they would never part.

Daniel and she would never part. She had given him her heart. When he finally got around to proposing! Dan Reiter was not a man to be pushed or pulled.

He was hard to resist, and Marta didn't try. She admired his certainty and self-confidence. (His body she adored! The heavy chest and strong arms, the athlete's legs with the thick developed muscles; she had surprised and charmed him again and again with her ready lustiness, her pleasure in the physical.)

That single-minded self-reliance of his, whether it was cause or effect, had come with a long string of successes. Going from the top of his high-school class to honor student at the university, to decorated captain in the infantry, he took it all in stride with quiet pride and natural modesty. He had known at the age of nine (the biggest and smartest boy in his class, according to his mother) that he wanted to be a businessman like his father.

Sitting on the couch that cold January night in 1946, wrapped tightly together, his battle ribbons rubbing at her cheek, she had listened to the outline of his future. Perry Como was singing softly to them, "Till the End of Time," while Dan talked about his new job and the master's in business he was going to get at night at the university.

371

She had said dreamily, "I always knew what I wanted to be too."

He had moved his head so that he could look down at her, grinning. "Somebody's wife!" he had said teasingly.

Her reaction had been swift and angry. He had never once discussed their future together. "That's not what I meant, Captain Know-it-all! I meant career-wise."

He hadn't responded, but stroking her shoulder, he kissed the tip of her nose, gently, lovingly. Disarmed once more, she had found herself relaxing despite her best intentions to tell him off.

She knew he didn't like an argument. ABF (After the Big Fight), things between them had subtly changed. On a brief leave home after officer-candidate school, he had peremptorily informed her that it was better to cool their affair for the present, to wait for the end of the war before seeing each other again. He had shocked her because he had offered no reason, no excuse. They had finally gotten back together after several weeks, after many unanswered telephone calls and letters from him, and a dramatic silence from her. But from then on, she had tended to tred lightly with him, curbing her natural inclination to battle back. His rejection had come so swiftly and abruptly on the heels of their tender embraces and open declarations of passion that she had been knocked totally off balance.

She had never quite regained it. She had been her brassy high-school self when they first met at the army canteen in the center of Philadelphia during the war. Saucy, bright, and almost completely honest with him. Since Vincent (whose name she never mentioned), Daniel was the only guy she had met whom she wanted to respond to. Physically and mentally! He was her equal in all departments and her superior in several. He understood the role that music played in her life and, beyond trying to please her, he seemed deeply interested. Hearing her sing or play, he would stop what he was doing, his expression rapt, his eyes focused on her.

The joy in all the arts that came spontaneously like breathing to Marta, she shared eagerly with him. Listening to music together, she observed how attentive and sensitive he was to the nuances. She was thrilled too by his responsiveness to literature and painting. With no obvious effort, he became a willing audience to her theories, her endless pleasure rambles on the nature of the arts, the interrelationships, the symbols, the crossovers.

He seemed to remember everything that was said and most of what he read in the books she recommended. If he didn't come on as a big authority among her intellectual college friends, it was because he had no need to. At unexpected moments he had his fund of information at hand, and he frequently astonished her by making reference to some artistic fact he had observed and analyzed independently.

But he didn't believe in her career. Her parents didn't believe in it either. And even Steven, her biggest rooter and most admiring booster, couldn't see how a nice Jewish girl could either go up to New York all alone and break into the music business (whatever it was, there being no clearly marked path to the marketplace!) or pursue it from Philadelphia. She might as well be in Timbuktu as in Woodlyn, trying to write and sell songs to some mythical publisher in New York City.

Steven understood, but couldn't see a way out. "It's a question of what you really want," he had said, as always skipping the fancy rhetoric and getting right to the heart of the matter. "You won't get much encouragement from the folks." Looking at her sheepishly, "Nor from Dan, I imagine. You'd have to walk out on the whole combo here. . . ."

Not really hearing him, she had said accusingly, "You said you were going to do it!"

"And I am," he had agreed. "But it's different for me."

"Why the hell is it different for you?"

"Oh, Mart." Steven had looked crushed when she blustered at him. "I think you're a big talent. I always did. You know that. But you can't have a house in the suburbs and a banker husband and follow the yellow-brick road to the big city."

This final comment she had heard clearly, and it had stopped her short. It had never occurred to her that falling in love and wanting to be with big Captain Reiter had represented some deep, no-options decision.

She had worked hard for three years at the university on music history, theory, and composition. But she never once relinquished her passion for the popular field, jotting down lyrics when they came to her at odd moments, inventing melodies, working them up with Steven whenever they both had a spare second. And she didn't have many. She had doubled up on her credits and was studying late into the night. She had gone to school two summers in a row. A young woman in a hurry!

In the spring of 1946, with the world formally at peace once more and the plans for graduation set, Marta realized that she had to stop moving and start thinking. There had to be some way to hook up with the professional music scene she loved without leaving Philadelphia. Then, the juncture of two events, like a signal, suggested a possibility for her. Out of the blue, she received a letter from Vincent Fanetti, telling her that he had graduated from medical school. He wrote that he had received his commission and was about to start a year's residency in a civilian hospital, before serving his time in the army. She understood the letter, not only because she understood him, but because she knew that the labyrinthine twistings of the past, hidden, semiforgotten, could unwind without special invitation. If you were watching the world for symbols, everything—from tea leaves in the bottom of your cup to the unlikely flash of lightning on a warm spring afternoon— prodded you with secret messages. .

She wrote back to him and then tore up her reply along with his letter. But his words remained in her mind, not quite buried yet in the folds of memory. One evening a week afterward, she and Dan went to see *Intermezzo* with Leslie Howard and Ingrid Bergman. When they came out of the movie, Marta's head filled with the romance and the drama of the music, they stopped at a luncheonette for coffee. As they sat waiting for their orders, she flipped the roller of the jukebox, remarking on the staying power of some of the hits and the fleetingness of others. Suddenly she stopped turning the lever. "Gee-zu!" she said. Their order came at that moment, with a hamburger for Dan. He began adding catsup to it, not asking a word about her exclamation, busy with his sandwich and french fries.

She looked closely again at the name on the juke, fished around in her bag for a dime, and started the music. Marcus Appleby and the City Five. He had a pretty big song there, somewhere in the top twenty-five at the moment, she figured. She listened to his sound, which was familiar but somehow seemed to have gotten religion into it! Although the harmonies were typical and the arrangement was identifiable, the song had a different swing and message. Planning to tell Dan all about Marcus when the song was over, she waited for the last bars. Then she had second thoughts. She knew she ought to be able to talk about Marcus without mentioning Vincent, but somehow

Vince was too integrated with the notes she was hearing. At once she was transported back to Nino's, singing, with Marcus behind them on the crowded little bandstand.... Then she was dancing ... in Vince's arms....

The song on the jukebox ended and she said nothing to Daniel. Private histories are laced with unprofitable memories. Begin unraveling and the threads lead where they will. And she had always been a lousy liar.

She woke at dawn the next morning hearing music. At first she thought it might be coming from across the alleyway, from somebody's house. She went to the window, where the cold spring morning was just beginning, the first flush of light silhouetting the row of houses across the back. But there was only silence out there and the chirps of the early birds. She tiptoed to Steven's room and gently opened his door. He was fast asleep and there was no music.

So the music had been in her head. Shivering in the dim heatless room, she climbed back into bed and curled her knees up under her chin, her pillows against her back, her quilt pulled high about her shoulders. Trying to hear the melody again. And then she knew what it was. Dreams reach down into private histories and are no respecters of profit or loss. She was engulfed with a sudden rising wave of sadness. It broke in her chest, leaving her sighing, weak, and breathy. She slid down in bed seeking sleep again as a refuge, dozing off. But the dream had unwound and the melody wanted out! "Let me touch your hand, your lips, your cheek / Let me hold you close, you'll hear it speak / This new love ..."

Her mother had to wake her. "Marta, you're going to miss your first class. What's the matter? You never oversleep."

Rushing her breakfast, tossing on her coat and rushing

out of the house, she ran for the trolley that took her down to the university. Lurching along through the cold gray morning, she tried to throw off the residue of sadness from the dream. It had been like an omen. She sat up so suddenly that her books tumbled off her lap and onto the slatted wooden floor. She knew what she was going to do. Marcus Appleby had once invited them, Vincent and her, to cut a record with him. She had declined, and Vince, of course, with his other big plans, had never followed up on it. Why not now? He would remember her. Marcus would remember.

"How would I find out how to get in touch with a recording artist?" she asked Steven that evening when they were sitting in the living room staring at the new TV with her father and mother.

"Who?" he asked, direct as usual.

"A guy named Appleby. Marcus Appleby."

"Oh yeah. I know him. He's got a nice number out now. He's had a couple pretty big ones."

"So how would I get in touch with him?"

Steven never blinked. She was speaking quietly, under her breath to him. He understood. "Let me get ahold of his last release and see who recorded him. Then you write a letter, asking for the name of his management, or his address directly. But they never give you that. They'll probably give you his A and R guy. You think he might be buying?"

She shrugged. "Who knows? They run out too. Even the great ones."

Steven nodded. "Try it. What have you got to lose!"

She wrote the note and enclosed it with a covering letter to the record company. Every day she charged at the mail, leafing through the family's pile. And then one afternoon, when she was exhausted from a full day at the university, dragging herself up the front steps, Steven was waiting for her at the front door. "Hey, you got an answer from RCA," he said.

She took the letter from the dining-room table and went up to her room. Closing the door, she sat on her bed and quickly ripped it open. They had sent her note on to him and the reply was from Appleby himself. In a large jagged hand he wrote, "Yes I do remember Miss Marty who sang so nice and clear and true with Doc Fanetti. He's really Doc Fanetti now! I seen him when I was out in California. He stopped in at a club where we was playing and sure looked great. If you are interested in selling some songs, I suggest you come up to New York and we'll talk about it. You have to have some agent, somebody to represent you so you can make a reasonable deal if somebody likes your song and wants to buy it. Here is my address and telephone number. You are welcome to call me when you get to New York."

She wrote him back directly and thanked him, telling him that yes, she had songs to sell and would very soon call for an appointment with him. She hoped he would listen to some of the pieces she had written with her partner, a very good composer. She added that she had some new ideas for lyrics if somebody else wanted to do the music.

Dreaming about the moment when she would get on the train to New York and try to make a career for herself writing songs, albeit long distance, she energetically attacked her heavy work schedule at the university. At last she mentioned her exciting plans to Daniel. He barely responded.

"Well?" she prodded on a Friday night after one of her mother's enormous, many-coursed Sabbath dinners. They were sitting on the couch together, looking at the new TV in the living room. "What do you think of my idea? I want to work after I graduate. This could be it!"

He barely moved his head. "Mm-hm," was all he said, his eyes focused on the tiny screen.

"What the heck is 'mm-hm'?" Her irritation was out of hand.

He laughed. "Sorry," he said.

"Don't be sorry, Daniel. Tell me what you think!"

"I think it's better for you to find something to do in Philadelphia," he said evenly.

A dozen rejoinders leaped to her tongue and she squelched them all. "Oh boy!" she said under her breath. Pursing her lips, she got up from the couch and went in to help her mother with the dishes. The subject was not mentioned again.

A week later Marta's father brought up the question of postgraduate plans. "What do you say, Marta? You'll stay at Penn for the master's? Why shouldn't you? It will solidify that major for you."

"I thought about working, Daddy."

Dr. Resnick, his eyes as always on the world around him, answered, "The times are still unsettled. Nobody knows yet what is coming. Stay in school for a while longer. Get the advanced degree! You can do it in a year."

"I ought to get a job, Papa."

He was shaking his gray head, the sparse front hair slipping down onto his creased forehead. "It's all right. It's all right. You will—if you have to—one day. Finish your education. Dan's going on to get his master's. You should have yours too!"

The war was over but the world, as her father said, was a very unsettled place. The Yalta conference in February 1945, when Allied victory was in sight, had left the seeds of the Cold War planted. At least that was what the mavens agreed.

"Personally, I don't like it," Dr. Resnick said, sitting at the pinochle table with his doctor friends a few nights later in the living room. Mrs. Resnick was reading a novel on the porch, and Marta was curled up on the living-room couch studying her Brahms scores for a midterm music final.

Dr. Berkow, Aaron Resnick's best friend, nodded in agreement to the doctor's statement. "Truman's got some problems! Roosevelt was too sick. He didn't know what he was doing. He gave the Russians too much."

"Thieves . . . buggers . . ." the other men agreed.

The Russians had gotten a big piece of Germany, including East Berlin. They had rapidly installed Communist regimes in Rumania and Bulgaria. Despite Allied promises to the Polish government in exile in England, Stalin recognized instead a local Polish committee of liberation. Poland, like all of eastern Europe and the Balkans, dropped solidly and silently behind the Iron Curtain.

"I'm taking a day off, Ma," Marta said casually the following week, a few days after her examinations.

"What for?" Her mother's face creased. "College you don't miss! It has to be something very important!"

"I want to go up to New York."

Her mother carefully put down the egg beater she was holding over the chocolate cake batter. "New York? What's in New York?"

"A guy I used to know, Mom. In the music business. I want to talk to him . . . just talk . . . about how you get started selling material. I'm coming right back. The same night. I'll probably be home for dinner."

And her mother shifted into the logic of the common dream. It wasn't meant to be expertly devious. It was out in the open, simple, right from its source. "What does Daniel say?"

Marta sighed and looked at the shared hope. It was all the same cul-de-sac, no matter whose shoulder you were looking over. She lied, and they both knew it. "He doesn't care, really. It's okay with him."

She planned to tell him that night, but when he called her on the phone after dinner, he was filled with his own good news. "I'm being moved up at the bank, Mart!"

"My God! That didn't take you long, Daniel-genius!"

He was calling from the university, on the way to a class. It was a public phone, she knew, hanging on the wall somewhere in one of the old buildings. All around him people were rushing to classes. She could hear the noise in the background.

Daniel was chuckling on the other end of the wire. "Well, it's a start!"

"You may own that bank by summer, Dan." She was smiling to herself in the mirror of her dressing table, stretched out on her bed, all her original lyrics and music around her.

"Not quite, but I'm on my way, Mart!"

And kiddingly, referring to her independent dreams, she said, "We'll be so rich and famous we'll hardly be able to talk to the common folk, Dan!" Right then she had meant to tell him about her plans for the following day. But there was a moment of deep silence between them that was suddenly heavy with his unspoken thoughts. Floating like thick clouds over the telephone, the stillness held all his unexpressed wishes. She was mind reading, and she knew immediately what those portentous puffs of sentiment were signaling. He had never proposed. And he would soon. Her heart flopped about in her chest. This was obviously a time when he couldn't speak freely and say all the proper things.

But he didn't propose then. And she didn't mention that she was going to be rich and famous on her own by going up to New York the following day, laying the groundwork for a nebulous but inevitable success. Clouds, she thought, hanging up, great bumpy mounds of cover.

Nobody said a word at breakfast the next morning. Her father sat quietly eating his oatmeal and reading the morning paper, his glasses low on his nose. Her brother was stuffing himself, his face right over his cereal bowl, the sports page propped close in front of him. Mrs. Resnick as usual was on her feet moving between the stove and the sink and the table. Marta came rushing in for a quick slug of coffee, all dressed up in her high heels and sheared-beaver coat.

"So sit down!" Mrs. Resnick tapped her shoulder. "Eat a little something. You have time."

Marta glanced at her wristwatch. "No time!" she said, gulping a cup of steaming milky coffee while her mother's lips pursed disapprovingly. "I'm okay, Mom. I'll be back by dinner." She held a briefcase filled with her material, and her leather pocketbook dangled from its strap across her shoulder.

"Carry your bag!" Mrs. Resnick warned. "You shouldn't get robbed!"

On her way out, Marta glanced at herself in the dining-room mirror, across the expanse of the old mahogany table. Standing straight, then leaning forward to check the makeup on the fair skin, as always pleased, maybe even a little surprised by the shine in the wide-spaced green eyes, the curves of the red mouth, the winged brows, and the delicate pinkness above the cheekbones. Nice face. Beautiful face, Dan said. Often, kissing, touching, or just sitting across from her while they were munching hamburgers. "You're beautiful, Marta!" And trying to take the compliment gracefully, not turn it from embarrassment into a gag, she would smile and murmur, "Thank you," always knowing that thanking him, anyone, was silly, not sure what could be said in response that would be modest and loving. How to say what you mean! So that when facing the empty paper, she could frame the deep thoughts in simple lines, tell the truth for the music, making it shoot straight to the heart. She sighed to herself, tucking the curly ends of bright blond hair back under the soft, felt cloche hat. She had had her hair shingled short and it spilled in waves and ringlets around her face. She was all set. And nodding to the successful, composer-lyricist in the glass, she saluted and said silently, Okay, kid. Your turn!

Only Steven came to the front door with her, his paper napkin floating from the neck of his sweater. "Good luck!" he said.

Winking back at him happily, she slammed out the front door and ran down the steps. She kept moving fast up the hill, hurrying to catch the eight-fifteen trolley in order to make a quick bus transfer for the train station. Out of the corner of her eye she spotted the unexpected colors of tiny crocuses on front lawns and thought of them as further good omens.

Sitting on the train, concentrating on the material spread on her lap, she reviewed what her expectations might be. At the top of the list of hopes was the first: Marcus will love this song, and this one, and this . . . will record them; they'll make the hit parade; I'm established, I keep on writing, I have my own little studio. Daniel will approve and Daddy will be proud. I'm set, set, set! Or, number two: Marcus will send a few of the songs to his publisher.

At least one will be accepted. Some good recording artist, Vaughn Monroe or Art Lund, or—God! Sinatra!—will go for it, will cut it. And I'm set, set, set! Or, number three: Marcus will send me to somebody who is looking for material. He'll like what I have, at least some of it, hand it off; the lyrics will be bought and I'll be set, set, set!

Staring out the window at north Jersey sliding past, the April landscape still dun gray in the pale, lemony sunshine, she saw her own hopeful, light eyes reflecting back at her. She heard the clacking rhythm of the train on its tracks: You're set, you're set, you're set! By the time she got to Pennsylvania Station in New York, toting her case, her pocketbook locked tightly under her arm, she could see all around her the crowds noticing that interesting lyricist from Philadelphia, the tall young blonde who turned out all the hits!

She hadn't given any thought to where Marcus Appleby lived. On the telephone with him the preceding week, she had simply asked if she could come up and bring some of her material. He had been polite and friendly, and had given her his address but no instructions. Nothing tough about finding your way around New York. She had been there many times. Simple city, laid out in a grid; east opposite west, and up opposite down . . . all there is to it. But the cab driver looked at her strangely when she climbed in the back and gave him the address. He shrugged and began to crawl uptown through the heavy morning traffic. The meter ticked as he drove and drove.

And drove. She tapped the glass separating them. "Where is this place?" She had been taken for a hick; the cabbie was giving her the classic tourist runaround. The meter was relentless.

Over his shoulder, out of the corner of his mouth, thick New Yorkese larding his every word, he said, "You asked to go to Harlem, lady. I don't fly there! It's a helluva ride!''

She had never been in Harlem. She had no idea what to expect. And the minute the taxi pulled up in front of a towering old building on a busy crowded street filled with colored people, some just standing and holding up the buildings, laughing, talking, others sitting in the door-ways, others rushing up and down the sidewalks, she began to worry. All dressed up, it was mistake number one. All made up, mistake number two. Coming up here at all, probably the biggest mistake!

She sat in the back of the cab for a minute trying to collect her thoughts. A group of young men standing on the sidewalk leaned down to look into the taxi windows. ''Well, lady?'' The cabbie was getting impatient.

''Say, mister,'' she leaned over the front seat to pay him, ''is it safe . . . around here? You know, am I . . . okay?''

''How the hell do I know?'' He gave her the change and she handed him a very small tip. He grumbled. She got out clutching her bag and pocketbook; and as the cab sped off, she looked neither right nor left but hurried into the building directly in front of her. Nobody followed, and as the door took a while to shut behind her, she heard no catcalls, no whistles, no gibes. Still, her heart was knocking as she walked into the small lobby, heading for the elevators in the rear. A woman with a baby in her arms was pushing the up button. Marta said to her, ''Is this 9087 . . . the building number?''

The woman looked at her quizzically over the baby's head. ''Gee, I don't know. They call this the Chatsford, that's all I ever heard.''

The elevator was grinding to a noisy start somewhere in the shaft overhead. Marta said quickly, ''Well, do you know Mr. Appleby . . . Marcus Appleby. Does he live here?''

She was worried about having to walk outside once more and check the building number.

"You got me, honey," the girl answered. The elevator door swung open and several black people came out. "My mother live here," the girl said, shifting the baby in her arms. She moved into the creaky car. "What apartment you lookin' for?"

Marta got in behind her. "Uh . . ." She pulled the piece of paper with her information on it out of her coat pocket. "Six-B?"

"My mother's in six D. You get off with me."

Marta sighed with temporary relief. The tension had given her an instant, pounding headache. The pain was circling the back of her head and speeding down between her shoulder blades. She rolled her head around to relieve the pressure. At the sixth floor, the girl moved off first and Marta trailed her. "Right here." She indicated a door to Marta.

"Uh, would you, would you mind just sort of waiting . . . ?"

The girl interrupted her, "Well sure, but . . . it's okay. This is a family place. You don't have to be worried. My mother live here forty years. It's just that I don't see everybody around. You know?"

Marta knocked lightly at the door. There was silence within.

Reaching around the infant, the girl pushed a buzzer on the door frame. Marta could hear it resounding within the apartment. She heard footsteps on a bare floor and a second later the door opened. A woman with a plaid dish towel over her arm stood there. "Yes?"

"I'm looking for Mr. Appleby. Marcus Appleby?"

The woman made a gesture with her thumb over her shoulder, indicating the interior. "He here. Come on in."

Marta turned to the girl who was still standing in the hall, the baby balanced on her hip. "Thanks a million!" She walked into the sunny apartment, saying to the woman who closed the door behind her, "I'm Marta. He's expecting me, I think."

"Okay. You set down here. He work late last night. He just gettin' dressed. He be in in a minute." She disappeared quickly into the kitchen off the living room. Marta heard the lids of pots clattering, and the sudden, pungent aroma of spicy food filled the air. When the woman came back into the living room, Marta was still standing in the center, clutching her things. "Go 'head and set down now. I tell him you here." She walked toward the back of the apartment, returning a minute later. "He be right with you."

Marta perched herself uneasily on the edge of the couch, holding her case and pocketbook on her lap. The woman had gone back into the kitchen. A few minutes later, when Marta's nerves were stretched almost to their breaking point, Marcus came through the hallway leading from the back of the apartment. His arms were straight out in front of him and his big dark face was creased into the old familiar grin. "Well now, look who's here!"

She jumped to her feet and he put his arm around her, giving her a quick hug. "How you doin', Marty?"

He hadn't changed much, a little heavier, a little grayer. There were creases on either side of his wide mouth and his thick jowls hung down over his open collar. Time fell away as she grabbed his hand and pumped it. "Oh, Marcus . . . boy, am I glad to see you!"

He motioned to a large dining table near the sunny front window of the apartment. "We have a cup of java . . . something to eat maybe. And we talk it up some. You singin' any?"

"Well, not professionally. I'm still in school."

"Oh yeah? Vince still in school too, I think." He scratched his head and peered at her. "Is that right?"

There was something in the hooded, bloodshot eyes that told her he knew all about Vince and her. He always had. She said, "Vince is finished now, Marcus. But his training has to continue for a year in a hospital."

Marcus clucked. "He one smart cat. You know he was lookin' around out there in LA when I was on tour last year. He come right into this café. I couldn't believe my eyes! I say, 'Hey Vince! I'm out of the army too, man. My back done give out playin' all over Europe, entertainin' the boys. Now,' I ask him, 'what you doin'? Any new stuff, Vince?' He say, 'Oh no way, man. I'm studying to be a doc now.'"

Marta felt the musician's focus on her, serious, measuring, although his tone was light.

She looked up into his strained pouchy eyes, and decided instantly that this road had no place to go. She sighed and shrugged. After a second she said, "I got some terrific songs here to show you."

Marcus pointed again to the dining table. "Okay, honey. Let's set down and we'll just take a look at 'em." He pulled out a chair for her, then called, "Izzy?" There was bustling in the kitchen. "You bring us some coffee, girl."

The woman stuck her head out the doorway. "Lissen, you gotta eat now, Marcus. Aren't you hungry? It's after noon."

Marcus had sat down across from Marta. "You hungry, Marta? Isabel the best cook I know. What you got, Izzy?"

Isabel looked up at the ceiling, reading an invisible menu: "I got soup, I got greens and beans. I got roast pork. I got biscuits. I got a chicken. I got yams. I got . . ."

Marcus chuckled and held up a hand. "That's enough!

You see what that girl do to old Marcus' waistline, Marta? Whatchya wanta eat now?''

Marta shook her head and said to Isabel, "Gosh, it all sounds wonderful. But I never eat much during the day. I mean, I'd like to try the biscuits," she added as she saw the disappointment on Isabel's face.

"Give her java an' some biscuits and some of that strawberry jam I brought home. And gimme a platter, honey. I'll skip the soup."

"The soup is good, Marcus." Isabel leaned out of the kitchen.

"I eat the soup later!" He looked back at Marta. "So you wanta start in the business, huh?"

Marta chose her words carefully. "I think I have some good numbers here." She got up and opened her case. Taking out the music, carefully done in Steven's hand, with her lyrics typed in over the top. She handed Marcus several songs. He looked them over as Isabel put his piled-up steaming platter in front of him. "You eat now, boy," Isabel said to him. "You worked late last night and you never did eat nothin'."

Marcus nodded. "Okay, okay!" He had put on a pair of reading glasses and was looking over the music. Marta waited, almost holding her breath.

"Mm-hm!" He shuffled through the papers. "They looks pretty good." Marta exhaled, realizing she was sitting as rigid as a statue. She tried to relax and sipped the coffee that Isabel had placed in front of her, nibbling at the hot buttered biscuits. She had made up her mind to wait for his suggestions. She knew she would get a truer picture of her chances if she let him talk first, off the top of his head as he got the feel of the music.

In a few minutes he said, "Why don't we hit the ivories?" He glanced up at her over his glasses. "We try these on for size in a couple a minutes. . . ." He began to eat. Isabel brought him a pot of coffee from which he poured several times, refilling his cup and Marta's. "It's a tough game, this here! You know that, I think, Marty. If you don't," he lifted his brow, "you gonna learn it real quick!"

"Yes," she said firmly. "But, Marcus, I know I have talent."

"Sure you do," he said, mopping up the chicken gravy with a biscuit. "I know you do! It's just awful tough to peddle songs! Everybody and his uncle is a song pusher in this here burg."

"But the record companies need constant stuff, Marcus. Records are big business!"

He nodded. "That's true . . . if you got a hit. But don't nobody know what makes a hit, girl! Least of all them big shots! You take it from me! Of course, we all tryin' all the time."

"All I ask is a hearing."

"Absolutely," he said, finishing his last swallow of coffee. He pushed his heavy body away from the table and walked over to a small grand piano that stood angled against a wall. Sitting down on the bench, with almost no effort and no preamble, he began to read the music, to play and sing softly. He went through one song after another without comment. Then he pushed back the piano bench and swung around to face her. "They sure are nice songs, Marty." And her heart sank.

He wasn't jumping up and down as she had dreamed. He wasn't buying and offering and projecting and conjuring the big time with her. He wasn't hearing the applause and the clink of the cash register. He got up, sighing, and came back to the dining table. "Fill up the coffeepot,

Izzy." Pointing to the chair near him, he said, "Set down now, Marty. Lets jaw this over a little."

She was trying to control her impulse to scream, Well . . . well . . . please! She was trying to collect herself, to look professional and capable and not destroyed. But she knew her face had gone pale and her hands were trembling.

If he noticed, he ignored her terrible disappointment. "They real nice songs. All of 'em. Now I jes' can't use 'em, honey. Because they not in my current style. I'm into some new rhythms now. You hear my last release, 'Country Girl in the City'?"

She nodded mutely.

"I'm into a little bit of gospel sound, Marta. I was in the special services, you know? An' we had some country boys along with us. I likes that! We mix it up with a little yokel, kinda old-fashioned."

"But you used to do such sophisticated stuff! Gosh, Marcus, Vince used to say you were a miniature Goodman band. I mean, you think that style is done?"

He shook his head, drawing down the corners of his mouth. "I don't mean nothin', honey. I ain't got a crystal ball. No way to tell what's comin' . . . all I try to do is what feels right—right now! Not one of us in the business can do more than that! An' for me, right now there's a slightly different sound . . . hits my ear real good!" He caught a glimpse of the undisguised dismay on her face. "But now look here. . . . You doin' real hit-parade ballads, and they damned good! You tell your brother that for me. Nice melodies, nice key shifts. Okay stuff. Now, you want me to send your stuff on to somebody? I can do that for you. Or I can make a telephone call or two and get you in to see some people in the business."

She swallowed hard, took a deep breath, and knew she

was starting again from the top of the score. "Yes," she said thoughtfully. "I think I'd like to try to see somebody else today. And then maybe in addition, you can give my stuff to whoever you think might be interested."

Marcus put out his hand and touched her arm. "Look here, honey, don't you go and be disappointed now. You plannin' to come up here and be in New York when you finish with your school? You may have to pound the pavement a little bit, girl! It don't come easy, and you may have to go back to singin'. I knows lots of talented songwriters who are performin' right now—to eat! You hear! And then you keep pushin' and maybe somebody need some stuff and they like what you got!"

"Would you make that call for me now, Marcus? Who do you think would be the right one to take this to?"

"I'll call my rep. He half work for me and half work for the record company. You go see him. Do you have copies of these songs?"

She nodded and reached into her case. "I have duplicates of everything. And others at home, of course."

"That's right. You don't ever want to hand off nothin' that ain't got a seal, and that ain't got a copy. Now . . ." He got to his feet and reached for the phone. Sitting down once more on the couch and holding the receiver, he dialed.

She listened to the conversation and knew it wasn't encouraging. His A and R was a busy man; he had a full day of appointments.

Marcus put on the pressure. "Now look, Mickey, you hear me, this a friend of mine! She comin' down. When can you see her?" And he nodded, writing something on a pad beside the phone. When he hung up he pulled off the sheet of paper and scribbled something. "Here's his name

and address—Michael Morgan—and he'll see you today.
He may have some good news for you."

"Will he listen to the songs right away?"

"I doubt that. You'll have to leave 'em."

She took a deep breath. "Is there anybody else? You
know, that maybe I can go see today?"

"They won't see you the same day. Not these busy
guys! You gotta make an appointment. I'll do that for you.
Now don't you worry, you hear! You gonna get there,
honey!" He stood up and helped her on with her coat.

Isabel came back into the room. Shyly, not looking
directly at Marta, she said, "I sure liked those songs."

"Oh thank you! I hope one day you hear them on the
radio!"

"We all wants that!" said Isabel. "You jes' keep
tryin'!"

"Thank you, Izzy, and thanks for the coffee and biscuits, and," turning to Marcus, "for the hospitality and
the help!"

"Everybody need a little help, Marty!" He chuckled.
"Course, the biggest boot up gotta come from you yourself! You understand what I mean!"

"Oh yes, Marcus. I do!"

He went down in the elevator with her, came out onto
the sidewalk, and hailed a passing cab. She turned and
hugged him as he held the door open for her. "However
this all turns out, Marcus, now . . . ever . . . you are my
friend, and I appreciate the time you gave me. And I thank
you for whatever you do for me."

She was whirled off into the afternoon traffic, going
back downtown. When she got to Mickey Morgan's office
on Fifty-seventh Street, her hopes began to rise again.
There were posters and photographs in the office where his
secretary sat typing and answering a constantly ringing

telephone. All the best-known recording stars of the day, and a few Marta remembered from before the war, filled the walls. She was in the right place.

But when she finally got into Morgan's office and he gestured to a seat in front of his desk, without even glancing at her, her heart sank again. This guy wasn't going to take her seriously either. She cleared her throat, sitting on the edge of the chair, clutching her pocketbook and case. Finally, he looked up at her. And then, with no apparent embarrassment or hesitation, he lifted himself slightly from his seat and stared down at her crossed legs. Leaning back again in his chair, a small smile moved on his thin mouth, and his pale eyes took on a peculiar sheen. He was middle-aged, dressed in gray flannels, going bald at the hairline. He looked well fed and pleased with himself as he drummed on the desk in front of him. "Well now, you're a friend of Marcus's. That's a surprise! I expected some little nigger chick!"

Marta hated him with all her soul and had to control her impulse to leap up and rush out of his office. Swallowing hard, she repeated to herself, He can help you, he can help you.

So she smiled sweetly. "Marcus is a special friend. I knew him when he was based in Philadelphia."

"Where do you live?" Morgan asked suddenly, his mouth pulled to one side in a speculative grin.

"In Philadelphia," she said. "In the suburbs to be exact."

"I mean, here in New York?"

"Well, I'm not staying in New York . . . yet. I'm going back to Philadelphia."

He raised his brows and his mouth opened slightly. "You're not living here?"

"No . . ." she said, and added lamely, "well, not yet."

He pushed his lips together in a pout and stroked his chin. "Hard to sell stuff from out of town, honey. You better stick around." His eyes were wide and smiling again. "I'll find you a place."

"Well . . ." She took a deep breath. "I will come up here eventually, you see, Mr. Morgan. But what I wanted to do right now was to start circulating my material, to make some contacts."

"Mm-hm. You free tonight?" he asked abruptly. And she knew it wouldn't be business.

"No, I'm not," she said. Morgan stood up behind his desk. Marta rose too. She was dismissed. "Thanks for seeing me, Mr. Morgan. I hope you like my songs. They're all in here." She handed him a manila envelope with copies of all the numbers. "I mainly do the lyrics," she began to say, but he had lost interest, she knew. "And I can work with anybody," she added.

His laugh was a sudden cackle. "There's a happy thought!" He started to come around toward her. She had been in his office five minutes. She had the sudden certainty that if he got close enough he would put his hands on her. She moved fast, tugging at the office door. Standing in the doorway, she said, "My home phone number is on all the copies. If you have any news for me."

"Yeah," he said vaguely, leaning back against the edge of his desk. "Listen, you call me, honey. In about two or three weeks. Not much doing right in here. And I advise you to shift up to New York. Soon." He stood up and turned his back on her. "You're going about it the hard way!"

Back on the street outside, navigating through the heavy crowds on the sidewalk, she tried to breathe deeply and collect herself. The afternoon sun was fading and with it the spring disappeared. A cold wintry wind swept down from the north, and she held her coat wrapped around her as she walked down Sixth Avenue toward the station. She couldn't afford another taxi. Hanging on to her briefcase, her hat pulled down on her forehead, and her pocketbook locked under her arm, she wondered if she had really accomplished anything at all. There was no way to know. She had started things up. Marcus would try for her; and he might prod Morgan. A couple of things could still open up.

But sitting on the train going back home as the daylight dimmed, she faced the fact for the first time that it might take months or years to get established as a lyricist. The rotten experts are right on this one, she thought grimly.

She gave Steven the highlights but decided to spare him the harsh details. She had a feeling, from the way he looked at her, nodded his head but made few comments, that her brother understood the field better than she ever could. He had spent a lot of time poking about in the business locally, talking to musicians, performing at little clubs, and reading *Variety* (which he kept hidden from their parents but left out for her, underlining certain pertinent facts!). Steven's response to failure had always been quiet and unmeasurable in the usual ways. He had never had Marta's successes and had learned how to retreat and retrench better than she. There was something to be said for getting knocked off your perch periodically!

"It can be done," she said to him that night while they sat together at the piano after their parents had gone up to bed. Then, looking directly into the wide blue eyes behind the thick glasses, "Oh, but it's tough out there, Steven!"

He grinned and ran his fingers up and down the keyboard. "Man, it's tough out there," he sang to a fast boogie-woogie beat, and she had to laugh with him.

"That's the way!" she said, hugging his thin shoulders. At that moment she knew that in his own time Steven could make it.

To Daniel she confessed the stark truth. "It was awful!"

He shook his head. "Because there's no real route. That's the problem. It's all hit or miss in the entertainment field." Then, seeing her dejection, "There are big rewards, of course. If you can handle them after having handled the disappointments!"

They didn't discuss her career again. The following week she went in to see her adviser and signed up for the master's program in music beginning that summer. She had already taken the graduate record exam, had received a top grade, and had been accepted into the graduate school. She would have only a ten-day vacation, but Daniel was going to school all summer too, taking his courses on Saturdays and after work. They made elaborate plans for meeting on the campus every day.

And then graduation was upon her! Outdoors in the early summer afternoon, she walked down the aisle with a lot of strangers, in the largest class in university history, her family and Dan watching. Most of her friends had elected to do the traditional four-year program. With her black gown blowing gently in the warm June air, she shifted the tassel on her mortar cap to signify the conferring of the B.A. degree and ran to her sweetheart and parents for their congratulations.

With the summer term the work grind began again, on an ever more intense level. Marta began studying piano as part of her course, with a world-famous musician who had come to the university during the war years, two steps ahead of the Nazis. He was meticulous, brilliant, demanding, and cast very much in the new mode of the technical virtuoso. She found herself practicing long hours in the hot afternoons. Her parents were pleased, her brother was awed, and she was vaguely aware of harboring buried resentments that kept trying to surface. Her professors were thrilled with her, and the famous pianist told her she had a concert career ahead if she would continue to work for it. She immediately began to slack off from the practicing and concentrated instead on her theory and history. She wanted out of the university! She knew it now and was working to complete the degree as quickly as she could.

In September there was another brief vacation before the fall term began. Dan had been as busy and engrossed as she all during the summer months, taking his business courses and working hard at the bank. They came together like two people crossing the desert, thirsty, in need of comfort and refreshment.

She said to him one afternoon on the phone, "We must be nuts!"

His only reply was a deep chuckle on the other end of the wire.

"I mean it, Daniel!" she insisted. "What the hell are we killing ourselves for?"

There was a moment's silence. "I like my work, Mart. I'm sorry you feel so overloaded."

She knew then that he was thriving on the pressure. And that she was not. She needed time to dream.

The fall term reconvened while summer was still officially with them, and the work load got even heavier.

"Let's go to the Dell tonight," she said suddenly one evening at dinner in the campus cafeteria. "It's the last concert of the open-air season."

"I have my class in an hour." Dan glanced at his wristwatch.

She reached over and covered it with her palm. "I don't care," she said solemnly.

"What are they playing?" he asked.

"I don't know. It doesn't matter."

He was staring at her, frowning, his eyes boring into hers. "Are you fed up, Marta?"

"And how!" She took a deep breath, glancing restlessly around the crowded, familiar room.

"Okay," he said, picking up his books. "Let's go listen to music."

"Oh, Daniel, you are my pal!" She held his arm tightly, squeezing the biceps, making him grin with pleasure.

He had an old blanket in the trunk of his car. They drove to the trolley barn in the park and left the car. Carrying their blanket, they rode the rickety, open trolley, swaying and clacking across the bridge, high above the Schuylkill River. They traveled on through the park, with the leaf-heavy trees all around them, and the summer light filled the western sky with a bright pink glow. She sighed again and again with happiness. At the Dell, they spread their blanket on a hillside looking down into the grassy knoll where the orchestra was seated on the stage, in front of a large acoustical shell. Side by side, arms around their knees, they listened to Rudolph Serkin play the Chopin Second Piano Concerto. The orchestra was mellow in the background as the piano's melodies softened and diffused in the evening breeze. From high in the leafy branches behind them came the faint hum of tree crickets. Night lowered slowly; the stars appeared and fireflies lit up the wooded hillside all around them.

In the dark, Daniel gently pushed Marta down and wrapped himself around her. "I love you," he said.

"Oh I hope so," she answered softly. "Because I love you too, Daniel!"

"We're right together, Mart." He was kissing and nibbling her ear. "We're perfect!"

She giggled. "And also we're modest, and humble and . . ." She never finished because his mouth was on hers, hard and urgent. Breathless between kisses, she whispered, "We won't make it to the end of the concert. . . ." His hands were caressing her all over, making her tremble. His scent rose in her nostrils, skin and hair fresh with lime, masculine and exciting.

"Oh, Daniel," she said, sighing.

"We'll get married," he said softly, directly in her ear.

She moved her head, trying to see his eyes through the darkness. "Are you proposing?" she whispered.

He held her shoulders, burying his head in her soft neck. "Mm-hm."

This time she shoved him hard. "Well! That's one heck of a way to do it, Banker Reiter!" She began to sit up.

He reached up, took hold of her, and pulled her back against him. Holding on to her tightly, he said clearly, "I love you, Marta. I want you to be my wife. Will you marry me?"

She sank closer to him, her arms creeping up around his neck. "I will," she said. "I will, Daniel."

She knew her parents heard them come in, although it was almost two in the morning. She could hear them murmuring softly in their front bedroom. "Do you want to go up and tell them?" asked Dan.

"No," she said. "I want it all for myself tonight! Tomorrow we kiss and cry!"

"No crying for us, Mart. Only joy."

But nobody tried to stop the mothers from their tears of elation. The families were wild with glee. They entertained each other at large and lavish meals, exchanged histories and childhood anecdotes, and were properly impressed

400

with each other's backgrounds. The Resnicks had culture and the Reiters had money.

The wedding was planned for the following June. There were moments during that winter when Marta thought the time would never pass, that she would forever be coming home alone from classes, loaded with books and papers and work, to her same little proper bedroom, still filled with childhood mementos.

In January, General George C. Marshall, one of the true heroes of the war, was appointed secretary of state by President Truman. Surveying the desolation in the world at large around him, he began his plans for feeding the hungry and for rebuilding Europe. In June, two days after Dan and Marta got their masters' degrees, Marshall spoke at Howard University and proposed the European Recovery Plan.

"It will unquestionably have political strings attached," said Dr. Resnick at dinner that night, shaking his head worriedly.

"It will reconstruct the world economy," said Daniel. "It's the correct response!"

"I hope you're right, Dan," said the doctor.

The following week, on June 12, a bright and sunny Saturday, Marta and her mother and her bridesmaid, Doris Molner, were driven by her father in his new Mercury to the large center-city hotel where the wedding was scheduled to take place that evening after sundown. Steven was Dan's best man. Marta had wanted Kathryn Caplan to be her matron of honor, but Kathy had sadly and reluctantly declined. "Not because I don't love you, Marta dearest," she said when Marta asked her, "but because it's not right for me to put on a fancy gown and be part of a bridal party. I will come to the wedding as a guest and share your joy. Please understand!"

Marta did understand, but Mrs. Resnick was annoyed. "I don't know why you asked her. She goes her own way. Let her alone!"

Marta and Doris spent the long afternoon curling their hair, doing their nails, lounging around in the rented hotel room, laying out bridge hands on the bed, sipping Cokes to keep cool. Marta spoke to Dan five times during the day, kidding him that she might change her mind, going over the honeymoon plans for their trip to Maine. She played the radio, hummed along with it to the familiar tunes, and unaccountably, on and off, shed sudden tears.

"Well," said Doris, turning her own engagement ring around and around on her finger. "I'm next!"

"Herby Brenner is a lucky man," said Marta, hugging her friend.

"We'll be able to play bridge any afternoon we want," said Doris, giggling.

"Aren't you going to work?"

"What for? He can support me!"

Marta shrugged, playing an ace to take in one of the exposed tricks. "That's not the point, Dor."

"So what's the point?" Doris lost the finesse she tried.

"The point is, I now have two very fancy degrees. What am I going to do with them?"

Doris lifted her brow. "Play classical records for the *kinder*."

At seven-thirty as the summer sun lowered and the rabbi arrived with the documents to be signed before the wedding, Marta in her white lace gown and tiara, Mrs. Resnick in her tan chiffon, Mrs. Reiter in her beige crepe, Dr. Resnick, Steven, Daniel, and Mr. Reiter in their rented white dinner jackets and magenta carnations, all nervously assembled in the foyer outside the wedding chamber. They listened to the instructions of the rabbi's daughter who was explaining the simple procedure to them. Mrs. Resnick peered through the crack in the french doors, checking the seated crowd, the massed flowers, the silken canopy, the white runner down the aisle. Behind them, off the ante-chamber where they awaited the signal to begin, they could hear the dance combo hired by Steven, tuning up softly in the dining room. Mrs. Resnick hurriedly checked the tables all set with flowers and candles for the dinner that followed the wedding and reception.

The rabbi's daughter carefully opened the double doors and they heard the soft strains of Mozart played by the classical trio seated down in the front of the hall, Marta's musician friends from the famous Eustace Academy. The violin was sweet over the vibrations of the cello and the deep strains of a viola. The rabbi entered and the wedding procession began. Daniel walked down with his father, followed by Mrs. Reiter and Mrs. Resnick, leaning against each other, their mouths smiling, their eyes full of bright tears. Doris, for once totally silent, came down the aisle in her yellow chiffon beside Steven. They all mounted the steps to the flower-banked canopy, standing on either side of the rabbi, who waited, book in hand, prayer shawl over his shoulders, a tall white yarmulka on his gray head.

Dr. Resnick took Marta's arm outside the door as the Mendelssohn began. His eyes were full of love and tenderness. And pride. She leaned over, kissed him, and lowered the white veil across her face. They walked together, keeping time to the Wedding March. Her heart pounding with the music, she stopped halfway, and waited as Daniel came forward, lifted her veil, and escorted her down the aisle and up the steps. Her father joined them under the canopy. ''Baruch ata . . .'' the rabbi began.

The receiving line afterward stood in a chamber that connected with the larger dining room. All the rooms had

Suzanne Diamond

gilded ceilings adorned by flying cupids and plaster wreaths of garlands, marble columns and floors, and heavy carved moldings on the silk-lined walls. The guests passed down the line, kissing and shaking hands with the two families, until the last of the two hundred people had gone through and were circulating around the room sipping cocktails and nibbling from the long buffet that was laden with all varieties of hors d'oeuvres. The trio had shifted out of the wedding hall into the reception room and was playing Schubert in the corner, away from the traffic.

When the dinner was announced, the guests, holding their tiny name cards on which appeared their table numbers, all moved slowly into the dining room. The five-man combo was already up on the stage and playing dance music, a saxophone deep and sweet in counterpoint to a sharp clarinet. Marta heard the sounds of the two instruments as she and Dan waited outside the ballroom for the signal to enter.

When the guests were all at their tables, Steven said loudly from the doorway, "The bride and groom!" The orchestra began to play "My Darling," Dan's favorite. There was applause from the standing guests as Marta and Dan walked in arm-in-arm, smiling. "My Darling, My Darling" . . . he had always called her his darling. They made their way to the head table to take their seats with the two families. As she sat down Marta glanced toward the band. Steven had told them which was Daniel's favorite song, which was hers, which was "theirs." She suddenly caught her breath. Dominic Perrina was out front, playing the clarinet. And Buster Mackie was beside him on the sax. She glanced away quickly, and then to make sure her eyes were not fooling her, she looked back. The two men faced the head table and were playing directly to her. When the song ended, Steven, rising to his full six

404

feet two inches, toasted the bride and groom. The rabbi offered the prayer over the bread. And the orchestra began the first dance for the young couple to do alone on the dance floor. It was the song the two of them had shared from the beginning, a song of young love and partings and hopes for the future, "You'll Never Know." Marta stood up and, led by Daniel, they moved together onto the dance floor. "You'll Never Know," the clarinet sang. Daniel knew her heart had gone away with him. He knew how much she cared. She leaned into his arms as the orchestra took on volume. The clarinet and sax were together in harmony, clear, above the other sounds as the young couple danced past the bandstand. She glanced up and smiled at Dom and Buster. Both nodded, saluting her with their instruments.

Everybody said it was a perfect wedding.

CHAPTER 16

January 1982

TIME IS A MAGIC BALLOON; FILLED OR FLATTENED, IT
takes on the shapes of that which it holds. The kids surprised
Marta and Dan and came home for the holidays after all.
The blues were blown away with the snowy December
winds, the house was filled with holly and fresh flowers,
and the wonderful aromas of fresh bread and chocolate
cake and cinnamon buns and cookies. Marta was in the
kitchen nonstop for three days after Diane called and said,
"I just want to be at home, doing nothing, Mom." Which
meant that the new boyfriend, whose family lived nearby,
would be camping in the Reiter house, and that Diane,
tired from school and the bleakness of dormitory living,
needed a little charm in her life, a little coddling. Marta
always remembered her own mother and father, Lillian and
Aaron, approaching the holidays in an old-fashioned, ritu-
alistic way, as they no doubt in turn remembered with
mixed pleasure and sadness their parents' traditions giving
comfort and continuity. And if Marta had felt a second's
disappointment that having her daughter under her roof did

not mean late-night gabbing and lunches out together and shopping for new clothes, if they were to be confronted with the discomfort of new personalities (the boyfriend was brilliant and "difficult" according to Diane), the pleasures would outweigh somehow. The silly heart had its reasons that reason ought to skip inspecting at close range.

When their son, Allen, called, Marta and Dan were in the library reading in front of the fire. Outside was a cold clear night that made the snow-packed grounds glitter. Dan answered the phone and, grinning from ear to ear, said, "That's marvelous! That's terrific!" Marta tried to get her head as close to the receiver as she could to hear that special voice. "When? When?" she whispered and her son heard her. "On my way, Mom," she heard.

"When does he get here?" she said as Dan hung up.

"Tonight."

"When?"

"His plane gets in at ten-thirty. He said to please have sandwiches and coffee for them."

She was already walking toward the kitchen to get the bread she had baked out of the freezer and to defrost hamburgers, when she suddenly stopped in the doorway and turned back to her husband. "Them?"

"He's bringing his girl." Dan had a look of triumph on his face that instantly irritated Marta. "My God! You're thrilled," she said, coming back into the room.

He pulled her down on the couch. "Yes. He ought to have his own girl."

"But who is she?"

Dan kissed his wife gently and then deeply on the lips. "Somebody special. A guy knows when he finds that one." He held her tightly. "I knew."

She said, "We were different. I just hope our kids know what they're doing."

"We weren't so different, Marta. When most things are right, you know it. It was the same then as it is now. Just a few stylistic changes, that's all."

A dozen rebuttals sprang to her lips, but she shook her head and swallowed them.

"Anyway," he said, smoothing her hair, following the line of her brows with the tips of his fingers, "how can the kids miss when they had you as their mother?"

"Uh!" She pulled away from him. "You're full of soup!" She started to get up but he pulled her back.

She returned his kiss and leaned against his shoulder. "Darling Daniel! It's you who gets all the credit." She sighed. "The truth is, I've never known what the hell I'm doing. Still don't!"

"Good instincts," he said in her ear.

"Do you believe that?"

"Oh yes," he said seriously. Then mocking himself he added, "Of course, I taught you a great deal, Mart!"

"Like what?" She laughed, trying to get up. But he had her around the waist.

"You don't think I did?" He let her go.

She stood up in front of him, enjoying as always the way his neck and head rose strongly from his broad shoulders, the thick curly gray hair that was tousled, the playful gleam in his brown eyes. "Sure you did," she said to him. "You taught me lots of wonderful things. And all I ever taught you was how to make a decent cup of coffee."

He nodded and went back to his book. "My mother never did know how to make coffee," he murmured. Marta stood in the doorway looking at him reflectively for a second or two and then went to fix the midnight feast for Allen and his girl.

*   *   *

Diane's boyfriend turned out to be "familiar" and neither Dan nor Marta found him "difficult." He was bright and well educated and Marta assumed his reputation as a problem had been earned by his determination to do his own thinking. Diane Reiter had at last met her match! His father was a prominent local lawyer and his mother was the guiding spirit behind one of the charitable organizations patronized by the Reiters. Thinking back to that charity's previous spring dance, and trying to place his mother, Marta had a memory of a carefully groomed blonde in a Halston. "Familiar," indeed. The young man was finishing up at law school and already had a job with a firm in the city. He had, it appeared, done his bit for the spirit of uncertainty said to be the keynote of the times, by spending two years in Europe looking at Gothic architecture and bumming around. He came home quite willingly, went back to school, and took the best job he was offered, although emphatically not with his father's firm. He was pleasant company, came to the house to be with Diane every day, and spent every evening with them. He clearly wanted to please them. Above all, he was in love with Diane! It was obvious to anyone who spent time with the young couple. Diane, on the other hand, was trying to be cool and told her mother she didn't want to get too deeply ensnared. Marta, making a valiant effort to hold her tongue, commented dispassionately that he was a nice boy and let it go at that. It didn't do to take sides. Nobody knew that better than Marta. Still, it wasn't easy, because this attractive young man was different from, and certainly more acceptable than, the peculiar, angry, antiestablishment types Diane had always brought home before. What particularly charmed and amused Marta was how much the boyfriend was like Dan: quiet, tall, broad, strong featured, and strong willed.

Allen's girl, quite the contrary, was not "familiar." She was a flaxen-haired beauty from Minnesota, almost as tall as he, her Nordic heritage apparent in the length of limb and squareness of shoulders, in the blushing fair skin and light eyes. After the first astonishment wore off (Allen had always taken out little dolls!), Marta found herself warming to the shy pretty girl. She was, however, almost knocked off her feet when Dan said, as they were getting ready for bed one bitter-cold night in the middle of the holiday week, "Of course, he picked her because she looks like you."

Marta stood naked in the center of the room, stunned, forgetting the cold and the nightgown over her arm as she stared at her husband. "Like me? She's . . . she's . . . a Swede!"

He merely shrugged, getting comfortable under the covers. "Well, maybe you had Swedish ancestors . . . somewhere."

"Poor Poles, more likely," she murmured, rolling against him and clinging to his warm chest. "Do you think . . . ?" she began, but Dan interrupted her by kissing her lips. "Don't think!" he ordered. "Just react . . . naturally. She's a nice girl. He's crazy about her, and she's in love with him. Everything will be fine. Maybe we'll have two weddings next year."

She drifted off to sleep, dreaming about Christmas trees under a floating silken canopy surrounded by laughing blond babies.

It snowed on and off all week right up to New Year's Eve, and the holidays turned into a winter houseparty for six. (Seven, when Aunt Kathy Caplan showed up.) It was pleasant, lively, and there was too much food. (They all groaned whenever Marta appeared again out of the kitchen

bearing another plate of something or other). Becoming a
group without any effort, they relaxed into one another's
company. For the first time in months, Marta stopped
listening to the news, stopped worrying about her major
decisions, stopped thinking about her dying friend Doris.
They were all together every evening in front of the fire,
the kids sprawled on the floor on cushions, Dan's records
on the stereo, sipping hot rum drinks (the boyfriend's
specialty). "Why don't you do a movie?" she asked both
Allen and Diane privately. "You don't have to hang
around here with us!"

But they got more and more comfortable and couldn't
be pried loose. Each of them was a little sorry to see it end
as New Year's Eve approached. With it came separate
plans, dress-up occasions in which no one seemed interested. When she had heard that the kids were home, Kathy
Caplan came twice for dinner during the week. Spending
the long evening with them in an easy chair that Dan
moved close to the fire for her, Kathy's eyes strayed again
and again to Diane's and Allen's faces. More than once
Marta watched fleeting emotions playing across the small
delicate features. She came as usual by herself and wouldn't
stay overnight, a gently, intensely involved visitor, moving
with silence and speed on her own determined track. All of
them individually invited Kathy to spend New Year's Eve
with them and as usual she declined. But when Allen
mentioned that they were all leaving, alas, on January 2,
Kathy herself suggested that she spend that last evening
with them.

On New Year's Day she came promptly at six, fresh
faced and lively, to find the group exhausted from the
evening before and gloomy over the end of the vacation.
Marta was especially saddened by her son's departure,
unsure when she would see him again. She was asking no

questions, trying not to let it matter so much. As the week ground to a close, there were two sudden, separate surprises that portended change. It was after dinner on their last evening together and Dan was casually discussing with Allen the routine of life out west, the mundane bits and problems of adjusting to a new environment. Allen, for the first time, answered unenthusiastically, and Marta and Kathy exchanged surreptitious glances. Each then looked away guiltily, lest she betray her involvement. During a momentary silence, Allen's girl suddenly spoke up, remarking as if they already knew that Allen was considering coming back to Philadelphia to resume the practice of law.

Never blinking, staring straight ahead into the fire, Marta caught her breath. When nobody commented, the girl added, "I personally think it would be wonderful! He's suited to a big-city practice. He's just wasted in that bookshop!"

Marta was aware that her son had turned his head and was contemplating her. She was struck at that instant by the dramatic references inherent in the situation. A movie-reel flicked on and was rerunning familiar frames, scenes from her own girlhood. Events and feelings that were buried played out before her in the firelight, directed by messages in her son's eyes, and so vivid that she wondered for a crazy moment if they could all see them too: Aaron and Lillian watching her obliquely, guarded and silent, trying to finesse as best they could the capricious, brooding sixteen-year-old Marta and her smiling, talented, difficult brother. If the past became the present, then it was all spliced onto one long film; the fears and hopes were the same and only the hair styles and the beat of the music had changed.

The moment moved on. All past memories and present ambivalences were stored away again. The conversation rippled around the group, covering those private discoveries with tact and manners. And almost immediately came the second big shock of the evening. Quietly, almost carelessly, Dan said to Diane, "Did you hear? Mom's going to help Uncle Steve with a TV special. She's been writing some terrific lyrics for him."

They turned to her with a rush. "How could you keep it a secret?" Diane asked.

"I thought . . ." she looked up at Daniel, "it would be better to wait and think about it some more."

"Wait for what?" her daughter insisted.

Allen said, "What's to think about if you want to do it?"

"Oh I want to do it," she responded at once as Kathy's eyes signaled her good wishes. "Yes," Marta repeated, "I do want to!" Daniel was staring into the fire, concentrating on the colors leaping up into the chimney. Hearing her comment, he nodded slightly. As if by common consent they discussed it no more and the evening came to a close.

The good-nights were farewells; they all had early starts in the morning. Beginnings for the winter, beginnings for plans. They kissed Kathy good-night and Allen saw her to her car. Shaking hands with Diane's boyfriend, they invited him to stop by even if she was not at home. To Marta's amusement, Diane beamed with approval at their invitation.

And then the house was quiet, the holiday done, and Daniel and Marta were alone in their bedroom. She pulled off her shoes and her pantyhose and sat down on their bed, watching him as he quietly and efficiently undressed. He had switched on the radio and was humming softly with the vocalist. "Through the years / You never let me down / You turned my life around. . . ."

Almost too languorous to continue undressing herself,

she stretched out on the bed. "Do you like that song?" she asked.

Dan grinned, folding his trousers neatly over a hanger. "Mm-hm."

"Do you know what it is? I mean do you know who that is singing?"

Still grinning and raising his brows, he looked over at her. "That's Kenny Rogers," he said, and when she broke into laughter, he came over to her and sat down beside her on the bed. Sliding his hand under her skirt, he rubbed his palm up and down her thigh. "Really think I'm out of it, don't you!"

She liked the feel of his fingers on her bare flesh. "Not you, Daniel! I never sold you short, my love."

He leaned over and lightly brushed her lips with his. "You're my love. . . ."

"Thank you, Dan. . . ."

He sat back looking at her seriously for a second and then got up, unbuttoned his shirt, and continued to undress. He said softly, "What for? For letting you do what you were going to do anyway?"

"For accepting it gracefully."

He shrugged. "I hope it makes you happy."

Kenny sang, "I love the life we made / And I'm so glad I stayed / Right here with you / Through the years. . . ."

She sat in bed in her nightgown at last, ready for sleep, listening to the shower running behind the half-closed bathroom door. Dan was still singing the song, slightly off key. "The sweetest days I found, I found with you"; first a little sharp, then a little flat, but with full volume. Switching off the lights and lying back relaxed, she listened to the song on the airwaves, and its approximate counterpoint coming from the bathroom.

When Dan climbed in beside her she was already

half-asleep as she curled against him. He stretched out to his full length, relaxing, breathing quietly, smelling of soap and aftershave lotion and toothpaste, his chin up in the air, his arms folded under his head. The light of the January moon shone in through the undraped windows and etched his profile against the darkened wall beyond: straight nose, stubborn chin, high forehead. She reached up and traced his features with the tip of her finger. His thick curly hair was still damp from the shower.

"Dan?"

She thought he might have fallen instantly asleep as he always did, but she could see the blink of his lashes and knew his eyes were wide open. The shadows made valleys on his face. He didn't answer and she said again, "Dan? It's going to be okay. You'll see."

He turned on his side facing her and his features disappeared in the dark, only his hair and ear in silhouette. Kissing her nose and upper lip, he said, "I hope so, Mart." When he reached back to turn off the radio, Kenny was winding it down: "Through all the good and bad / I know how much we had. . . ."

"Happy New Year, darling!"

"And to you . . ." he said.

Steven was thrilled and Marta was scared. Having misgivings of all varieties, many of them brand new, she heard herself whining into the phone, "Gee whiz Steve, suppose the damn lyrics are lousy. . . ." She was sitting at the piano in the living room staring out at the grim winter, which was already setting records for cold. The telephone cord curled around her arm and her fingers were on the keyboard as she listened to her own childish fears out loud. Her brother's reaction was quick and infectious. He roared back over the wire with joyous laughter, the Steven she remembered from their childhood, full of fun and hope, "You just let me worry about it! I'm so happy that you're going to go through with it! It really means a lot to me right now."

"I know you're flattering me," she said and saw her reflection smiling in the ice-etched window pane.

"No!" he said firmly. "I am not! I need you! Will you bring everything soon? Tomorrow?"

"At the end of the week," she said, "I'll be all ready."

When she hung up, her hand lingered on the phone, the impulse to call Vincent instantaneous and strong. But she held back; the family holiday was still in the house, still in her eyes and ears.

And then one evening at the end of the week his name came up naturally. Dan mentioned casually that he and Dr. Fanetti had had another impromptu meeting. "So," she said, without meeting Dan's eyes, "do you think he'll take the post?"

He didn't answer at once and she glanced at his face. His eyes were focused on her, weighing and watchful. Finally he answered, "I don't know." And as soon as she could she changed the subject.

The next morning she was sipping coffee at the kitchen table, her typed lyrics in front of her, rereading, reevaluating, worrying anew at certain rhythmic liberties she had taken; wondering if they would be construed as weaknesses or ignorance; trying as always to be that ubiquitous listener, the one with the universal taste and the most enthusiasm; testing the innovations against the usual; struggling to be at least for this moment on the other side of the creator-audience equation, just to see if images were alive and feelings were being stirred.

She thought about Vincent. Again and again the impulse to call him rose and was quelled. And yet when the phone rang as she sat thoughtfully at the kitchen table, she was so startled she jumped. Even before she heard his voice, she knew it was he on the other end. She sat staring at the receiver for a split second as if it were a conjuring rod.

He asked her and she answered, "Yes," softly, "I'll meet you."

"What time can you?"

"Early please. Will Mikko be open by eleven-thirty?"

"A quarter to twelve."

So easy. They would see each other again. And if they were to meet in the middle of the Sahara sometime in the future, the energy between them would flow unbroken, making the same complete circuit, as always.

For the first time in two weeks she switched on the news station as she was driving to the restaurant. The even, unemotional voice of the announcer told her that martial law was firmly in place in Poland; that the union Solidarity was officially outlawed and its leaders detained; the Iraquis and Iranians were in a bloody war; the Russians were skirmishing with resisting guerrillas in Afghanistan and deaths were mounting; the Christians and Muslims were at each other in Lebanon, with PLO guerrillas waiting like hungry tigers on the sidelines, as the time approached for the Israelis to return the last third of the Sinai to Egypt; the Quebecois were once again threatening to go on the warpath; India and Pakistan were eyeing each other, Madame Ghandi making threats that would affect the rest of the world, considering that either side might soon have nuclear weapons; Latin America was a tinder box; Castro, backed by his Soviet armorers was speeding aid to Nicaragua's Sandinista regime, helping the rebels in El Salvador and encouraging the continuous fighting in Guatamala; the orange and green Irish were still murdering each other; a bomb had killed a woman and young children

418

outside Belfast; the United States was having problems with Europe, its traditional allies, over nuclear arms and warheads to be aimed at Russia (Russia's warheads were already in place, pointing directly at the continent); Greece was squirming around in NATO and threatening to close its U.S. bases; the English were going bankrupt; the French, who had voted a Socialist government into power, were having severe employment and monetary problems.

She flipped off the radio. Driving through unrestored West Philly, the whole panorama of human instability, fear, and aggression created waves of revulsion in her. By chance she caught a glimpse of her anguished face in the rear-view mirror and, shocked at her own expression, tried to keep her focus on the street ahead, narrowing the area of vision. She wanted to avoid seeing the poor old scarred city. But the human eye was constructed to view a wide field and Marta couldn't help taking in the rubbish, the rubble, the decay, the graffiti climbing in wild and helpless messages all over houses and public buildings, even on the side of a church.

Aaron had said, "Daughter, the world is yours . . . if you follow the rules." Lillian had said, "It will all be wonderful for you, my darling."

But the world ran its own race and didn't necessarily keep pace with the correct, thoughtful protocol of the proper achievers. The population swerved and dodged and jiggled and the ground was not perfectly solid and time was not forever. Mom and Pop's conscientious goals, like overstretched imaginations, became exhausted from the onslaught of the unthinkable. Who ever won the race?

She got to Mikko's before Vincent and went right to the little table in the back. Mikko saluted her as she came in. Who she was and why she was there was no concern to him. He had just opened up and was placing small containers of fresh blossoms on each table. His wife, Sally, was setting the tables in the front, and she smiled at Marta but made no attempt at conversation either. Marta was glad. She needed the few minutes before Vince came to collect herself. Her small overnight bag was stowed in the trunk of her car along with her portfolio. It wasn't easy to make everything orderly. Mikko switched on the stereo and Stevie and his piano came wondering softly from the amplifiers in the ceiling corners ... You don't know, we don't know, if you'll ever come back. . . . Always the same questions . . .

Marta ordered a glass of white wine. It was already noon. He was going to be late. She had expected it, always knew in advance what it was going to be with him, just as he always knew with her. Their prescient, fine-tuned antennae functioned for each other. The stereo was turned down and the music was sweet, noting that it could be goodbye this time. . . .

She was nursing her glass of wine, trying not to look at her watch, and then all at once he was there. He filled the doorway, his raincoat flung open, his heavy tweed jacket underneath hanging unbuttoned, his tie askew, his jaw taut, the straight black-gray hair tossed on his forehead.

"Sorry . . ."

"It's okay."

"You have to make a train." He took off his coat and tossed it over a chair.

"We have . . ." she glanced again at her wrist, "well . . . about an hour."

"I'll run you to the station."

She didn't answer. She would tell him later, when they were leaving together, that she had her car parked down the street. Stevie Wonder was crooning about how strange his emotions were lately. . . .

420

Vince took Marta's hand and pressed it hard against his palm. "They expect my answer today." He placed his other hand on top and she was so disoriented by her feelings that for a minute she stared at him uncomprehendingly. "But some things are tough to figure out, aren't they, Mart?" She knew as he knew that she would not change her mind.

"Twice in one lifetime is too much, Vince," she said, her chest flooding with aching sadness. She couldn't stop the tears from welling under her lids. She blinked and they ran down her cheeks.

"Don't," he said, wiping them away with his fingers. "It's all right. I understand."

"When did you decide?" she asked.

He shrugged. "I try not to kid myself, but this time I really didn't know. . . ." He held both her hands in his. "One thing I do know—twice in one lifetime is not too much. It's just, not enough."

"You love California."

"Yes," he said and looked up as Mikko brought him his wine.

"Hey, Doc, wanta hear how good the piana sounds now? I had this kid tune it. I think he did a good job."

Vincent couldn't let her go and her tears wouldn't stop. "Let's try the man's piano, Mart. Come on . . ." Still holding her arm, he handed her a sheet of paper and they walked over to the piano together. She read through a blue blur: "A few notes and a little melody / Is all that's left to share / We cannot play in harmony / Our world's apart out there." He pulled the bench away from the piano and she sat down beside him at the keyboard as his long fingers moved quietly over the notes. Their backs were to the rest of the room, arms and shoulders pressed against each other. Mikko shut off the radio. Marta began to hum the melody and then she softly sang the verse. "This is the last song I'll write for you / The last tune / The last time / There isn't any future left / For us, a bar or two, some rhyme." When she stopped, her throat filled up, her voice quavering to a bleat. He smiled at her. "Go on," he said. She sang, "My arms are empty in advance / There's nothing I can do / The music's over with the dance / This is the last song I'll write for you."

Mikko was standing behind them. "Hey, Doc, that's a nice song. Sing it louder, missy. The guys at the bar want to hear."

Vince shut the lid over the keyboard and they both stood up. Without looking at each other he took her hand again; and it wasn't clear whether he did it to steady her or himself. Their palms gripped, he wouldn't let her go and had to rummage awkwardly in his pocket with his other hand. Her coat was half off her shoulders and they still couldn't let go of each other.

When they came out onto the street the north wind was whipping wildly at the already bare trees, beating at the little awning over the entranceway. "Put your coat on," he said and finally let go of her hand to help her into it. "I'll drive you to the station."

"I don't want you to."

He said, "I love you, Marta Portia."

"Remember me, Fanetti. . . . I was your first fan."

"And I was yours. I'll be listening for you on TV. . . ."

"You're better than I am, Vincent. . . ."

"How can that be, Marta? How can one half be better than its other?"

"There was no way, Vince."

"No way."

He held her bundled in his arms as the wind whistled

under the awning and tugged at their coats and blew her hair all over his face.

She pulled away from him and ran for her car. She had twenty minutes to make her train.